W9-BLD-521

Praise for David Lagercrantz's

THE GIRL IN THE SPIDER'S WEB

"**Masterful.... Intricate and ambitious**.... Salander is an extraordinary heroine whose hacker skills are more relevant than ever in an increasingly high-tech surveillance society." —*The Atlantic*

"**Lagercrantz has more than met the challenge.** Larsson's brainchildren are in good hands and may have even come up a bit in the world." —*The Wall Street Journal*

"Lisbeth Salander remains, in Lagercrantz's hands, the most **enigmatic** and **fascinating** anti-heroine in fiction." —*Financial Times*

"A thrillingly layered book every bit as **addictive** as the originals." —*O, The Oprah Magazine*

"[A] **worthy, crowd-pleasing** fourth installment.... Lagercrantz, his prose more assured than Larsson's, keeps Salander's fiery rage at the white-hot level her fans will want." —*Publishers Weekly* (starred review)

"This whirlwind of nonstop action and intrigue is **compulsively readable** to the electrifying end." —*Library Journal* (starred review)

"[A] **smart, action-packed thriller** that is true to the spirit of the characters Larsson created while adding interesting new ones and updating the political backdrop that made the Millennium series so compelling."

—*The Buffalo News*

"**Engrossing**.... In spinning a complex and intriguing new chapter in the adventures of Blomkvist and Salander, Lagercrantz has written a worthy successor to one of the more uniquely compelling thriller sagas of his generation."

—*Paste*

"Fans of the original trilogy will be pleased with [Lagercrantz's] new installment. The novel is a **smart, propulsive** thriller and espionage tale with a timely digital age plot (think Snowden and Wikileaks)."

—*The Hollywood Reporter*

"Lagercrantz pulls it off, and with a great deal of style....
Elegantly paced, slickly executed, and properly thrilling.... A welcome treat."   —*The Guardian*

"Passion and fire, check: there are plenty of both here....
Fast-moving, credible, and intelligently told.
Larsson fans won't be disappointed."   —*Kirkus Reviews*

"**Action-packed and thoroughly enjoyable**.... [A] finely wrought thriller.... I will eagerly devour the next adventure for Lisbeth Salander and Mikael Blomkvist, especially now that we know their fate lies in the hands of a writer worthy of their story." —William O'Connor, *The Daily Beast*

David Lagercrantz

THE GIRL IN THE SPIDER'S WEB

David Lagercrantz is an acclaimed Swedish journalist and author. He has worked as a crime reporter for *Expressen*, and has written several novels, including *Fall of Man in Wilmslow*. He worked with international soccer star Zlatan Ibrahimović on his memoir, *I Am Zlatan Ibrahimović*, which was shortlisted for the William Hill Sports Book of the Year award and was nominated for the August Prize in Sweden.

THE MILLENNIUM SERIES BY STIEG LARSSON

The Girl with the Dragon Tattoo

The Girl Who Played with Fire

The Girl Who Kicked the Hornet's Nest

ALSO BY DAVID LAGERCRANTZ
IN ENGLISH TRANSLATION

I Am Zlatan Ibrahimović

Fall of Man in Wilmslow

THE GIRL IN THE
SPIDER'S WEB

David Lagercrantz

Translated from the Swedish by George Goulding

VINTAGE CRIME/BLACK LIZARD
Vintage Books
A Division of Penguin Random House LLC
New York

FIRST VINTAGE CRIME/BLACK LIZARD PREMIUM
MASS-MARKET MTI EDITION, OCTOBER 2018

Translation copyright © 2015 by George Goulding

All rights reserved. Published in the United States by Vintage Books,
a division of Penguin Random House LLC, New York. Originally
published in Sweden as *Det som inte dödar oss* by Norstedts,
Stockholm, in 2015. Copyright © 2015 by Norstedts Agency.
This translation simultaneously published in Great Britain by
MacLehose Press, an imprint of Quercus, London, by agreement
with Norstedts Agency. Published by arrangement with
Quercus Publishing PLC (U.K).

Vintage is a registered trademark and Vintage Crime/Black Lizard
and colophon are trademarks of Penguin Random House LLC.

This is a work of fiction. Names, characters, places, and incidents
either are the product of the author's imagination or are used
fictiously. Any resemblance to actual persons, living or dead,
events or locales is entirely coincidental.

The Cataloging-in-Publication Data is on file at
the Library of Congress.

**Vintage Crime/Black Lizard Premium
Mass-Market MTI ISBN: 978-0-525-56457-7
Vintage Crime/Black Lizard Premium
Mass-Market ISBN: 978-0-525-43476-4
eBook ISBN: 978-0-385-35429-5**

www.vintagebooks.com

Printed in the United States
1 0 9 8 7 6 5

CONTINUING CHARACTERS FROM THE MILLENNIUM SERIES

LISBETH SALANDER, an exceptionally talented hacker with tattoos, piercings, and a troubled past.

MIKAEL BLOMKVIST, an investigative journalist at *Millennium* magazine. Salander assisted him with one of the biggest stories of his career, about the disappearance of Harriet Vanger. He later helped to vindicate Salander when she was on trial for murder.

ALEXANDER ZALACHENKO, also known as Zala, or by the alias Karl Axel Bodin. A Soviet spy who defected to Sweden and was protected for years by a special group within the Swedish Security Police who later murdered him. He is Lisbeth Salander's father, and used to violently abuse her mother, Agneta. He was also the head of a criminal empire.

RONALD NIEDERMANN, Salander's half-brother, a blond giant impervious to pain. Salander arranged for his murder.

CAMILLA SALANDER, Lisbeth Salander's twin sister, from whom she is estranged.

HOLGER PALMGREN, Salander's former guardian, a lawyer. One of the few people who know Salander well and whom she trusts.

DRAGAN ARMANSKY, Salander's former employer, the head of Milton Security. Another of the few she trusts.

PETER TELEBORIAN, a sadistic psychiatrist at the clinic where Salander was institutionalized as a child. The chief prosecution witness in her murder trial.

ERIKA BERGER, editor-in-chief of *Millennium* magazine, occasional lover of Blomkvist.

GREGER BECKMAN, Erika Berger's husband.

MALIN ERIKSSON, managing editor of *Millennium*.

CHRISTER MALM, art director and part owner of *Millennium*.

ANNIKA GIANNINI, Blomkvist's sister, a lawyer who represented Salander in her trial.

HARRIET VANGER, scion of a wealthy industrial family, who disappeared as a girl and was found by Blomkvist and Salander at the behest of her great-uncle, Henrik Vanger. She became a shareholder in *Millennium*.

HANS-ERIK WENNERSTRÖM, a corrupt financier who tricked Blomkvist into publishing a defamatory article in *Millennium* about his business, landing Blomkvist in prison for libel. Salander emptied Wennerström's bank accounts in retribution.

SVAVELSJÖ MC, a motorcycle gang closely associated with Zalachenko. Members of the gang were critically injured by Salander.

HACKER REPUBLIC, a coalition of hackers, among whom Salander, who goes by the handle "Wasp," is the star. Includes the hackers Plague, Trinity, and Bob the Dog.

SÄPO, the Swedish Security Police, which harbored a secret faction known as "the Section," dedicated to protecting Zalachenko.

JAN BUBLANSKI, a detective inspector with the Stockholm police, who headed the team investigating the Salander case. Now promoted to chief inspector. Known as "Officer Bubble."

SONJA MODIG, a police officer who works closely with Bublanski.

JERKER HOLMBERG, a crime scene investigator on Bublanski's team.

HANS FASTE, a police officer who clashed with Bublanski and leaked information to Ekström during the Salander investigation.

RICHARD EKSTRÖM, the prosecutor who brought the case against Salander. Now chief prosecutor. A manipulative and venal man, believed within the police to be interested only in self-advancement.

THE GIRL IN THE
SPIDER'S WEB

ONE YEAR EARLIER

This story begins with a dream, and not a particularly spectacular one at that. Just a hand beating rhythmically and relentlessly on a mattress in a room on Lundagatan.

Yet it still gets Lisbeth Salander out of her bed in the early light of dawn. Then she sits at her computer and starts the hunt.

PART 1

THE WATCHFUL EYE

NOVEMBER 1–21

The NSA, or National Security Agency, is a U.S. federal authority that reports to the Department of Defense. The head office is in Fort Meade, Maryland, by the Patuxent Freeway.

Since its founding in 1952, the NSA has been engaged in signals surveillance—these days mostly in connection with Internet and telephone traffic. Time after time its powers have been increased, and now it monitors more than twenty billion conversations and messages every twenty-four hours.

CHAPTER 1

EARLY NOVEMBER

Frans Balder had always thought of himself as a lousy father.

He had hardly attempted to shoulder the role of father before and he did not feel comfortable with the task now that his son was eight. But it was his duty, that is how he saw it. The boy was having a rough time living with Balder's ex-wife and her obnoxious partner, Lasse Westman.

So Balder had given up his job in Silicon Valley, gotten on a plane home to Sweden, and was now standing at Arlanda airport, almost in shock, waiting for a taxi. The weather was hellish. Rain whipped onto his face and for the hundredth time he wondered if he was doing the right thing.

That he of all self-centred idiots should become a full-time father, how crazy an idea was that? He might as well have gotten a job at the zoo. He knew nothing about children and not much about life in general. The strangest thing of all was nobody had asked him to do it. No mother or grandmother had called him, pleading and telling him to face up to his responsibilities.

It was his own decision. He was proposing to defy a long-standing custody ruling and, without warning, walk into his ex-wife's place and bring home his boy, August. No doubt all hell would break loose. That damn Lasse Westman would probably give him a real beating. But he put that out of his mind and got into a taxi with a woman driver who was dementedly chewing gum and at the same time trying to strike up a conversation with him. She would not have succeeded even on one of his better days. Balder was not one for small talk.

He sat there in the backseat, thinking about his son and everything that had happened recently. August was not the only—or even the main—reason why he had stopped working at Solifon. His life was in turmoil and for a moment he wondered if he really knew what he was getting himself into. As the taxi came into the Vasastan neighbourhood Balder felt as if all the blood was draining from his body. But there was no turning back now.

He paid the taxi on Torsgatan and took out his luggage, leaving it just inside the building's front entrance. The only thing he took with him up the stairs was an empty suitcase covered with a brightly coloured map of the world, which he had bought at San Francisco International. He stood outside the apartment door, panting. With his eyes closed he imagined all the possible scenarios of fighting and screaming, and actually, he thought, you could hardly blame them. Nobody just turns up and snatches a child from his home, least of all a father whose only previous involvement had consisted of depositing money into a bank account. But this was an emergency, so he steeled himself and rang the doorbell, resisting the urge to run away.

At first there was no answer. Then the door flew open and there was Westman with his piercing blue eyes and massive chest and enormous fists. He seemed built to hurt people, which was why he so often got to play the bad guy on screen, even if none of the roles he played—Balder was convinced of this—were as evil as the person he was in real life.

"Christ," Westman said. "Look what we have here. The genius himself has come to visit."

"I'm here to fetch August," Balder said.

"You what?"

"I'm taking him away with me, Lasse."

"You must be joking."

"I've never been more serious," he tried, and then Hanna appeared from a room across to the left. True, she was not as beautiful as she had once been. There had been too much unhappiness for that and probably too many cigarettes and too much drink as well. But still he felt an unexpected wave of affection, especially when he noticed a bruise on her throat. She seemed to want to say something welcoming, even under the circumstances, but she never had time to open her mouth.

"Why should you care all of a sudden?" Westman said.

"Because August has been through enough. He needs a stable home."

"And you think you can provide that, you freak? Since when have you done anything except stare at a computer screen?"

"I've changed," he said, feeling pathetic, in part because he doubted that he had changed one little bit.

A shiver ran through Balder as Westman came towards him with his mighty bulk and his pent-up rage. It became crushingly clear that he would have no means of resistance if that madman let fly. The whole idea had been insane from the start. But surprisingly there was no outburst, no scene, just a grim smile and then the words:

"Well, isn't that just great!"

"What do you mean?" Hanna asked.

"That it's about time, isn't it, Hanna? Finally some sense of responsibility from Mr. High and Mighty. Bravo, bravo!" Westman clapped his hands theatrically. Afterwards that was what Balder found the most frightening—how easily they let the boy go.

Perhaps they saw August only as a burden. It was hard to tell. Hanna shot Balder some glances which were difficult to read and her hands shook and her jaw was clenched. But she asked too few questions. She should really have been cross-examining him, making thousands of demands, warning him and worrying that the boy's routine would be upset. But all she said was:

"Are you sure about this? Will you manage?"

"I'm sure," he said. Then they went to August's room. Balder had not seen him for more than a year and he felt ashamed. How could he have abandoned such a boy? He was so beautiful and strangely wonderful with his curly, bushy hair and slender body and serious blue eyes, engrossed in a gigantic jigsaw puzzle of a sailboat. His body seemed to cry out, "Don't disturb me," and Balder walked up to him slowly, as if approaching an exotic creature.

He nonetheless managed to get the boy to take hold of his hand and follow him out into the corridor. He would never forget it. What was August thinking? What did he imagine was happening? He neither looked up at him nor at his mother and of course he ignored all the waving and the words of farewell. He just vanished into the lift with Balder. It was as simple as that.

. . .

August was autistic. He was most likely also mentally disabled, even though they had not received unequivocal advice on that point and anyone who saw him from afar might suspect the opposite. His exquisite face radiated an air of majestic detachment, or at least suggested that he did not think it worth bothering with his surroundings. But when you looked at him closely there was something impenetrable in his gaze. He had yet to say his first word.

In this he had failed to live up to all the prognoses made when he was two years old. At the time, the doctors had said that August probably belonged to that minority of autistic children who had no learning impairment, and that provided he was given intensive behavioural therapy his prospects were quite good. But nothing had turned out as they had hoped and Balder had no idea what had become of all that remedial care and assistance or even the boy's schooling. Balder had run away to the United States and lived in his own world. He had been a fool. But now he was going to repay his debt and take care of his son.

Right away he ordered casebooks and called specialists and educational experts and it became immediately apparent that none of the money he had been sending had gone towards August's care, but instead had trickled out to pay for other things, probably Westman's extravagances and gambling debts. The boy seemed to have been left pretty much to his own devices, allowed to become set in his compulsive ways, and probably worse—this was also the reason why Frans had come home.

A psychologist had called to express concern about unexplained bruises covering August's arms and legs, chest and shoulders. According to Hanna they were because the boy had fits and hurt himself thrashing back and forth. Balder had witnessed one already on the second day, and it scared him out of his wits. But that could not account for the sheer number and type of bruises, he thought. He suspected violence and turned for help to a GP and a former policeman whom he knew privately. Even if they were not able to confirm his fears with any degree of certainty he grew more and more angry about it and set about submitting a series of formal letters and reports.

He almost forgot all about the boy. It was easy to forget him. August spent most of his time sitting on the floor in the room Balder had prepared for him in the house in Saltsjöbaden, doing his exceedingly difficult jigsaws, assembling hundreds of pieces only to break them up and start afresh.

At first, Balder had observed him in fascination. It was like watching a great artist at work, and sometimes he was taken by the fantasy that the boy would glance up at any moment and say something grown-up. But August never uttered a word. If he raised his head from the puzzle it was to look straight past him towards the window overlooking the sea and the sunshine reflected on the water, and eventually Balder just left him alone. Balder seldom even took him outside into the garden.

From a legal point of view he did not have custody of the boy and he did not want to take any chances until he had sorted this out. So he let the housekeeper, Lottie Rask, do all the shopping—and all the cooking and cleaning. Balder was no good at that side of things. He understood computers and algorithms but not much else, and he immersed himself in them even more. At night he slept as badly as he had in California.

Lawsuits and storms loomed on the horizon and every evening he drank a bottle of red wine, usually Amarone, and that probably did little good either, except in the short term. He began to feel worse and worse and fantasized about vanishing in a puff of smoke or taking himself off to some inhospitable place, somewhere remote. But then, one Saturday in November, something happened.

It was a cold, windy evening and he and August were walking along Ringvägen in the Södermalm district, feeling frozen. They had been having dinner at Farah Sharif's on Zinkens väg. August should have long since been asleep, but dinner had gone on late and Balder had revealed far too much. Farah Sharif tended to have that effect on people. She and Balder had known each other since they had read computer sciences at Imperial College in London and now Sharif was one of the few people at his level in Sweden, or at least one of the few who was by and large able to follow his thinking. It was an incredible relief for him to meet someone who could understand.

He also found her attractive, but despite numerous attempts he had never managed to seduce her. Balder was not much good at seducing women. But this time he had received a farewell hug that almost turned into a kiss, which was a big step forward. He was still thinking about it as he and August passed Zinkensdamm sports centre. Maybe next time he should get a babysitter and then perhaps . . . Who knows? A dog was barking some ways off and there was a woman's voice shouting behind him, but it was hard to tell if she was upset or happy. He looked over towards Hornsgatan and the intersection where he could pick up a taxi or take the tunnelbana down to Slussen. It felt like it might rain. Once they got to the crossing, the light turned to red and on the other side of the street stood a worn-looking man in his forties who seemed vaguely familiar. At precisely that moment Balder took hold of August's hand.

He only wanted to make sure his son stayed on the sidewalk, but then he felt it: August's hand tensed as if the boy were reacting strongly to something. His look was intense and clear, as though the veil which always seemed to cover his eyes had been magically drawn aside, and instead of staring inwards at his own complexities, August had apparently understood something uniquely deep and great about that intersection. So Balder ignored the fact that the light had turned green. He just let his son stand there and observe the scene, and without knowing why, he was overcome by a strong emotion, which he found strange. It was only a look, after all, and not even an especially bright or joyful one at that. Yet it rang a distant bell, stirred something long dormant in his memory. For the first time in an age he felt hopeful.

CHAPTER 2

NOVEMBER 20

Mikael Blomkvist had slept for only a few hours because he had stayed up reading a detective novel by Elizabeth George. Not a particularly sensible thing to do. Ove Levin, the newspaper guru from Serner Media, was due to present a strategy session for *Millennium* magazine later that morning and Blomkvist ought to be rested and ready for combat.

But he had no desire to be sensible. Only reluctantly did he get up and make himself an unusually strong cappuccino with his Jura Impressa X7, a machine which had been delivered to his home a while ago with a note saying, "According to you, I don't know how to use it anyway." It now stood there in the kitchen like a memorial to a better time. He no longer had any contact with the person who had sent it. Nor did he feel that his work was particularly stimulating these days. Over the weekend he had even considered looking around for something new, and that was a pretty drastic idea for a man like Mikael Blomkvist. *Millennium* had been his passion and his life, and many of his life's best, most dramatic events had occurred in connection with the magazine. But nothing lasts forever, perhaps not even a love for *Millennium*. Besides, this was not a good time to own a magazine dedicated to investigative journalism. All publications with ambitions for greatness were bleeding to death and he could not help but reflect that while his own vision for *Millennium* may have been beautiful and true on some higher plane, it would not necessarily help the magazine survive.

He went into the living room sipping his coffee and looked out at the waters of Riddarfjärden. There was quite a storm blowing out there. From an Indian summer, which had kept the city's outdoor restaurants and cafés open well into October, the weather had turned nightmarish with gusts of wind and cloudbursts, and people hurried bent double through the streets. Blomkvist had stayed in all weekend, not only because of the weather. He had been planning revenge on an ambitious scale, but the scheme had come to nothing, and that was not like him, neither the former nor the latter.

He was not an underdog, and unlike so many other big media figures in Sweden he did not suffer from an inflated ego which needed constant boosting and soothing. On the other hand, he had been through a few tough years. Barely a month ago the financial journalist William Borg had written a piece in Serner's *Business Life* magazine under the heading: MIKAEL BLOMKVIST'S DAYS ARE OVER.

The fact that the article had been written in the first place and been given such prominence was of course a sign that Blomkvist's position was still strong. No-one would say that the column was well written or original, and it should have been easy to dismiss as yet another attack from a jealous colleague. But for some reason, incomprehensible in retrospect, the whole thing blew up. At first it might have been interpreted as a spirited discussion about journalism, but gradually the debate began to go off the rails. Although the serious press stayed out of it, all kinds of invective were being spewed out in social media. The offense came not only from financial journalists and industry types, who had reason to set upon their enemy now that he was temporarily weakened, but also from a number of younger writers who took the opportunity to make a name for themselves. They pointed out that Blomkvist was not on Twitter or Facebook and should rather be seen as a relic of a bygone age in which people could afford to work their way through whichever strange old volumes happened to take their fancy. And there were those who took the opportunity to join in the fun and create amusing hashtags like #inblomkvistsday. It was all a lot of nonsense and nobody could have cared less than Blomkvist—or so he persuaded himself.

It certainly did not help his cause that he had not had a major story since the Zalachenko affair and that *Millennium* really was in a crisis. The circulation was still OK, with 21,000 subscribers. But since advertising revenue was falling dramatically and there was no longer additional income from their successful books, and since one of the shareholders, Harriet Vanger, was not willing to put up any more capital, the board of directors had, against Blomkvist's wishes, allowed the Norwegian Serner newspaper empire to buy 30 percent of the shares. That was not as odd as it seemed, or not at first sight. Serner published weekly magazines and evening papers and owned a large online dating site and two premium TV channels as well as a football team in Norway's top division and ought not to have anything to do with a publication like *Millennium*.

But Serner's representatives—especially the head of publications, Ove Levin—had assured them that the Group needed a prestige product and that "everybody" in the management team admired *Millennium* and wanted only for the magazine to go on exactly as before. "We're not here to make money!" Levin said. "We want to do something significant." He immediately arranged for the magazine to receive a sizeable injection of funds.

At first Serner did not interfere in the editorial work. It was business as usual, but with a slightly better budget. A new feeling of hope spread among the editorial team, sometimes even to Blomkvist, who felt that for once he would have time to devote himself to journalism instead of worrying about finances. But then, around the time the campaign against him got under way—he would never lose the suspicion that the Serner Group had taken advantage of the situation—the tone changed and they started to apply pressure.

Levin maintained that of course the magazine should continue with its in-depth investigations, its literary reporting, its social fervour. But surely it was not necessary for all the articles to be about financial irregularities, injustices, and political scandals. Writing about high society—about celebrities and premieres—could also produce brilliant journalism, so he said, and he spoke with passion about *Vanity Fair* and *Esquire* in America, about Gay Talese and his classic piece "Frank Sinatra Has a Cold," and about Norman Mailer and Truman Capote and Tom Wolfe and heaven knows who else.

Blomkvist did not actually have any objections to that, not at the time. Six months earlier he had himself written a long piece about the paparazzi industry, and as long as he could find a serious angle then he was content to profile just about any lightweight. In fact he always said it isn't the subject that determines good journalism, it's the reporter's attitude. No, what he objected to was what he sensed was there between the lines: that this was the beginning of a longer-term assault and that, to the Group, *Millennium* was just like any other magazine, a publication you can damn well shift around any which way you want until it becomes profitable—and colourless.

So on Friday afternoon, when he heard that Levin had hired a consultant and commissioned several consumer surveys to present on Monday, Blomkvist had simply gone home. For a long time he had sat at his desk or lain in bed composing various impassioned speeches about why *Millennium* had to remain true to its vision: There is rioting in the suburbs; an openly racist party sits in Riksdagen, the parliament; intolerance is growing; fascism is on the rise and there are homeless people and beggars everywhere. In many ways Sweden has become a shameful nation. He came up with lots of fine and lofty words and in his daydreams he enjoyed a series of fantastic triumphs in which what he said was so relevant and compelling that the whole editorial team and even the entire Serner Group were roused from their delusions and decided to follow him as one.

But when sobriety set in, he realized how little weight such words carry if nobody believes in them from a financial point of view. Money talks, bullshit walks. First and foremost the magazine had to pay its way. Then they could go about changing the world. He began to wonder whether he could rustle up a good story. The prospect of a major revelation might boost the confidence of the editorial team and get them all to forget about Levin's surveys and forecasts.

Blomkvist's big scoop about the Swedish government conspiracy that had protected Zalachenko turned him into a news magnet. Every day he received tips about irregularities and shady dealings. Most of it, to tell the truth, was rubbish. But just occasionally the most amazing story would emerge. A run-of-the-mill insurance matter or a trivial report of a missing person could be concealing something crucial. You never knew for sure. You had to be methodical and look through it all with an open mind, and so on Saturday morning he sat down with his laptop and his notebooks and picked his way through what he had.

He kept going until 5:00 in the afternoon. He did come across the odd item which would probably have gotten him going ten years ago, but which did not now stir any enthusiasm. It was a classic problem, he of all people knew that. After a few decades in the profession most things feel pretty familiar and even if something looks like a good story in intellectual terms it still might not turn you on. So when yet another squall of freezing rain whipped across the rooftops he stopped working and turned to Elizabeth George.

It wasn't just escapism, he persuaded himself. Sometimes the best ideas occur to you while your mind is occupied with something completely different. Pieces of the puzzle can suddenly fall into place. But he failed to come up with anything more constructive than the thought that he ought to spend more time lying around like this, reading good books. When Monday morning came and with it yet more foul weather he had ploughed through one and a half George novels plus three old copies of the *New Yorker* which had been cluttering up his bedside table.

So there he was, sitting on the living-room sofa with his cappuccino, looking out at the storm. He had been feeling tired and listless until he got to his feet with an abrupt start—as if he had suddenly decided to pull himself together and do something—and put on his boots and his winter coat and went out.

It was a parody of hell out there. Icy, heavy, wet squalls bit into his bones as he hurried down towards Hornsgatan, which lay before him looking unusually grey. The whole of Södermalm district seemed to have been drained of all colour. Not even one tiny bright autumn leaf flew through the air. With his head bent forward and his arms crossed over his chest he continued past Maria Magdalena kyrka to Slussen, all the way until he turned right onto Götgatsbacken and as usual he slipped in between the Monki boutique and the Indigo pub, then went up to the magazine on the fourth floor, just above the offices of Greenpeace. He could already hear the buzz when he was in the stairwell.

An unusual number of people were up there. Apart from the editorial team and the key freelancers, there were three people from Serner, two consultants and Levin, who had dressed down for the occasion. He no longer looked like an executive and had picked up some new expressions, among others a cheery "Hi."

"Hi, Micke, how's things?"

"That depends on you," Blomkvist said, not actually meaning to sound unfriendly.

But he could tell that it was taken as a declaration of war and he nodded stiffly, walked in and sat down on one of the chairs which had been set out to make a small auditorium in the office.

· · · ·

Levin cleared his throat and looked nervously in Blomkvist's direction. The star reporter, who had seemed so combative in the doorway, now looked politely interested and showed no sign of wanting to have a row. But this did nothing to set Levin's mind at ease. Once upon a time he and Blomkvist had both temped for *Expressen*. They mostly wrote quick news stories and a whole lot of rubbish. But afterwards in the pub, they had dreamed about the big stories and talked for hours of how they would never be satisfied with the conventional or the shallow but instead would always dig deep. They were young and ambitious and wanted it all, all at once. There were times when Levin missed that, not the salary, or the working hours, or even the easy life in the bars and the women, but the dreams—he missed the power in them. He sometimes longed for that throbbing urge to change society and journalism and to write so that the world would come to a standstill and the mighty powers bow down. Even a hotshot like himself wondered: Where did the dreams go?

Micke Blomkvist had made every single one of them come true, not just because he had been responsible for some of the big exposés of modern times, but also because he really wrote with that passion and power that they had fantasized about. Never once had he bowed to pressure from the establishment or compromised his ideals, whereas Levin himself . . . Well, really *he* was the one with the big career, wasn't he? He was probably making ten times as much as Blomkvist these days and that gave him an enormous amount of pleasure. What use were Blomkvist's scoops when he couldn't even buy himself a country place nicer than that little shack on the island of Sandhamn? My God, what was that hut compared to a new house in Cannes? Nothing!

No, it was Levin who had chosen the right path. Instead of slogging it out in the daily press, he had taken a job as media analyst at Serner and developed a personal relationship with Haakon Serner himself, and that had changed his life and made him rich. Today he was the most senior journalist responsible for a whole series of newspaper houses and channels and he loved it. He loved the power, the money, and all that went with it, yet he was not above admitting that even he sometimes dreamed about that other stuff, in small doses, of course, but still. He wanted to be regarded as a fine writer, just like Blomkvist, and that was probably why he had pushed so hard for the Group to buy a stake in *Millennium*. A little bird had told him that the magazine was up against it and that the editor-in-chief, Erika Berger, whom he had always secretly fancied, wanted to keep on her two latest recruits, Sofie Melker and Emil Grandén, and she would not be able to do so unless they got some fresh capital.

In short, Levin had seen an unexpected opportunity to buy into one of the most prestigious brands in Swedish media. But Serner's management was not enthusiastic, to put it mildly. On the contrary, people were heard to mutter that *Millennium* was old-fashioned and had a left-wing bias and a tendency to end up in fights with important advertisers and business partners, and if Levin had not argued his case so passionately, the plan would have come to nothing. But he had insisted. In a broader context, he argued, investing in *Millennium* represented a negligible amount, which might not yield vast profits but could give them something much greater, namely credibility. Right now, after the cutbacks and blood-letting, Serner's reputation wasn't exactly their prime asset. Taking a stake in *Millennium* would be a sign that the

Group did after all care about journalism and freedom of expression, even if Serner's board was not conspicuously keen on either. This much they were able to understand, and Levin got his acquisition through, and for a long time it looked like a winning outcome for all parties.

Serner got good publicity and *Millennium* kept its staff and was able to concentrate on what it did best: carefully researched, well-written reportage, with Levin himself beaming like the sun and even taking part in a debate at the Writers' Club, where he said in his usual modest way, "I believe in virtuous enterprise. I have always fought for investigative journalism."

But then . . . he did not want to think about it. At first he was not bothered by the campaign against Blomkvist. Ever since his former colleague's meteoric rise in the reporting firmament, Levin had rejoiced secretly whenever Blomkvist was sneered at in the media. This time, though, his joy did not last. Serner's young son Thorvald spotted the commotion—social media made a big thing of it. Even though he was not a man who took any interest in what journalists had to say, he did like power and intrigue, and here he saw a chance to score some points or simply to give the older generation on the board a good drubbing. Before long Thorvald had encouraged the CEO—who until quite recently had not concerned himself with such trivial matters—to declare that *Millennium* could not be given any special treatment, but would have to adapt to the new times like all of the other products in the Group.

Levin, who had just given Berger a solemn promise that he would not interfere in the editorial line, save perhaps as a "friend and adviser," all of a sudden felt that his hands were tied. He was forced to play some intricate games behind the scenes. He did everything he could to get Berger, Malin Eriksson, and Christer Malm at the magazine to buy into the new policy, which was never in fact clearly expressed—something that flares up in a panic rarely is—but which somehow entailed making *Millennium* younger and more commercial.

Naturally Levin kept repeating that there could be no question of compromising the magazine's soul and provocative attitude, even if he was not sure what he meant by that. He only knew that to keep the directors happy he needed to get more glamour into the magazine and reduce the number of lengthy investigations into industry, since they were liable to irritate advertisers and make enemies for the board. But of course he did not tell Berger this.

He wanted to avoid unnecessary conflict and, standing there in front of the editorial team, he had taken the trouble to dress more casually than usual. He did not want to provoke anyone by wearing the shiny suits and ties which had become all the rage at the head office. Instead he had opted for jeans and a white shirt and a dark-blue V-necked pullover which was not even cashmere. His long curly hair—which had always been his rebellious little gimmick—was tied in a ponytail, just like the edgiest journalists on TV. But most important of all, he kicked off in the humble tone he had been taught in his management courses:

"Hello, everybody," he said. "What foul weather! I've said it many times before, but I'm happy to repeat it: We at Serner are incredibly proud to be accompanying you on this journey, and for me personally it amounts to even more than that. It's the commitment to magazines like *Millennium* which makes my job meaningful; it reminds me why I went into this profession in the first place. Micke, do you remember how we used to sit in the Opera Bar and dream about everything we were going to achieve together? And we weren't exactly holding back on the booze, ha ha!"

Blomkvist did not look as if he remembered. But Levin was not put off.

"Don't worry, I'm not going to get all nostalgic," he said, "and there's no reason to do so. In those days there was much more money in our industry. Just to cover some piddling little murder in the middle of nowhere we would hire a helicopter and book an entire floor at the poshest hotel, and order champagne for the after party. You know, when I was about to go off on my first overseas trip I asked Ulf Nilson, foreign correspondent at the time, what the Deutschmark exchange rate was. 'I have no idea,' he said, 'I set my own exchange rate.' Ha! We used to pad our expenses, do you remember, Micke? Maybe we were at our most creative back then. In any case, all we had to do was knock out some quick copy and we still managed to sell any number of issues. But a lot has changed since then—we all know that. We now face cut-throat competition and it's not easy these days to make a profit in journalism, not even if you have Sweden's best editorial team, as you do. So I thought we should talk a little bit today about the challenges of the future. Not that I imagine for one moment that I can teach you anything. I'm just going to provide you with some context for discussion. We at Serner have commissioned some surveys about your readership and the public perception of *Millennium*. Some of it may give you a bit of a fright. But instead of letting it get you down you should see it as a challenge, and remember, there are some totally crazy changes happening out there."

Levin paused for a moment and wondered if the term "totally crazy" had been a mistake, if he had tried too hard to appear relaxed and youthful and whether he had started off in too chatty and jocular a vein. As Haakon Serner would say, "It is impossible to overestimate how humourless underpaid journalists can be." But no, he decided, I'll fix this. I'll get them on my side.

Blomkvist had stopped listening more or less at the point when Levin explained that they all needed to reflect on their "digital maturity," so he did not hear them being told that the younger generation were not aware of *Millennium* or Mikael Blomkvist. Unfortunately that was precisely the moment at which he decided he had had enough and went out to the coffee room. So he had no idea either that Aron Ullman, the Norwegian consultant, quite openly said, "Pathetic. Is he so scared that he's going to be forgotten?"

In fact nothing could have worried Blomkvist less at that moment. He was angry that Levin seemed to think consumer surveys might be their salvation. It was no bloody market analysis that had created the magazine. It was passion and fire. *Millennium* had gotten to where it was because they had all put their faith in it, and in what felt right and important, without trying to guess which way the wind was blowing. For a time he just stood there in the pantry, wondering how long it would take before Berger came to join him.

The answer was about two minutes. He tried to calculate how angry she was by the sound of her heels. But when she was standing next to him she only gave him a dejected smile.

"What's going on?" she said.

"I just couldn't bear to listen."

"You do realize that people feel incredibly uncomfortable when you behave like that?"

"I do."

"And I assume you also understand that Serner can do nothing without our agreement. We still have control."

"Like hell we do. We're their hostages, Ricky! Don't you get it? If we don't do as they say they'll withdraw their support and then we'll be sitting there with our arses hanging out," he said, loudly and angrily. When Berger hushed him and shook her head he added sotto voce:

"I'm sorry. I'm being a brat. But I'm going home now. I need to think."

"You've started to work extremely short hours."

"Well, I reckon I'm owed a fair bit of overtime."

"I suppose you are. Would you like company this evening?"

"I don't know. I honestly don't know, Erika," he said, and then he left the magazine offices and went out onto Götgatsbacken.

The storm and the freezing rain lashed against him and he swore, and for a moment considered dashing into Pocketshop to buy yet another English detective novel to escape into. Instead he turned onto Sankt Paulsgatan and as he was passing the sushi restaurant on the right-hand side his mobile rang. He was sure that it would be Berger. But it was Pernilla, his daughter, who had chosen the worst possible time to get in touch with a father who already felt bad about how little he did for her.

"Hello, my darling," he said.

"What's that noise?"

"It's the storm, I expect."

"OK, OK, I'll be quick. I've been accepted into the writing course at Biskops Arnö school."

"So, now you want to be a writer," he said, in a tone which was too harsh and almost sarcastic, and that was unfair in every way.

He should have simply congratulated her and wished her luck, but Pernilla had had so many difficult years hopping between one Christian sect and another, and from one course to another without finishing anything, that he felt exhausted by yet another change of direction.

"I don't think I detected a whoop of joy there."

"Sorry, Pernilla. I'm not myself today."

"When are you ever?"

"I'm just not sure writing is such a good idea, given how the profession is looking right now. I only want you to find something that will really work for you."

"I'm not going to write boring journalism, like you."

"Well, what are you going to write, then?"

"I'm going to write for real."

"OK," he said, without asking what she meant by that. "Do you have enough money?"

"I'm working part-time at Wayne's Coffee."

"Would you like to come to dinner tonight, so we can talk about it?"

"Don't have time, Pappa. It was just to let you know," she said, and hung up. Even if he tried to see the positive side in her enthusiasm it just made his mood worse.

He took a shortcut across Mariatorget and Hornsgatan

to reach his apartment on Bellmansgatan. It felt as if he had only just left. He got a strange sense that he no longer had a job and that he was on the verge of entering a new existence where he had oceans of time instead of working his fingers to the bone. For a brief moment he considered tidying the place up. There were magazines and books and clothes everywhere. But instead he fetched two Pilsner Urquell from the fridge and sat down on the sofa in the living room to think everything through more soberly, as soberly as one can with a bit of beer in one's body.

What was he to do?

He had no idea, and most worrying of all was that he was in no mood for a fight. On the contrary, he was strangely resigned, as if *Millennium* were slipping out of his sphere of interest. Isn't it time to do something new? he asked himself, and he thought of Kajsa Åkerstam, a quite charming person whom he would occasionally meet for a few drinks. Åkerstam was head of Swedish Television's "Investigative Taskforce" programme and she had for years been trying to recruit him. It had never mattered what she had offered or how solemnly she had guaranteed backing and total integrity. *Millennium* had been his home and his soul. But now . . . maybe he should take the chance. Perhaps a job on the "Investigative Taskforce" programme would fire him up again.

His mobile rang and for a moment he was happy. Whether it was Berger or Pernilla, he promised himself he would be friendly and really listen. But no, it was a withheld number and he answered guardedly.

"Is that Mikael Blomkvist?" said a young-sounding voice.

"Yes," he said.

"Do you have time to talk?"

"I might if you introduced yourself."

"My name is Linus Brandell."

"OK, Linus, how can I help?"

"I have a story for you."

"Tell me."

"I will if you can drag yourself down to the Bishops Arms across the street and meet me there."

Blomkvist was irritated. It wasn't just the bossy tone. It was the intrusion on his home turf.

"The phone will do just fine."

"It's not something which should be discussed on an open line."

"Why do I feel so tired talking to you, Linus?"

"Maybe you've had a bad day."

"I *have* had a bad day. You're right about that."

"There you go. Come down to the Bishop and I'll buy you a beer and tell you something amazing."

Blomkvist wanted only to snap: Stop telling me what to do! Yet without knowing why, or perhaps because he didn't have anything better to do than sit in his attic apartment and brood over his future, he said, "I pay for my own beers. But OK, I'm coming."

"A wise decision."

"But Linus . . ."

"Yes?"

"If you get long-winded and give me a load of wild conspiracy theories to the effect that Elvis is alive and you know who shot Olof Palme, then I'm going straight home."

"Fair enough," Brandell said.

CHAPTER 3

NOVEMBER 20

Edwin Needham—Ed the Ned, as he was sometimes called—
was not the most highly paid security technician in the
United States. But he may have been the best.

He grew up in South Boston, Dorchester, and his father
had been a monumental good-for-nothing, a drunk who
took on casual work in the harbour but often disappeared
on binges which not infrequently landed him in jail or in
hospital. These benders were the family's best time, a sort
of breathing space. When Ed's father could be bothered to
be around, he would beat his mother black-and-blue. Sometimes she would spend hours or even whole days locked
inside the toilet, crying and shaking. Nobody was very surprised when she died from internal bleeding at only forty-
six, or when Ed's older sister became a crack addict, still less
when the remains of the family soon afterwards stood teeter-
ing on the brink of homelessness.

Ed's childhood paved the way for a life of trouble and
during his teenage years he belonged to a gang that called
themselves "The Fuckers." They were the terror of Dorchester and got mixed up in everything from muggings to rob-
bing grocery stores. There was something brutal about Ed's

appearance from an early age and this was not improved by the fact that he never smiled and was missing two upper teeth. He was sturdy, tall, and fearless, and his face usually bore the traces of brawls with his father or gang fights. Most of the teachers at his school were scared to death of him. All were convinced that he would end up in jail or with a bullet in his head. But there were some adults who began to take an interest in him—no doubt because they discovered that there was more than aggression and violence in his intense blue eyes.

Ed had an irrepressible thirst for knowledge, an energy which meant that he could devour a book with the same vigour with which he could trash the inside of a public bus. Often he was reluctant to go home at the end of the school day. He liked to stay on in what was known as the technology room, where there were a couple of computers. He would sit there for hours. A physics teacher with the Swedish-sounding name of Larson noticed how good he was with machines, and after social services got involved he was awarded a scholarship and transferred to a school with more motivated students.

He began to excel at his studies and was given more scholarships and distinctions and eventually—something of a miracle in view of the odds against him—he went on to study Electrical Engineering and Computer Science at MIT. In his doctoral thesis he explored some specific fears around new asymmetric cryptosystems like RSA, and then went on to senior positions at Microsoft and Cisco before being recruited by the National Security Agency in Fort Meade, Maryland.

He did not have the ideal CV for the job, even leaving aside his criminal behaviour as a teenager. He had smoked a

lot of grass at college and flirted with socialist or even anar-
chist ideals. He had also been arrested twice for assault: bar
fights. He still had a volcanic temper and everyone who knew
him thought better of crossing him.

But at the NSA they recognized his other qualities.
Besides which it was the autumn of 2001, and the American
security services were so desperate for computer technicians
that they hired pretty much anybody. During the ensuing
years, nobody questioned Needham's loyalty—or patriotism,
for that matter—and if anyone thought to do so, his advantages always outweighed his shortcomings.

Needham was not just amazingly gifted. There was an
obsessive streak to his character, a manic precision and a furious efficiency which boded well for a man in charge of building IT security at America's most highly classified agency.
Nobody was damn well going to crack his system. It was a
matter of personal pride for him. At Fort Meade he quickly
made himself indispensable to the point where people were
constantly lining up to consult him. Not a few were terrified of him. He was often verbally abusive and had even told
the head of the NSA himself, the legendary Admiral Charles
O'Connor, to go to hell.

"Use your own busy fucking head for things you might
just be able to understand," Needham had roared when the
admiral had attempted to comment on his work.

But O'Connor and everyone else let it happen. They knew
that Needham screamed and yelled for the right reasons—
because colleagues had been careless about security regula-
tions, or because they were talking about things beyond their
understanding. Not once did he interfere in the rest of the
agency's work, even though his level of clearance gave him

access to pretty much everything, and even though in recent years the agency had found itself at the centre of a heated storm of opinion, advocates of both the right and the left seeing the NSA as the devil incarnate, Orwell's Big Brother. As far as Needham was concerned, the organization could do whatever the hell it wanted, so long as his security systems remained rigorous and intact.

And since he did not yet have a family he more or less lived at the office. Apart from the occasional drinking session, during which he sometimes turned alarmingly sentimental about his past, there was no suggestion that he had ever told outsiders what he was working on. In that other world he remained as silent as the grave, and if ever questioned about his profession, he stuck to a well-rehearsed cover story.

It was not by chance, nor was it the result of intrigue or manipulation, that he had risen through the ranks and become the NSA's most senior security chief. Needham and his team had tightened internal surveillance "so that no new whistle-blowers can pop up and punch us in the nose" and during countless sleepless nights created something which he alternately called "an unbreakable wall" or "a ferocious little bloodhound."

"No fucker can get in, and no fucker can dig around without permission," he said. And he was enormously proud of that.

He had been proud, that is, until that disastrous morning in November. The day had begun beautiful and clear. Needham, who had put on a belly over the years, came wad-dling over from the coffee machine in his characteristic way. Because of his seniority he completely ignored dress codes. He was wearing jeans and a red-checked lumberjack shirt, not quite buttoned at the waist, and he sighed as he settled down at his computer. He was not feeling great. His back and right knee hurt and he cursed the fact that his long-time colleague Alona Casales had managed to persuade him to come out for a run the night before. Sheer sadism on her part.

Luckily there was nothing super-urgent to deal with. He only had to send an internal memo with some new procedures for those in charge of COST, a programme for cooperation with the large IT companies—he had even changed the codenames. But he did not get far. He was just beginning to write, in his usual turgid prose:

```
<To keep you all on your toes as good par-
anoid cyber agents, so that no-one will be
tempted to fall back into idiotic habits,
I would just like to point out>
```

when he was interrupted by one of his alerts.

He was not particularly worried. His warning systems were so sensitive that they reacted to the slightest divergence in the information flow. It was going to be an anomaly, a notification perhaps that someone was trying to exceed the limits of their authorization, or some minor interference.

As it turned out, he never had time to investigate. In the next moment something so uncanny happened that for several seconds he refused to believe it. He just sat there, staring at the screen. Yet he knew exactly what was going on. A RAT had been put on the intranet, NSANet. Anywhere else he would have thought, *Those fuckers, I'll crush them.* But in here, the most tightly closed and controlled place of all, which he and his team had gone over with a fine-toothed comb a million times just this last year to detect every minuscule little vulnerability, here, no, no, it was impossible, it could not be happening.

Without realizing it he had closed his eyes, as if hoping that it would all vanish so long as he wasn't watching. But when he looked at the screen again, the sentence he had begun was being completed. His `<I would just like to point out>` was continuing on its own with the words: `<that you should stop with all the illegal activity. Actually it's pretty straightforward. Those who spy on the people end up themselves being spied on by the people. There's a fundamental democratic logic to it.>`

"Jesus, Jesus," he muttered—which was at least a sign that he was beginning to recover some of his composure.

But then the text went on: `<Chill out, Ed. Why don't you stick around for a ride? I've got Root>` at which point he gave a loud cry. The word "Root" brought down his whole world. For about a minute, as the computer raced through the most confidential parts of the system at lightning speed, he genuinely believed that he was going to have a heart attack. He was only vaguely aware that people were beginning to gather around his desk.

There was not much of a crowd down at the Bishops Arms. It was only early in the afternoon, and the weather was not encouraging people to venture out, not even to the local pub. Blomkvist was nevertheless met by shouts and laughter, and by a hoarse voice bawling:

"Kalle Blomkvist!"

It came from a man with a puffy red face, a halo of frizzy hair, and a fussy moustache whom Blomkvist had seen many times in the area. He thought his name was Arne. Arne would turn up at the pub as regularly as clockwork at 2:00 every afternoon, but today he had clearly come earlier than that and settled down at a table to the left of the bar with three drinking companions.

"Mikael Blomkvist," Blomkvist corrected him, with a smile.

Arne and his friends laughed as if Blomkvist's actual name was the greatest joke ever.

"Got any good scoops?" Arne said.

"I'm thinking about blowing wide open the whole murky scene at the Bishops Arms."

"You reckon Sweden's ready for a story like that?"

"No, probably not."

In truth Blomkvist quite liked this crowd, not that he ever talked to them more than in throwaway lines and banter. But these men were a part of the local scene which made him feel at home in the area, and he was not in the least bit offended when one of them shot out, "I've heard that you're washed up."

Far from upsetting him, it brought the whole campaign against him down to the low, almost farcical level where it belonged.

"I've been washed up for the last fifteen years, hello to you brother bottle, all good things must pass," he said, quoting the poet Fröding and looking around for someone who might have had the gall to order a tired journalist down to the pub. Since he saw no-one apart from Arne and his gang, he went up to Amir at the bar.

Amir was big and fat and jolly, a hardworking father of

four who had been running the pub for some years. He and Blomkvist had become good friends. Not because Blomkvist was an especially regular customer, but because they had helped each other out in completely different ways; once or twice when Blomkvist had not had the time to get to the state liquor store and was expecting female company, Amir had supplied him with a couple of bottles of red wine, and Blomkvist in turn had helped a friend of Amir's, who had no papers, to write letters to the authorities.

"To what do we owe this honour?" Amir said.

"I'm meeting someone."

"Anyone exciting?"

"I don't think so. How's Sara?"

Sara was Amir's wife and had just had a hip operation.

"Complaining and taking painkillers."

"Sounds like hard work. Give her my best."

"Will do," Amir said, and they chatted about this and that.

But Linus Brandell had not shown up and Blomkvist thought it was probably a practical joke. On the other hand there were worse tricks to fall victim to than to be lured down to your local pub, so he stayed for fifteen minutes discussing a number of financial and health-related concerns before he turned and walked towards the door, and that is when Brandell appeared.

Nobody understood how Gabriella Grane had ended up at Säpo, Swedish Security Police, least of all she herself. She had been the sort of girl for whom everybody had predicted a glittering future. Her old girlfriends from the classy suburb of Djursholm worried that she was thirty-three and neither famous nor wealthy nor married, either to a rich man or to any man at all for that matter.

"What's happened to you, Gabriella? Are you going to be a policeman all your life?"

Most of the time she could not be bothered to argue, or point out that she was not a police officer but had been head-hunted for the position of analyst, and that these days she was writing far more challenging texts than she ever had at the Foreign Ministry or during her summers as a lead writer for *Svenska Dagbladet*. Apart from which, she was not allowed to talk about most of it in any case. So she might as well keep quiet and simply come to terms with the fact that working for the Swedish Security Police was considered to be about as low as you can go—both by her status-obsessed friends and even more so by her intellectual pals.

In their eyes, Säpo was a bunch of clumsy right-leaning idiots who went after Kurds and Arabs for what were fundamentally racist reasons and who had no qualms about committing serious crimes or infringements of civil rights in order to protect former senior Soviet spies. And indeed, sometimes she was on their side. There was incompetence in the organization, values that were unsound, and the Zalachenko affair remained a major blot. But that was not the whole truth. Stimulating and important work was being done as well, especially now after the shakeout, and sometimes she had the impression that it was at Säpo, not in any editorial or lecture hall, that people best understood the upheavals that were taking place across the world. But she still often asked herself: How did I end up here, and why have I stayed?

Presumably some of it came down to flattery. No less

a person than Helena Kraft, the newly appointed chief of Säpo at the time, had contacted her and said that after all the disasters and bad press they had to rethink their approach to recruitment. We need to "bring on board the real talents from the universities and, quite honestly, Gabriella, there's no better person than you." That was all it had taken.

Grane was hired as an analyst in counter-espionage and later in the Industry Protection Group. Even though as a young woman, attractive in a slightly proper sort of way, she got called a "daddy's girl" and "snotty upper-class bitch," she was a star recruit, quick and receptive and able to think outside the box. And she could speak Russian. She had learned it alongside her studies at the Stockholm School of Economics, where needless to say she had been a model student but never that keen. She dreamed of something bigger than a life in business, so after her graduation she applied for a job at the Foreign Ministry and was accepted. But she did not find that especially stimulating either—the diplomats were too stiff and neatly combed. It was then that Helena Kraft had gotten in touch. Grane had been at Säpo for five years now and had gradually been accepted for the talent that she was, even if it was not always easy.

It had been a trying day, and not just because of the ghastly weather. The head of the division, Ragnar Olofsson, had appeared in her office looking surly and humourless and told her that she should damn well not be flirting when she was out on an assignment.

"Flirting?"

"Flowers have been delivered."

"And that's my fault?"

"Yes, I do think you have a responsibility there. When

we're out in the field we have to show discipline and reserve at all times. We represent an absolutely key public agency."

"Well, that's great, Ragnar dear. One always learns something from you. Now I finally understand that I'm responsible for the fact that the head of research at Ericsson can't tell the difference between normal polite behaviour and flirting. Now I realize that I should blame myself when men indulge in such wildly wishful thinking that they see a sexual invitation in a simple smile."

"Don't be stupid," Olofsson said, and he disappeared.

Later she regretted having answered back. That kind of outburst rarely does any good. On the other hand, she had been taking shit for far too long. It was time to stand up for herself. She quickly tidied her desk and got out a report from GCHQ in Britain about Russian industrial espionage against European software companies, which she had not yet had time to read. Then the telephone rang. It was Kraft, and that made Grane happy. She had never yet called to complain or moan. On the contrary.

"I'll get straight to the point," Kraft said. "I've had a call from the United States, it may be a bit of an emergency. Can you take it on your Cisco? We've arranged a secure line."

"Of course."

"Good, I'd like you to interpret the information for me, see if there's anything in it. It sounds serious, but I can't get a handle on the person who's passing it on—who, by the way, says that she knows you."

"Put me through."

It was Alona Casales at the NSA—although for a moment Grane wondered if it really *was* her. When they had last met, at a conference in Washington, D.C., Casales had been a self-assured and charismatic lecturer in what she somewhat euphemistically described as active signals surveillance: hacking, in other words. Afterwards she and Grane had gone out for drinks, and almost against her will, Grane had been enchanted. Casales smoked cigarillos and had a dark, sensuous voice well suited to her punchy one-liners and frequent sexual allusions. But now on the telephone she sounded confused and sometimes unaccountably lost the thread of what she was saying.

Blomkvist did not really know what to expect, a fashionable young man, presumably, some cool dude. But the fellow who had arrived looked like a tramp, short and with torn jeans and long, dark, unwashed hair, something slightly sleepy and shifty in his eyes. He was maybe twenty-five, perhaps younger, had bad skin, and a rather ugly mouth sore. Linus Brandell did not look like someone who was sitting on a major scoop.

"Linus Brandell, I presume."

"That's right. Sorry I'm late. Happened to bump into a girl I knew. We were in the same class in ninth grade, and she—"

"Let's get this over with," Blomkvist interrupted him, and led the way to a table towards the back of the pub.

When Amir appeared, smiling discreetly, they ordered two pints of Guinness and then sat quietly for a few seconds. Blomkvist could not understand why he felt so irritated. It was not like him; perhaps the whole drama with Serner was getting to him after all. He smiled at Arne and his gang, all of whom were studying them keenly.

"I'll come straight to the point," Brandell said.

"That sounds good."

"Do you know Supercraft?"

Blomkvist did not know much about computer games, but even he had heard of Supercraft.

"By name, yes."

"No more than that?"

"No."

"In that case you won't know that what makes this game different, or at least so special, is that it has a particular AI function: it allows you to communicate with a player about war strategy without being really sure, at least to begin with, whether you're talking to a real person or a digital creation."

"You don't say," Blomkvist said. Nothing interested him less than the finer points of a damn game.

"It's a minor revolution in the industry and I was actually involved in developing it," Brandell said.

"Congratulations. In that case you must have made a killing."

"That's just it."

"Meaning what?"

"The technology was stolen from us and now Truegames is making billions while we don't get a single öre."

Blomkvist had heard this line before. He had even spoken to an old lady who claimed that it was actually she who had written the Harry Potter books and that J. K. Rowling had stolen everything by telepathy.

"So how did it happen?" he said.

"We were hacked."

"How do you know that?"

"It's been established by experts at the National Defence

Radio Establishment. I can give you a name there if you want, and also by a . . ."

Brandell hesitated.

"Yes?"

"Nothing. But even the Security Police were involved, you can talk to Gabriella Grane there. She's an analyst and I think she'll back me up. She mentioned the incident in a report which she published last year. I have the reference number here . . ."

"In other words, this isn't news," Blomkvist interrupted.

"No, not in that sense. *New Technology* and *Computer Sweden* wrote about it. But since Frans didn't want to talk and on a couple of occasions even denied that there had been any breach at all, the story never went very far."

"But it's still old news."

"I suppose so."

"So why should I be listening to you, Linus?"

"Because now Frans seems to have understood what happened. I think he's sitting on pure dynamite. He's become completely manic about security. Only uses hyper-encryption for his phones and e-mail and he's just got a new burglar alarm with cameras and sensors and all that crap. I think you should talk to him. That's why I got in touch with you. A guy like you could get him to open up. He doesn't listen to me."

"So you order me down here because it seems as if someone called Frans may be sitting on some dynamite."

"Not someone called Frans, Blomkvist, it's none other than Frans Balder, didn't I say that? I was one of his assistants."

Blomkvist searched his memory: the only Balder he could think of was Hanna Balder, the actress, whatever might have become of her.

"Who's he?" he said.

The look he got was so full of contempt that he was taken aback.

"Where've you been living, Mars? Frans Balder is a legend. A household name."

"Really?"

"Christ, yes!" Brandell said. "Google him and you'll see. He became a professor of computer sciences at just twenty-seven and for two decades he's been a leading authority on research in artificial intelligence. There's hardly anyone who's as far advanced in the development of quantum computing and neural networks. He has an amazingly cool, back-to-front brain. Thinks along completely unorthodox, ground-breaking lines and as you can probably imagine the computer industry's been chasing him for years. But for a long time Balder refused to let himself be recruited. He wanted to work alone. Well, not altogether alone, he's always had assistants he's driven into the ground. He wants results, and he's always saying: 'Nothing is impossible. Our job is to push back the frontiers, blah blah blah.' But people listen to him. They'll do anything for him. They'll just about die for him. To us nerds he is God Almighty."

"I can hear that."

"But don't think that I'm some starstruck admirer, not at all. There's a price to be paid, I know that better than anyone. You can do great things with him, but you can also go to pieces. Balder isn't even allowed to look after his own son. He messed up in some unforgivable way. There are a lot of different stories, assistants who've hit the wall and wrecked their lives and God knows what. But although he's always been obsessive he's never behaved like this before. I just know he's onto something big."

"You just know that."

"You've got to understand, he's not normally a paranoid person. Quite the opposite. He's never been anywhere near paranoid enough, given the level of the things he's been dealing with. But now he's locked himself into his house and hardly goes out. He seems afraid and he really doesn't do scared."

"And he was working on computer games?" Blomkvist said, without hiding his scepticism.

"Well . . . since he knew we were all gaming freaks he probably thought we should get to work on something that we liked. But his AI programme was also right for that business. It was a perfect testing environment and we got fantastic results. We broke new ground. It was just . . ."

"Get to the point, Linus."

"Frans and his lawyers wrote a patent application for the most innovative parts of the technology, and that's when the first shock came. A Russian engineer at Truegames had thrown together an application just before, which blocked our patent. It can hardly have been a coincidence. But that didn't really matter. The patent was only a paper tiger. The interesting thing was how the hell they had managed to find out about what we'd been doing. Since we were all devoted to Frans even to the point of death, there was only one possibility: we must have been hacked, in spite of all our security measures."

"Is that when you got in touch with Säpo and the National Defence Radio Establishment?"

"Not at first. Balder is not too keen on people who wear ties and work from nine to five. He prefers obsessive idiots who are glued to their computers all night long, so instead he got in touch with some weirdo hacker he had met somewhere and she said straightaway that we'd had a breach. Not that she seemed particularly credible. I wouldn't have hired her, if you see what I mean, and perhaps she was just talking drivel. But her main conclusions were nevertheless subsequently borne out by people at the NDRE."

"But no-one knew who had hacked you?"

"No, no, trying to trace hacker breaches is often a complete waste of time. But they must have been professionals. We had done a lot of work on our IT security."

"And now you suspect that Balder may have found out something more about it?"

"Definitely. Otherwise he wouldn't be behaving so strangely. I'm convinced he got wind of something at Solifon."

"Is that where he worked?"

"Yes, oddly enough. As I told you before, Balder had previously refused to let himself be tied up by the big computer giants. No-one has ever banged on as much as he did about being an outsider, about the importance of being independent and not being a slave to commercial forces. But out of the blue, as we stood there with our trousers down and our technology stolen, he suddenly accepted an offer from Solifon, of all companies. Nobody could understand it. OK, they were offering a megasalary, free rein, and all of that crap, like: Do whatever the hell you want, just work for us, and that probably sounded cool. It would definitely have been cool for anyone who wasn't Frans Balder. But he'd had any number of offers like that from Google, Apple, and all the others. Why was this suddenly so interesting? He never explained. He just packed his stuff and disappeared and from what I've heard it went swimmingly at first. Balder continued to develop our technology and I think Solifon's owner, Nicolas Grant, was beginning to fantasize about revenues in the billions. There was great excitement. But then something happened."

"Something that you don't actually know so much about."

"No, we lost contact. Balder lost contact with pretty much everyone. But I understand enough to know that it must have been something serious. He had always preached openness and enthused about the Wisdom of Crowds, all that stuff; the importance of using the knowledge of many, the whole Linux way of thinking. But at Solifon he apparently kept every comma secret, even from those who were closest to him, and then—wham bam—he gave notice and went home, and now he's sitting there in his house in Saltsjöbaden and doesn't even go out into the garden or give a damn how he looks."

"So what you've got, Linus, is a story about a professor who seems to be under pressure and who doesn't care what he looks like—though it's not clear how the neighbours can see that, if he never goes outside?"

"Yes, but I think . . ."

"Listen, this could be an interesting story. But unfortunately it isn't for me. I'm no IT reporter—as someone so wisely wrote the other day, I'm a caveman. I'd recommend you contact Raoul Sigvardsson at the *Swedish Morning Post*. He knows everything about that world."

"No, no, Sigvardsson is a lightweight. This is way above his head."

"I think you underestimate him."

"Come on, now, don't chicken out. This could be your comeback, Blomkvist."

Blomkvist made a tired gesture towards Amir, who was wiping a table not far from them.

"Can I give you some advice?" Blomkvist said.

"What? Yes . . . sure."

"Next time you have a story to sell, don't try to explain to the reporter what's in it for him. Do you know how many times people have played me that tune? 'This is going to be the biggest thing in your career. Bigger than Watergate!' You'd do better with just some basic matter-of-fact information, Linus."

"I just meant . . ."

"Yes, what actually *did* you mean?"

"That you should talk to Frans. I think he would like you. You're the same uncompromising kind of guy."

It was as if Brandell had suddenly lost his self-confidence and Blomkvist wondered if he had not been unnecessarily tough. As a general principle, he tended to be friendly and encouraging towards people who gave him tip-offs, however weird they sounded. Not just because there might be a good story even in something that sounded crazy, but also because he recognized that often he was their last straw. There were many who turned to him when everyone else had stopped listening. He was the last hope, and there was never any excuse to be scornful.

"Listen," he said. "I've had a really bad day and I didn't mean to sound sarcastic."

"That's OK."

"And you know," Blomkvist said. "There's one thing

which interests me about this story. You said you had a visit
from a female hacker."

Alona Casales was not one to become nervous easily and she
rarely had trouble staying on topic. She was forty-eight, tall,
and outspoken, with a voluptuous figure and small intelligent eyes which could make anybody feel insecure. She often
seemed to see straight through people and did not suffer
from a surfeit of deference to superiors. She would give anyone a dressing down, even the Attorney General if he came
calling. That was one of the reasons why Ed the Ned got on
so well with her. Neither of them attached much importance
to status; all they cared about was ability.

Nevertheless, she had completely lost it with the head
of Sweden's Security Police. This had nothing to do with
Helena Kraft. It was because of the drama unfolding in the
open-plan office behind her. Admittedly they were all used to
Needham's explosions of rage. But something told her right
away that what was going on now was on an altogether different scale.

The man seemed paralyzed. While Casales sat there
blurting some confused words down the line, people gathered around him and all of them, without exception, looked
scared. But perhaps because she was in a state of shock, Casales did not hang up or say that she would call back later. She
let herself be put through to Gabriella Grane, that charming young analyst whom she had met and tried to seduce in
Washington. Even though Alona had not succeeded in taking
her to bed, she had been left with a deep feeling of pleasure.

"Hello, my dear," she said. "How are you?"

"Not so bad," Grane answered. "We're having some terrible storms, but otherwise everything's fine."

"I really enjoyed that last time we saw each other."

"Absolutely, it was nice. I was hungover the whole of the next day. But I don't suppose you're calling to ask me out."

"Unfortunately not. I'm calling because we've picked up signs of a serious threat to a Swedish scientist."

"Who?"

"For a long time we had trouble understanding the information, or even working out which country it concerned. The communication was encrypted and used only vague codenames, but still, once we got a few small pieces of the puzzle we managed . . . what the *hell* . . ."

"What?"

"One second . . ."

Casales's computer screen blinked, then went blank, and as far as she could see the same thing was happening all over the office floor. For a moment she wondered what to do, but carried on the conversation; it might just be a power outage, after all, although the overhead lights seemed to be working.

"I'm still here," said Grane.

"Thanks, I appreciate it. Sorry about this. It's complete chaos here. Where was I?"

"You were talking about pieces of the puzzle."

"Right, yes, we put two and two together, because there's always one person who's careless, however professional they try to be, or who . . ."

"Yes?"

"Um . . . talks, gives an address or something, in this case it was more like . . ."

Casales fell silent again. None other than Commander

Jonny Ingram, one of the most senior people in the NSA with contacts high up in the White House, had come onto the office floor. Ingram was trying to appear as composed as usual. He even cracked some joke to a group sitting further away. But he was not fooling anyone. Beneath his polished and tanned exterior—ever since his time as head of the cryptological centre in Oahu he was suntanned all year round—you could sense something nervous in his expression. Now he seemed to want everybody's attention.

"Hello, are you still there?" Grane said on the other end of the line.

"I'm going to have to leave you, unfortunately. I'll call you back," Casales said, and hung up.

At that moment she became very worried indeed. There was a feeling in the air that something terrible had happened, maybe another major terrorist attack. But Ingram carried on with his soothing act and, even though there was sweat on his upper lip and forehead, he kept repeating that it was nothing serious. Most likely a virus, he said, which had found its way into the intranet, despite all the security precautions.

"To be on the safe side, we've shut down our servers," he said, and for a moment he really did manage to calm things down. "What the hell," people seemed to be saying, "a virus isn't such a big deal."

But then Ingram started spouting such vague statements that Casales could not stop herself from shouting:

"Tell us what's actually happening!"

"We don't know that much yet. But it's possible that our systems have been hacked. We'll get back to you as soon as we know more," Ingram said, looking concerned, and a murmur ran through the room.

"Is it the Iranians again?" somebody wondered.

"We think . . ." Ingram said.

He got no further. Ed Needham, the person who should have been standing there in the first place, explaining what was happening, interrupted him brusquely and got to his feet, a bear of a man. At that moment there was no denying that he was an imposing sight. Gone was the deflated Needham from a minute before; he now exuded a tremendous sense of determination.

"No," he hissed. "It's a hacker, a fucking superhacker, and I'm going to cut his balls off."

"The female hacker doesn't really have anything to do with this story," said Brandell, nursing his beer. "She was more like Balder's social project."

"But she seemed to know her stuff."

"Or she was just lucky. She talked a lot of rubbish."

"So you met her?"

"Yes, just after Balder took off for Silicon Valley."

"How long ago was that?"

"Almost a year. I'd moved our computers into my apartment on Brantingsgatan. My life was not great, to put it mildly. I was single and broke and hungover, my place looked like hell. I had just spoken to Frans on the telephone, and he'd been going on like some boring old dad. There was a lot of: Don't judge her by how she looks, appearances can be deceptive blah blah, and hey, he said that to *me*! I'm not exactly the ideal son-in-law myself. I've never worn a jacket and tie in my entire life, and if anyone knows what people look like in the hacker community, then I do. Whatever, so I was sitting there waiting for this girl. Thought that she would at least knock. But she just opened the door and walked in."

"What did she look like?"

"Bloody awful . . . but then, she was also sexy in a weird way. But dreadful!"

"Linus, I'm not asking you to rate her looks. I just want to know what she was wearing and if she maybe mentioned what her name was."

"I have no idea who she was," Brandell said, "although I did recognize her from somewhere—I had the feeling that it was something bad. She was tattooed and pierced and all that crap and looked like a heavy rocker or goth or punk, plus she was as thin as hell."

Hardly aware that he was doing it, Blomkvist gestured to Amir to pull him another Guinness.

"What happened?" Blomkvist said.

"Well, what can I say? I guess I thought that we didn't have to get going right away, so I sat down on my bed—there wasn't much else to sit on—and suggested that we might have a drink or something first. But do you know what she did then? She asked me to leave. She ordered me out of my own home, as if that was the most natural thing in the world. Obviously I refused. I was like: 'I do actually live here.' But she said: 'Piss off, get lost,' and I didn't see what choice I had so I was out for a while. When I got back she was lying there on my bed, smoking—how sick is that? And reading a book about string theory or something. Maybe I gave her some sort of dodgy look, what do I know, and she said that she wasn't planning on having sex with me, not even a little. 'Not even a little,' she said, and I don't think she looked me in the eye even once. She just announced that we'd had a Trojan, a

RAT, and that she recognized the pattern in the breach, the level of originality in the programming. 'You've been blown,' she said. And then she walked out."

"Without saying goodbye?"

"Without a single damn word."

"Christ."

"But to be honest I think she was bullshitting. The guy at the NDRE, who did the same investigation a little while later, and who probably knew much more about these kinds of attacks, was very clear that you couldn't draw any conclusions like that, and that however much he searched through our computer he couldn't find any spyware. But still his guess was—Molde was his name, by the way, Stefan Molde—that we'd been hacked."

"This woman, did she ever introduce herself in any way?"

"I did actually press her, but all she would say was that I could call her Pippi. Pretty surly she was too. It was obvious that that wasn't her real name, but still . . ."

"What?"

"I thought it suited her somehow."

"You know," Blomkvist said, "I was just about to head home again."

"Yes, I noticed that."

"But now everything's changed in a pretty major way. Did you say that your professor Balder knew this woman?"

"Well, yes."

"In that case I want to talk to him as soon as possible."

"Because of the woman?"

"Something like that."

"OK, fine," Brandell said thoughtfully. "But you won't

find any contact details for him. He's become so bloody secretive, like I said. Do you have an iPhone?"

"I do."

"In that case you can forget it. Frans sees Apple as more or less in the pocket of the NSA. To talk to him you'll have to buy a Blackphone or at least borrow an Android and download a special encryption programme. But I'll see to it that he gets in touch with you, so you can arrange to meet in some secure place."

"Great, Linus, thanks."

CHAPTER 4

NOVEMBER 20

Grane had just put on her coat to go home when Casales
called again, and at first she was irritated, not only because
of the confusion last time. She wanted to get going before the
storm got out of hand. The news on the radio had forecast
winds of up to sixty-seven miles per hour and the temperature falling to –10°C, and she was not dressed for it.

"I'm sorry it took a while," Casales said. "We've had an
insane morning. Total chaos."

"Here too," Grane said politely, looking at her watch.

"But I do have something important to tell you, as I said,
at least I think I do. It isn't that easy to analyze. I just started
checking out a group of Russians, did I mention that?" Casales said.

"No."

"Well, there are probably Germans and Americans involved and possibly one or more Swedes."

"What sort of group are we talking about?"

"Criminals, sophisticated criminals who don't rob banks
or sell drugs. Instead they steal corporate secrets and confidential business information."

"Black hats."

"They're not just hackers. They also blackmail and bribe people. Possibly they even commit old-fashioned crimes, like murder. I don't have much on them yet, to be honest, mostly codenames and unconfirmed links, and then a couple of real names, some young computer engineers in junior positions. The group is active in suspected industrial espionage and that's why the case has ended up on my desk. We're afraid that cutting-edge American technology has fallen into Russian hands."

"I understand."

"But it isn't easy to get at them. They're good at encryption and, no matter how hard I try, I haven't been able to get any closer to their leadership than to catch that their boss goes by the name of Thanos."

"Thanos?"

"Yes, derived from Thanatos, the god of death in Greek mythology, the one who's the son of Nyx—night—and twin brother to Hypnos—sleep."

"Real cloak-and-dagger stuff."

"Actually, it's pretty childish. Thanos is a supervillain in Marvel Comics, you know that comic book series with heroes like the Hulk, Iron Man and Captain America. First of all it's not particularly Russian, but more than that it's . . . how do I put this . . . ?"

"Both playful and arrogant?"

"Yes, like a bunch of cocky college kids messing around, and that really annoys me. In fact there's a whole lot that worries me about this story, and that's why I got so worked up when we learned through our signals surveillance that someone in the network may have defected, somebody who could maybe give us some insight—if only we could get our hands on this guy before they do. But now that we've looked more carefully, we realize it wasn't at all what we thought."

"Meaning what?"

"The guy who quit wasn't some criminal, but the opposite, an honest person who resigned from a company where this organization has moles, someone who presumably stumbled on some key information . . ."

"Keep going."

"In our view this person is now seriously under threat. He needs protection. But until recently we had no idea where to look for him, we didn't even know which company he'd worked at. But now we think we've zeroed in," Casales said. "You see, in the last few days one of these characters mentioned something about this guy, said that 'with him all the bloody Ts went up in smoke.'"

"The bloody Ts?"

"Yes, cryptic and strange, but it had the advantage of being specific and highly searchable. While 'bloody Ts' didn't give us anything, Ts generally, words beginning with T in conjunction with companies, high-tech firms of course, kept leading us to the same place—to Nicolas Grant and his maxim: Tolerance, Talent, and Teamwork."

"We're talking Solifon here, right?" Grane said.

"We think so. At least it felt like everything had fallen into place, so we began to investigate who had left Solifon recently. The company always has such high staff turnover, it's part of their philosophy—that talent should flow in and out. But then we started to think specifically about those Ts. Are you familiar with them?"

"Not really."

"They're Grant's recipe for creativity. By tolerance he

means that you need to be open to unconventional ideas and unconventional people. Talent—it doesn't just achieve results, it attracts other gifted people and helps create an environment that people want to be in. And all these talents have to form a team. As I'm sure you know, Solifon was a remarkable success story, producing pioneering technology in a whole series of fields. But then this new genius popped up, a Swede, and with him . . ."

". . . all the bloody Ts went up in smoke."

"Exactly."

"And it was Frans Balder."

"I don't think he normally has any problem with tolerance, or with teamwork for that matter. But from the beginning there was apparently something toxic about him. He refused to share anything and in no time at all he managed to destroy the rapport among the elite researchers at the company, especially when he started accusing people of being thieves and copycats. There was a scene with the owner, too. But Grant has refused to tell us what it was about— just that it was something private. Soon after, Balder gave notice."

"I know."

"Most people were probably relieved when he took off. The air at work became easier to breathe, and people began to trust each other again, at least up to a point. But Grant wasn't happy, and more importantly his lawyers weren't happy either. Balder had taken with him whatever he had been developing at Solifon, and there was a rumour—maybe because no-one really knew what it was—that he was onto something sensational that could revolutionize the quantum computer, which Solifon was working on."

"And from a purely legal point of view whatever he'd produced belonged to the company and not to him personally."

"Correct. So even though Balder had been going on about theft, when all was said and done he himself was the thief. Any day now things are likely to blow up in court, as you know, unless Balder manages to use whatever he has to frighten the lawyers. That information is his life insurance, so he says, and it may well be true. But in the worst-case scenario it could also be . . ."

". . . the death of him."

"That's what I'm afraid of," Casales said. "We're picking up stronger indications that something serious is getting under way, and your boss tells me that you might be able to help us."

Grane looked at the storm that was now raging outside, and longed desperately to go home and get away from it all. Yet she took off her coat and sat down again, feeling uneasy.

"How can I help?"

"What do you think he found out?"

"Do I take that to mean that you haven't managed either to bug him or hack him?"

"I'm not going to answer that one, sweetheart. But what do you think?"

Grane remembered how Frans Balder had stood in the doorway of her office not so long ago and muttered about dreaming of "a new kind of life"—whatever he may have meant by that.

"I assume you know," she said, "I met him before he joined Solifon, because he claimed that his research had been stolen. I didn't warm to him much, at first. Then there was talk in-house of getting him some form of protection, so I met him again. His transformation over the last few weeks was incredible. Not only because he had shaved off his beard, tidied up his hair and lost some weight. He was also mellower, even a little bit unsure of himself. I could tell he was rattled and at one point he did say that he thought there were people who wanted to harm him."

"In what way?"

"Not physically, he said. It was more his research and his reputation they were after. But I'm not so sure, deep down, he believed it would stop there, so I suggested he get a guard dog. I thought a dog would be excellent company for a man who lived out in the suburbs in far too big a house. But he wouldn't hear of it. 'I can't have a dog now,' he said rather sharply."

"Why's that, do you think?"

"I really don't know. But I got the feeling there was something weighing on him: he didn't protest too much when I arranged for a sophisticated alarm system in his house. It has just been installed."

"By whom?"

"A company we often use, Milton Security."

"Good. But my recommendation is to move him to a safe house."

"Is it that bad?"

"We think the risk is real."

"OK," Grane said. "If you send over some documentation I'll have a word with my superior right away."

"I'll see what I can do, but I'm not sure what I can get my hands on. We've been having . . . some computer issues."

"Can an agency like yours really afford that sort of thing?"

"No, you're right. Let me get back to you, sweetheart," she said, and hung up.

Grane remained quite still and looked out at the storm lashing against the window with increasing fury. Then she picked up her Blackphone and rang Balder. She let it ring and ring. Not just to warn him and see to it that he move to a safe place at once, but also because she suddenly wanted to know what he had meant when he said: "These last few days I've been dreaming about a new kind of life."

No-one would have believed that at that moment Balder was fully occupied with his son.

Blomkvist remained sitting for a while after Brandell had left, drinking his Guinness and staring into the distance. Behind him, Arne and his gang were laughing at something. But Blomkvist was so engrossed in his thoughts that he heard nothing, and hardly even noticed that Amir had sat down next to him and was giving him the latest weather forecast.

The temperature was dropping. The first snow of the year was expected to fall, and not in any pleasant or picturesque way. The misery was going to come blasting in sideways in the worst storm the country had seen for a long time.

"Could get hurricane-force winds," Amir said, and Blomkvist, who still was not listening, just said, "That's good."

"Good?"

"Yes . . . well . . . better than no weather at all."

"I suppose. But are you all right? You look shaken up. Was it a useful meeting?"

"Sure, it was fine."

"But what you got to hear rattled you, didn't it?"

"I'm not certain. Things are just a mess right now. I'm thinking of quitting *Millennium*."

"I thought you basically *were* that magazine."

"I thought so, too. But I guess there's an end to everything."

"That's probably true," Amir said. "My old man used to say that there's even an end to eternity."

"What did he mean by that?"

"I think he was talking about love everlasting. It was shortly before he left my mother."

Blomkvist snorted. "I haven't been so good at everlasting love myself. On the other hand . . ."

"Yes, Mikael?"

"There's a woman I used to know, she's been out of my life for some time now."

"Tricky."

"Well, yes it is. But now I've suddenly had a sign of life from her, or at least I think I did, and perhaps that's what's got me looking a bit funny."

"Right."

"I'd better get myself home. What do I owe you?"

"We can settle up another time."

"Great, take care, Amir," he said. He walked past the regulars, who threw a few random comments at him, and stepped into the storm.

It was a near-death experience. Gusts of wind blew straight through his body, but in spite of them he stood still for a while, lost in old memories. He thought about a dragon tattoo on a skinny, pale back, a cold snap on Hedeby Island in the midst of a decades-old missing person case, and a dug-up grave in Gosseberga that was nearly the resting place of a woman who refused to give up. Then he walked home slowly. For some reason he had trouble getting the door open, had to jiggle the key around. He kicked off his shoes and sat at his computer and searched for information on Frans Balder, Professor.

But he was alarmingly unfocused and instead found himself wondering, as he had so many times before: Where had she disappeared to? Apart from some news from her one-time employer, Dragan Armansky, he had not heard a word about her. It was as if she had vanished off the face of the earth and, although they lived in more or less the same part of town, he had never caught a glimpse.

Of course, the person who had turned up at Brandell's apartment that day could have been someone else. It was possible, but not likely. Who else would come stomping in like that? It must have been Salander, and Pippi . . . that was typical.

The nameplate on her apartment door on Fiskargatan was V. Kulla and he could well see why she did not use her real name. It was all too searchable and associated with one of the most high-profile trials the country had ever seen. Admittedly, it was not the first time that the woman had vanished in a puff of smoke. But ever since that day when he had knocked on her door on Lundagatan and given her hell for having written a personal investigation report about him which was rather too thorough, they had never been apart for so long. It felt a little strange, didn't it? After all, Salander was his . . . well, what the hell was she in point of fact?

Hardly his friend. One sees one's friends. Friends don't only get in touch by hacking into your computer. Yet he still felt this bond with Salander and, above all, he worried about her. Her old guardian Holger Palmgren used to say that Lisbeth Salander would always manage. Despite her appalling childhood, or maybe because of it, she was one hell of a survivor, and there was probably a lot of truth in that. But one could never be sure, not with a woman of such a background, and with that knack for making enemies.

Perhaps she really had gone off the rails, as Armansky had hinted when he and Blomkvist met over lunch at Gondolen about six months ago. It was a spring day, a Saturday, and Armansky had offered to buy beer and snaps and all the rest of it. Even though they were ostensibly meeting as two old friends, there was no doubt that Armansky only wanted to talk about Salander and, with the help of a few drinks, indulge in a spot of sentimentality.

Among other things, Armansky told Blomkvist that his company, Milton Security, had supplied a number of personal alarms to a nursing home in Högdalen, good equipment, he said.

But not even the best equipment in the world will help you if the electricity goes off and nobody can be bothered to fix it, and that is precisely what happened. There was a power outage at the home late one evening, and in the course of that night one of the residents, a lady called Rut Åkerman, fell and broke her femur, and she lay there for hour after hour pressing the button on her alarm to no avail. By the morning she was in critical condition and, since the papers were just then focusing heavily on negligence in care for the elderly, the whole thing became a big deal.

Happily, the old lady pulled through. But she also happened to be the mother of a senior figure in the Swedish Democrats party. When it emerged on the party's website, Unpixelated, that Armansky was an Arab—which incidentally he was not at all, although it was true that he was occasionally called "the Arab" in jest—there was an explosion in the posted comments. Hundreds of anonymous writers said that's what happens "when you let coons supply your technology." Armansky took it very badly, especially when the trolling affected his family.

But then suddenly, as if by magic, all those posts were no longer anonymous. You could see the names and addresses of those responsible, their job titles and how old they were. It was beautifully neat, as if they had all filled in a form. You could say that the entire site had been unpixelated, and of course it became clear that the posts did not just come from crackpots, but also from many established citizens, even some of Armansky's competitors in the security business. For a long time the hitherto-anonymous perpetrators were completely powerless. They could not understand what had happened. Eventually someone managed to close the site down, but nobody had any idea who lay behind the attack—except for Dragan Armansky himself.

"It was classic Salander," he said. "You know, I hadn't heard from her for ages and was convinced that she couldn't give a damn about me, or anybody else for that matter. But then this happened, and it was fantastic. She had stood up for me. I sent an effusive thanks by e-mail, and to my surprise an answer came back. Do you know what she wrote?"

"No."

"Just one single sentence: 'How the hell can you protect that creep Sandvall at the Östermalm clinic?'"

"And who's Sandvall?"

"A plastic surgeon to whom we gave personal protection because he'd been threatened. He'd pawed a young Estonian woman on whom he had performed breast surgery and she happened to be the girlfriend of a known criminal."

"Oops."

"Precisely, not such a clever thing to do. I answered Salander to say that I didn't think Sandvall was one of God's little angels any more than she did. But I pointed out that we don't have the right to make that kind of judgment. Even male chauvinist pigs are entitled to some degree of security. Since Sandvall was under serious threat and asked for our help we gave it to him—at double the usual rate."

"But Salander didn't buy your argument?"

"Well, she didn't reply, at least not by e-mail. But I suppose you could say she gave a different sort of answer."

"What do you mean?"

"She marched up to our guards at the clinic and ordered them to keep calm. I even think she gave them my regards. Then she walked straight past all the patients and nurses and doctors, went into Sandvall's office and broke three of his fingers and made the most terrifying threats against him."

"Jesus!"

"That's putting it mildly. Stark staring mad. I mean, to do something like that in front of so many witnesses and in a doctor's office on top of it all. And of course there was a huge fuss afterwards, a lot of brouhaha about lawsuits and prosecutions and the whole damn thing. You can just imagine: breaking the fingers of a surgeon who's lined up to perform a string of lucrative nips and tucks . . . It's the kind of thing that gets top lawyers seeing dollar signs everywhere."

"What happened?"

"Nothing. It all came to nothing, apparently because the

surgeon himself didn't want to take things any further. But still, Mikael, it was insane. No person in their right mind steams into a top surgeon's office in broad daylight and breaks his fingers. Not even Salander."

Blomkvist actually thought that it sounded pretty logical, according to Salander logic, that is, a subject in which he was more or less expert. He did not doubt for one second that that doctor had done far worse than grope the wrong girlfriend. But even so, he could not help wondering if Salander hadn't screwed up in this case, if only on the score of risk analysis.

It occurred to him that she might have *wanted* to get into trouble again, maybe to put some spice back into her life. But that was probably unfair. He knew nothing of her motives or her current circumstances. As the storm rattled the windowpanes and he sat there in front of his computer Googling Frans Balder, he tried to see beauty in the fact that they had now bumped into each other in this indirect way. It would seem that Salander was the same as ever and perhaps, who knows, she had given him a lead. Linus Brandell had irritated him from the word "go," but when Salander dropped into the story, he saw it all with new eyes. If she had taken the time to help Frans Balder then he could at least take a closer look at it, and with some luck find out a bit more about Salander at the same time.

Why had she gotten herself involved in the first place?

She was not just some itinerant IT consultant, after all. Yes, she could fly into a rage over life's injustices, but for a woman who had no qualms about hacking to get indignant about a computer breach, that was a little bit surprising. Breaking the fingers of a plastic surgeon, fine. But hackers? That was very much like throwing stones at glass houses.

There must be some backstory. Maybe she and Balder knew each other. It was not inconceivable and so he tried Googling their names together, but without getting any hits, at least not any that had relevance.

He focused on Frans Balder. The professor's name generated two million hits but most of them were scientific articles and commentaries. It did not seem as if Balder gave interviews, and because of that, there was a sort of mythological gloss over the details of his life, as if they had been romanticized by admiring students.

Apparently it had been assumed that Balder was more or less mentally disabled as a child until one day he walked into the headmaster's office at his school on Ekerö island and pointed out a mistake in the ninth grade maths books to do with so-called imaginary numbers. The mistake was corrected in subsequent editions and the following spring Balder won a national mathematics competition. He was reported as being able to speak backwards and create his own long palindromes. In an early school essay later published online he took a critical view of H. G. Wells's novel *The War of the Worlds* on the grounds that he could not understand how beings superior to us in every way could fail to grasp something so basic as the differences between bacterial flora on Mars and on Earth.

After graduating from secondary school he studied computer sciences at Imperial College in London and defended his thesis on algorithms in neural networks, which was considered revolutionary. He became the youngest ever professor at the Royal Institute of Technology in Stockholm and was elected to the Royal Swedish Academy of Engineering Sciences. These days he was regarded as a world authority on the

hypothetical concept of "technological singularity," the state
at which computer intelligence will have overtaken our own.

In most photographs he looked like a dishevelled troll
with small eyes, his hair standing on end. Yet he married the
glamorous actress Hanna Lind. The couple had a son who,
according to evening newspaper coverage, under the headline HANNA'S GREAT SORROW, was mentally disabled, even
though the boy did not—at least not in the picture accompanying the article—look in the least bit impaired. The
marriage fell apart and, amidst a heated custody battle in
Nacka district court, the *enfant terrible* of the theatre, Lasse
Westman, stepped into the fray to declare aggressively that
Balder should not be allowed to look after his son because
he cared more about "the intelligence of computers than
that of children." Blomkvist concentrated his efforts on trying to understand Balder's research, and for a long time he
sat engrossed in a complicated text about quantum processors in computers.

Afterwards he went into Documents and opened a file he
had created a year or so earlier. It was called [*Lisbeth stuff*].
He had no idea whether she was still hacking into his computer, but he could not help hoping that she did and wondered if he should not after all type out a little greeting. Long,
personal letters were not her thing. He would do better to go
for something brisk and a bit cryptic. He wrote:

```
<What should we make of Frans Balder's
artificial intelligence?>
```

CHAPTER 5

NOVEMBER 20

The words blinked onto the computer screen:

    <Mission accomplished!>

Plague gave a hoarse, almost deranged, yell, and that may have been unwise. But even if the neighbours had happened to hear, they could not have dreamed what it was about. Plague's home was not an obvious setting for high-level international security coups.

It felt more like a place where a social welfare case might hang out. Plague lived on Högklintavägen in Sundbyberg, a markedly unglamorous area with dull, four-storey, faded brick houses, and the apartment itself had nothing much going for it. It had a sour, stale smell, and his desk was covered in all sorts of rubbish: McDonald's containers and Coca-Cola cans, crumpled-up pages from notebooks, unwashed coffee cups, and empty candy wrappers. Even though some had actually made it into the wastepaper basket—which had not been emptied for weeks—you could hardly take a step in the room without getting crumbs or grit under your feet. But none of this would have surprised anyone who knew him.

Plague was not a man who normally showered or changed his clothes much. He spent his whole life in front of the computer even when he was not working: a giant of a man, overweight, bloated, and unkempt, with an attempt at an imperial beard that had long since turned into a shapeless thicket. His posture was dreadful and he had a habit of groaning when he moved.

But the man had other talents. He was a wizard on the computer, a hacker who flew unconstrained through cyberspace and was probably second only to one person in the field, a woman in this particular case. The mere sight of his fingers dancing across the keyboard was a joy to behold. He was as light and nimble online as he was heavy and clumsy in the other, more material world, and as a neighbour somewhere upstairs, presumably Herr Jansson, now banged on the floor, he answered the message he had received:

```
<Wasp, you bloody genius. They ought to
put up a statue to you!>
```

Then he leaned back with a delighted smile and tried to run through in his mind the sequence of events, savouring the triumph for a little while longer before going on to pump Wasp for every detail, and to ensure that she had covered her tracks. No-one must be able to trace them, no-one!

This was not the first time they had messed with a powerful organization. But this was on a new level, and many in Hacker Republic had actually been against the idea, Wasp herself most of all.

Wasp could take on just about any authority or person you would care to name, if it was necessary. But she did not like picking a fight for its own sake. She disliked that sort of childish hacker nonsense. She was not someone who hacked into supercomputers merely to show off. Wasp wanted to have a clear objective, and she always damn well analyzed the potential consequences. She weighed long-term risks against whatever need was being satisfied in the short term, and from that point of view it could not be said it made sense to hack into the NSA. Still, she let herself be talked into it. Nobody could quite understand why.

Maybe she was bored and wanted to stir up a bit of chaos so as not to die of tedium. Or else, as some in the group claimed, she was already in conflict with the NSA and therefore the breach amounted to little more than her personal revenge. But others in the group questioned even that and maintained she was looking for information, that she had been on the hunt for something ever since her father, Alexander Zalachenko, had been murdered at Sahlgrenska hospital in Göteborg.

Nobody knew for sure. Wasp had always had her secrets and actually her motives were unimportant, or so they tried to persuade themselves. If she was prepared to help, then they should just accept gratefully and not worry about the fact that, to begin with, she had not shown much enthusiasm, or hardly any feelings at all for that matter. At least she was no longer being awkward about it, and that seemed as much as anyone could expect.

Hacker Republic knew better than most that the NSA had outrageously overstepped its boundaries in recent years. These days the organization did not confine itself to eavesdropping on terrorists and potential security risks, or even just foreign heads of state and other powerful figures, but listened in on everything, or nearly everything. Millions, billions, trillions of communications and activities online were spied on and archived, and with each passing day the NSA went further and further and pried deeper and deeper into every private life. The agency had become one immeasurable, watchful, evil eye.

It was true that nobody in Hacker Republic could claim the moral high ground here. Every single one of them had made their way into parts of the digital landscape where they had no business being. Those were the rules of the game, so to speak. A hacker was someone who crossed the line, for better or for worse, someone who by virtue of his occupation broke rules and broadened the frontiers of his knowledge, without always being concerned about the distinction between private and public.

But they were not without ethics and above all they knew, also from their own experience, how power corrupts, especially power without control. None of them liked the thought that the worst, most unscrupulous hacking was no longer carried out by solitary rebels or outlaws, but by state behemoths who wanted to control their populations. Plague and Trinity and Bob the Dog and Flipper and Zod and Cat and the whole Hacker Republic gang had therefore decided to strike back by hacking the NSA and messing with them in one way or another.

That was no simple task. It was a little bit like stealing the gold from Fort Knox, and like the arrogant idiots they were they did not content themselves with breaking into the system. They also wanted superuser status, or "Root," in Linux language, and for that they needed to find unknown vulnerabilities in the system, for what was called a Zero-day

Exploit—first on the NSA's server platform and then further into the organization's intranet, NSANet, from which the authority's signals surveillance went out across the world.

They began as usual with a little social engineering. They had to get hold of the names of systems administrators and infrastructure analysts who held the complex passwords for the intranet. It would not do any harm either if there was a chance that some careless oaf was being negligent about security routines. Through their own contacts they came up with four or five names, among them one Richard Fuller.

Fuller worked in the NISIRT, the NSA Information Systems Incident Response Team, which supervised the intranet, and he was constantly on the lookout for leaks and infiltrators. Fuller was a decent sort of fellow: a Harvard law graduate, Republican, former quarterback, a dream patriot if one were to believe his CV. But through a former lover, Bob the Dog managed to discover that he was also bipolar, and possibly a cocaine addict.

When Fuller got excited he would do all sorts of stupid things, such as opening files and documents without first putting them in a so-called sandbox, a required security protocol. Furthermore he was very handsome and a little smarmy. Someone, probably Bob the Dog himself, came up with the idea that Wasp should travel to his home in Baltimore, go to bed with him, and catch him in a honey trap.

Wasp told them all to go to hell.

She also rejected their next idea, that they would compile a document containing information which looked like dynamite, specifically about infiltrators and leaks at the head office in Fort Meade. This would then be infected with malware containing an advanced Trojan with a high level of originality, which Plague and Wasp were to develop. The plan was to put out leads online which would lure Fuller to the file, and with a bit of luck get him so worked up that he would be careless with security. Not a bad plan at all—it could take them into the NSA's computer system without an active breach that might be traceable.

But Wasp said that she was not going to sit around waiting for that blockhead Fuller to put his foot in it. She did not want to have to rely on other people making mistakes. She was being generally contrary and bloody-minded, so no-one was surprised when she suddenly wanted to take over the whole operation herself. Even though there was a certain amount of protest, in the end they all gave in, but not without issuing a series of instructions. Wasp did carefully write down the names and details of the systems administrators which they had managed to obtain, and she did ask for help with the so-called fingerprinting: the mapping of the server platform and operating system. But after that she closed the door on Hacker Republic and the world, and Plague had no reason to think that she paid any attention to his advice, for example that she should not use her handle, her alias, and that she should not work from home but rather from some remote hotel under a false identity, in case the NSA's bloodhounds managed to track her down. Needless to say, she did everything her own way and all Plague could do was sit at his desk in Sundbyberg and wait, his nerves in tatters. Which is why he still had no idea how she had gone about it.

He knew one thing for certain: what she had achieved was legendary, and while the storm howled outside he pushed aside some of the rubbish on his desk, leaned forward, and typed on his computer:

<Tell me! How does it feel?>

<Empty>, came the answer.

Empty.

That was how it felt. Salander had hardly slept for a week and she had probably also had too little to drink and eat, and now her head ached and her eyes were bloodshot and her hands shook and what she wanted above all was to sweep all of her equipment to the floor. In one sense she was content, though hardly for the reason Plague or anyone else in Hacker Republic would have guessed. She was content because she had been able to get some new information on the criminal group she was mapping out; she had found evidence of a connection which she had previously only suspected. But she kept that to herself, and she was surprised that the others could have imagined that she would have hacked the system for the hell of it.

She was no hormone-fuelled teenager, no idiot show-off looking for a kick. She would only embark on such a bold venture because she was after something very specific, although it was true that once upon a time hacking had been more than just a tool for her. During the worst moments of her childhood it had been her way of escaping, a way to make life feel a little less boxed in. With the help of computers she could break through barriers which had been put in her way and experience periods of freedom. There was probably an element of that in the current situation too.

First and foremost she was on the hunt and had been ever since she woke up in the early light of dawn with her dream of that fist beating rhythmically, relentlessly on a mattress on Lundagatan. Her enemies were hiding behind smoke screens and this could be the reason why Salander had been unusually difficult and awkward of late. It was as if a new darkness emanated from her. Apart from a large, loudmouthed boxing coach called Obinze and two or three lovers of both sexes, she saw hardly anyone. More than ever she looked like trouble; her hair was straggly, her eyes threatening, and even though she sometimes made an effort she had not become more fluent at small talk. She spoke the truth or said nothing at all. As for her apartment here on Fiskargatan . . . that was a story in itself. It was big enough for a family with seven children, although in the years since she had acquired the place nothing had been done to decorate it or make it homey. There were only a few pieces of Ikea furniture, placed seemingly at random, and she did not even have a stereo system, perhaps because she did not understand music. She saw more melody in a differential equation than in a piece by Beethoven. Yet she was as rich as Croesus. The money she had stolen from that crook Hans-Erik Wennerström had grown to a little more than five billion kronor, so she could afford whatever she wanted. But in some way—which was typical of her—her fortune had not made any mark on her personality, unless perhaps it had made her yet more fearless. She had certainly done some increasingly drastic things of late.

She may have crossed a line by wandering into the NSA's intranet. But she had judged it necessary, and for several days and nights she had been totally absorbed. Now that it was over she peered out of tired, squinting eyes at her two work desks, set at a right angle. Her equipment consisted of the regular computer and the test machine she had bought, on which she had installed a copy of the NSA's server and operating system.

She had run her own fuzzing programme, which searched for errors and tiny vulnerabilities in the platform against the test computer. She then followed that up with debugging and black box penetration testing and various beta test attacks. The outcome of all that formed the basis of her root kit, including her RAT, so she could not afford to neglect a single point. She was scrutinizing the system from top to bottom and that was why she had installed a copy of the server here at home. If she had set to work on the real platform, the NSA technicians would have noticed it immediately.

This way she was able to work without distraction, day after day, and if she did happen to leave the computer, then it was only to doze off for a while on the sofa or to put a pizza in the microwave. Apart from that, she kept at it until her eyes hurt, especially with her Zero-day Exploit, the software which exploited the unknown security vulnerabilities and which would update her status once she had actually gotten in. It was completely mind-boggling. Salander had written a programme which not only gave her ownership over the system, but also the power to control remotely pretty much anything on an intranet of which she had only patchy knowledge.

That was the most extraordinary part. She was not just going to break in. She was going further, into NSANet, which was a self-contained universe barely connected to the ordinary net. She might look like a teenager who had failed all of her subjects at school, but give her source codes in computer programmes and a logical context and her brain just went click, click. What she had created was nothing less than wholly new and improved malware, an advanced Trojan with a life of its own.

She found the pay-as-you-go card she had bought from T-Mobile in Berlin and put it into her telephone. Then she used it to go online. Maybe she should have been far away in another part of the world, dressed up as her alter ego, Irene Nesser. If the security people at the NSA were diligent and on top of things, they just might be able to trace her to Telenor's base station here on the block. They would not get all the way through, at least not with the technology now available, but it would still be close enough and that would be very bad news. Yet she reckoned the advantages of sitting here at home outweighed the risk, and she did take all the security precautions she could. Like so many other hackers, she used Tor, a network by which her traffic bounced about among thousands and thousands of users. But she also knew that not even Tor was watertight—the NSA used a programme called EgotisticalGiraffe to crack the system—so she spent a long time further improving her own personal security. Only then did she go on the attack.

She sliced into the platform like a blade through paper, but she could not afford to become over-confident as a result. Now, quickly, she had to locate the systems administrators whose names she had been given and inject her Trojan into one of their files, thereby creating a bridge between the server network and the intranet, none of which was simple, not by any means. No warning bells or antivirus programmes must be allowed to start ringing. In the end she used the identity of a man called Tom Breckinridge to penetrate NSANet and then . . . every muscle in her body tensed. Before her eyes, her over-worked, sleepless eyes, the magic unfolded.

Her Trojan took her further and further in, into this, the most secret of the secret, and she knew exactly where she was going. She was on her way to Active Directory—or its equivalent—to upgrade her status. She would go from unwelcome little visitor to superuser in this teeming universe, and only once that was done would she try to get some sort of overview of the system. It wasn't easy. It was more or less impossible, in fact, and she did not have much time either.

She worked fast to get a grip on the search system and to pick up all the passwords and expressions and references, all the internal gibberish. She was at the point of giving up when she finally found a document marked TOP SECRET, NOFORN—no foreign distribution—not particularly remarkable in itself. But together with a couple of communications links between Zigmund Eckerwald at Solifon and cyber agents at the Department for the Protection of Strategic Technologies at the NSA, it turned into dynamite. She smiled and memorized every little detail. Then she caught sight of yet another document that seemed relevant. It was encrypted and she saw no alternative but to copy it, even if that would set alarm bells ringing at Fort Meade. She swore ferociously.

The situation was becoming critical. Besides, she had to get on with her official assignment, if "official" was the right word. She had solemnly promised Plague and the others at Hacker Republic to pull down the NSA's trousers, so she tried to work out whom she should be communicating with. Who was to get her message?

She settled for Edwin Needham, Ed the Ned. His name invariably came up in connection with IT security and as she quickly picked up some information about him on the intranet, she felt a grudging respect. Needham was a star. But she had outwitted him.

For a moment she thought twice about giving the game away. Her attack would create an uproar. But an uproar was exactly what she was looking for, so she went ahead. She had no idea what time it was. It could have been night or day, autumn or spring, and only vaguely, deep in her conscious-ness, was she aware that the storm over the city was building up, as if the weather was synchronized with her coup. In dis-tant Maryland, Needham began to write his e-mail.

He didn't get far, because in the next second she took over his sentence and then continued: <Those who spy on the people end up themselves being spied on by the people. There's a fundamental democratic logic to it>, and for a moment it felt as if those sentences hit the mark. She savoured the hot, sweet taste of revenge and after-wards she dragged Ed the Ned along on a journey through the system. The two of them danced and tore past a whole flickering world of things that were supposed to remain hid-den at all costs.

It was a thrilling experience, no question, and yet . . . when she disconnected and all her log files were automati-cally deleted, then came the hangover. It was like the after-math of an orgasm with the wrong partner. Those sentences that had seemed so absolutely right a few seconds ago began to sound increasingly childish and more and more like the usual hacker nonsense. Suddenly she longed to drink herself into oblivion. With tired, shuffling steps she went into the kitchen and fetched a bottle of Tullamore D.E.W. and two or three beers to rinse her mouth with, and sat down at her computers and drank. Not in celebration. There was no sense of victory left in her body. Instead there was . . . well, what? Defiance perhaps.

She drank and drank while the storm roared and congratulatory whoops came streaming in from Hacker Republic. But none of it touched her now. She hardly had the strength to stay upright and with a wide, hasty movement she swept her hand across the desktops and watched with indifference as bottles and ashtrays crashed to the floor. Then she thought about Mikael Blomkvist.

It must have been the alcohol. Blomkvist had a way of popping up in her thoughts when she was drunk, as old flames do, and without quite realizing what she was doing she hacked into his computer. She still had a shortcut into his system—it was not exactly the NSA—and at first she wondered what she was doing there.

Could she care less about him? He was history, just an attractive idiot she had once happened to fall in love with, and she was not going to make that mistake again. She'd much rather get out of there and not look at another computer for weeks. Yet she stayed on his server and in the next moment her face lit up. Kalle Fucking Blomkvist had created a file called [*Lisbeth stuff*] and in that document there was a question for her:

```
<What should we make of Frans Balder's
artificial intelligence?>
```

She gave a slight smile, in spite of it all, and that was partly because of Frans Balder. He was her kind of computer nerd, passionate about source codes and quantum processors and the potential of logic. But mostly she was smiling at the fact that Blomkvist had stumbled into the very same situation she was in. Even though she debated for some time whether just to shut down and go to bed, she wrote back:

> <Balder's intelligence isn't in the least
> bit artificial. How's your own these days?>
> <And what happens, Blomkvist, if we create
> a machine which is a little bit cleverer
> than we are?>

Then she went into one of her bedrooms and collapsed with her clothes on.

CHAPTER 6

NOVEMBER 20

Despite his best intentions to be a full-time father, and in spite of the intense moment of hope and emotion on Hornsgatan, Frans Balder had sunk back into that deep concentration which could be mistaken for anger. Now his hair was standing on end and his upper lip was shiny with sweat. It was at least three days since he had shaved or taken a shower. He was even grinding his teeth. For hours the world and the storm outside had ceased to exist for him, and he even failed to notice what was going on at his feet. They were small, awkward movements, as if a cat or an animal had crept in under his legs; it was a while before he realized that August was crawling around under his desk. Balder gave him a dazed look, as if the stream of programming codes still lay like a film over his eyes.

"What are you after?"

August looked up at him with a pleading, clear look in his eyes.

"What?" Balder said. "What?" And then something happened.

The boy picked up a piece of paper covered in quantum algorithms which was lying on the floor and feverishly moved his hand back and forth over it. For a moment Balder thought the boy was about to have another attack. But no, it was rather as if August were pretending to write. Balder felt his body go tense and again he was reminded of something important and remote, the same feeling as at the crossing on Hornsgatan. But this time he understood what it was.

He thought back to his own childhood, when numbers and equations had been more important than life itself. His spirits rose and he burst out, "You want to do sums, don't you? Of course, you want to do sums!" and the next moment he hurried off to fetch some pencils and ruled A4 paper, which he put on the floor in front of August.

Then he wrote down the simplest series of numbers he could think of, Fibonacci's sequence, in which every number is the sum of the preceding two, 1, 1, 2, 3, 5, 8, 13, 21, and left a space for the next number: 34. Then it occurred to him that this was likely too simple, so he also wrote down a geometric sequence: 2, 6, 18, 54 . . . in which every number is multiplied by three and the next number should therefore be 162. To solve a problem like that, he thought, a gifted child would not need a great deal of prior knowledge. Balder slipped into a daydream that the boy was not disabled at all, rather an enhanced copy of himself; he, too, had been slow to speak and interact socially, but he had understood mathematical relationships long before he uttered his first word.

He sat beside the boy for a long time and waited. But nothing happened. August just stared at the numbers with his glassy look. In the end Balder left him alone, went upstairs and drank some fizzy water, and then settled down at the kitchen table to continue to work. But now his concentration had vanished and he started absentmindedly flicking through the latest issue of *New Scientist*. After half an hour or so he went back downstairs to August, who was still sitting on his heels in the same immobile posture in which he had left him. Then Balder noticed something intriguing.

A second later he had the sense of being confronted by something totally inexplicable.

Hanna Balder was standing in the kitchen on Torsgatan smoking a filterless Prince. She had on a blue dressing gown and worn grey slippers and although her hair was thick and beautiful and she was still attractive, she looked haggard. Her lip was swollen and the heavy make-up around her eyes was not there purely for aesthetic reasons. Hanna Balder had taken another beating.

It would be wrong to say that she was used to it. No-one gets used to that sort of abuse. But it was part of her everyday existence and she could scarcely remember the happy person she had once been. Fear had become a natural element of her personality and for some time now she had been smoking sixty cigarettes a day and taking tranquilizers.

She had known for a while that Lasse regretted having been so generous to Frans. In fact it had been a mystery from the start. Westman had been relying on the money Balder sent them for August. For long periods they had been living off it and often he would make Hanna write an e-mail full of lies about unforeseen expenses for some educational expert or remedial therapy, which obviously the funds had never gone anywhere near. That's what made it so odd. Why had he given up all of that and let Balder take the boy away?

Deep down Hanna knew the answer. It was hubris brought on by alcohol. It was the promise of a part in a new detective series on TV4 which had boosted his confidence still further. But most of all it was August. Westman found the boy creepy and weird even though to her that was incomprehensible. How could anyone detest August?

He sat on the floor with his puzzles and did not bother anyone. Yet he had that strange look which was turned inwards rather than outwards, which usually made people smile and say that the boy must have a rich inner life, but which got under Westman's skin.

"Jesus, Hanna! He's looking straight through me," he would burst out.

"But you say that he's just an idiot."

"He is an idiot, but there's something funny about him all the same. I think he hates me."

That was nonsense, nothing more. August did not even look at Westman or at anyone else for that matter, and he did not have it in him to wish anybody ill. The world out there disturbed him and he was happiest inside his own bubble. But Westman in his drunken ravings believed that the boy was plotting some form of revenge, and that must have been the reason he let August and the money slip out of their lives. Pathetic. That at least is how Hanna had interpreted it. But now as she stood there by the sink smoking her cigarette so furiously and nervously that she got tobacco on her tongue, she wondered if there had not been something in it after all. Maybe August *did* hate Westman. Maybe he *did* want to punish him for all the punches he had taken, and maybe— Hanna closed her eyes and bit her lip—the boy hated her too.

She had started having these feelings of self-loathing and wondered whether she and Westman might not actually have damaged August.

It was not the fact that August had filled in the right answers to the numerical sequences. That sort of thing did not particularly impress a man like Balder. No, it was something he saw lying next to the numbers. At first sight it looked like a photograph or a painting but it was in fact a drawing, an exact representation of the traffic light on Hornsgatan which they had passed the other evening. It was beautifully captured, in the minutest detail, with a sort of mathematical precision.

There was a glow to it. No-one had taught August anything at all about three-dimensional drawing or how an artist works with shadow and light, yet he seemed to have a perfect mastery of the techniques. The red eye of the traffic light flashed towards them and Hornsgatan's autumn darkness closed around it, and in the middle of the street you could see the man whom Balder had noticed and vaguely recognized. The man's head was cut off above the eyebrows. He looked frightened or at least uncomfortable and troubled, as if August had disconcerted him, and he was walking unsteadily, though goodness knows how the boy had managed to capture that.

"My God," said Balder. "Did you do this?"

August neither nodded nor shook his head but looked over towards the window, and Balder had the strangest feeling that his life would never be the same again.

. . . .

Hanna Balder needed to do some shopping. The refrigerator was empty. Lasse could come home at any moment and he would not be happy if there was not even a beer for him. But the weather outside looked ghastly so she put it off, and instead she sat in the kitchen smoking, even though it was bad for her skin and bad in general.

She scrolled through her contacts two or three times, in the hope that a new name would come up. But of course there were just the same old people, and they were all tired of her. Against her better judgment she called Mia. Mia was her agent and once upon a time they had been best friends and dreamed of conquering the world together. These days Hanna was Mia's guilty conscience and she had lost count of all her agent's excuses: "It's not easy for an actress to grow older, blah blah." Why not just say it straight out: "You look worn out, Hanna. The public doesn't love you anymore."

But Mia did not answer and that was probably just as well. The conversation would not have done either of them any good. Hanna could not help looking into August's room just to feel that stinging sense of loss which made her realize that she had failed her life's most important mission, motherhood. In some perverse way she took comfort in her self-pity, and she was standing there wondering whether she shouldn't go out and get some beer after all, when the telephone rang.

It was Frans. She made a face. All day she had been tempted—but did not dare—to call him to say that she wanted August back, not just because she missed the boy, still less because she thought her son would be better off with her. It was simply in order to avoid a disaster.

Lasse wanted to get the child support again. God knows what would happen, she thought, if he were to turn up in

Saltsjöbaden to claim his rights. He might even drag August out of the house, scare him out of his wits, and beat Frans to a pulp. She would have to warn him. But when she picked up and tried to say that to Frans, it was impossible to get a word in edgewise. He just went on and on about some strange story which was apparently "totally fantastic and completely amazing" and all that sort of thing.

"I'm sorry, Frans, I don't understand. What are you talking about?" she said.

"August is a savant. He's a genius."

"Have you gone mad?"

"Quite the opposite, my love. I've come to my senses at last. You have to get over here, yes, really, right now! I think it's the only way. You won't be able to understand otherwise. I'll pay for the taxi. I promise, you'll flip out. He must have a photographic memory, you see? And in some incomprehensible way he must have picked up the secrets of perspective drawing all by himself. It's so beautiful, Hanna, so precise. It shines with a light from another world."

"What shines?"

"His traffic light. Weren't you listening? The one we passed the other evening—he's been drawing a whole series of perfect pictures of it, actually more than perfect . . ."

"More than . . ."

"Well, how can I put it? He hasn't just copied it, Hanna, not just captured it exactly. He's also added something, an artistic dimension. There's such a strange fervour in what he's done, and paradoxically enough also something mathematical, as if he even has some understanding of axonometry."

"Axo . . . ?"

"Never mind! You have to come here and see," he said, and gradually she began to understand.

Out of the blue August had started to draw like a virtuoso, or so Frans claimed, and that would of course be fantastic if it were true. But the sad thing was that Hanna was still not happy, and at first she could not understand why. Then it dawned on her. It was because it had happened at Frans's house. The fact was, the boy had been living with her and Lasse for years and absolutely nothing like this had happened. He had sat there with his puzzles and building blocks and not uttered a word, just having those unpleasant fits when he screamed with that piercing voice and thrashed backwards and forwards. Now, hey presto, a few weeks with pappa and he was a genius.

It was too much. Not that she was not happy for August. But still, it hurt, and the worst thing was: she was not as surprised as she should have been. On the contrary, it felt as if she had almost seen it coming, not that the boy would draw accurate reproductions of traffic lights, but that there was something more beneath the surface.

She had sensed it in his eyes, in that look which, when he was excited, seemed to register every little detail of his surroundings. She had sensed it in the way the boy listened to his teachers, and the nervous way he leafed through the maths books she had bought for him, and most of all she had sensed it in his numbers. There was nothing so strange as those numbers. Hour after hour he would write down series of incomprehensibly large sums, and Hanna really did try to understand them, or at least to grasp the point of it all. But however hard she tried she had not been able to work it out, and now she supposed that she had missed something important. She had been too unhappy and wrapped up in herself to fathom what was going on in her son's mind, wasn't that it?

"I don't know," she said.

"Don't know what," Frans said in irritation.

"I don't know if I can come," she said, and at the same time she heard a racket at the front door.

Lasse was coming in with his old drinking buddy Roger Winter, and that made her flinch in fear, mutter an apology to Frans, and for the thousandth time dwell on the fact that she was a bad mother.

Balder stood on the chequered floor in the bedroom, the telephone in his hand, and swore. He had had the floor laid because it appealed to his sense of mathematical order, with the squares repeating themselves endlessly in the wardrobe mirrors on either side of the bed. There were days when he saw the multiplication of the squares reflected there as a teeming riddle, something with a life of its own rising up out of the schematic in the same way that thoughts and dreams arise from neurons or computer programmes emerge from binary codes. But just then he was lost in quite different thoughts.

"Dear boy. What has become of your mother?" he said.

August, who was sitting on the floor beside him eating a cheese-and-gherkin sandwich, looked up with a concentrated expression, and Balder was seized by a strange premonition that he was about to say something grown-up and wise. But that was obviously idiotic. August remained as silent as ever and knew nothing about women who were neglected and had faded away. The fact that the idea had even occurred to Balder was due to the drawings.

The drawings—by now there had been three—seemed to him to be proof not only of artistic and mathematical gifts, but also of some sort of wisdom. The works seemed so mature and complex in their geometric precision that Balder could not reconcile them with August's mental limitations. Or rather, he did not want to reconcile them, because he had long ago worked out what this was about.

As the father of an autistic son, Balder had suspected that many parents hoped the notion of a savant would be the consolation prize to make up for a diagnosis of cognitive deficiencies. But the odds were against them.

According to a common estimate, only one in ten children with autism have some kind of savant gift, and for the most part these talents, though they often entail a fantastic memory and observation of detail, are not as startling as those depicted in films. There are, for example, autistic people who can say on which day of the week a certain date falls, within a range of several hundred years—in extreme cases within a range of forty thousand years.

Others possess encyclopaedic knowledge within a narrow field, such as bus timetables or telephone numbers. Some can calculate large sums in their heads, or remember what the weather had been like every day of their lives, or are able to tell time to the second without looking at a watch. There are all kinds of more or less remarkable talents and, from what Balder gathered, people with these skills are called talented savants and capable of quite outstanding accomplishments given the fact that they are otherwise handicapped.

Another far less common group is where Balder hoped

that August belonged: the so-called prodigious savants, individuals whose talents are sensational whichever way one looks at them. Kim Peek, for example, who was the basis for Rain Man, was severely mentally handicapped and could not get dressed by himself. Yet he had memorized twelve thousand books and could give a lightning-quick answer to almost any factual question. He was known as Kimputer.

Or Stephen Wiltshire, an autistic English boy who was extremely withdrawn as a child and uttered his first word when he was six—it happened to be "paper." By the age of seven Stephen was able to draw groups of buildings perfectly and in the minutest detail, having seen them for just one brief moment. He was flown above London in a helicopter and when he landed he drew the entire city in a fantastic, dizzying panorama, and with a wonderfully individual touch.

If Balder understood it all correctly, he and August must have looked at that traffic light in very different ways. Not only because the boy was plainly so much more focused, but also because Balder's brain had with lightning speed eliminated all nonessential elements in order to concentrate on the traffic light's key message: go or stop. In all probability his perception was also clouded by his thinking about Farah Sharif, while for August the crossing must have appeared exactly as it was, in precise detail.

Afterwards he had taken the image away with him like a fine etching, and it was not until a few weeks later that he had felt the need to express it. The strangest thing of all was, he had done more than simply reproduce the traffic light and the man. He had charged them with a disquieting light, and Balder could not rid himself of the thought that August had wanted to say something more to him than: Look what I can do! For the hundredth time he stared at the drawings and it was as if a needle had gone into his heart.

It frightened him. He did not entirely understand it. But there was something about that man. His eyes were bright and hard. His jaw was tense and his lips strangely thin, almost nonexistent, although that could hardly be held against him. Still, the longer he stared at him, the more frightening he looked, and all of a sudden Balder was gripped by an icy fear.

"I love you, my boy," he murmured, hardly aware of what he was saying, and possibly he repeated the sentence once or twice because the words began to sound increasingly unfamiliar to his ears.

He realized with a new sort of pain that he had never uttered them before and once he had recovered from the first shock it occurred to him that there was something contemptible in that. Did it take an exceptional talent to make him love his own child? It would be only too typical, if so. All his life he had had an absolute obsession with achievement.

He had never bothered with anything which was not innovative or highly skilled, and when he left Sweden for Silicon Valley he had hardly given a thought to August. Basically his son was no more than an irritant in the scheme of brilliant discoveries which Balder himself was busy making.

But now, he promised himself, things would be different. He would set aside his research and everything that had tormented him these last few months, and devote his full attention to the boy.

He would become a new person.

CHAPTER 7

NOVEMBER 20

Something else had happened at the magazine, something bad. But Berger did not want to give any details over the telephone. She suggested coming round to his place. Blomkvist had tried to put her off.

"You're going to freeze off that beautiful bum of yours!"

Berger had paid no attention and, but for the tone in her voice, he would have been happy that she was so stubborn. Ever since he left the office he had been longing to speak to her, and maybe also pull her into the bedroom and tear all her clothes off. But something told him this was not going to happen now. She had sounded upset and mumbled "I'm sorry," and this only made him more worried.

"I'll get a taxi right away," she said.

It was a while before she appeared, and out of boredom he went into the bathroom and looked in the mirror. He had certainly seen better days. His hair was dishevelled and needed a cut and he had bags under his eyes. That was basically Elizabeth George's fault. He swore and left the bathroom to set about cleaning up.

That was one thing at least that Berger would not be able to complain about. However long they had known each

other, and however interwoven their lives were, he still suffered a complex when it came to tidiness. He was a labourer's
son and a bachelor, she the upper-class married woman with
the perfect home in Saltsjöbaden. In any case it could do no
harm for his place to look a little respectable. He filled the
dishwasher and wiped the sink and put out the rubbish.

He even had time to vacuum the living room, water the
flowers on the windowsill, and tidy up the bookshelf and
magazine rack before the doorbell rang. There was both a
ring and an impatient knock. When he opened the door he
was horrified. Berger was frozen stiff.

"Ricky!" he said. "Are you all right?"

She shook like a leaf, and not just because of the weather.
She was not even wearing a hat. The wind had ruined her neat
hairstyle and there was something that looked like a graze on
her right cheek, which had not been there that morning.

"I've frozen off that beautiful bum of mine. Couldn't get
a taxi."

"What happened to your face?"

"I slipped and fell. Three times, I think."

He looked down at her dark-red high-heeled Italian
boots.

"You've got perfect snow boots on, too."

"Yes. Ideal. Not to mention my decision to go without
thermals this morning. Brilliant!"

"Come on in and I'll warm you up."

She fell into his arms and shook even more as he hugged
her tightly.

"I'm sorry," she said again.

"What for?"

"For everything. For Serner. I've been a fool."

"Don't exaggerate, now, Ricky."

He brushed the snowflakes from her hair and forehead and took a careful look at her cheek.

"No, no, I'll tell you everything," she said.

"But first get your clothes off and climb into a hot bath. Would you like a glass of red?"

She would, and she stayed in the bath for a long while with her glass, which he refilled two or three times. He sat on the lid of the toilet listening to her story, and despite all the ominous news there was something of a reconciliation about their conversation, as if they were breaking through a wall they had lately been building up between themselves.

"I know you thought I was being a fool right from the start," she said. "No, don't argue, I know you too well. But you have to understand that Christer and Malin and I could see no other solution. We had recruited Emil and Sofie, and we were so proud of that. They were just about the hottest reporters around, weren't they? It was incredibly prestigious for us. It showed that *Millennium* was on the move and there was a great buzz, with really positive coverage in *Resumé* and *Dagens Media*. It was like the good old days, and personally I felt strongly about the fact that I had promised both Sofie and Emil a secure future at the magazine. Our finances are stable, I said. We have Harriet Vanger behind us. We're going to have the money for fantastic, in-depth reporting. You know I really believed it, too. But then . . ."

"Then the sky fell in."

"Exactly, and it wasn't just the newspaper crisis, or the collapse of the advertising market. There was also that whole situation at the Vanger Corporation. I'm not sure you realize what a mess it was. Sometimes I see it almost as a political coup. All those reactionary old men in the family, and women too for that matter—well, you know them better than anyone. The old racists and regressives got together and stabbed Harriet in the back. I'll never forget that call from her. I've been steamrolled, she said. Crushed. Of course it was her efforts to revive and modernize the corporation which had annoyed them, and then her decision to appoint David Goldman to the board, the son of Rabbi Viktor Goldman. But we were also part of the picture, as you know: Andrei had just written his report on beggars in Stockholm, which we all thought was the best thing he'd ever done, and which was quoted everywhere, even abroad. But which the Vanger people—"

"Thought was lefty rubbish."

"Worse than that, Mikael, they called it propaganda for 'lazy buggers who can't even be bothered to get themselves a job.'"

"Is that what they said?"

"Something along those lines. My guess is that the story itself was irrelevant, it was just their excuse, a pretext for further undermining Harriet's role within the corporation. They wanted to put a stop to everything that Henrik and Harriet had stood for."

"Idiots."

"My God, yes, but that didn't exactly help us. I remember those days. It was as if the rug had been pulled from under our feet, and I know, I know—I should have involved you more. But I thought we'd all benefit if we left you to concentrate on your stories."

"And still I didn't deliver anything decent."

"You tried, Mikael, you really tried. But what I'm coming

to is that it was then, when it seemed as if we'd hit rock bottom, that Levin rang."

"Someone had presumably tipped him off about what had happened."

"Without a doubt, and I don't even need to tell you that I was sceptical at first. Serner felt like the trashiest sort of tabloid. But Levin gave it the works, with his usual torrent of words, and invited me down to his big new villa in Cannes."

"What?"

"Yes, I'm sorry, I didn't tell you that either. I suppose I felt ashamed. But I was going down to the film festival in any case, to do a profile on the Iranian film director. You know, the one being persecuted because she made the documentary about nineteen-year-old Sara, who had been stoned, and I didn't think it would do any harm if Serner helped us with the travel costs. In any event, Levin and I sat up all night and talked and I remained sceptical. He was absurdly boastful and came on with all this sales talk. But eventually I began to listen to him, and do you know why?"

"He was a fantastic lay?"

"Very funny, no, it was his relationship to you."

"Did he want to sleep with me, then?"

"He has boundless admiration for you."

"Bullshit."

"No, Mikael, that's where you're wrong. He loves his power and his money and his villa in Cannes. But more than that, it bugs him that he's not as cool as you. If we're talking cred, he's poor and you're stinking rich. Deep down he wants to be like you, I felt that right away, and yes, I should have realized that that sort of envy can become dangerous. You do know what the campaign against you is all about, don't you?

Your uncompromising attitude makes people feel pathetic. Your very existence reminds them just how much they've sold out, and the more you're acclaimed, the punier they themselves appear. When it's like that the only way they can fight back is by dragging you down. The bullshit gives them back a little bit of dignity—at least that's what they imagine."

"Thanks, Erika, but I really couldn't care less about that campaign."

"I know, at least I hope I do. But what I realized was that Levin really wanted to be in with us, and feel like one of us. He wanted some of our reputation to rub off on him and I thought that was a good incentive. If his ambition was to be cool like you then it would be devastating for him to turn *Millennium* into a run-of-the-mill commercial Serner product. If he became known as the man who destroyed one of the most fabled magazines in Sweden, any cred he might still have would be scuttled for good. That's why I really believed him when he said that both he and the Group needed a prestigious magazine, and that he only wanted to help us produce the kind of journalism we believed in. Admittedly he did want to be involved in the magazine, but I put that down to vanity, that he wanted to be able to show off and say to his yuppie friends that he was our spin doctor or something. I never thought he would dare to have a go at the magazine's soul."

"And yet that's precisely what he's doing now."

"Unfortunately, yes."

"And where does that leave your fancy psychological theory?"

"I underestimated the power of opportunism. As you saw, Levin and Serner's behaviour were exemplary before this campaign against you got going, but since then . . ."

"He's been taking advantage of it."

"No, no, somebody else has. Somebody who wanted to get at him. I only realized later that Levin didn't have an easy time persuading the others to support him in buying a stake in the magazine. As you might imagine, not everybody at Serner suffers from a journalistic inferiority complex. Most of them are just ordinary businessmen. They despise all talk of standing up for things that matter. They were irritated by what they described as Levin's 'fake idealism,' and in the campaign against you they saw an opportunity to put the squeeze on him."

"Dear, oh dear."

"You have no idea. At first it looked OK. We were to adapt somewhat to the market, and, as you know, I thought some of that sounded pretty good. I have, after all, spent a fair amount of time wondering how we could reach a younger readership. I really thought that Levin and I were having a productive dialogue so I didn't worry too much about his presentation today."

"I noticed that."

"But that was before all hell broke loose."

"What are you talking about?"

"The uproar when you sabotaged his presentation."

"I didn't sabotage anything, Erika. I just left."

Berger lay in the bath, took a sip of her wine, and then she smiled a wistful smile.

"When will you learn that you're Mikael Blomkvist?" she said.

"I thought I was beginning to get the hang of that."

"Apparently not, because otherwise you'd have realized that when Mikael Blomkvist walks out in the middle of a presentation about his own magazine it's a big deal, whether Mikael Blomkvist intends it to be or not."

"In that case I apologize for my sabotage."

"I'm not blaming you, not anymore. Now I'm the one saying sorry, as you can see. I'm the one who's put us in this position. It probably would have gone pear-shaped anyway, whether you'd walked out or not. They were just waiting for an excuse to take a swing at us."

"What actually happened?"

"After you disappeared we all felt deflated, and Levin, whose self-esteem had taken yet another knock, no longer gave a damn about his presentation. 'There's no point,' he said. He rang his boss to report back, and he probably laid it on a bit thick. I suspect that the envy on which I had been pinning my hopes had changed into something petty and spiteful. He was back again after an hour or so and said that the Group was prepared to give *Millennium* its full backing and use all its channels to market the magazine."

"You didn't like the sound of that."

"No, and I knew before he'd even said one word about it. You could tell by the look on his face. It radiated a mixture of fear and triumph and at first he couldn't find the right words. He was mostly waffling and said that the Group wanted to have more insight into the business, plus content aimed at a younger readership, plus more celebrity news. But then . . ."

Berger shut her eyes, drew her hand through her wet hair, then knocked back the last of her wine.

"Yes?"

"He said that he wanted you off the editorial team."

"He *what*?"

"Of course neither he nor the Group could say it straight

out, still less could they afford to get headlines like 'Serner sacks Blomkvist,' so Ove put it neatly by saying that he wanted you to have a freer rein and be allowed to concentrate on what you're best at: writing reportage. He suggested a strategic relocation to London and a generous stringer arrangement."

"London?"

"He said that Sweden's too small for a guy of your calibre, but you get what this is about."

"They think they can't push through their changes if I stay on the editorial team?"

"Something like that. Still, I don't think any of them was surprised when Christer, Malin, and I just said no, that it wasn't even negotiable. Not to mention Andrei's reaction."

"What did he do?"

"I'm almost embarrassed to tell you. Andrei stood up and said that it was the most shameful thing he'd heard in his whole life. That you were one of the best things we had in this country, a source of pride for democracy and journalism, and that the whole Serner Group should hang their heads in shame. He said that you were a great man."

"He does tend to exaggerate."

"But he's a good kid."

"He really is. What did the Serner people do then?"

"Levin was prepared for it, of course. 'You're always welcome to buy us out,' he said. 'It's just—'"

"That the price has gone up," Blomkvist completed the sentence.

"Exactly. He claimed that whichever basis you use for valuing the business would show that any price for Serner's interest should be at least double what it was when the Group went in, given the additional value and goodwill they've created."

"Goodwill! Have they gone mad?"

"Not at all, apparently, but they're bright, and they want to mess us about. And I wonder if they don't want to kill two birds with one stone: pull off a good deal and get rid of a competitor by breaking us financially, all in one go."

"What the hell should we do?"

"What we're best at, Mikael: slug it out. I'll take some of my own money and we'll buy them out and fight to make this northern Europe's best magazine."

"Sure, Erika, but then what? We'll end up with a lousy financial situation which even you won't be able to do anything about."

"I know, but it'll be OK. We've come through more difficult situations than this. You and I can waive our salaries for a while. We can manage, can't we?"

"Everything has to end some time, Erika."

"Don't say that. Ever."

"Not even if it's true?"

"Especially not then."

"Right."

"Don't you have anything in the pipeline?" she said. "Something, anything that will stun Sweden's media?"

Blomkvist hid his face in his hands and for some reason he thought of Pernilla, his daughter. She had said that unlike him she was going to write "for real," whatever it was that was not "real" about his writing.

"I don't think so," he said.

Berger smacked her hand hard on the bath water so that it splashed out onto his socks.

"Jesus, you must have something. There's no-one in this country who gets as many tip-offs as you do."

"Most of it's junk," he said. "But maybe . . . I was just in the process of checking something."

Berger sat up in the tub.

"What?"

"No, it's nothing," he backtracked. "Only wishful thinking."

"In a situation like this we have to think wishfully."

"Yes, but it's a load of smoke and nothing you can prove."

"Yet there's something inside you that believes in it, isn't there?"

"Maybe, but that's because of one little detail which doesn't have anything to do with the story itself."

"What?"

"That my old comrade-in-arms has also been at the story."

"The one with a capital S?"

"The very one."

"Well, that does sound promising," Berger said, and stepped out of the bath, naked and beautiful.

CHAPTER 8

NOVEMBER 20—EVENING

August was kneeling on the chequered floor in the bedroom, looking at a still-life arrangement with a lit candle on a blue plate, two green apples, and an orange which his father had set out for him. But nothing was happening. August stared emptily out at the storm and Balder wondered: Does it make sense to present the boy with a subject?

His son only had to glance at something for it to be embedded in his mind, so why should his father of all people choose what he was supposed to draw? August must have thousands of images of his own in his head. Maybe a plate and some pieces of fruit were as wrong as could be. Once again Balder asked himself: Was the boy trying to convey something in particular with his traffic light? The drawing was no casual little observation. On the contrary, the stop light shone like a baleful glowering eye and maybe—what did Balder know?—August had felt threatened by the man on that pedestrian crossing.

Balder looked at his son for the umpteenth time that day. It was shameful, wasn't it? He used to think that August was simply weird and unfathomable. Now he wondered if he and his son were not in actual fact alike. When Balder was young, the doctors did not go in so much for diagnoses. In those days, there was a far greater tendency to dismiss people as being odd. He himself had definitely been different from other children, much too serious—his facial expression never changed—and no-one on the school playground thought he was much fun. Nor did he find the other children particularly entertaining either—he sought refuge in numbers and equations and avoided talking more than he was required to.

He would probably not have been considered autistic in the same sense as August. But nowadays they probably would have stuck an Asperger's label on him. He and Hanna had believed that the early diagnosis of August would help them, yet so little had been done, and it was only now, now that his son was eight, that Balder discovered the boy had a special mathematical and spatial talent. How come Hanna and Westman had not noticed?

Even if Westman was a bastard, Hanna was fundamentally a sensitive and good person. Balder would never forget their first meeting. It was an evening function of the IVA, the Royal Swedish Academy of Engineering Sciences, at Stockholm's Rådhus, where he was being given some prize that he cared nothing about. He had spent a boring evening longing to get home to his computer when a beautiful woman whom he vaguely recognized—Balder's knowledge of the world of celebrity was limited—came up to him and started to talk. Balder still thought of himself as the nerd from Tappström school who got nothing but contemptuous looks from the girls. He could not understand what a woman like Hanna saw in him. At the time—as he was soon to find out—she was at the height of her career. But she seduced him and made love to him that night like no woman had done before.

Then followed maybe the happiest time in his life and yet . . . the binary codes won out over love.

He worked until the marriage fell apart. Lasse Westman arrived on the scene and Hanna went downhill and probably August did as well, which should of course have made Balder wild with fury. But he knew that he too was to blame. He had bought his freedom and not bothered about his son and perhaps what was said during the custody hearing was true, that he had chosen the dream of artificial life over that of his own child. What a monumental idiot he had been.

He got out his laptop and went on Google to learn more about savant skills. He had already ordered a number of books, and in his usual way meant to teach himself every-thing there was to know. No damn psychologist or educa-tionalist would be able to catch him out and tell him what August needed at this point. He would know that better than any of them and so he continued searching until his atten-tion was caught by the story of an autistic girl called Nadia.

What happened to her was described in Lorna Selfe's book *Nadia: A Case of Extraordinary Drawing Ability in an Autistic Child* and in Oliver Sacks's *The Man Who Mis-took His Wife for a Hat.* Balder read in fascination. It was a gripping story and in many ways there were parallels. Like August, Nadia had seemed perfectly healthy when she was born, and only gradually did her parents realize that some-thing was amiss.

The girl did not start speaking. She did not look people in the eye. She disliked physical contact and did not respond to her mother's smiles or attempts at communication. She was for the most part quiet and withdrawn and compulsively tore paper into narrow strips. By the time she was six she had still not spoken a word.

Yet she could draw like Leonardo da Vinci. Already at the age of three, and out of the blue, she had begun to draw horses. Unlike other children she did not begin with the entire animal, but instead with some little detail, a hoof, a rider's boot, a tail, and the strangest thing of all was that she drew fast. In a tearing hurry she put together the parts, one here, one there, until she had a perfect whole, a horse which galloped or walked. From his own efforts when he was a teenager, Balder knew how exceptionally difficult it is to draw an animal in motion. However hard you try, the result is unnatural or stiff. It takes a master to tease out the lightness in the movements. Nadia was a master already at the age of three.

Her horses were like perfect stills, drawn with a light touch, and obviously not the result of any long training. Her virtuosity burst out like a breaking dam, and that fascinated her contemporaries. How was it possible for her to leapfrog centuries of development in the history of art with just a few quick hand movements? The Australian specialists Allan Snyder and John Mitchell studied the drawings and in 1999 presented a theory, which has gradually won general acceptance, to the effect that we all have an inherited capacity to reach that level of virtuosity, but that in most of us it is blocked.

If we see a football, for example, we do not immediately understand that it is a three-dimensional object. Instead, the brain processes a series of details at lightning speed: the way in which shadows fall and the differences in depth and nuance, from which it then draws certain conclusions about shape. We are not conscious of this. But it requires an examination of the separate parts before we can register something as simple as the fact that what we see is a ball and not a circle.

It is the brain which then produces the final form and, when it does, we no longer see all the detail we first registered. We cannot see the trees for the forest, so to speak. But what struck Mitchell and Snyder was that if only we could reproduce the original image in our minds, we would be able to see the world in an entirely new way, and perhaps even recreate it, as Nadia had done without any training whatsoever.

Nadia saw the myriad details before they had been processed, which is why she began each time with an individual part, such as a hoof or a nose, because the totality as we perceive it did not yet exist in her mind. Balder found the idea appealing, even if he saw a number of problems with the theory, or at least had a number of questions.

In many ways this was the sort of original thinking he always looked for in his research; an approach which took nothing for granted but looked beyond the obvious, down to the small details. He grew more obsessed with the subject and read on with increasing fascination until, quite suddenly, he shuddered and even swore out loud, staring at his son with a stab of anxiety. It had nothing to do with the research findings, rather with the description of Nadia's first year at school.

Nadia had been put in a school for autistic children, where the teaching was focused on getting her to talk for the first time. The girl made some progress—the words came, one by one. But there was a high price to pay. As she started to talk, her brilliance with crayons disappeared and, according to the author Lorna Selfe, it was likely that one language was being replaced by another. From having been an artistic genius, Nadia became a severely handicapped autistic girl who was able to speak a little but who had entirely lost the gift that had astounded the world. Was it worth it, just to be able to say a few words?

No, Balder wanted to shout out, possibly because he had always been prepared to do whatever it took to become a genius in his field. Anything but the ordinary! That had been his guiding principle all his life, and yet . . . he was clever enough to understand that his own elitist principles were not necessarily a good pointer to the right way forward now. Maybe a few fabulous drawings were nothing as compared to being able to ask for a glass of milk, or exchange a few words with a friend, or a father. What did he know?

Yet he refused to be faced with such a choice. He could not bear to give up the most wonderful thing that had happened in August's life. No . . . that was simply not an option. No parent should have to decide. After all, no-one could anticipate what was best for the child.

The more he thought about it, the more unreasonable it seemed, and it occurred to him that he did not believe it, or perhaps that he simply did not *want* to believe it. Nadia's was after all only one case.

He had to find out more. But just then his mobile rang. It had been ringing a lot over the last few hours. One call had been from a withheld number and another from Linus, his former assistant. He had less and less time for Linus; he was not even sure he trusted him—certainly he did not feel like talking to him now.

Yet he answered, maybe out of sheer nervousness. It was Gabriella Grane, the lovely analyst at the Security Police, and that put a little smile on his face. After Farah Sharif, Gabriella came a close second. She had sparklingly beautiful eyes and she was sharp-witted. He had a weakness for smart women.

"Gabriella," he said. "I'd love to talk, but I don't have the time. I'm right in the middle of something."

"You've definitely got time for what I have to tell you," she said with uncharacteristic severity. "You're in danger."

"Oh, nonsense, Gabriella! I told you, they may try to sue the shirt off my back—but that's all."

"Frans, I'm sorry, but some new information has come through, and from an extremely well-informed source at that. There does appear to be a genuine risk."

"What do you mean?" he said, distracted. With the telephone clamped between his shoulder and ear, he was skimming another article on Nadia's lost gift.

"I'm finding it hard to assess the information, I admit, but it's worrying me, Frans. It does have to be taken seriously."

"In that case, I promise I'll be extra-careful. I'll stay indoors as usual. But I'm a bit busy just now, as I was saying. Besides, I'm all but convinced that you're wrong. At Solifon—"

"Sure, sure, I could be wrong," she cut in. "That's possible. But what if I'm right, what if there's even a tiny risk that I am?"

"Well—"

"Frans, listen to me. I think you're right. Nobody at Solifon wants to do you physical harm. It's a civilized company, after all. But it seems as if someone or even more than one person in the company is in touch with a criminal organization operating out of Russia and Sweden. That's where the threat is coming from."

Balder took his eyes off the computer screen for the first time. He knew that Zigmund Eckerwald, head of a special division of Solifon, was cooperating with a group of criminals. He had even picked up some codenames for the leader of that group, but could not understand why they would go after him. Or could he?

"A criminal organization?" he muttered.

"Yes," Grane said. "And isn't it logical, in a way? That's more or less what you've been saying, isn't it? That once you've started stealing someone else's ideas, and made money from them, then you've already crossed the line. It's downhill from there on."

"I think what I actually said was that all you needed was a gang of lawyers and you could safely steal whatever you like. Lawyers are the hit men of our times."

"OK, maybe so. But listen to me: I haven't yet got approval for your personal protection, so I want to move you to a secret location. I'm coming to collect you."

"What are you saying?"

"I think we have to act immediately."

"Not a chance. Me and . . ."

He hesitated.

"Do you have someone else there?"

"No, no, but I can't go anywhere right now."

"Aren't you listening to what I'm saying?"

"I hear you loud and clear. But with all due respect it sounds to me as if it's mostly speculation."

"Speculation is an essential tool in assessing risk, Frans. And the person who got in touch with me . . . I suppose I shouldn't really be saying this . . . is an agent from the NSA who has this particular organization under surveillance."

"The NSA!" He snorted.

"I know you're sceptical of them."

"Sceptical doesn't even begin to describe it."

"OK. But this time they're on your side, at least this agent is. She's a good person. By eavesdropping she's picked up something which could very well be a plan to eliminate you."

"Me?"

"There's a lot to suggest that."

"'Could very well' and 'suggest' . . . it all sounds vague."

August reached for his pencils, and Balder concentrated on that for a moment.

"I'm staying where I am," he said.

"You've got to be joking."

"No, I'm not. I'd be happy to move if you get more information, but not right now. Besides, the alarm Milton installed is excellent. I've got cameras and sensors everywhere. And you know I'm a stubborn bastard."

"Do you have a weapon of any kind?"

"What's got into you, Gabriella? A weapon! The most dangerous thing I own is my new cheese slicer."

"You know . . ." she said, letting the words hang.

"Yes?"

"I'm going to arrange protection for you, whether you want it or not. I doubt you'll even notice it. But since you're going to be so damn obstinate, I have another piece of advice for you."

"Tell me."

"Go public. Tell the media what you know—then if you're lucky there'll be no point in someone getting rid of you."

"I'll think about it." Balder had detected a note of distraction in Grane's voice. "Yes?" he said.

"Wait a moment," she said. "I've got someone else on the line. I have to . . ."

She was gone, and Balder, who should have had much else to mull over, found himself thinking of only one thing: Will August lose his ability to draw if I teach him to talk?

"Are you still there?" Grane asked after a short while.

"Of course."

"I'm afraid I have to go. But I promise to see to it that you get some sort of protection as rapidly as possible. I'll be in touch. Take care!"

He hung up with a sigh and thought again of Hanna, and of August and the chequered floor reflected in the wardrobe doors, and of all kinds of things which seemed irrelevant just then. Almost absentmindedly he said to himself, "They're after me."

He could see that it was not unreasonable, even though he had always refused to believe that it would actually come to violence. But what, in fact, did he know? Nothing. Besides, he could not be bothered to address it now. He continued his search for information on Nadia, and what implications this might have for his son, but that was insane. He was burying his head in the sand. Despite Grane's warning he kept surfing and soon came upon the name of a professor of neurology, an expert on savant syndrome named Charles Edelman. Instead of reading on as he normally would—Balder always preferred the written to the spoken word—he called the switchboard at the Karolinska Institute.

He soon realized how late it was. Edelman was unlikely to be at work still, and his home number was not on the website. But wait a moment . . . he was also the head of Ekliden, an institution for autistic children with special abilities.

Balder tried calling there. The telephone rang a number of times before a woman answered and introduced herself as Nurse Lindros.

"I'm sorry to disturb you so late in the evening," Balder said. "I'm looking for Professor Edelman. Might he possibly still be there?"

"Yes, in fact he is. No-one is setting off for home in this dreadful weather. Who may I say is calling?"

"Frans Balder," he said, and in case it might help he added: "Professor Frans Balder."

"Just a moment," Nurse Lindros said, "I'll see if he's available."

Balder stared down at August, who was once again gripping his pencil hesitantly, and that worried him somehow, as if it were an ominous sign. "A criminal organization," he muttered again.

"Charles Edelman," a voice said. "Am I really talking to Professor Balder?"

"The very same. I have a little—"

"You can't know what an honour this is," Edelman said. "I'm just back from a conference at Stanford where we discussed your work on neural networks; in fact we were even asking ourselves if we neurologists don't have a great deal to learn about the brain through the back door, as it were, through AI research. We were wondering—"

"I'm flattered," Balder interrupted. "But right now I have a quick question for you."

"Oh, really? Is it something to do with your research?"

"Not at all. I have an autistic son. He's eight years old and hasn't yet said a single word, but the other day we passed a traffic light on Hornsgatan and afterwards . . ."

"Yes?"

"He just sat down and drew it at lightning speed, completely perfectly. It was astonishing!"

"And you want me to come and take a look at what he's done?"

"I'd like that. But that's not why I called. The fact is that I'm worried. I've read that perhaps drawing is the way in which he interacts with the world around him, and that he might lose this ability if he learns to talk."

"I can tell you've been reading about Nadia."

"How do you know that?"

"Because she's always mentioned in this context. But . . . may I call you Frans?"

"Of course."

"Excellent, Frans, and I'm so glad you called. I can tell you straightaway that you have nothing to worry about, on the contrary. Nadia is the exception that proves the rule, no more than that. All research shows that speech development actually enhances savant abilities. It can happen, of course, that children lose those skills, but that is mostly due to other factors. They get bored, or there's a significant event in their lives. You probably read that Nadia lost her mother."

"I did."

"Maybe that was the reason, even though neither I nor anyone else can know for sure. But there's virtually no other documented case of a similar evolution, and I'm not just saying this off the top of my head, or because it happens to be my own hypothesis. There is broad consensus today to the effect that savants have everything to gain from developing their intellectual skills on all levels."

"Do you mean that?"

"Yes, definitely."

"He's also good at numbers."

"Really?" Edelman said thoughtfully.

"Why do you say that?"

"Because it is extremely rare for artistic ability to be combined with mathematical talent in a savant. These two different skills have nothing in common, and sometimes they seem even to block each other."

"But that's how it is with my son. There's a kind of geometric precision about his drawings, as if he had worked out the exact proportions."

"How fascinating. When can I see him?"

"I don't know. For the time being I only wanted some advice."

"In that case my advice is clear: Make an effort with the boy. Stimulate him. Let him develop his skills in every way."

"I . . ." Balder felt a strange pressure in his chest and found it hard to get the words out. "I want to thank you," he said. "Really thank you. Now I have to . . ."

"It's been such an honour to talk to you, it would be wonderful to be able to meet you and your son. I've developed quite a sophisticated test for savants, if I may boast a little. I could help you get to know the boy better."

"Yes, of course, that would be terrific. But now I must . . ." Balder mumbled, without knowing what he wanted to say. "Goodbye, and thank you."

"Oh, my pleasure. I hope to hear from you again soon."

Balder hung up and sat still for a moment, his hands crossed over his chest, and looked at his son. August was still looking at the burning candle, the yellow pencil in his hand. A shudder went across Balder's shoulders, and the tears came. Whatever else you might say about Professor Balder, he was not one to cry easily.

In fact he could not remember when it had last happened. Not when his mother died, and definitely not when watching or reading anything. He thought of himself as a block of stone. But now, in front of his son with his rows of pencils and crayons, the professor cried like a child and he just let it happen.

It had been Charles Edelman's words. August would be able to learn to speak and could keep drawing, and that was overwhelming news. But Balder was not crying just because of that. There was also the drama at Solifon. The death threat. The secrets he was privy to and the longing for Hanna or Farah or anyone who could fill the gap in his heart.

"My little boy!" he said, so emotional he failed to notice his laptop switch itself on and show pictures from one of the surveillance cameras outside the house.

Out in the garden, in the blustering storm, there was a tall, thin man in a padded leather jacket, with a grey cap pulled down to conceal his face. Whoever it was knew that he was being filmed, and even if he seemed lean and agile there was something in his swaying walk which was reminiscent of a heavyweight boxer on his way into the ring.

Grane was sitting in her office at Säpo searching the Web and the agency's records. She did not really know what she was looking for. But something worrying was gnawing away at her.

Her conversation with Balder had been interrupted by Helena Kraft, chief of Säpo, who was looking for her again to discuss the same matter as before. Then Alona Casales at the NSA had called to continue their conversation; this time she sounded calmer, and again a little flirtatious.

"Have you managed to sort out your computers?" Grane said.

"Yes, that was a circus, but I don't think it's anything serious. I'm sorry if I was a little cryptic last time. I don't have much of a choice. I just want to stress again that the level of threat against Professor Balder is both real and serious, even though we know nothing for certain. Did you have time to deal with it?"

"I've spoken to him. He refuses to leave his house, told me he was in the middle of something. I'm going to arrange protection."

"Fine. As you might have guessed I've done more than quickly check you out. I'm very impressed, Miss Grane. Shouldn't someone like you be working for Goldman Sachs and earning millions?"

"Not my style."

"Not mine either. I wouldn't say no to the money, but this underpaid snooping is more my thing. Now, honey, here's the situation. As far as my colleagues are concerned this isn't a big deal—which I happen to disagree with. And not just because I'm convinced that this group represents a threat to our national economic interests. I also think there are political implications. One of those Russian computer engineers I mentioned, a guy called Anatoli Chabarov, is also linked to Ivan Gribanov, a member of the Russian Duma. He's notorious, and a major shareholder in Gazprom."

"I understand."

"But most of it so far is just dead ends. I've spent a lot of time trying to crack the identity of the person at the top."

"The man they call Thanos."

"Or woman."

"Woman?"

"I could be wrong. This type of group tends to *exploit* women, not promote them to leadership positions, and this figure has mostly been referred to as a he."

"Then what makes you think it might be a woman?"

"A sort of reverence, you could say. They talk about 'Thanos' in the same way men through the ages have spoken about women they desire."

"A beauty, in other words."

"Right. But maybe I'm just picking up some homoeroticism. Nothing would make me happier than if Russian gangsters and bigwigs were to indulge more in that department."

"Ha, true!"

"In fact I mention it only so that you'll keep an open mind if this mess ends up on your desk. You understand, there are also quite a few lawyers mixed up in it. What else is new, right? Hackers steal and lawyers legitimize the theft."

"True. Balder's said to me that we're equal before the law—if we pay the same amount."

"If you can afford a strong defence you can get away with whatever you want these days. You do know who Balder's legal opponents are, don't you? The Washington firm Dackstone & Partner."

"Sure."

"In that case you know that the firm is also used by large

tech companies to sue the shit out of inventors and innovators hoping to get some modest reward for their creations."

"I discovered that when we were dealing with the lawsuits of that inventor Håkan Lans."

"Grim, wasn't it? But the interesting thing is that Dackstone crops up in one of the few conversations we've managed to track down and decrypt from this criminal network, although there the firm is simply referred to as DP, or even D."

"So Solifon and these crooks have the same lawyers?"

"It looks like it, and that's not all. Dackstone is about to open an office in Stockholm—do you know how we found that out?"

"No," said Grane, who was beginning to feel stressed. She wanted to finish the conversation and ensure that Balder got police protection.

"Through our surveillance of this group," Casales went on. "Anatoli Chabarov mentions it in passing, which suggests that there are ties to the firm. They knew about the office opening even before it became public. Also Dackstone & Partner is setting up in Stockholm together with a Swedish lawyer named Brodin. He used to be a criminal lawyer, and if you remember he was known for getting a little too cozy with his clients."

"I do remember that classic picture in the evening papers—Kenny Brodin out on the town with some gangsters, his hands all over some call girl," Grane said.

"I saw that. I'd bet Mr. Brodin is a good place to start if you want to check out this story. Who knows, maybe he's the link between big business and this group."

"I'll take a look at it," Grane said. "But right now I've got a number of other things to deal with. I'm sure we'll be in touch again soon."

She called the duty officer for Säpo's Personal Protection Unit, who that evening was none other than Stig Yttergren. Her heart sank. Yttergren was sixty, overweight, known to be a heavy drinker, and most of all he liked to play cards online. He was sometimes called "Officer No-Can-Do." She proceeded to explain the situation in her most authoritative tone and demanded that Professor Frans Balder in Saltsjöbaden be given a bodyguard as quickly as possible. As usual Yttergren responded by saying that it would be extremely difficult, perhaps not possible at all. When she countered by saying that this was an order from the chief of Säpo herself, he muttered something which might even have been "that stroppy cunt."

"I didn't hear that," Grane said. "Just make sure this is put in place immediately." Which of course it was not. While she was waiting and drumming her fingers on her desk, she searched for information on Dackstone & Partner and anything else she could find linked to what Casales had been telling her—and that is when she was overcome by a sense of something horribly familiar.

She could not put her finger on it. Before she could find what she was looking for, Yttergren called back to say that no-one from Personal Protection was available. There was an unusual amount of activity for the royal family that evening, he said, some sort of public engagement with the Norwegian crown prince and princess, and the leader of the Swedish Democrats had had an ice cream thrown at his head before his guards could intervene, which meant that they had to provide reinforcements for his late speech in Södertälje.

So Yttergren had sent out "two great guys from the regular police," Peter Blom and Dan Flinck, and Grane had to make do with that, even if their names reminded her of Kling and Klang in *Pippi Longstocking*. For a moment she had serious misgivings. Then she got angry with herself.

It was so typical of her snobbish background to judge people by their names. She might have had more cause for concern if they had a posh name like Gyllentofs or something and been irresponsible layabouts. *I'm sure this'll be fine,* she thought.

She got back to work. It was going to be a long night.

CHAPTER 9

NOVEMBER 20–21—NIGHT

Salander woke up lying straight across the king-size bed and realized that she had been dreaming about her father. A feeling of menace swept over her like a cloak. But then she remembered the start of the evening and concluded that it could as easily be a chemical reaction in her body. She had a terrible hangover. She got up on wobbly legs and went into the large bathroom—with the jacuzzi and the marble and all the idiotic luxuries—to be sick. But nothing happened; she just sank to the floor, breathing heavily.

Then she stood up and looked at herself in the mirror, which was not particularly encouraging either. Her eyes were red. On the other hand it was not long after midnight. She must have slept for only a few hours. She took a glass from the bathroom cupboard and filled it with water. But at the same moment the details of her dream came flooding back and she crushed the glass in her hand. Blood dripped to the floor, and she swore and realized that she was unlikely to be going back to sleep.

Should she try to crack the encrypted NSA file she had downloaded? No, that would be pointless, at least for now. Instead she wound a towel around her hand and took from her bookshelves a new study by Princeton physicist Julie Tammet, which described how a big star collapses into a black hole. She lay down on the sofa by the windows over-looking Slussen and Riddarfjärden.

As she began to read she felt a little better. Blood from the towel did seep onto the pages and her head would not stop hurting, but she became more and more engrossed in the book, every now and then making a note in the margin. None of it was new to her. She knew better than most that a star stays alive as a result of two opposing actions, the fusion at its core forcing it outwards and the gravitational pull keep-ing it together. She saw it as a balancing act, a tug of war from which a victor eventually emerges, once the fuel for the reac-tions runs out and the explosions weaken.

When gravity gains the upper hand, the celestial body shrinks like a punctured balloon and becomes smaller and smaller. In this way, a star can vanish into nothing. Salander liked black holes. She felt an affinity to them.

Yet, like Julie Tammet, she was not interested in black holes per se, but rather in the process which creates them. Salander was convinced that if only she could describe that process, she would be able to draw together the two irrecon-cilable languages of the universe, quantum physics and the theory of relativity. But it was no doubt beyond her capabili-ties, just like the bloody encryption, and inevitably she began again to think about her father.

When she was a child, that revolting specimen had raped her mother over and over again, right up until the time her mother received injuries from which she would never recover. Salander herself, then twelve, hit back with a horrific force. At the time she could have no idea that her father was an important spy who had defected from the GRU, the Soviet military intelligence service, nor could she know that a special department within the Swedish Security Police, referred to as the Section, was protecting him at any cost. Yet even then she understood that there was some mystery surrounding the man, a darkness no-one was allowed to approach in any way. That even applied to so simple a thing as his name: Zala, or Alexander Zalachenko, to be more precise.

Other fathers could be reported to the social services and the police. But Zala had forces behind him which were above all that.

It was this and one other thing which for her were true black holes.

The alarm went off at 1:18 a.m. and Balder woke with a start. Was there someone in the house? He felt an inexplicable fear and reached across the bed. August was lying beside him. The boy must have crept in as usual, and now he whimpered with worry, as if the wailing of the siren had made its way into his dreams. My little boy, Balder thought. Then he stiffened. Were those footsteps?

No, he must be imagining things. All you could hear was the alarm. He cast a worried look towards the storm beyond the windows. It seemed to have grown worse. The sea was beating against the jetty and the shore. The windowpanes shook and arched. Could the alarm have been set off by a gust of wind? Perhaps it was as simple as that.

He still had to check to see if that protection Gabriella Grane was organizing had arrived at last. Two men from the regular police were supposed to have been there hours ago.

It was a farce. They had been delayed by the storm and by a series of conflicting orders. It was either one thing or another and he agreed with Grane, it seemed hopelessly incompetent.

He would have to deal with that in due course. Now he had to make a call. But August was beginning to wake up and a hysterical child banging his body against the headboard was the last thing Balder needed right now. The earplugs, it occurred to him, those old green earplugs he had bought at Frankfurt airport.

He took them from the bedside table and gently pushed them into his son's ears. Then he tucked him in and kissed him on the cheek and stroked his curly, tousled hair, straightened the collar on the boy's pyjamas, and made sure that his head was resting comfortably on the pillow. Balder was frightened and should have been in a hurry, or had every reason to be. Yet he took his time and fussed over his son. Perhaps it was a sentimental moment in the midst of a crisis. Or he wanted to put off confronting whatever awaited him out there. For a moment he wished he did have a weapon. Not that he would have known how to use it.

He was a programmer, for heaven's sake, who had developed some paternal instinct in his old age, that was all. He should never have gotten into this mess. To hell with Solifon and the NSA and all criminal gangs! But now he had to get a grip. With stealthy, uncertain steps he went into the hallway, and before doing anything else, before even looking out at the road, he turned off the alarm. The racket had set his nerves on edge and in the sudden silence which followed he stood stock-still. Then his mobile rang and even though it startled him he was grateful for the distraction.

"Yes," he said.

"Hello, this is Jonas Anderberg, I'm on duty tonight at Milton Security. Is everything all right?"

"What, well . . . I think so. My alarm went off."

"I know that and, according to our instructions, when this happens you're supposed to go down to a special room in the cellar and lock the door. Are you down there?"

"Yes," he lied.

"Good, very good. Do you know what's happened?"

"No idea. The alarm woke me up. I have no clue what set it off. Could it have been the storm?"

"Unlikely . . . One moment please."

Anderberg's voice sounded a bit unfocused.

"What is it?" Balder said nervously.

"It seems . . ."

"For God's sake, tell me what's going on."

"Sorry, just take it easy, take it easy . . . I'm going through the picture sequence from your cameras, and it does look as if . . ."

"As if what?"

"As if you've got a visitor. A man, well, you can see for yourself later, a lanky man with dark glasses and a cap has been prowling around your property. He's been there twice, as far as I can see, but as I said . . . I've only just noticed it now. I'd have to look at it more closely to be able to say more."

"What sort of person is it?"

"Well, it's hard to say."

Anderberg seemed to be studying the picture sequences again.

"But maybe . . . I don't know . . . no, it's too soon to be speculating," he said.

"Go on, please go on. I need something specific. It would make me feel better."

"OK, in that case there's at least one reassuring thing I can tell you."

"And what's that?"

"His walk. The man walks like a junkie—like a guy who's just taken a load of speed. There's something cocky and stilted about the way he moves, and that could be a sign that he's just an ordinary druggie and petty thief. On the other hand . . ."

"Yes?"

"He's done a very good job of hiding his face and then . . ."

Anderberg fell silent again.

"Keep going!"

"One moment."

"You're making me nervous, you know that?"

"Don't mean to. But you know . . ."

Balder froze. The sound of a car engine could be heard from his garage drive.

". . . you're getting a visitor."

"What should I do?"

"Stay where you are."

"OK," said Balder, more or less paralyzed. But he was not where Anderberg thought he was.

When the telephone rang at 1:58, Blomkvist was still awake. But his mobile was in the pocket of his jeans on the floor and he did not manage to answer it in time. In any case the call was from a withheld number, so he swore and crawled back into bed and closed his eyes.

He could really do without another sleepless night. Ever since Berger had fallen asleep a little before midnight, he had been tossing and turning and thinking about his life. Not much of it felt right, not even his relationship with Berger. He had loved her for many years, and there was every reason to think that she felt the same way about him. But it was no longer as simple as it had once been. Perhaps Blomkvist had started to feel some sympathy for Greger. Greger Beckman was Erika's husband, an artist, and he could not be accused of being grudging or small-minded. On the contrary, when Greger had realized that Erika would never get over Blomkvist or even be able to stop herself from tearing his clothes off, he had not lost his temper. He had made a deal:

"You can be with him—just so long as you always come back to me." And that's how it became.

They set up an unconventional arrangement with Berger mostly sleeping at home with her husband in Saltsjöbaden, but sometimes here with Blomkvist on Bellmansgatan. Over the years Blomkvist had thought that it really was an ideal solution, one which many couples who lived under the dictatorship of monogamy ought to have adopted. Every time Berger said "I love my husband more when I can also be with you," or when at some cocktail party Beckman put his arm around him in a brotherly embrace, Blomkvist had thanked his lucky stars for the arrangement.

Yet he had lately begun to have doubts, perhaps because he had had more time to think and it had occurred to him that an agreement is not necessarily always agreeable to all.

On the contrary, one party might advance their self-interest under the guise of a common decision, and in the long run it often becomes clear that someone is suffering, despite assurances to the contrary. Berger's call to her husband that evening evidently had not been well received. Who knows, maybe Beckman was also lying awake right now.

Blomkvist tried to put it out of his mind. For a little while he even tried daydreaming. But that did not help much, and in the end he got up, determined to do something more useful. Why not do some reading on industrial espionage or, better still, sketch out an alternative funding plan for *Millennium*? He got dressed, sat down at his computer, and checked his in-box.

Most of it was rubbish as usual, even if some of the e-mails did give him a bit of a boost. There were shouts of encouragement from Malm and Eriksson, also from Andrei Zander and Harriet Vanger in the light of the coming battle with Serner, and he answered them with more of a fighting spirit than he actually felt. After that he checked Salander's document, without expecting to find anything there. But then he lit up. She had answered. For the first time in ages she had given a sign of life:

```
<Balder's intelligence isn't in the least
bit artificial. How's your own these days?>
<And what happens, Blomkvist, if we create
a machine which is a little bit cleverer
than we are?>
```

Blomkvist smiled and thought of the last time they had met at Kaffebar on St. Paulsgatan. It took a while before he noticed that her message contained two questions, the first one a friendly little jibe which perhaps regrettably contained a grain of truth. What he had written in the magazine lately had lacked intelligence and genuine newsworthiness. Like so many journalists, he had just been plugging away, occasionally trotting out clichés. But that's how it was for the moment and he was much keener to ponder Salander's second question, her riddle, not so much because in itself it interested him especially, but because he wanted to think of some clever response.

If we create a machine that is cleverer than we ourselves are, he thought, what happens then? He went to the kitchen, opened a bottle of Ramlösa mineral water, and sat at the kitchen table. Downstairs Fru Gerner was coughing rather painfully, and in the distance amid the hubbub of the city an ambulance wailed away in the storm. Well, he mused, then we get a machine that can do all the clever things which we ourselves can do, plus a little bit more, for example ... He laughed out loud and understood the point of the question. A machine like that could go on to produce something more intelligent than itself in turn, and then what happens?

The same would be true of the next machine and the next one and the next one, and soon the very source of it all, man himself, would be no more interesting to the latest computer than a lab rat. An explosion of intelligence beyond all control, as in the *Matrix* films. Blomkvist smiled and went back to his computer and wrote:

```
<If we create such a machine then we'll
get a world where not even Lisbeth is so
cocksure.>
```

After that he sat looking out through the window, insofar as one could see anything beyond the swirling snow. Every now and then he looked through the open door at Berger, who was sleeping soundly and who knew nothing about machines more intelligent than human beings, or at least was not concerned about that right now.

He thought he heard his mobile give a ping, and sure enough: he had a new voicemail. That worried him, he was not sure why. Apart from ex-girlfriends who call when they're drunk and want to have sex, you usually only get bad news at night. The voice in the message sounded harried:

> *My name is Frans Balder. I know it's rude to call this late. I apologize for that. But my situation has become somewhat critical, at least that's how I see it. I've just discovered that you were looking for me, which is really a strange coincidence. There are a few things I've been wanting to tell you about for some time now, I think they might interest you. I'd be grateful if you could get in touch as soon as possible. I have a feeling that this might be a bit urgent.*

Balder left a telephone number and an e-mail address and Blomkvist jotted them down and sat still for a while, drumming his fingers on the kitchen table. Then he dialled the number.

Balder was lying in bed, agitated and scared. Yet he was feeling a little calmer now. The car coming up his drive had been the police guard arriving at long last. Two men in their forties, one tall and one quite short, both looking cocky and with the same short, trendy haircut. But they were perfectly polite and apologized for the delay in taking up their post.

"Milton Security and Gabriella Grane at the Security Police briefed us on the situation," one said.

They were aware that a man wearing a cap and dark glasses had been snooping around the property and that they had to be on their guard. Therefore they turned down the offer of a cup of hot tea in the kitchen. They wanted to check out the house and Balder thought that sounded sensible. Otherwise they did not make a hugely positive impression, but then he did not get an overwhelmingly negative impression either. He had taken their telephone numbers and gone back to bed to join August, who was still sleeping, curled up with his green earplugs.

But Balder had not been able to fall asleep again. He was listening for noises out there in the storm and eventually he sat up in bed. He had to do something, or he would go mad. He checked his mobile. He had two messages from Linus Brandell, who sounded bad-tempered and defensive all at the same time. At first Balder felt like hanging up. But then he caught a couple of things which were interesting after all. Linus had spoken to Mikael Blomkvist at *Millennium* magazine and now Blomkvist wanted to get in touch and Balder began to think. "Mikael Blomkvist," he muttered.

Is he to be my link with the outside world?

Balder knew very little about Swedish journalists. But he did know who Blomkvist was, and was aware of his reputation as someone who always went right to the heart of his stories, never yielding to pressure. That in itself did not necessarily make him the right man for the job—plus, somehow Balder seemed to recall hearing other, less flattering things—so he called Gabriella Grane again. She knew just about everything there was to know about the media scene and had said that she would be staying up late.

"Hello," she answered right away. "I was about to get in touch. I'm looking at that man on the CCTV. We really ought to move you now, you know."

"But, my God, Gabriella, the police are here—finally. They're sitting right outside the front door."

"There's nothing to suggest that the man will come through the front door."

"Why would he come back at all? The man from Milton said he looked like an old junkie."

"I'm not so sure about that. He was carrying some sort of box, something technical. We should play this safe."

Balder glanced at August lying next to him.

"I'm quite happy to move tomorrow. That might help my nerves. But I'm not going anywhere tonight—your policemen seem professional, professional enough at any rate."

"If you're going to be stubborn I'll see to it that Flinck and Blom make themselves conspicuous and cover the entire property."

"Fine, but that's not why I'm calling. You said I ought to go public, remember?"

"Well . . . yes . . . That's not the kind of advice you would expect from the Security Police, is it? I still think it would be a good idea, but first I'd like you to tell *us* what you know. I'm feeling a little apprehensive about this story."

"In that case let's talk tomorrow morning, when we've had a good sleep. But one thing, what do you think of Mikael

Blomkvist at *Millennium*? Could he be the right sort of person to talk to?"

Grane gave a laugh.

"If you want my colleagues to have an apoplectic fit, then definitely talk to him."

"Is it as bad as that?"

"At Säpo people avoid him like the plague. If you find Blomkvist on your doorstep, then you know your whole year is shot, they say. Everybody here, including Helena Kraft, would advise against it in the strongest terms."

"But it's you I'm asking."

"Well, my answer is that your reasoning is sound. He's a damn fine journalist."

"Hasn't he also come in for some criticism?"

"For sure, people have been saying that he's past his prime and that his writing isn't positive or upbeat enough, or whatever. But he's an old-fashioned investigative reporter of the highest calibre. Do you have his contact details?"

"My ex-assistant gave them to me."

"Good, great. But before you get in touch with him, you must first tell us what you have. Do you promise?"

"I promise, Gabriella. Now I'm going to sleep for a few hours."

"Do that, and I'll keep in touch with Flinck and Blom and arrange a safe house for you first thing in the morning."

After he had hung up he tried again to get some sleep. But it proved as impossible this time as before. The storm made him increasingly restless and worried. It felt as if something evil was travelling across the sea towards him, and he could not help listening anxiously for any unusual sounds.

It was true that he had promised Grane he would talk to her first. But he could not wait—everything he had kept bottled up for so long was throbbing to get out. He knew it was irrational, nothing could be that urgent. It was the middle of the night and, regardless of what Grane had said, he was by any reckoning safer than he had been for a long time. He had police protection and a first-rate security system. But that did not help. He was agitated and so he got out the number Linus had given him and dialled it, but of course Blomkvist did not answer.

Why would he? It was far too late. Balder left a voice message instead in a slightly forced, whispered voice so as not to wake August. Then he got up and put on his bedside light. On the bookshelf by the bed there was some literature which had nothing to do with his work, and both absentminded and worried, he flicked through an old novel by Stephen King, *Pet Sematary*. But that made him think even more about evil figures travelling through the night. For a long time he just stood there with the book in his hand—then he felt a stab of apprehension, which he might have dismissed as nonsense in broad daylight but which now seemed totally plausible. He had a sudden urge to speak to Farah or better still Steven Warburton at the Machine Intelligence Research Institute in Los Angeles, who would be certain to be awake, and while imagining all sorts of unpleasant scenarios, he looked out to sea and the night and the clouds scudding across the sky. At that moment his mobile rang, as if it had heard his prayer. But it was neither Farah nor Warburton.

"My name is Mikael Blomkvist," the voice said. "You've been looking for me."

"Correct. I'm sorry to have called so late."

"No problem. I was awake anyway."

"Can you talk now?"

"Absolutely, I was actually just answering a message from a person whom I think we both know. Lisbeth Salander."

"Who?"

"Sorry, maybe I've gotten hold of the wrong end of the stick. I thought you had hired her to go through your computers and trace a suspected data breach."

Balder laughed.

"Yes, my God, she's a strange girl, that one," he said. "She never revealed her surname, even though we had a lot of contact for a while. I assumed she had her reasons, and I never pushed her. I met her at one of my lectures at the Royal Institute of Technology. I'd be happy to tell you about it; it was pretty astonishing. But what I meant to ask was . . . well, you'll probably think it's a crazy idea."

"Sometimes I like crazy ideas."

"You wouldn't feel like coming over right now? It would mean a lot to me. I'm sitting on a story which I think could be explosive. I'll pay for your taxi here and back."

"Thanks, but I always pick up my own tab. Tell me, why do we have to talk now, in the middle of the night?"

"Because . . ." Balder hesitated. "Because I have a feeling this is urgent, or actually it's more than a feeling. I've just been told that I'm under threat, and an hour or so ago someone was snooping around my property. I'm frightened, to be honest, and I want to get this information off my chest. I no longer want to be the only one in the know."

"OK."

"OK what?"

"I'll come—if I can manage to get hold of a taxi."

Balder gave him the address and hung up, then called Professor Warburton in Los Angeles, and had an intense conversation with him on an encrypted line for about thirty minutes. Then he put on a pair of jeans and a black cashmere polo and went in search of a bottle of Amarone, in case that was the kind of thing Blomkvist might enjoy. But he got no further than the doorway before he started in fright.

He thought he had seen a movement, something flashing past, and looked anxiously towards the jetty and the sea. But it was the same desolate, storm-lashed scene as before, and he dismissed whatever it was as a figment of his imagination, a product of his nervous frame of mind, or at least he tried to. He left the bedroom and walked along the large window on his way towards the upper floor. Suddenly gripped by a new fear, he spun around again and this time he really did glimpse something over by the house next door.

A figure was racing along in the shelter of the trees, and even if Balder did not see the person for more than a matter of seconds, he could make out that it was a powerfully built man with a backpack and dark clothes. The man ran in a crouch and something about the way he moved had a trained look to it, as if he had run like that many times before, perhaps in a distant war.

It took a few moments for Balder to fumble for his mobile, and he tried to work out which of the numbers on his call list belonged to the policemen out there. He had not put their names into his contacts, and now was uncertain. With a shaking hand he tried one which he thought was right. No-one answered, not at first. The ring tone sounded three, four, five times before a voice panted out, "Blom here, what's up?"

"I saw a man running along the line of trees by my neighbour's house. I don't know where he is now. But he could very well be up by the road near you."

"OK, we'll check it out."

"He seemed . . ." Balder said.

"What?"

"I don't know, quick."

Dan Flinck and Peter Blom were sitting in the police car chatting about their young colleague, Anna Berzelius, and the size of her bum.

Both had recently gotten divorced. Their divorces had been painful at first. They both had young children, wives who felt let down, and parents-in-law who to varying degrees called them irresponsible shits. But once the dust had settled and they had gotten shared custody of the children and new, if modest, homes, they had both been struck by the same realization: that they missed their bachelor days. Lately, during the weeks when they were not looking after the kids, they had lived it up as never before. Afterwards, just like when they were in their teens, they had discussed all the parties in detail, especially the women they had met, reviewing their physiques from top to bottom, and their prowess in bed. But on this occasion they had not had time to discuss Anna Berzelius in as much depth as they would have liked.

Blom's mobile rang and they both jumped, partly because he had changed his ringtone to an extreme version of "Satisfaction," but mainly because the night and the storm and the emptiness out here had made them edgy. Besides, Blom had his telephone in his pocket, and since his trousers were tight—his waistline had expanded as a result of all the partying—it took a while before he could get it out. When he hung up he looked worried.

"What's that about?" Flinck said.

"Balder saw a man, a quick bastard, apparently."

"Where?"

"Down by the trees next to the neighbour's house. The guy's probably on his way up towards us."

Blom and Flinck stepped out of the car. They had been outside many times over the course of this long night, but this was the first time they shivered right down to the bone. For an instant they just stood looking awkwardly to the right and the left, shocked by the cold. Then Blom—the taller of the two—took command and told Flinck to stay up by the road while he himself went down towards the water.

It was a short slope which extended along a wooden fence and a small avenue of newly planted trees. A lot of snow had fallen, it was slippery and at the bottom lay the sea. Baggensfjärden, Blom thought, and in fact he was surprised that the water had not frozen over, but that may have been because of the waves. Blom cursed at the storm and at this night duty which wore him out and ruined his beauty sleep. He tried to do his job all the same, not with his whole heart perhaps, but still.

He listened and looked around, and at first he could not pick out anything. It was dark. Only the light from a single lamppost shone into the property, immediately in front of the jetty, so he went down towards it, past a garden chair which had been flung about in the storm.

In the next moment he could see Balder through the large windowpane. Balder was standing some way inside the house, bent over a large bed, his body in a tensed position. Perhaps he was straightening the covers, it was hard to tell. He seemed busy with some small detail in the bed. Blom should not be bothering about it—he was meant to be keeping watch over the property—yet there was something in Balder's body language which fascinated him and for a second or two he lost his concentration before he was brought back to reality again.

He had a chilling feeling that someone was watching him, and he spun around, his eyes searching wildly. He saw nothing, not at first, and had just begun to calm down when he became aware of two things—a sudden movement by the shiny steel bins next to the fence, and the sound of a car up by the road. The engine stopped and a car door was opened.

Neither occurrence was noteworthy in itself. There could easily be an animal by the trash bins and cars could come or go here even late at night. Yet Blom's body stiffened and for a moment he just stood there, not knowing how to react. Then Flinck's voice could be heard.

"Someone's coming!"

Blom did not move. He felt that he was being observed and almost unconsciously he fingered the service weapon at his hip and thought of his mother and his ex-wife and his children, as if something serious really was about to happen. Flinck shouted again, now with a desperate tone in his voice, "Police! Stop right there!" and Blom ran up towards the road, although it did not seem the obvious option even then. He could not rid himself of the apprehension that he was leaving something threatening and unpleasant down by the steel bins. But if his partner shouted like that, he did not have a choice, did he? and he felt secretly relieved. He had been more frightened than he cared to admit and so he hurried off and came stumbling onto the road.

Up ahead, Flinck was chasing after an unsteady man with a broad back and clothes that were far too thin. Even though he hardly fit the description of a "quick bastard," Blom ran after him. Soon afterwards they brought him down by the side of the ditch, right next to a couple of mailboxes and a small lantern which cast a pale light over the whole scene.

"Who the hell are you?" Flinck bellowed with surprising aggression—he had also been scared—and the man looked at them in confusion and terror.

He was not wearing a hat, he had hoarfrost in his hair and in the stubble on his chin, and you could tell that he was cold and in pretty bad shape. But above all there was something extraordinarily familiar about his face.

For a few seconds Blom thought that they had arrested a known and wanted criminal and he swelled with pride.

Balder had gone back to the bedroom and tucked August in again, perhaps to hide him under the blanket if anything should happen. Then he had a crazy thought, prompted by the sense of foreboding he felt, accentuated by his conversation with Warburton. Probably his mind was just clouded by panic and fear.

He realized it was not a new idea but something which had been developing in his subconscious during many sleepless nights in California. So he got out his laptop, his own little supercomputer connected to a series of other machines for sufficient capacity, opened the AI programme to which he had dedicated his life, and then . . .

He deleted the file and all of the backup. He barely thought it through. He was like an evil God snuffing out a life, and perhaps that was exactly what he *was* doing. Nobody knew, not even he himself, and he sat there for a little while, wondering if he would be floored by remorse and regret. It was incomprehensible, wasn't it? His life's work was gone, with just a few taps of a key.

But oddly enough it made him calmer, as if at least one aspect of his life was protected. He got to his feet and once more looked out into the night and the storm. Then the telephone rang. It was Flinck, the second policeman.

"I just wanted to say that we apprehended the man you saw," the policeman said. "In other words, you can relax. We have the situation under control."

"Who is it?" Balder said.

"I couldn't say. He's very drunk and we have to get him to quiet down. I just wanted to let you know. We'll get back to you."

Balder put the mobile down on the bedside table, next to his laptop, and tried to congratulate himself. Now the man was under arrest, and his research would not fall into the wrong hands. Yet he was not reassured. At first he did not understand why. Then it hit him: the man who had run along the trees had been anything but drunk.

It took a full minute or more before Blom realized that they had not in fact arrested a notorious criminal but rather the actor Lasse Westman, who did often enough play bandits and hit men on screen, but who was not actually wanted for any crime. The realization did not make Blom feel any calmer.

Not just because he again suspected it had been a mistake to leave the area by the trees and the bins, but because this whole episode could lead to scandal and headlines in the press.

He knew enough about Westman to be aware that whatever that man did all too often ended up in the evening papers, and you could not say that the actor was looking particularly happy. He puffed and swore as he scrambled to get to his feet and Blom tried to work out what on earth the man was doing out here in the middle of the night.

"Do you live in the area?" he said.

"I don't have to tell you a fucking thing," Westman hissed, and Blom turned to Flinck in an attempt to understand how the whole drama had begun.

But Flinck was already standing a little way off talking into his telephone, apparently with Balder. He probably wanted to show how efficient he was by passing on the news that they had seized the suspect, if indeed he was the suspect.

"Have you been snooping around Professor Balder's property?" Blom said.

"Didn't you hear what I said? I'm not telling you a fucking thing. What the hell, here I am strolling around perfectly peacefully and along comes that maniac waving his pistol. It's outrageous. Don't you know who I am?"

"I know who you are, and if we have over-reacted then I apologize. I'm sure we'll have a chance to talk about it again. But right now we're in the middle of a tense situation and I demand that you tell me at once what brought you here to Professor Balder. Oh, no, don't you try to run away now!"

Westman was probably not trying to escape at all. He was just having trouble keeping his balance. Then he cleared his throat rather dramatically and spat right out into the air. The phlegm did not get far but flew back like a projectile and froze to ice on his cheek.

"Do you know something?" he said, wiping his face.

"No?"

"I'm not the bad guy in this story."

Blom looked nervously down towards the water and the avenue of trees and wondered yet again what he had seen there. Still he remained standing where he was, paralyzed by the absurdity of the situation.

"Well then, who is?"

"Balder."

"How so?"

"He's taken my girlfriend's son."

"Why would he have done that?"

"You shouldn't bloody well be asking me! Ask the computer genius in there! That bastard has absolutely no right to him," Westman said, and fumbled in the inside pocket of his coat.

"He doesn't have a child in the house, if that's what you think," Blom said.

"He sure as hell does."

"Really?"

"Really!"

"So you thought you'd come along here in the middle of the night, pissed as a newt, and fetch the child," Blom said, and he was about to make another crushing comment when he was interrupted by a sound, a soft clinking sound coming up from the water's edge.

"What was that?" he said.

"What was what?" answered Flinck, who was standing next to him and did not seem to have heard anything at all.

It was true that the sound had not been all that loud, at least not up here.

Yet it still made Blom shudder. He was just about to go down to investigate when he hesitated again. As he looked around anxiously he could hear another car approaching.

It was a taxi which drove past and stopped at Balder's front door, and that gave Blom an excuse to stay up on the road. While the driver and the passenger settled up he cast yet another worried look down to the water. He thought he heard another sound—that didn't reassure him.

He did not know for sure, and now the car door opened and a man climbed out whom Blom, after a moment's confusion, identified as the journalist Mikael Blomkvist, though God only knew why the hell all these celebrities had to congregate right here in the middle of the night.

CHAPTER 10

NOVEMBER 21—EARLY MORNING

Balder was standing in the bedroom next to his computer and his mobile, looking at August, who was whimpering restlessly in the bed. He wondered what the boy was dreaming. Was it about a world which he could even understand? Balder wanted to know. He wanted to start living, to no longer bury himself in quantum algorithms and source codes and paranoia. He wanted to be happy, not tormented by that constant weight in his body; he wanted instead to launch himself into something wild and magnificent, a romance even. For a few intense seconds he thought about the women who had fascinated him: Gabriella, Farah, and others too.

He also thought about the woman who it turned out was called Salander. He had been spellbound by her, and as he now remembered her he saw something new in her, something both familiar and strange: she reminded him of August. That was absurd of course. August was a small autistic boy. Salander was not that old either, and there may have been something boyish about her, but otherwise she was his polar opposite. Dressed in black, a bit of a punk, totally uncompromising. Still it occurred to him now that her eyes had that same strange shine as August's, when he had been staring at the traffic light on Hornsgatan.

Balder had encountered Salander at the Royal Institute of Technology in Stockholm, while he was giving a lecture on technical singularity, the hypothetical state when computers become more intelligent than the human being. He had just begun by explaining the concept of singularity in terms of mathematics and physics when the door opened and a skinny girl in black strode into the lecture hall. His first thought was that it was a shame there was no other place for junkies to go. Then he wondered if the girl really was an addict. She did not seem strung out, but on the other hand she did look tired and surly, and did not appear to be paying any attention to his lecture. She just sat there slouched over a desk. Eventually, in the middle of a discussion of the moment of singularity in complex mathematical calculation, the point where the solution hits infinity, he asked her straight out what she thought of it all. It was mean of him to pick on her. But what had happened?

The girl looked up and said that, instead of bandying fuzzy concepts about, he should become sceptical when the basis for his calculations fell apart. It was not some sort of real world physical collapse, more a sign that his own mathematics were not up to scratch, and therefore it was sheer populism on his part to mystify singularities in black holes when it was so obvious that the main problem was the absence of a quantum mechanical method for calculating gravity.

With icy clarity—which set off a buzz in the hall—she then presented a sweeping critique of the singularity theorists he had quoted, and he was incapable of coming up with any answer other than a dismayed: "Who the hell are you?"

That was their first contact. The girl was to surprise him a few times more after that. With lightning speed or just one bright glance she immediately grasped what he was working on. When he realized that his technology had been stolen, he had asked for her help, and that had created a bond between them—they shared a secret.

Now he was standing there in the bedroom thinking of her. But his thoughts were interrupted. He was overcome by a new chilling sense of unease and he looked through the doorway towards the large window overlooking the water.

In front of it stood a tall figure in dark clothes and a tight black cap with a small lamp on his forehead. He was doing something to the window. He pulled across it with a swift and powerful movement, like an artist starting work on a fresh canvas, and before Balder even had time to cry out, the whole window fell in and the figure moved towards him.

Jan Holtser usually told people that he worked on industrial security issues. In actual fact he was a former Soviet special forces soldier who spent his time breaking into security systems. He had a small skilled staff, and for operations like this one, as a rule the preparations were so painstaking that the risks were not as great as one might imagine.

It's true that he was no longer a young man, but for fifty-one he kept himself in good shape with hard training and was known for his efficiency and ability to improvise. If fresh circumstances cropped up, he thought about them and took them into consideration in his planning.

His experience tended to make up for his lack of youthful vigour, and occasionally, in the limited circle within which he could talk openly, he would speak of a sort of sixth sense, an acquired instinct. He had learned over the years when to wait and when to strike and although he had been through a bad patch a couple of years earlier and betrayed signs of weakness—humanity, his daughter would say—he now felt more accomplished than ever before.

He was once more able to take pleasure in his work, that old sense of excitement. Yes, he did still dose himself with ten milligrammes of Stesolid before a mission, but that was only because it enhanced his accuracy with weapons. He remained crystal clear and alert at critical moments, and most important: he always carried out the tasks he was assigned. Holtser was not someone who let people down or bailed out. That was how he thought of himself.

And yet tonight, even though his client had stressed that the job was urgent he had considered calling it off. The bad weather was a factor. But the storm in itself would never have been enough to get him to consider cancelling. He was Russian and a soldier who had fought in far worse conditions than these—he hated people who moaned about trivial things.

What bothered him was the police guard, which had appeared out of nowhere. He did not think much of the policemen on the property. From his hiding place he had seen them snooping around with the vague reluctance of small boys told to go outside in bad weather. They would rather have stayed sitting in their car talking rubbish, and they were easily frightened, especially the taller of the two, who seemed to dislike the dark and the storm and the black water. As he stood there staring from among the trees a little while ago, he had appeared terrified, presumably because he had sensed Holtser's presence, but that was not something that worried Holtser. He could have slit the man's throat swiftly and soundlessly.

Still, the policemen were not good news.

Their presence considerably raised the level of risk; above all it was an indication that some part of the plan had leaked out, there was a heightened readiness. Maybe the professor had started to talk, in which case the operation would be meaningless, it might even make their situation worse. Holtser was determined not to expose his client to any unnecessary risks. He regarded that as one of his strengths. He always saw the bigger picture and, despite his profession, he was often the one who counselled caution.

He had lost count of the number of criminal gangs in his home country that had gone under because they had resorted too often to violence. Violence can command respect. Violence can silence and intimidate, and ward off risks and threats. But violence can also cause chaos and a whole chain of unwanted consequences.

All those thoughts had gone through his mind as he sat hidden behind the trees and the line of bins. For a few seconds he was resolved to abort the operation and go back to his hotel room. Yet that did not happen.

A car arrived, occupying the policemen's attention, and he spotted an opportunity. Without stopping to evaluate his motivations he fitted the elastic of the lamp over his head. He got out the diamond saw from his left-hand jacket pocket and drew his weapon, a 1911 R1 Carry with a custom-made silencer, and weighed them, one in each hand. Then, as ever, he said:

"Thy will be done, amen."

Yet he could not shake off the uncertainty. Was this right? He would have to act with lightning speed. True, he knew the house inside out and Jurij had been here twice and hacked the alarm system. Plus the policemen were hopeless amateurs. Even if he were delayed in there—say the professor did not have his computer next to his bed, as everyone had said, and they had time to come to his aid—Holtser would be able to dispose of them too without any problem. He looked forward to it. He therefore muttered a second time:

"Thy will be done, amen."

Then he disengaged the safety on his weapon and moved rapidly to the large window overlooking the water. It may have been due to the uncertainty of the situation, but he felt an unusually strong reaction when he saw Balder standing there in the bedroom, engrossed in something. He tried to persuade himself that everything was fine. The target was clearly visible. Yet he still felt apprehensive: Should he call the job off?

He did not. Instead he tensed the muscles in his right arm and with all his strength drew the diamond saw across the window and pushed. The window collapsed with a disturbing crash and he rushed in and raised his weapon at Balder, who was staring hard at him, waving his hand as though in a desperate greeting. The professor began to say something confused and ceremonious which sounded like a prayer, a litany. But instead of "God" or "Jesus," Holtser heard the word "disabled." That was all he managed to catch, and in any case it did not matter. People had said all sorts of things to him.

He showed no mercy.

. . .

Quickly and almost soundlessly the figure moved through the hallway into the bedroom. In that time Balder registered with surprise that the alarm had not gone off and noticed a motif of a grey spider on the man's sweater, also a narrow, oblong scar on his pale forehead beneath the cap and the lamp.

Then he saw the weapon. The man was pointing a pistol at him. Balder raised his hand in a vain attempt to protect himself. But even though his life was on the line and fear had set its claws into him he thought only of August. Whatever else happens, even if he himself has to die, let his son be spared. He burst out:

"Don't kill my child! He's disabled, he doesn't understand anything."

Balder did not know how far he got. The whole world froze and the night and the storm seemed to bear down on him and then everything went black.

Holtser fired and as he had expected there was nothing wrong with his aim. He hit Balder twice in the head and the professor collapsed to the floor like a flapping scarecrow. There was no doubt that he was dead. Yet something did not feel right. A blustery wind swept in off the sea and brushed across Holtser's neck as if it were a cold, living being, and for a second or two he had no idea what was happening.

Everything had gone according to plan and over there was Balder's computer, just as he had been told. He should take it and go. He needed to be efficient. Yet he stood as if frozen to the spot and it was only after a strangely long delay that he realized why.

In the large double bed, almost completely hidden by a duvet, lay a small boy with unruly, tousled hair watching him with a glassy look. Those eyes made him uncomfortable, and that was not just because they seemed to be looking straight through him. There was more to it than that.

Then again it made no difference. He had to carry out his assignment. Nothing must be allowed to jeopardize the operation. Here was someone who was clearly a witness, especially now that he had exposed his face, and there must be no witnesses, so he pointed his weapon at the boy and looked into his glowing eyes and for the third time muttered:

"Thy will be done, amen."

Blomkvist climbed out of the taxi in a pair of black boots and a white fur coat with a broad sheepskin collar, which he had dug out of the cupboard, as well as an old fur hat that had belonged to his father.

It was then 2:40 in the morning. The Ekot news bulletin had reported a serious accident involving an articulated truck which was now blocking the main Värmdö road. But Blomkvist and the taxi driver had seen nothing of that and had travelled together through the dark, storm-battered suburbs. Blomkvist was sick with exhaustion. All he had wanted was to stay at home, creep into bed with Erika again, and go back to sleep.

But he had not felt able to say no to Balder. He could not understand why. It might have been out of some sense of duty, a feeling that he could not allow himself any easy options now that the magazine was facing a crisis, or it might have been that Balder had sounded lonely and frightened, and Blomkvist was both sympathetic and curious. Not that he thought he was going to hear anything sensational. He was cynically expecting to be disappointed. Maybe he would find himself acting as a therapist, a night watchman in the storm. On the other hand, one never knew, and once again he thought of Salander. Salander rarely did anything without good reason. Besides, Balder was a fascinating figure, and he had never before given an interview. It could well turn out to be interesting, Blomkvist thought, as he looked about him in the darkness.

A lamppost cast a blueish light over the house, and a nice house it was too, architect-designed with large glass windows, and built to look a little like a train. Standing by the mailbox was a tall policeman in his forties, with a fading tan and somewhat strained, nervous features. Further down the road was a shorter colleague of his, arguing with a drunk who was waving his arms about. More was happening out here than Blomkvist had expected.

"What's going on?" he said to the taller policeman.

He never got an answer. The policeman's mobile rang and Blomkvist overheard that the alarm system did not seem to be working properly. There was a noise coming from the lower part of the property, a crackling, unnerving sound, which instinctively he associated with the telephone call. He took a couple of steps to the right and looked down a hill which stretched all the way to a jetty and the sea and another lamppost which shone with the same blueish light. Just then a figure came charging out of nowhere and Blomkvist realized that something was badly wrong.

· · ·

Holtser squeezed the first pressure on the trigger and was just about to shoot the boy when the sound of a car could be heard up by the road, and he checked himself. But it was not really the car. It was because of the word "disabled," which cropped up again in his thoughts. He realized that the professor would have had every reason to lie in that last moment of his life, but as Holtser now stared at the child he wondered if it might not in fact be true.

The boy's body was immobile, and his face radiated wonder rather than fear, as if he had no understanding of what was happening. His look was too blank and glassy to register anything properly.

Holtser recalled something he had read during his research. Balder did have a severely mentally handicapped son. Both the press and the court papers had said that the professor did not have custody. But this must surely be the boy and Holtser neither could nor needed to shoot him. It would be pointless and a breach of his own professional ethics. This recognition came to him as a huge relief, which should have made him suspicious had he been more aware of himself at that moment.

Now he just lowered the pistol, picked up the computer and the mobile from the bedside table and stuffed them into his backpack. Then he ran into the night along the escape route he had staked out for himself. But he did not get far. He heard a voice behind him and turned around. Up by the road stood a man who was neither of the policemen but a new figure in a fur coat and fur hat and with quite a different aura of authority. Perhaps this was why Holtser raised his pistol again. He sensed danger.

. . .

The man who charged past was athletic and dressed in black, with a headlamp on his cap, and in some way Blomkvist could not quite explain why he had the feeling that the figure was part of a coordinated operation. He half expected more figures to appear out of the darkness, and that made him very uncomfortable. He called out, "Hey you, stop!"

That was a mistake. Blomkvist understood it the instant the man's body stiffened, like a soldier in combat, and that was doubtless why he reacted so quickly. By the time the man drew a weapon and fired a shot as if it were the most natural thing in the world, Blomkvist had already ducked down by the corner of the house. The shot could hardly be heard, but when something smacked into Balder's mailbox there was no doubt what had happened. The taller of the policemen abruptly ended his call, but did not move a muscle. The only person who said anything was the drunk.

"What the fuck's going on here? What's happening?" he roared in a voice which sounded oddly familiar, and only then did the policemen start talking to each other in nervous, low tones:

"Is someone shooting?"

"I think so."

"What should we do?"

"Call for reinforcements."

"But he's getting away."

"Then we'd better take a look," the taller one said, and with slow, hesitant movements, as if they wanted the assailant to escape, they drew their weapons and went down to the water.

A dog could be heard barking in the winter darkness, a small, bad-tempered dog, and the wind was blowing hard from the sea. The snow was whirling about and the ground was slippery. The shorter of the two policemen nearly fell over and started flailing his arms like a clown. With a bit of luck they might avoid running into the man with the weapon. Blomkvist sensed that the figure would have no trouble at all in getting rid of those two. The quick and efficient way in which he had turned and raised his weapon suggested that he was trained for situations like these.

Blomkvist wondered if he should do something. He had nothing with which to defend himself. Yet he got to his feet, brushed the snow from his coat, and looked down the slope again. The policemen were working their way along the water's edge towards the neighbour's house. There was no sign of the black-clad man with the gun. Blomkvist made his way down too, and it was at once clear that a window had been smashed in. There was a large gaping hole in the house. But before he could summon the policemen, he heard something, a strange, low whimpering sound, so he stepped through the shattered window into a corridor with a fine oak floor whose pale glow could be seen in the darkness. He walked slowly towards a doorway where the sound was coming from.

"Balder," he called out. "It's me, Mikael Blomkvist. Is everything all right?"

There was no answer. But the whimpering grew louder. He took a deep breath, walked into the room—and froze, paralyzed with shock. Afterwards he could not say what he had noticed first, or even what had frightened him most. It was not necessarily the body on the floor, despite the blood and the empty, rigid expression on its face.

It could have been the scene on the large double bed next to Balder, though it was difficult to make sense of it. There was a small child, perhaps seven, eight years old, a boy with fine features and dishevelled, dark-blond hair, wearing blue checked pyjamas, who was banging his body against the headboard and the wall, methodically and with force. The boy's wailing did not sound like that of a crying child, more like someone trying to hurt himself as much as he could. Before Blomkvist had time to think straight he hurried over to him. The boy was kicking wildly.

"There," Blomkvist said. "There, there," and wrapped his arms around him.

The boy twisted and turned with astonishing strength and managed—possibly because Blomkvist did not want to hold him too tightly—to tear himself from his embrace and rush through the door and out into the corridor, barefoot over the glass shards towards the shattered window, with Blomkvist racing after him shouting, "No!"

That was when he ran into the two policemen. They were standing out in the snow with expressions of total bewilderment.

CHAPTER 11

NOVEMBER 21

Afterwards it was said that the police had a problem with their procedures, and that nothing had been done to cordon off the area until it was too late. The man who shot Professor Balder must have had all the time in the world to make good his escape. The first policemen on the scene, Detectives Blom and Flinck, known rather scornfully at the station as "the Casanovas," had taken their time before raising the alarm, or at least had not done so with the necessary urgency or authority.

The forensic technicians and investigators from the Violent Crimes Division arrived only at 3:40, at the same time as a young woman who introduced herself as Gabriella Grane and who was assumed to be a relative because she was so upset, but who they later came to understand was an analyst from Säpo, sent by the head of the agency herself. That did not help Grane; thanks to the collective misogyny within the force, or possibly to underline the fact that she was regarded as an outsider, she was given the task of taking care of the child.

"You look as if you know how to handle this sort of thing," Erik Zetterlund said. He was the leader of the duty investigating team that night. He had watched Grane bending to examine the cuts on the boy's feet, and even though she snapped at him and declared that she had other priorities, she gave in when she looked into the boy's eyes.

August—as he was called—was paralyzed by fear and for a long time he sat on the floor at the top of the house, wrapped in a duvet, mechanically moving his hand across a red Persian carpet. Blom, who in other respects had not proved to be especially enterprising, managed to find a pair of socks and put sticking plasters on the boy's feet. They noticed too that he had bruises all over his body and a split lip. According to the journalist Mikael Blomkvist—whose presence created a palpable nervousness in the house—the boy had been throwing himself against the bed and the wall downstairs and had run in bare feet across the broken glass on the ground floor.

Grane, who for some reason was reluctant to introduce herself to Blomkvist, realized at once that August was a witness, but she was not able to establish any sort of rapport with him, nor was she able to give him comfort. Hugs and tenderness of the usual kind were clearly not the right approach. August was at his calmest when Grane simply sat beside him, a little way away, doing her own thing, and only once did he appear to be paying attention. This was when she was speaking on her mobile with Kraft and mentioned the house number, 79. She did not give it much thought at the time, and soon after that she reached an agitated Hanna Balder.

Hanna wanted to have her son back at once and told Grane, to her surprise, that she should get out some jigsaw puzzles, particularly the one of the warship *Vasa,* which she said the boy's father would have had lying around some-where. She did not describe her ex-husband as having taken the boy unlawfully, but she had no answer when asked why Westman had been out at the house demanding to have the boy back. It certainly did not seem to be concern for the child that had brought him here.

The fact of the boy's presence did, however, shed light on some of Grane's earlier questions. She now understood why Balder had been evasive about certain things, and why he had not wanted to have a guard dog. In the early morning Grane arranged for a psychologist and a doctor to take August to his mother in Vasastan, unless it turned out that he needed more urgent medical attention.

Then she was struck by a different thought. It occurred to her that the motive for murder might not have been to silence Balder. The killer could as easily have been wanting to rob him—not of something as obvious as money, but of his research. Grane had no idea what Balder had been work-ing on during the last year of his life. Perhaps no-one knew. But it was not difficult to imagine what it might have been: in all likelihood a development of his AI programme, which was already regarded as revolutionary when it was stolen the first time.

His colleagues at Solifon had done everything they could to get a look at it and according to what Balder had once let slip he guarded it as a mother guards her baby, which must mean, Grane thought, that he kept it next to him while he was asleep. So she told Blom to keep an eye on August and went down to the bedroom on the ground floor where the forensic team were working.

"Was there a computer in here?" she said.

The technicians shook their heads and Grane got out her mobile and called Kraft again.

It was soon established that Westman had disappeared. He must have left the scene amid the general turmoil, and that made Zetterlund swear and shout, the more so when it transpired that Westman was not to be found at his home either.

Zetterlund considered putting out a search bulletin, which prompted his young colleague Axel Andersson to enquire whether Westman should be treated as dangerous. Maybe Andersson was unable to tell Westman himself apart from the characters he played on screen. But to give the investigator his due, the situation was looking increasingly messy.

The murder was evidently no ordinary settling of scores within the family, no booze-up gone wrong, no crime committed in a fit of passion, but a cold-blooded, well-planned assault. Matters did not improve when the chief of provincial police, Jan-Henrik Rolf, weighed in with his assessment that the killing must be treated as an attack on Swedish industrial interests. Zetterlund was finding himself at the heart of an incident of major domestic political importance and even if he were not the brightest mind in the force he realized that what he did now would have a significant long-term impact.

Zetterlund, who had turned forty-one two days earlier and was still suffering some of the after-effects of his birthday party, had never been close to taking charge of an investigation of this importance. The reason he had now been detailed to do it, if only for a matter of hours, was that there had not been very many competent people on duty during the night and his superior had chosen not to wake the National Murder Squad or any of the more experienced investigators in the Stockholm police.

Accordingly Zetterlund found himself in the midst of this confusion, feeling less and less sure of himself, and was soon shouting out his orders. In the first place he was trying to set in motion an effective door-to-door enquiry. He wanted quickly to gather as much testimony as possible, even if he was not expecting to get very much out of it. It was night-time and dark and there was a storm blowing. The people living nearby had presumably not seen anything at all. But you never knew.

So he had himself questioned Blomkvist, though God only knows what he was doing there. The presence of one of Sweden's best-known journalists did not make matters any easier and for a while Zetterlund imagined that Blomkvist was examining him critically with a view to writing a tell-all. Probably that was just his insecurity. Blomkvist himself was shaken and throughout the interview he was unfailingly polite and keen to help. But he was not able to provide much in the way of information. It had all happened so quickly and that in itself was significant, the journalist told him.

There had been something brutal and efficient about the way in which the suspect moved, and Blomkvist said it would not be too far-fetched to speculate that the man either was or had been a soldier, possibly even special forces. His way of spinning around to aim and fire his weapon had seemed practised. He had a lamp strapped to his tight-fitting black cap, but Blomkvist had not been able to make out any of his features.

He had been too far away, he said, and had thrown himself to the ground the instant the figure had turned around.

He should thank his lucky stars that he was still alive. He could only describe the body and the clothes, and that he did very well. According to the journalist, the man did not seem all that young, he could have been over forty. He was fit and taller than average, over six feet tall, powerfully built with a slim waist and broad shoulders, wearing boots and black, military-style clothes. He was carrying a backpack and looked to have a knife strapped to his right leg.

Blomkvist thought that the man had vanished down along the water's edge, past the neighbouring houses, and that also matched Blom and Flinck's account. The policemen had admittedly not seen the man at all. But they had heard his footsteps and set off in vain pursuit, or so they claimed. Zetterlund had his doubts about that.

Blom and Flinck had chickened out, he presumed, and had stood there in the darkness, fearful and doing nothing. In any event, that was the moment when the big mistake was made. Instead of identifying escape routes from the area and trying to cordon them off, nothing much seems to have happened. At that point Flinck and Blom were not yet aware that someone had been killed and as soon as they knew, they had had their hands full coping with a barefoot boy running hysterically out of the house. Certainly it could not have been easy to keep a cool head. Yet they had lost precious time and, though Blomkvist exercised restraint when describing the events, it was plain to see that even he was critical. He had twice asked the policemen if they had sounded the alarm and got a nod for an answer.

Later on, when Blomkvist overheard a conversation between Flinck and the operations centre, he realized that the nod was most likely a no, or at best some sort of bewildered failure to grasp the enormity of what had happened. It had taken a long time for the alarm to be raised and even then things had not proceeded as they should have, probably because Flinck's account of the situation had not been clear.

The paralysis had spread to other levels. Zetterlund was infinitely glad he could not be blamed for that—at that point he had not yet become involved in the investigation. On the other hand he was here, and he should at least avoid making a mess of things. His personal record had not been so impressive recently and this was an opportunity to put his best foot forward.

He was at the door to the living room and had just finished a call to Milton Security about the character who had been seen on camera earlier that night. He did not at all fit the description Mikael Blomkvist had given of the presumed murderer. He looked like a skinny old junkie, albeit one who must have possessed a high level of technical skill. Milton Security believed that the man had hacked the alarm system and put all the cameras and sensors out of action.

That did not exactly make matters any easier. It was not only the professional planning. It was the idea of committing a murder in spite of police protection and a sophisticated alarm system. How arrogant is that? Zetterlund had been about to go down to the forensic team on the ground floor, but he stayed upstairs, deeply troubled, staring into space until his gaze fastened on Balder's son. He was their key witness but incapable of speech, nor did he understand a word they said. In other words pretty much what one might expect in this shambles.

The boy was holding a small, single piece of an extremely complex puzzle. Zetterlund started towards the curved staircase leading to the ground floor—then he stopped dead. He thought back to his initial impression of the child. When he arrived on the scene, not knowing very much about what had happened, the boy had seemed the same as any other child. Zetterlund would have described him as an unusually pretty but normal-looking boy with curly hair and a shocked look in his eyes. Only later did he learn that the boy was autistic and severely handicapped. That, he thought, meant that the murderer either knew him from before or else was aware of his condition. Otherwise he would hardly have let him live and risk being identified in a witness parade, would he? Although Zetterlund did not give himself time to think this through in full, the hunch excited him and he took a few hurried paces towards the boy.

"We must question him at once," he said, in a voice that came out louder and more urgent than he had intended.

"For heaven's sake, take it easy with him," Blomkvist said.

"Don't you interfere," Zetterlund snapped. "He may have known the killer. We have to get out some pictures and show them to him. Somehow we must . . ."

The boy interrupted him by slamming the puzzle with his hand in a sudden sweeping movement. Zetterlund muttered an apology and went downstairs to join his forensic team.

Blomkvist remained there, looking at the boy. It felt as if something else was about to happen with him, perhaps a new outburst, and the last thing he wanted was for the child to hurt himself again. The boy stiffened and began to make furiously rapid circular movements over the rug with his right hand.

Then he stopped and looked up pleadingly. Though Blomkvist asked himself what that might mean, he dropped the thought when the policeman whose name he now knew to be Blom sat down with the boy and tried to get him to do the puzzle again. Blomkvist went into the kitchen to get some peace and quiet. He was exhausted and wanted to go home. But apparently he first had to look at some pictures from a surveillance camera. He had no idea when that was going to happen. It was all taking a long time and seemed disorganized and Blomkvist was longing for his bed.

He had spoken to Berger twice by then and told her what had happened. They agreed that Blomkvist should write a longer piece about the murder for the next issue. Not just because the crime itself was obviously major and Professor Balder's life was worth describing, but Blomkvist had a personal connection to the story and that would raise its quality and give him an advantage over the competition. The dramatic telephone call alone, in the middle of the night, which had gotten him here in the first place, would give his article an edge.

The Serner situation and the crisis at the magazine were implicit in their conversation. Berger had already planned for their temp Andrei Zander to do the preliminary research while Blomkvist got some sleep. She had said rather firmly— like someone halfway between a loving mother and an authoritative editor-in-chief—that she refused to have her star reporter dead from exhaustion before the work had even begun.

Blomkvist accepted without protest. Zander was ambitious and pleasant and it would be nice to wake up and find all the spadework done, ideally also with lists of people close to Balder whom he should be interviewing. For a little while Blomkvist welcomed the distraction of reflecting on Zander's persistent problems with women, which had been confided to him during evening sessions at the Kvarnen beer hall. Zander was young, intelligent, and handsome. He ought to be a catch. But because there was something soft and needy in his character, he was time and again being dropped, and that was painful for him. Zander was an incorrigible romantic, forever dreaming about love with a capital L and the big scoop.

Blomkvist sat down at Balder's kitchen table and looked out at the darkness. In front of him, next to a matchbox, a copy of *New Scientist,* and a pad of paper with some incomprehensible equations on it, lay a beautiful but slightly ominous drawing of a street crossing. A man with watery, squinting eyes and thin lips was standing next to a traffic light. He was caught in a fleeting moment and yet you could see every wrinkle in his face and the folds in his quilted jacket and trousers. He did not look pleasant. He had a heart-shaped mole on his chin.

But the striking thing about the drawing was the traffic light. It shone with an eloquent, troubling glow, and was skilfully executed according to some sort of mathematical technique. You could almost see the underlying geometrical lines. Balder must have enjoyed doing drawings on the side. Blomkvist wondered, though, about the unconventional choice of subject. On the other hand, why would a person like Balder draw sunsets and ships? A traffic light was probably just as interesting to him as anything else. Blomkvist was intrigued by the fact that the drawing looked like a snapshot. Even if Balder had sat and studied the traffic light, he could hardly have asked the man to cross the street over and over again. Maybe he was imagined, or Balder had a photographic memory, just like . . . Blomkvist grew thoughtful. He picked up his mobile and for the third time called Berger.

"Are you on your way home?" she asked.

"Not yet, unfortunately. There are a couple of things I still need to look at. But I'd like you to do me a favour."

"What else am I here for?"

"Could you go to my computer and log in. You know my password, don't you?"

"I know everything about you."

"Then go into Documents and open a file called [*Lisbeth stuff*]."

"I think I have an idea where this is going."

"Oh? Here's what I'd like you to write . . ."

"Wait a second, I have to open it first. OK, now . . . Hold on, there are already a few things here."

"Ignore them. This is what I want, right at the top. Are you with me?"

"Yes, I'm with you."

"Write: 'Lisbeth, maybe you already know, but Frans Balder is dead, shot in the head. Can you find out why someone wanted to kill him?'"

"Is that all?"

"Well, it's rather a lot considering that we haven't been in touch for ages. She'll probably think it's cheeky of me to ask. But I don't think it would hurt to have her help."

"A little illegal hacking wouldn't go amiss, you mean?"

"I didn't hear that. I'll see you soon I hope."

"I hope so."

. . .

Salander had managed to go back to sleep, and woke again at 7:30. She was not in top form—she had a headache and she felt nauseated. Yet she felt better than she had during the night. She bandaged her hand, had a quick breakfast of two microwaved meat piroshki and a large glass of Coca-Cola, then she stuffed some workout clothes into a sports bag and left the apartment. The storm had subsided, leaving trash and newspapers lying all over the city. She walked down from Mosebacke torg and along Götgatan, muttering to herself.

She looked angry and at least two people were alarmed enough to get out of her way. But Salander was merely determined. She was not looking forward to working out, she just wanted to stick to her routine and drive the toxins out of her body. So she continued down to Hornsgatan, and right before Hornsgatspuckeln she turned into Zero boxing club, which was in the basement down one flight of stairs. It seemed more run-down than ever that morning.

The place could have used a coat of paint and some general freshening up. It seemed as if no improvements had been made since the '70s. Posters of Ali and Foreman were still on the walls. It still looked like the day after that legendary bout in Kinshasa, possibly due to the fact that Obinze, the man in charge of the premises, had seen the fight live as a small boy and had afterwards run around in the liberating monsoon rain shouting "Ali Bomaye!" That double-time canter was not just his happiest memory, it also marked what he called the last moment of "the days of innocence."

Not long after that he and his family had been forced to flee Mobutu's terror and nothing had ever been the same again. Maybe it was not so strange that he wanted to preserve that moment in history, carry it with him to this godforsaken boxing hall in the Södermalm district of Stockholm. Obinze was still constantly talking about the fight. But then he was always constantly talking about something or other.

He was tall and mighty and bald-headed, a chatterbox of epic proportions and one of many in the gym who quite fancied Salander, even if like many others he thought she was more or less crazy. Periodically she would train harder than anyone else in there and go at the punch-balls, punch-bags, and her sparring partners like a madwoman. She possessed a kind of primitive, furious energy which Obinze had seldom come across.

Once, before he got to know her, he had suggested that she take up competitive boxing. The derisive snort he got in response stopped him from asking again, though he had never understood why she trained so hard. Not that he really needed to know—one could train hard for no reason at all. It was better than drinking hard. It was better than lots of things.

Maybe it was true, as she said to him late one evening about a year ago, that she wanted to be physically prepared in case she ever ended up in difficulties again. He knew that there had been trouble before. He had read every single word about her online and understood what it meant to be prepared in case some evil shadow from the past turned up. Both his parents had been murdered by Mobutu's thugs.

What he did not understand was why, at regular intervals, Salander gave up training altogether, not exercising at all, eating nothing but junk food. When she came into the gym that morning—as demonstratively dressed in black and pierced as ever—he had not seen her for two weeks.

"Hello, gorgeous. Where have you been?"

"Doing something highly illegal."

"I can only imagine. Beating the crap out of some motor-bike gang or something."

But she did not even rise to the jest. She just marched angrily in towards the changing room and he did something he knew she would hate: he stepped in front of her and looked her straight in the face.

"Your eyes are bright red."

"I've got the mother of all hangovers. Out of my way!"

"In that case I don't want to see you in here, you know that."

"Skip the crap. I want you to drive the shit out of me," she spat, and ducked past him to get changed. When she emerged wearing her outsized boxing shorts and white T-shirt with the black skull on the chest, he saw nothing for it but to go ahead and let her have it.

He pushed her until she threw up three times in his wastepaper bin. He gave her as much grief as he could. She gave him plenty of lip back. Then she went off and changed and left the gym without even a goodbye. As so often at such moments Obinze was overcome by a feeling of emptiness. Maybe he was even a little in love. He was certainly stirred—how could one not be by a girl who boxed like that?

The last he saw of her was her calves disappearing up the stairs, so he could not know that the ground swayed beneath her feet as she came out onto Hornsgatan. Salander braced her-self against the wall of the building and breathed heavily. Then she set off in the direction of her apartment on Fiskargatan. Once home she drank another large glass of Coca-Cola and half a litre of juice, then she crashed onto her bed and looked at the ceiling for ten, fifteen minutes, thinking about this and that, about singularities and event horizons and certain special aspects of Schrödinger's equation, and Ed Needham.

She waited for the world to regain its usual colours before she got up and went to her computer. However reluctant she might be, she was drawn to it by a force which had not grown weaker since her childhood. But this morning she was not in the mood for any wild escapades. She hacked into Mikael Blomkvist's computer. In the next moment she froze. They had been joking about Balder and now Blomkvist wrote that he had been murdered, shot in the head.

"Jesus," she muttered, and had a look at the online evening papers.

There was no explicit mention of Balder, but it was not difficult to work out that he was the "Swedish academic shot at his home in Saltsjöbaden." For the time being, the police were being tight-lipped and journalists had not managed to turn up a great deal, no doubt because they had not yet cottoned on to how big the story was. Other events from the night took precedence: the storm and the power outage right across the country and the scandalous delays on the railways. There was also the odd celebrity news item which Salander could not be bothered to try to understand.

The only facts reported on the murder were that it had taken place around 3:00 in the morning and that the police were seeking witnesses in the neighbourhood, for reports of anything untoward. So far, there were no suspects, but apparently witnesses had spotted unknown and suspicious persons on the property. The police were looking for more information on them. At the end of the articles it said that a press conference was going to be held later that day, led by Chief Inspector Jan Bublanski. Salander gave a wistful smile. She had a fair bit of history with Bublanski—or Officer Bubble, as he was sometimes called—and she thought that so long as they didn't put any idiots onto his team the investigation would turn out to be reasonably effective.

Then she read Blomkvist's message again. He needed help and without thinking twice she wrote "OK." Not only because he was asking her. It was personal. She did not do grief, not in the conventional way at least. Anger, on the other hand, yes, a cold ticking rage. And though she had a certain respect for Jan Bublanski she was not usually inclined to trust the forces of law and order.

She was used to taking matters into her own hands and she had all sorts of reasons to find out why Frans Balder had been murdered. Because it was no coincidence that she had sought him out and taken an interest in his situation. His enemies were most likely her enemies too.

It had begun with the old question of whether in some sense her father lived on. Alexander Zalachenko—Zala—had not only killed her mother and destroyed her childhood, he had also established and controlled a criminal network, sold drugs and arms, and made a living exploiting and humiliating women. She was convinced that that sort of evil never goes away. It merely migrates into other forms.

Ever since that day just over a year ago when she had woken up at dawn at Hotel Schloss Elmau in the Bavarian Alps, Salander had been pursuing her own investigation into what had become of his legacy.

For the most part his old comrades seemed to have turned into losers, depraved bandits, revolting pimps, or small-time crooks. Not one of them was a villain on her father's level, and for a long time Salander remained convinced that the organization had changed and dissolved after Zalachenko's death. Yet she did not give up, and eventually she stumbled onto something which pointed in a wholly unexpected direction. It was a reference to one of Zala's young acolytes, a certain Sigfrid Gruber.

Already during Zala's lifetime, Gruber was one of the more intelligent people in the network, and unlike his colleagues he had earned himself degrees in both computer science and business administration, which had apparently given him access to more exclusive circles. These days he cropped up in a couple of alleged crimes against high-tech companies: thefts of new technology, extortion, insider trading, hacker attacks.

Normally, Salander would have followed the lead no further. Nothing could worry her less than a couple of rich business groups being fleeced of some of their innovations. But then everything had changed.

In a classified report from Government Communications Headquarters in Cheltenham, England, which she had gotten her hands on, she had come across some codenames associated with a gang Gruber seemed now to belong to. The names had set some bells ringing, and after that she had not been able to let go of the story. She assembled all the information she could find about the group and kept coming across a rumour that the organization had stolen Balder's AI technology and then sold it to the Russian-American games company Truegames. Her source was unreliable—a half-open hacker site—but it was for this reason that she had turned up at the professor's lecture at the Royal Institute of Technology and given him a hard time about singularities deep within black holes. Or that was part of the reason.

PART 2

THE LABYRINTHS OF MEMORY

NOVEMBER 21–23

People with a photographic memory are also said to have an eidetic memory, an ability to recall images, sounds, or objects after only a few instants of exposure.

Research shows that people with eidetic memories are more likely to be nervous and stressed than others.

Most, though not all, people with eidetic memories are autistic. There is also a connection between photographic memory and synaesthesia—the condition where two or more senses are connected, for example when numbers are seen in colour and every series of numbers forms an image in the mind.

CHAPTER 12

NOVEMBER 21

Jan Bublanski had been looking forward to a day off and a long conversation with Rabbi Goldman in the Söder congregation about certain questions which had been troubling him recently, chiefly concerning the existence of God.

It would be going too far to say that he was becoming an atheist. But the very notion of a God had become increasingly problematic for him and he wanted to discuss his persistent feelings of the meaninglessness of it all, often accompanied by dreams of handing in his notice.

Bublanski certainly considered himself to be a good investigator. His record of clearing up cases was on the whole outstanding and occasionally he was still stimulated by the job. But he was not sure he wanted to go on investigating murders. He could learn some new skill while there was time. He dreamed about teaching, helping young people to find their path and believe in themselves, maybe because he himself suffered from bouts of the deepest self-doubt—but he did not know which subject he would choose. He had never specialized in one particular field, aside from that which had become his lot in life: sudden, evil death, and morbid human perversions. That was definitely not something he wanted to teach.

It was 8:10 in the morning and he was at his bathroom mirror. He felt puffy, worn out, and bald. Absentmindedly he picked up I. B. Singer's novel *The Magician of Lublin,* which he had loved with such a passion that for many years he had kept it next to the lavatory in case he felt like reading it at times when his stomach was playing up. But now he managed only a few lines. The telephone rang and his mood did not improve when he recognized the number: Chief Prosecutor Richard Ekström. A call from Ekström meant not just work, but probably work with a political and media element to it. Ekström would otherwise have wriggled out of it like a snake.

"Hi, Richard, nice to hear from you," Bublanski lied. "But I'm afraid I'm busy."

"What . . . no, no, not too busy for this, Jan. You can't miss out on this one. I heard that you'd taken the day off."

"That's right, and I'm just off to"—he did not want to say his synagogue. His Jewishness was not popular in the force— "see my doctor," he went on.

"Are you sick?"

"Not really."

"What's that supposed to mean? Nearly sick?"

"Something like that."

"Well, in that case there's no problem. We're all nearly sick, aren't we? This is an important case, Jan. The Minister of Enterprise has been in touch, and she agrees that you should handle the investigation."

"I find it very hard to believe the minister even knows who I am."

"Well, maybe not by name, and she's not supposed to be interfering anyway. But we're all agreed that we need a big player."

"Flattery no longer works with me, Richard. What's it about?" he said, and immediately regretted it. Just asking was halfway to saying yes and he could tell that Ekström accepted it as such.

"Last night Professor Frans Balder was murdered at his home in Saltsjöbaden."

"Who?"

"One of our best-known scientists, of international renown. He's a world authority on AI technology."

"On *what*?"

"He was working on neural networks and digital quantum processes, that sort of thing."

"I have no idea what you're talking about."

"He was trying to get computers to think, to replicate the human brain."

Replicate the human brain? Bublanski wondered what Rabbi Goldman would make of that.

"They say he's been a victim of industrial espionage in the past," Ekström said. "And that's why the murder is attracting the attention of the Ministry of Enterprise. No doubt you're aware of the solemn declarations the minister has made about the absolute requirement to protect Swedish research and new technology."

"Maybe."

"It would seem that this Balder was under some sort of threat. He had police protection."

"Are you saying he was killed while under police protection?"

"Well, it wasn't the most effective protection in the world. It was Flinck and Blom from the regular force."

"The Casanovas?"

"Yes. They were assigned late last night at the height of the storm and the general confusion. But in their defence it has to be said that the whole situation was a shambles. Balder was shot while our men were dealing with a drunk who had turned up at the house, out of nowhere. Unsurprisingly, the killer took advantage of that moment of inattention."

"Doesn't sound good."

"No, it looks very professional, and on top of it all the burglar alarm seems to have been hacked."

"So there were several of them?"

"We believe so. Furthermore, there are some tricky details."

"Which the media are going to like?"

"Which the media are going to love," Ekström said. "The lush who turned up, for example, was none other than Lasse Westman."

"The actor?"

"The same. And that's a real problem."

"Because it'll be all over the front pages?"

"Partly that, yes, but also because there's a risk we'll end up with a load of sticky divorce issues on our hands. Westman claimed he was there to bring home the eight-year-old son of his partner. Balder had the boy with him, even though . . . hang on a moment . . . I want to get this right . . . according to a custody ruling, Balder is not competent to look after him."

"Why wouldn't a professor who can get computers to behave like people be capable of looking after his own child?"

"Because previously he had shown a shocking lack of responsibility. He was a completely hopeless father, if I've understood it right. It's all rather sensitive. This little boy, who wasn't even supposed to have been at Balder's, probably witnessed the killing."

"Jesus! And what does he say?"

"Nothing."

"Is he in shock?"

"He must be, but he never says anything anyway. He's mute and apparently disabled, so he's not going to be much good to us."

"I see. So there's no suspect."

"Unless there was a reason why Westman appeared at precisely the same time as the killer entered the ground floor. You should get Westman in for questioning."

"If I decide to take on the investigation."

"As you will."

"Are you so sure of that?"

"You have no choice, in my view. Besides, I've saved the best for last."

"And that is?"

"Mikael Blomkvist."

"What about him?"

"For some reason he was out there too. I think Balder had asked to see him to tell him something."

"In the middle of the night?"

"So it would seem."

"And then he was shot?"

"Just before Blomkvist rang the bell—and it seems that the journalist caught a glimpse of the killer."

Bublanski snorted. It was an inappropriate reaction in every conceivable way and he could not have explained it even to himself. Perhaps it was a nervous reaction, or a feeling that life was repeating itself.

"I'm sorry?" Ekström said.

"Just got a bit of a cough. So you're worried that you'll end up with an investigative reporter on your back, one who'll show you all up in a bad light."

"Hmm, yes, maybe. We're assuming that *Millennium* has already gotten going with the story and right now I'm trying to find some legal justification for stopping them, or at least see to it that they're restricted in some way. I won't rule out that this case is a matter affecting national security."

"So we're saddled with Säpo as well?"

"No comment."

Go to hell, Bublanski thought.

"Are Olofsson and the others at Industry Protection working on this?"

"No comment, as I said. When can you start?" Ekström said.

"I have some conditions," Bublanski said. "I want my usual team, Modig, Svensson, Holmberg, and Flod."

"Of course, OK, but you get Hans Faste as well."

"No way!"

"Sorry, Jan, that's not negotiable. You should be grateful you get to choose all the others."

"You're the bitter end, you know that?"

"I've heard it said."

"So Faste's going to be our own little mole from Säpo?"

"Nonsense. I happen to think that all teams benefit from someone who thinks differently."

"Meaning that when the rest of us have got rid of all our prejudices and preconceived notions, we're stuck with somebody who will take us back to square one?"

"Don't be absurd."

"Faste is an idiot."

"No, Jan, he isn't. He's just . . ."

"What?"

"Conservative. He's not someone who falls for the latest feminist fads."

"Or for the earliest ones, either. He may have just got his head around all that stuff about votes for women."

"Come on, Jan, pull yourself together. Faste is an extremely reliable and loyal detective, and I won't listen to any more of this. Any other requests?"

How about you go take a running jump, Bublanski thought.

"I need to go to my doctor's appointment, and in the meantime I want Modig to lead the investigation," he said.

"Is that really such a wise idea?"

"It's a damned wise idea," he growled.

"OK, OK, I'll see to it that Zetterlund hands it over to her," Ekström said with a wince.

Ekström was far from sure he should have agreed to take on this investigation.

Alona Casales rarely worked nights. She had managed to avoid them for a decade and justified her stance on the grounds that her rheumatism forced her from time to time to take strong cortisone tablets, which not only turned her face into the shape of a moon, but also raised her blood pressure. She needed her sleep and her routine. Yet here she was, 3:10 in the morning.

She had driven from her home in Laurel, Maryland, in a light rain, past the sign that read NSA NEXT RIGHT—STAFF ONLY, past the barriers and the electric fence, towards the black, cube-like main building in Fort Meade. She left her car in the sprawling parking area alongside the pale-blue golf-ball-like radome with its myriad dish aerials, and made her way through the security gates up to her workstation on the twelfth floor. She was surprised by the feverish atmosphere there and soon realized that it was Ed Needham and his young hacker team who were responsible for the heightened concentration hanging over the department.

Needham looked like a man possessed and was standing there bawling out a young man whose face shone with an icy pallor. A pretty weird guy, Casales thought, just like all those young genius hackers Needham had surrounded himself with. The kid was skinny, anaemic-looking, with a hairstyle from hell and strangely rounded shoulders which shook with some sort of spasm. Maybe he was frightened. He shuddered every now and then, and it did not help matters that Needham was kicking at his chair leg. The young man looked as if he were waiting for a slap, a clip across the ear. But then something unexpected happened.

Needham calmed down and ruffled the boy's hair like a loving father. That was not like him. He did not go in for demonstrative affection. He was a cowboy who would never do anything as dubious as hug another man. But perhaps he was so desperate that he was prepared to give normal humanity a go. Ed's zip was undone and he had spilled coffee or Coca-Cola on his shirt. His face was an unhealthy flushed colour, his voice hoarse and rough from shouting. Casales thought that no-one of his age and weight should be pushing himself so hard.

Although only half a day had gone by, it looked as if Needham and his boys had been living there for a week. There were coffee cups and fast-food remnants and discarded caps and sweatshirts everywhere, and a rank stench of sweat and tension in the air. The team was clearly in the process of turning the whole world upside down in their efforts to trace the hacker. She called out to them in a hearty tone:

"Go for it, guys! . . . Get the bastard!"

She did not really mean it. Secretly she thought the breach was amusing. Many of these programmers seemed to think they could do whatever they liked, as if they had *carte blanche,* and it might actually do them some good to see that the other side could hit back. Here in the Puzzle Palace their shortcomings showed only when they were confronted with something dire, as was happening now. She had been woken by a call saying that the Swedish professor had been murdered at his home outside Stockholm, and even though that in itself was not a big deal for the NSA—not yet at any rate—it did mean something to Casales.

The killing showed that she had read the signs right, and now she had to see if she could move forward one more step. She logged in and opened the diagrammatic overview of the organization she had been tracking. The evasive Thanos sat right at the top, but there were also names of real people like the member of the Russian Duma, Ivan Gribanov, and the German, Gruber, a highly educated former crook from a large and complex trafficking operation.

She did not understand why the NSA gave such low priority to the matter, and why her superiors kept suggesting that other, more mainstream law-enforcement agencies should be taking care of it. They could not rule out the possibility that the network had state backing, or links to Russian state intelligence, and that it was all to do with the trade war between East and West. Even though the evidence was sparse and ambiguous, there were indications that Western technology was being stolen and ending up in Russian hands.

But it was difficult to get a clear view of this tangled web, to know whether any crime had been committed or whether purely by chance a similar technology had been developed somewhere else. These days, industrial theft was an altogether nebulous concept. Assets were borrowed all the time, sometimes as a part of creative exchanges, sometimes just dressed up to seem legitimate.

Large businesses, bolstered by threatening lawyers, regularly scared the living daylights out of small companies, and nobody seemed to find it odd that individual innovators had almost no legal rights. Besides which, industrial espionage and hacker attacks were often regarded as little more than routine research in a competitive environment. You could hardly claim that the NSA crowd was helping to raise ethical standards in the field.

On the other hand, it was not so easy to view murder in relative terms, and Casales took a solemn vow to leave no stone unturned in trying to unseat Thanos.

She did not get far. In fact she managed only to stretch her arms and massage her neck before she heard puffing and panting behind her.

Needham looked dreadful. His back must have given out on him too. Her own neck felt better just looking at him.

"Ed, to what do I owe this honour?"

"I'm thinking you and I are working on the same problem."

"Park your butt, old man."

"You know, from my limited perspective . . ."

"Don't knock yourself, Ed."

"I'm not knocking myself. It's no secret, I couldn't care less who's high or low, who thinks this and who thinks that. I focus on my own stuff. I protect our systems, and the only thing that really impresses me is when people are good at their jobs."

"You'd hire the Devil himself if he was any good in IT."

"I can respect just about any enemy, if he knows what he's doing. Does that make sense to you?"

"It does."

"As I'm sure you've heard, a root kit has been used to access our server and install a RAT. And that programme, Alona, is like pure music. So compact and beautifully written."

"You've met a worthy opponent."

"Without a doubt, and my guys feel the same way. They're putting on this outraged patriotic act or whatever the hell it is we're supposed to do. But actually they want nothing more than to meet that hacker and pit their skills against his. For a while I thought: OK, get over it! Maybe the damage isn't so great after all. This is just one genius hacker who wants to show off, and maybe there's a silver lining. I mean, we've already learned a lot about our vulnerability chasing after this clown. But then I began to wonder if maybe I was conned— maybe the whole performance on my mail server was just a smoke screen, hiding something altogether different."

"Such as?"

"Such as a search for certain pieces of information."

"Now I'm curious."

"You should be. We identified which areas the hacker was checking out and basically it's all related to the same thing:

the network you've been working on, Alona. They call themselves the Spiders, don't they?"

"The Spider Society, to be precise. But I think it's some kind of joke."

"The hacker was looking for information on that group and their connections to Solifon, and that made me think maybe he's with them and wants to find out how much we know about them."

"That sounds possible. They know how to hack."

"But then I changed my mind."

"Why?"

"Because it looks like the hacker also wanted to show us something. You know, he got himself superuser status that gave him access to documents maybe even you haven't seen, highly classified stuff. But actually the file he uploaded is so heavily encrypted that we don't have the slightest chance of reading it unless the fucker who wrote it gives us the private keys. Anyway . . ."

"What?"

"The hacker revealed through our own system that we cooperate with Solifon, too, the same way the Spiders do. Did you know that?"

"No, my God, I did not."

"I didn't think so. But unfortunately what Solifon does for the Spiders, it also does for us. It's part of our own industrial espionage efforts. That must be why your project is such low priority. They're worried your investigation will drop us in the shit."

"Idiots."

"I'd have to agree with you there. Probably now you'll be taken off the job completely."

"That would be outrageous."

"Relax, there's a loophole. And that's why I dragged my sorry ass all the way over to your desk. Start working for me instead."

"What do you mean?"

"This goddamn hacker knows things about the Spiders, and if we can crack his identity we'll both get a break and then you'll be able to see your investigation through."

"I see what you're saying."

"So it's a yes?"

"It's a sort of," she said. "I want to focus on finding out who shot Frans Balder."

"And you'll keep me informed?"

"OK."

"Good."

"Tell me," she said, "if this hacker is so clever, won't he have covered his tracks?"

"No need to worry about that. No matter how smart he's been, we'll find him and we'll flay him alive."

"What happened to all that respect for your opponent?"

"It's still there, my friend. But we'll crush him all the same and lock him up for life. No fucker breaks into my system."

CHAPTER 13

NOVEMBER 21

Blomkvist did not get much sleep. He could not get the events of the night out of his head and at 11:15 he sat up in bed and gave up.

He went into the kitchen where he made himself two sandwiches with cheddar and prosciutto and a bowl of yoghurt and muesli. But he did not eat much of it. Instead he opted for coffee and water and some headache pills. He drank five glasses of Ramlösa, swallowed two Alvedon, took out a notebook and tried to write a summary of what had happened. He did not get far before the telephone started ringing.

The news was out: "Star reporter Mikael Blomkvist and TV star Lasse Westman" had found themselves at the centre of a "mysterious" murder drama, mysterious because no-one was able to work out why Westman and Blomkvist of all people, together or separately, had been on the scene when a Swedish professor was shot in the head. The questions seemed to be insinuating something sinister and that was why Blomkvist quite candidly said that he had gone there, despite the lateness of the hour, because Balder had asked to speak to him urgently.

"I was there because of my job."

He was being more defensive than he needed to be. He wanted to provide an explanation for the accusations out there, although that might prompt more reporters to dig into the story. Apart from that, he said "No comment" and if that was not the ideal response it was at least straightforward and unambiguous. After that he turned off his mobile, put his father's old fur coat back on and set out in the direction of Götgatan.

So much was going on at the office that it reminded him of the old days. All over the place, in every corner, there were colleagues sitting and working with concentration. Berger was bound to have made one or two impassioned speeches and everybody must have been aware of the significance of the moment. The deadline was just ten days away. There was also the threat from Ove Levin and Serner hanging over them and the whole team seemed up for the fight. They all jumped to their feet when they saw him and asked to hear about Balder and the night, and his reaction to the Norwegians' proposal. But he wanted to follow their good example.

"Later, later," he said, and went to Andrei Zander's desk.

Zander was twenty-six years old, the youngest person in the office. He had done his time as an intern at the magazine and had stayed on, sometimes as a temp, as now, and sometimes as a freelancer. It pained Blomkvist that they had not been able to give him a permanent job, especially since they had hired Emil Grandén and Sofie Melker. He would have preferred to take on Zander. But Zander had not yet made a name for himself, and still had a lot to learn.

He was a superb team player, and that was good for the magazine, but not necessarily good for him. Not in this cynical business. The boy was not conceited enough, although he had every reason to be. He looked like a young Antonio Banderas, and was quicker on the uptake than most. But he did not go to any lengths to promote himself. He just wanted to be a part of it all and produce good journalism and he thought the world of *Millennium*. Blomkvist suddenly felt that he loved everyone who loved *Millennium*. One fine day he would do something big for young Zander.

"Hi, Andrei," he said. "How are things?"

"Not bad. Busy."

"I expected nothing less. What have you managed to dig up?"

"Quite a bit. It's on your desk, and I've also written a summary. But can I give you some advice?"

"Good advice is exactly what I need."

"In that case go straight to Zinkens väg, to see Farah Sharif."

"Who?"

"A seriously gorgeous professor of computer science. She's taken the whole day off."

"Are you saying that what I really need right now is an attractive, intelligent woman?"

"Not exactly that, no. Professor Sharif just called and was under the impression that Balder had wanted to tell you something. She thinks she knows what it may have been all about, and she's keen to talk to you. Maybe to carry out his wishes. I think it sounds like an ideal place to start."

"Have you checked her out otherwise?"

"Sure, and we can't altogether rule out the possibility that she has an agenda of her own. But she was close to Balder. They were at university together and have co-authored a couple of scientific papers. There are also a few society-page photos which show the two of them together. She's a big name in her field."

"OK, I'll go. Will you let her know I'm on my way?"

"I will," Zander said, and gave Blomkvist the address.

So Blomkvist left the office almost immediately, just as he had the previous day, and began to leaf through the research material as he was walking down towards Hornsgatan. Two or three times he bumped into people, but he was concentrating so hard that he scarcely apologized and when at last he raised his head his feet had not taken him as far as Farah Sharif's.

So he stopped off at Mellqvist's coffee bar and drank two double espressos standing up. Not just to get rid of his tiredness. He thought a jolt of caffeine might help with his headache but afterwards he wondered if it had been the right cure. As he left the coffee shop he felt worse than he had when he'd arrived because of all the morons who had read about the night's dramatic events and were making idiotic remarks. They say that young people want nothing more than to become celebrities. He ought to explain to them that it is not worth aspiring to. It just drives you nuts, especially if you have not slept and have seen things that no human being should have to see.

Blomkvist went up Hornsgatan, past McDonald's and the Co-op, cut across to Ringvägen, and as he glanced to the right he stiffened, as if he had seen something significant. But what? It was just a street crossing with a high traffic accident rate and vast volumes of exhaust fumes, nothing more. Then it came to him.

It was the very traffic light Balder had drawn with his

mathematical precision, and so once again Blomkvist puzzled over the choice of subject matter. It was not an especially interesting crossing; it was run-down and banal. Maybe that was the point.

The work of art is in the eye of the beholder, and even that tells us no more than that Balder had been here, and had maybe sat on a bench somewhere studying the traffic light. Blomkvist went on past Zinkensdamm sports centre and turned right onto Zinkens väg.

Detective Sergeant Sonja Modig had been running around all morning. Now she was in her office and looked briefly at a framed photograph on her desk. It showed her six-year-old son, Axel, on the football field after scoring a goal. Modig was a single parent and had a hell of a time organizing her life. She was expecting to have a hell of a time at work the next few days too. There was a knock on the door. It was Bublanski at last, and she was supposed to be handing over responsibility for the investigation. Not that Officer Bubble looked as if he wanted to take responsibility for anything at all.

He was looking unusually dashing in a jacket and tie and a freshly ironed blue shirt. He had combed his hair over his bald patch. There was a dreamy and absent look on his face, as if murder investigations were the last thing on his mind.

"What did the doctor say?" she asked.

"The doctor said that what matters is not that we believe in God. God is not small-minded. What matters is for us to understand that life is serious and rich. We should appreciate it and also try to make the world a better place. Whoever finds a balance between the two is close to God."

"So you were with your rabbi?"

"Yes."

"OK, Jan, I'm not sure whether I can help with the bit about appreciating life, apart from offering you a piece of Swiss orange chocolate which I happen to have in my desk drawer. But if we nail the guy who shot Professor Balder then we'll definitely make the world a little better."

"Swiss orange chocolate and a solution to this murder sound like a decent start."

Modig broke off a piece of chocolate and gave it to Bublanski, who chewed it with a certain reverence.

"Exquisite," he said.

"Isn't it?"

"Just think if life could be like that sometimes," he said, pointing at the photograph of the jubilant Axel on her desk.

"What do you mean?"

"If joy could express itself with the same force as pain," he said.

"Yes, just imagine."

"How are things with Balder's son?" he said.

"Hard to tell," she said. "He's with his mother now. A psychologist has assessed him."

"And what have we got to go on?"

"Not much yet, unfortunately. We've found out what the murder weapon was. A Remington 1911 R1 Carry, bought recently. We're going to follow it up, but I feel sure we're not going to be able to trace it. We have the images from the surveillance cameras, which we are analyzing. But whatever angle we look at we still can't see the man's face, and we can't spot any distinguishing features either—no birthmarks, nothing, only a wristwatch which is just about visible in one sequence. It looks expensive. The guy's clothes are black. His cap is grey without any branding. Jerker tells me he moves like an old junkie. In one picture he's holding a small black box, presumably some kind of computer or GSM station. He probably used it to hack the alarm system."

"I'd heard that. How do you hack a burglar alarm?"

"Jerker has looked into that too and it isn't easy, especially not an alarm of this specification, but it can be done. The system was connected to the Net and to the mobile network and sent a feed of information to Milton Security over at Slussen. It's not impossible that the guy recorded a frequency from the alarm with his box and managed to hack it that way. Or else he'd bumped into Balder when he was out walking and stolen some information electronically from the professor's NFC."

"What's an NFC?"

"Near Field Communication, a function on Balder's mobile which he used to activate the alarm."

"It was simpler in the days when burglars had crowbars," Bublanski said. "Any cars in the area?"

"A dark-coloured vehicle was parked a hundred yards away by the side of the road with the engine running on and off, but the only person to have seen it is an old lady by the name of Birgitta Roos; she has no idea what make it was. Maybe a Volvo, according to her. Or like the one her son has. Her son has a BMW."

"Oh, wonderful."

"Yes, the investigation is looking a bit bleak," Modig said. "The killers had the advantage of the night and the weather. They could move around the area undisturbed, and apart from what Mikael Blomkvist told us we've only got one sighting. It's from a thirteen-year-old, Ivan Grede. A slightly odd, skinny figure who had leukaemia when he was small and who has decorated his room entirely in a Japanese style. He has a precocious way of expressing himself. Young Ivan went for a pee in the middle of the night and from the bathroom window he saw a tall man by the water's edge. The man was looking out over the water and making the sign of the cross with his fists. It looked both aggressive and religious at the same time, Ivan said."

"Not a good combination."

"No, religion and violence combined don't as a rule bode well. But Ivan wasn't sure that it really was the sign of the cross. It looked like it, but there was something else too, he says. Maybe it was a military oath. For a while he was afraid that the man was going to walk into the water and drown himself. There was something ceremonial about the situation, he said."

"But there was no suicide."

"No, the man jogged on in the direction of Balder's house. He had a backpack, and dark clothes, possibly camouflage trousers. He was powerful and athletic and reminded Ivan of his old toys, he said, his ninja warriors."

"That doesn't sound good either."

"Not good at all. Presumably this was the man who shot at Blomkvist."

"And Blomkvist didn't see his face?"

"No, he threw himself to the ground when the man turned and shot at him. It all happened very quickly. But according to Blomkvist the man looked as if he had military training and that fits with Ivan Grede's observations. I have to agree: the speed and efficiency of the operation point in that direction."

"Have you got to the bottom of why Blomkvist was there?"

"Oh, definitely. If anything was done properly last night, it was the interviews with him. Have a look at this." Modig handed over a transcript. "Blomkvist had been in touch with one of Balder's former assistants who claimed that the professor had been targeted by a data breach and had his technology stolen. The story interested Blomkvist. But Balder had been living as a recluse and had virtually no contact with the outside world. All the shopping and errands were done by a housekeeper called . . . just a second . . . Fru Rask, Lottie Rask, who incidentally had strict instructions not to say a word about the son living in the house. I'll come to that in a moment. Then last night, I'm guessing that Balder was worried and wanted to get some anxiety off his chest. Don't forget, he had just been told that he was subject to a serious threat. His burglar alarm had gone off and two policemen were guarding the house. Perhaps he suspected that his days were numbered. No way of knowing. In any case he called Mikael Blomkvist in the middle of the night and said he wanted to tell him something."

"In the olden days in situations like that you would call a priest."

"So now you call a journalist. Well, it's pure speculation. We only know what Balder said on Blomkvist's voicemail. Apart from that we have no idea what he was planning to tell him. Blomkvist says he doesn't know either, and I believe him. But I seem to be pretty much the only one who does. Ekström, who's being a massive nuisance by the way, is convinced Blomkvist is holding back things which he plans to publish in his magazine. I find that very hard to believe. Blomkvist is a tricky bugger, we all know that. But he isn't someone who will knowingly, deliberately sabotage a police investigation."

"Definitely not."

"Ekström is coming on strong and saying that Blomkvist should be arrested for perjury and obstruction and God knows what else."

"That's not going to do any good."

"No, and bearing in mind what Blomkvist is capable of I think we're better off staying on good terms with him."

"I suppose we'll have to talk to him again."

"I agree."

"And this thing with Lasse Westman?"

"We've just spoken to him, and it's not an edifying story. Westman had been to the Artists' Bar and the Theatre Grill and the Opera Bar and Riche, you get the idea, and was ranting and raving about Balder and the boy for hours on end. He drove his friends crazy. The more Westman drank and the more money he blew, the more fixated he became."

"Why was this important to him?"

"Partly it was a hang-up. You get that with alcoholics. I remember it from an old uncle. Every time he got loaded, he got something fixed in his mind. But obviously there's more to it than that. At first Westman went on about the custody ruling, and if he had been a different person one might believe that he really was concerned for the boy. But in this case . . . I suppose you know that Westman has a conviction for assault."

"No, I didn't."

"He had a relationship some years ago with some fashion blogger, Renata Kapusinski. He beat the crap out of her. I think he even bit her rather badly on the cheek. Also, Balder had intended to report him. He never sent in the paperwork—perhaps because of the legal position he found himself in—but it clearly suggests that he suspected Westman of being violent towards his son as well."

"What are you saying?"

"Balder had noticed unexplained bruises on the boy's body—and in this he's backed up by a psychologist from the Centre for Autism. So it was . . ."

". . . probably not love and concern which drove Westman out to Saltsjöbaden."

"More likely it was money. After Balder took back his son, he had stopped or at least reduced the child support he had agreed to pay."

"Westman didn't try to report him for that?"

"He probably didn't dare to, in the circumstances."

"What else does the custody ruling say?" Bublanski said after a pause.

"That Balder was a useless father."

"Was he?"

"He certainly wasn't evil, like Westman. But there'd been an incident. After the divorce, Balder had his son every other weekend, and at that time he was living in an apartment in Östermalm with books from floor to ceiling. One of those weekends, when August was six, he was in the sitting room—with Balder glued to his computer in the next room as usual. We don't know exactly what happened. But there was a small stepladder propped against one of the bookshelves. August climbed it and probably took hold of some of the books higher up and fell and broke his elbow. He knocked himself unconscious, but Balder didn't hear anything. He just kept working and only after several hours did he discover August lying on the floor next to those books, moaning. At that he became hysterical and drove the boy to the emergency room."

"And he lost custody altogether?"

"Not only that. He was declared emotionally immature and incapable of taking care of his child. He was not allowed to be alone with August. But frankly I don't think much of that ruling."

"Why not?"

"Because it was an uncontested hearing. The ex-wife's lawyer went at it hammer and tongs, while Balder grovelled and said he was useless and irresponsible and unfit to live and God knows what. What the tribunal wrote was malicious and tendentious, to my mind: to the effect that Balder had never been able to connect with other people and had always sought refuge with machines. Now that I've had time to look into his life a little, I'm not that impressed by how it was dealt with. His guilt-laden tirades and self-criticism were taken as gospel by the tribunal. At any rate Balder was extremely cooperative. As I said, he agreed to pay a large amount of child support, forty thousand a month, I believe, plus a one-off payment of nine hundred thousand kronor for unforeseen expenses. Not long after that he took himself off to America."

"But then he came back."

"Yes, and there were a number of reasons for that. He'd had his technology stolen, and maybe he identified who had done it. He found himself in a serious dispute with his employer. But I think it had also to do with his son. The woman from the Centre for Autism I mentioned, she'd been very optimistic about the boy's development at an early stage. But then nothing turned out as she'd hoped. She also received reports that Hanna Balder and Westman had failed to live up to their responsibilities when it came to his schooling. It had been agreed that August would be taught at home, but the special-needs teachers seem to have been played off against each other. Probably the money for his education was misappropriated and fake teachers' names used, all sorts of crap like that. But that's an altogether different story, which somebody will have to look into at some point."

"You were talking about the woman from the Centre for Autism."

"That's right. She smelled a rat and called Hanna and Westman and was informed that everything was fine. But she had a feeling that wasn't true. So against normal practice she made an unannounced home visit and, when they finally let her in, she could tell that the boy was not doing well, that his development had stagnated. She also saw those bruises. She rang Balder in San Francisco, had a long conversation with him, and soon after that he moved back and took his son with him to his new house in Saltsjöbaden, disregarding the custody order."

"How did he manage that, seeing how keen Westman was to get the child support?"

"Good question. According to Westman, Balder more or less kidnapped the boy. But Hanna has a different version of the story. She says that Frans turned up and seemed to have changed, so she let him take August. She even thought that the boy would be better off with his father."

"And Westman?"

"According to her, Westman was drunk and had just

landed a big part in a new TV production, and was feeling cocky and over-confident. So he agreed to it. However much he may have gone on about the boy's welfare, I think he was glad to be rid of him."

"But then?"

"Then he regretted it, and on top of everything else he was sacked from the series because he couldn't stay sober. He suddenly wanted to have August back, or not so much him, of course . . ."

"The child support."

"Exactly, and that was confirmed by his drinking pals. When Westman's credit card was rejected during the course of the evening, he really started ranting and raving about the boy. He bummed five hundred kronor off a young woman in the bar to pay for a taxi to Saltsjöbaden in the middle of the night."

Bublanski was lost in his thoughts for a while and gazed once again at the photograph of Modig's son.

"What a mess," he said.

"Right."

"Under normal circumstances we would be close to solving this one. We'd find our motive somewhere in that custody battle. But these guys who hack alarm systems and look like ninja warriors, they don't fit the picture."

"No."

"There's something else I'm wondering about."

"What's that?"

"If August can't read, then what was he doing trying to reach those books?"

.   .   .

Blomkvist was sitting opposite Farah Sharif at her kitchen table with a cup of tea, looking out at Tantolunden. Even though he knew it was a sign of weakness, he wished he did not have a story to write. He wished he could just sit there without having to press her for information.

She did not look as if talking would do her much good. Her whole face had collapsed and the intense dark eyes, which had looked straight through him at the front door, now seemed disoriented. Sometimes she muttered Balder's name like a mantra or an incantation. Maybe she had loved him. Farah was fifty-two years old and a very attractive woman, not beautiful in a conventional way but with a regal bearing. He had definitely loved *her*.

"Tell me, what was he like," Blomkvist said.

"Frans?"

"Yes."

"A paradox."

"In what way?"

"In all sorts of ways. But mainly because he worked so hard on the one thing which worried him more than anything else. Maybe a bit like Oppenheimer at Los Alamos. He was engrossed in something he believed could be our ruin."

"Now you've lost me."

"Frans wanted to replicate biological evolution on a digital level. He was working on self-teaching algorithms—the idea is they can enhance themselves through trial and error. He also contributed to the development of quantum computers, as people call them, which Google, Solifon, and the NSA are working on. His objective was to achieve AGI, or Artificial General Intelligence."

"And what is that?"

"Something with the intelligence of a human being, but the speed and precision of a computer. If a thing like that could be created, it would give us enormous advantages within numerous fields."

"I'm sure."

"There is an extraordinary amount of research going on in this area, and even though most scientists aren't specifically aiming for AGI, competition is driving us in that direction. Nobody can afford *not* to create applications which are as intelligent as possible. Nobody can afford to put the brake on development. Just think of what we have achieved so far. Just think back to what you had in your mobile five years ago compared to what's in there today."

"True."

"Before he became so secretive, Frans told me he estimated that we could get to AGI within thirty or forty years. That may sound ambitious, but for my part I wonder if he wasn't being too conservative. The capacity of computers doubles every eighteen months, and the human brain is bad at grasping that kind of exponential growth. It's like the grain of rice on the chessboard, you know? You put one grain of rice on the first square, two on the second, four on the third, eight on the fourth."

"And soon the grains of rice have flooded the world."

"The pace of growth goes on increasing and in the end it escapes our control. The interesting thing isn't actually when we reach AGI, but what happens after that. Just a few days after we've reached AGI, we'll have ASI—Artificial Super Intelligence—used to describe something more intelligent than we are. After that it'll just get quicker and quicker. Computers will start enhancing themselves at an accelerating pace, perhaps by a factor of ten, and become a hundred, a thousand, ten thousand times cleverer than we are. What happens then?"

"I dread to think."

"Quite. Intelligence in itself is not predictable. We don't know where human intelligence will take us. We know even less what will happen with a superintelligence."

"In the worst case we'll be no more interesting to the computer than little white mice," Blomkvist said, thinking of what he had written to Salander.

"In the worst case? We share ninety percent of our DNA with mice, and we're assumed to be about one hundred times as intelligent. Only one hundred times. Here's something completely new, not subject to these kinds of limitations, according to mathematical models. And it can become perhaps a million times more intelligent. Can you imagine?"

"I'm certainly trying to," Blomkvist said with a careful smile.

"I mean, how do you think a computer would feel when it wakes up to find itself captured and controlled by primitive little creatures like us. Why would it put up with that?" she said. "Why on earth should it show us any consideration, still less let us dig around in its entrails in order to shut down the process? We risk being confronted by an explosion of intelligence, a technological singularity, as Vernor Vinge put it. Everything that happens after that lies beyond our event horizon."

"So the very instant we create a superintelligence we lose control, is that right?"

"The risk is that everything we know about the world will cease to be relevant, and it'll be the end of human existence."

"You *are* joking."

"I know it sounds crazy, but it's a very real question. There are thousands of people all over the world working to prevent a development like this. Many are optimists, or even foresee some kind of utopia. There's talk of friendly ASI, superintelligences which are programmed from the start to do nothing but help us. The idea is something along the lines of what Asimov envisioned in his book *I, Robot:* built-in laws which forbid the machines to harm us. Innovator and author Ray Kurzweil has visions of a wonderful world in which nanotechnology allows us to integrate ourselves with computers, and share our future with them. But there are no guarantees. Laws can be repealed. The intent of initial programming can be changed and it's fatally easy to make anthropomorphic mistakes: to ascribe human characteristics to machines and misunderstand what drives them, inherently. Frans was obsessed with these questions and, as I said, he was of two minds. He both longed for intelligent computers and he also worried about them."

"He couldn't help but build his monsters."

"A bit like that, though that's putting it drastically."

"How far had he got?"

"Further, I think, than anyone could imagine, and that may have been yet another reason why he was so secretive about his work at Solifon. He was afraid his programme would end up in the wrong hands. He was even afraid the programme would come into contact with the Internet and merge with it. He called it August, after his son."

"And where is it now?"

"He never went anywhere without it. It must have been right by the bed when he was shot. But the terrible thing is that the police say there was no computer there."

"I didn't see one either. But then my focus was elsewhere."

"It must have been dreadful."

"Perhaps you heard that I also saw the man who killed him," Blomkvist said. "He was carrying a backpack."

"That doesn't sound good. But with a bit of luck the computer will turn up somewhere in the house."

"Let's hope so. Do you have any idea who stole his technology the first time around?"

"Yes, I do, as a matter of fact."

"I'm very interested."

"I can see that. But the sad thing is that I have some personal responsibility for this mess. Frans was working himself to death, you see, and I was worried he would burn out. That was about the time he had lost custody of August."

"When was that?"

"Two years ago. He was utterly worn out. He wasn't sleeping, and he went around blaming himself, yet he was incapable of dropping his research. He threw himself into it as if it were all he had left in life, and so I arranged for him to get some assistants who could take some of the load. I let him have my best students. I knew that none of them was a model of probity, but they were ambitious and gifted, and their admiration for Frans was boundless. Everything looked promising. But then . . ."

"His technology was stolen."

"He had clear proof of that when the application from Truegames was submitted to the U.S. Patent Office in August last year. Every unique aspect of his technology had been duplicated and written down there. It was obvious. At first they all suspected their computers had been hacked, but I was sceptical from the start—I knew how sophisticated

Frans's encryption was. But since there was no other plausible explanation, that was the initial assumption, and for a while maybe Frans believed it himself. That was nonsense, of course."

"What are you saying?" Blomkvist burst out. "Surely the data breach was confirmed by experts."

"Yes, by some idiot show-off at the NDRE. But that was just Frans's way of protecting his boys, or it could have been more than that. I suspect he also wanted to play detective, although heaven knows how he could be so stupid. You see . . ." Farah took a deep breath. "I learned all this only a few weeks ago. Frans and little August were here for dinner and I sensed at once that he had something important to tell me. It was hanging in the air. After a couple of glasses he asked me to put away my mobile and began to speak in a whisper. I have to admit that at first I was irritated. He was going on again about his young hacker genius."

"Hacker genius?" Blomkvist said, trying to sound neutral.

"A girl he spoke about so much that it was doing my head in. I won't bore you with the full story, but she'd turned up out of the blue at one of his lectures and practically lectured *him* on the concept of singularity. She impressed Frans, and he started to open up to her, it's understandable. A meganerd like Frans can't have found all that many people he could talk to on his own level, and when he realized that the girl was also a hacker he asked her to take a look at their computers. At the time they had all the equipment at the home of one of the assistants."

All Blomkvist said was "Linus Brandell."

"Yes," Farah said. "The girl came round to his place in Östermalm and threw him out. Then she got to work on the computers. She couldn't find any sign of a breach, but she didn't leave it at that. She had a list of Frans's assistants and hacked them all from Linus's computer. It didn't take long for her to realize that one of them had sold him out to none other than Solifon."

"And who was it?"

"Frans didn't want to tell me, even though I pressed him. But the girl apparently called him directly from Linus's apartment. Frans was in San Francisco at the time, and you can imagine: betrayed by one of his own! I was expecting him to report the guy right away and raise hell. But he had a better idea. He asked the girl to pretend they really had been hacked."

"Why would he do that?"

"He didn't want any traces of evidence to be tidied away. He wanted to understand more about what had happened. I suppose it makes sense—for one of the world's leading software businesses to steal and exploit his technology was obviously far more serious than if some good-for-nothing, unprincipled shit of a student had done the same. Because Solifon isn't just one of the most respected research groups in the States, they had also been trying to recruit Frans for years. He was livid. 'Those bastards were trying to seduce me and stealing from me at the same time,' he growled."

"Let me be sure I've got this right," Blomkvist said. "You're saying he took a job at Solifon in order to find out why and how they'd stolen from him?"

"If there's one thing I've learned over the years, it's just how difficult it can be to understand a person's motivation. The salary and the freedom and the resources obviously came into it. But apart from that: yes, I imagine you're right.

He'd worked out that Solifon was involved in the theft even before this hacker girl examined his computers. She gave him the specific information and that enabled him to dig into the mess. In the end it turned out to be much more difficult than he expected, and people started getting suspicious. It wasn't long before he became fantastically unpopular, so he kept more and more to himself. But he did find something."

"What?"

"This is where it all gets sensitive. I shouldn't really be telling you."

"Yet here we are."

"Yet here we are. Not only because I've always had the utmost respect for your journalism. It occurred to me this morning that it may not have been a coincidence that Frans rang you last night rather than Säpo's Industry Protection Group, who he had also been in touch with. I think he was beginning to suspect a leak there. It may have been no more than paranoia—Frans displayed a variety of symptoms of persecution mania. But it was you he called, and now I hope that I can fulfil his wish."

"I understand."

"At Solifon there's a department called 'Y,'" Farah said. "Google X is the model, the department where they work on 'moonshots,' as they call them, wild and far-fetched ideas like looking for eternal life or connecting search engines to brain neurons. If any place will achieve AGI or ASI, that's probably it. Frans was assigned to 'Y.' But that wasn't as smart as it may have sounded."

"And why not?"

"Because he had found out from his hacker girl that there was a secret group of business intelligence analysts at

'Y,' headed up by a character called Zigmund Eckerwald, also known as Zeke."

"And who is that?"

"The very person who had been communicating with Frans's treacherous assistant."

"So Eckerwald was the thief."

"A thief of the highest order. On the face of it, the work carried out by Eckerwald's group was perfectly legitimate. They compiled information on leading scientists and promising research projects. Every large high-tech firm has a similar operation. They want to know what's going on and who they should be recruiting. But Frans understood that the group went beyond that. They stole—through hacker attacks, espionage, moles, and bribery."

"But then why didn't he report them?"

"It was tricky to prove. They were careful, of course. But in the end Frans went to the owner, Nicolas Grant. Grant was horrified and apparently organized an internal investigation. But the investigation found nothing, either because Eckerwald had gotten rid of the evidence or because the investigation was just for show. It left Frans in a tight spot. Everyone turned on him. Eckerwald must have been behind it, and I'm sure he had no trouble getting the others to join in. Frans was already perceived as paranoid and became progressively isolated and frozen out. I can picture it. How he would sit there and become more and more awkward and contrary, and refuse to say a word to anyone."

"So he had no concrete evidence, you think?"

"Well, he did at least have the proof the hacker girl had given him: that Eckerwald had stolen Frans's technology and sold it on."

"And he knew that for sure?"

"Without a shadow of a doubt. Besides, he had realized that Eckerwald's group was not working alone. It had backing from outside, in all likelihood from the American intelligence services and also . . ."

Farah hesitated.

"Yes?"

"This is where he was a bit more cryptic, and it may be that he didn't know all that much. But he had come across an alias, he said, for the person who was the real leader outside Solifon. 'Thanos.'"

"Thanos?"

"That's right. He said that this individual was greatly feared. But he didn't want to say more than that. He needed life insurance, he claimed, for when the lawyers came after him."

"You said you didn't know which of his assistants sold him out. But you must have given it a great deal of thought," said Blomkvist.

"I have, and sometimes, I don't know . . . I wondered if it wasn't all of them."

"Why do you say that?"

"When they started working for Frans, they were young, ambitious, and gifted. By the time they finished, they were fed up with life and full of anxieties. Maybe Frans worked them too hard. Or maybe there's something else tormenting them."

"Do you have all their names?"

"I do. They're my boys—unfortunately, I'd have to say. First there's Linus Brandell, I've already mentioned him. He's twenty-four now, and just drifts around playing computer games and drinking too much. For a while he had a good job as a games developer at Crossfire. But he lost it when he started calling in sick and accusing his colleagues of spying on him. Then there's Arvid Wrange, maybe you've heard of him. He was a promising chess player, once upon a time. His father pushed him in a pretty inhuman way and in the end Arvid had enough and came to study with me. I'd hoped that he would have completed his PhD long ago. But instead he props up the bars around Stureplan and seems rootless. He came into his own for a while when he was with Frans. But there was also a lot of silly competition among the boys. Arvid and Basim, the third guy, came to hate each other—at least Arvid hated Basim. Basim Malik probably doesn't do hate. He's a sensitive, gifted boy who was taken on by Solifon Nordic a year ago. But he ran out of steam pretty quickly. Right now he's being treated for depression at Ersta hospital and it so happens that his mother, whom I know vaguely, rang me this morning to tell me that he's under sedation. When he found out what had happened to Frans, he tried to slash his wrists. It's devastating, but at the same time I do wonder: Was it just grief? Or was it also guilt?"

"How is he now?"

"He's not in any danger from a physical point of view. And then there's Niklas Lagerstedt, and he . . . well, what can I say about him? He's not like the others, at least not on the surface. He wouldn't drink himself into oblivion or even think of harming himself. He's a young man with moral objections to most things, including violent computer games and porn. He's a member of the Mission Covenant Church. His wife is a paediatrician and they have a young son called Jesper. On top of all that he's a consultant with the National

Criminal Police, responsible for the computer system coming into service in the new year; which means he's had to go through security clearance. But who knows how thorough it was."

"Why do you say that?"

"Because behind that respectable façade he's a nasty piece of work. I happen to know that he's embezzled parts of his in-laws' fortune. He's a hypocrite."

"Have these guys been questioned?"

"Säpo talked to them, but nothing came of it. At that time it was thought that Frans was the victim of a data breach."

"I imagine the police will want to question them again now."

"I assume so."

"Do you happen to know if Balder did much sketching in his free time?"

"Sketching?"

"Really detailed drawings of scenes."

"No, I haven't heard anything about that," she said. "Why do you ask?"

"I saw a fantastic drawing at his home, of a traffic light up here on the intersection of Hornsgatan and Ringvägen. It was flawless, a sort of snapshot in the dark."

"How strange. Frans wasn't usually in this part of town."

"There's something about that drawing that won't let go of me," Blomkvist said, and he realized to his surprise that Farah had taken hold of his hand. He stroked her hair. Then he stood up with a feeling that he was on the scent. He said goodbye and went out onto the street.

On the way back up Zinkens väg he called Berger and asked her to type another question in [*Lisbeth stuff*].

CHAPTER 14

NOVEMBER 21

Ove Levin was sitting in his office with a view over Slussen and Riddarfjärden and not doing much at all except Googling himself in the hope of coming across something to cheer him up. What he read instead was that he was sleazy and flabby and that he had betrayed his ideals. All that in a blog written by a slip of a girl at the Institute for Media Studies at Stockholm University. It made him so furious that he could not bring himself to write her name in the little black book he kept, of people who would never get a job in the Serner Group.

He could not be bothered to burden his brain with idiots who had no idea what it takes, and would only ever write underpaid articles in obscure cultural magazines. Rather than wallow in destructive thoughts he went into his online account and checked his portfolio. That helped a bit, at least to begin with. It was a good day in the markets. The Nasdaq and the Dow Jones had both gone up last night and the Stockholm index was 1.1 percent up too. The dollar, to which he was rather too exposed, had risen, and according to the update of a few seconds ago his portfolio was worth 12,161,389 kronor.

Not bad for a man who had once covered house fires and knife fights for the morning edition of *Expressen*. Twelve million, plus the apartment in Villastaden and the villa in Cannes. They could post whatever they wanted on their blogs. He was well provided for, and he checked the value of his portfolio again. 12,149,101. Jesus Christ, was it falling? 12,131,737. He grimaced. There was no reason why the market should be falling, was there? The employment figures had been good, after all. He took the tumble in value almost personally and could not help thinking about *Millennium,* however insignificant it might be in the bigger picture. He found himself getting worked up again as he kept remembering the openly hostile look on Erika Berger's beautiful face yesterday afternoon. Things had not improved this morning.

He had just about had a fit. Blomkvist had cropped up on every site, and that hurt. Not only because Levin had so gleefully registered that the younger generation hardly knew who Blomkvist was. He also hated the media logic which said that you became a star—a star journalist or a star actor or whatever the hell it might be—simply because you found yourself in some sort of trouble. He would have been happier to read about has-been Blomkvist who wasn't even going to keep his job at his own magazine, not if Ove Levin and Serner Media had anything to do with it. Instead they said: Why Frans Balder, of all people?

Why on earth did he have to be murdered right under Blomkvist's nose? Wasn't that just typical? So infuriating. Even if those useless journalists out there hadn't realized it yet, Levin knew that Balder was a big name. Not long ago Serner's own newspaper, *Business Daily,* had produced a special supplement on Swedish scientific research which had given him a price tag: four billion kronor, though God knows how they got to that figure. Balder was a star, no doubt about it. Most important, he was a Garbo. He never gave interviews, which made him all the more sought-after.

How many requests had Balder received from Serner's own journalists? As many as he had refused or, for that matter, simply not bothered to answer. Many of Levin's colleagues out there thought Balder was sitting on a fantastic story. He couldn't bear the idea that, so the newspaper reports said, Balder had wanted to talk to Blomkvist in the middle of the night. Could Blomkvist really have a scoop on top of everything else? That would be disastrous. Once more, almost obsessively, Levin went onto the *Aftonbladet* site and was met with the headline:

WHAT DID TOP SWEDISH SCIENTIST HAVE TO SAY TO MIKAEL BLOMKVIST?

MYSTERY CALL JUST BEFORE THE MURDER

The article was illustrated by a double-column photograph of Mikael Blomkvist which did not show any flab at all. Those bastard editors had of course chosen the most flattering photograph they could find, and that made Levin angrier still. I have to do something about this, he thought. But what? How could he put a stop to Blomkvist without barging in like some old East German censor and making everything worse? He looked out towards Riddarfjärden and an idea came to him. Borg, he thought. My enemy's enemy can be my best friend.

"Sanna!" he shouted.

"Yes, Ove?"

Sanna Lind was his young secretary.

"Book a lunch at once with William Borg at Sturehof. If he says he has something else on, tell him this is more important. He can even have a raise," he said, and thought, *Why not?* If he's prepared to help me in this mess then it's only fair he gets something out of it.

Hanna Balder was standing in the living room at Torsgatan looking in despair at August, who had yet again dug out paper and crayons. She had been told that she had to discourage him, and she did not like doing it. Not that she questioned the psychologist's advice and expertise, but she had her doubts. August had seen his father murdered and if he wanted to draw, why stop him? Even if it did not seem to be doing him much good.

His body trembled when he started drawing and his eyes shone with an intense, tormented light. The pattern of squares spreading out and multiplying in mirrors was a strange theme, given what had happened. But what did she know? Maybe it was the same as with his series of numbers. Even though she did not understand, it presumably meant something to him, and perhaps—who knows?—those squares were his own way of coming to terms with events. Shouldn't she just ignore the instructions? After all, who would find out? She had read somewhere that a mother should rely on her intuition. Gut feeling is often a better tool than all the psychological theories in the world. She decided to let August draw.

But suddenly the boy's back stiffened like a bow, and

Hanna could not help thinking back to what the psychologist had said. She took a hesitant step forward and looked down at the paper. She gave a start, and felt very uncomfortable. At first she could not make sense of it.

She saw the same pattern of squares repeating themselves in two surrounding mirrors and it was extremely skilfully done. But there was something else there as well, a shadow which grew out of the squares, like a demon, a phantom, and it frightened the living daylights out of her. She started to think of films about children who become possessed. She snatched the drawing from the boy and crumpled it up without fully understanding why. Then she shut her eyes and expected to hear that heart-rending toneless cry again.

But she heard no cry, just a muttering which sounded almost like words—impossible because the boy did not speak. Instead Hanna prepared herself for a violent outburst with August thrashing back and forth over the living-room floor. But there was no attack either, only a calm and composed determination as August took hold of a new piece of paper and started to draw the same squares again. Hanna had no choice but to carry him to his room. Afterwards she would describe what happened as pure horror.

August kicked and screamed and lashed out, and Hanna barely managed to keep hold of him. For a long time she lay in the bed with her arms knotted around him wishing that she could go to pieces herself. She briefly considered waking Lasse and asking him to give August one of those tranquilizing suppositories they now had, but then discarded that idea. Lasse was bound to be in a foul mood and she hated to give a child tranquilizers, however much Valium she herself took. There had to be some other way.

She was falling apart, desperately considering one option after the next. She thought of her mother in Katrineholm, of her agent, Mia, of the nice woman who rang last night, Gabriella Grane, and then of the psychologist again, Einar Fors-something, who had brought August to her. She had not particularly liked him. On the other hand he had offered to look after August for a while. He was the one who said August should not draw, so he should be sorting out this mess.

In the end she let go of her son and dug out the psychologist's card to call him. August immediately made a break for the living room to start drawing his damn squares again.

Einar Forsberg did not have a great deal of experience. He was forty-eight years old and with his deep-set blue eyes, brand-new Dior glasses, and brown corduroy jacket he could easily be taken for an intellectual. But anyone who had ever disagreed with him would know that there was something stiff and dogmatic about his way of thinking and he often concealed his lack of knowledge behind dogma and cocksure pronouncements.

It had only been two years since he qualified as a psychologist. Before that he was a gym teacher from Tyresö, and if you had asked his old pupils about him they would all have roared: "Silence, cattle! Be quiet, oh my beasts!" Forsberg had loved to shout those words, only half joking, when he wanted order in the classroom and even though he had hardly been anyone's favourite teacher he had kept his boys in line. It was this ability which persuaded him that he could put his skills to better use elsewhere.

He had been working at Oden's Medical Centre for Children and Adolescents for one year. Oden's was an emergency service which took in children and young people whose parents could not cope. Not even Forsberg—who had always been a staunch defender of whatever workplace he was in—believed that the centre functioned especially well. It was all crisis management and not enough long-term work. Children would come in after traumatic experiences at home and the psychologists were far too busy trying to manage breakdowns and aggressive behaviour to be able to devote themselves to resolving underlying causes. Even so, Forsberg thought he was doing some good, especially when he used his old classroom authority to calm hysterical children, or when he handled crisis situations out in the field.

He liked to work with policemen and he loved the tension in the air after dramatic events. He had been excited and expectant as he drove out to the house in Saltsjöbaden in the course of his night duty. There was a touch of Hollywood about the situation, he thought. A Swedish scientist had been murdered, his eight-year-old son was a witness, and none other than Forsberg had been sent to try to get the boy to open up. He straightened his hair and his glasses several times in the rearview mirror.

He wanted to make a stylish impression, but once he arrived he was not exactly a success. He could not make the boy out. Still, he felt acknowledged and important. The detectives asked him how they should go about questioning the child and—even though he did not have a clue—his answer was received with respect. That gave his ego a little boost and he did his best to be helpful. He found out that the boy suffered from infantile autism and had never spoken or been receptive to the world around him.

"There's nothing we can do for the time being," he said. "His mental faculties are too weak. As a psychologist I have to put his need for care first." The policemen listened to him with serious expressions and let him drive the boy home to his mother—who was another little bonus in the whole story.

She was the actress Hanna Balder. He had had the hots for her ever since he saw her in *The Mutineers* and he remembered her hips and her long legs—and even though she was now a bit older she was still attractive. Besides, her current partner was clearly a bastard. Forsberg did his best to appear knowledgeable and charming in a low-key way; within moments he got an opportunity to be authoritative, and that made him proud.

With a wild expression on his face the son began to draw black and white blocks, or squares, and Forsberg pronounced that this was unhealthy. It was precisely the kind of destructive compulsive behaviour that autistic children slip into, and he insisted that August stop at once. This was not received with as much gratitude as he had hoped for. Still, it had made him feel decisive and manly, and while he was at it he almost paid Hanna a compliment for her performance in *The Mutineers*. But then he decided that it was probably not the right time. Maybe that had been a mistake.

Now it was 1:00 in the afternoon and he was back home at his terraced house in Vällingby. He was in the bathroom with his electric toothbrush, feeling totally exhausted, when his mobile rang. At first he was irritated—but then he smiled. It was none other than Hanna Balder.

"Forsberg," he answered in an urbane voice.

"Hello," she said. "August, August . . ."

She sounded desperate and angry. But he could not understand why.

"Tell me, what's the problem?"

"All he wants to do is draw his chessboard squares. But you're saying he isn't allowed to."

"No, no, it's compulsive. But please, just stay calm."

"How the hell am I supposed to stay calm?"

"The boy needs you to be composed."

"But I can't be. He's yelling and lashing out at everything. You said you could help."

"Well, yes," he said, hesitant at first. Then he brightened, as if he had won some sort of victory. "Absolutely, of course. I'll see to it that he gets a place with us at Oden's."

"Wouldn't that be letting him down?"

"On the contrary, you're just taking account of his needs. I'll see to it personally that you can visit us as often as you like."

"Maybe that's the best solution."

"I'm sure of it."

"Will you come right away?"

"I'll be with you as soon as I can," he said. First he had to smarten himself up a bit. Then he added: "Did I tell you that I loved you in *The Mutineers*?"

It was no surprise to Levin that William Borg was already at the table at Sturehof, nor that he ordered the most expensive items on the menu, sole meunière and a glass of Pouilly-Fumé. Journalists generally made the most of it when he invited them to lunch. But it did surprise—and annoy—him that Borg had taken the initiative, as if he were the one with the money and the power. Why did he have to mention that raise? He should have kept Borg on tenterhooks, let him sit there and sweat instead.

"A little bird whispered in my ear that you're having difficulties with *Millennium*," Borg said, and Levin thought: I'd give my right arm to wipe that self-righteous smirk off his face.

"You've been misinformed," he said stiffly.

"Really?"

"We have the situation under control."

"How so, if you don't mind my asking?"

"If the editorial team is disposed to accept change and is ready to recognize the problems it has, we'll back them."

"And if not . . ."

"We'll pull out, and *Millennium* will be unlikely to stay afloat for more than a few months, which would of course be a great shame. But that's what the market looks like at the moment. Better magazines than *Millennium* have gone under. It's been only a modest investment for us and we can manage without it."

"Skip the bullshit, Ove. I know that this is a matter of pride for you."

"It's just business."

"I'd heard that you wanted to get Mikael Blomkvist off the editorial team."

"We've been thinking of transferring him to London."

"Isn't that a bit harsh, considering what he's done for the magazine?"

"We've made him a very generous offer," Levin said, feeling that he was being unnecessarily defensive and predictable.

He had almost forgotten the purpose of the lunch.

"Personally I don't blame you," Borg said. "You can ship him off to China, for all I care. I'm just wondering if it isn't going to be a bit tricky for you if Blomkvist makes a grand comeback with this Frans Balder story."

"Why would that happen? He's lost his sting. You of all people have pointed that out—and with considerable success, if I may say so," Levin said with an attempt at sarcasm.

"Well, yes, but I did get a little help."

"Not from me, you didn't, of that you can be sure. I hated that column. Thought it was badly written and tendentious. The one who kicked off the campaign against him was Thorvald Serner, you know that."

"But you can't be altogether unhappy about the way things are going right now?"

"Listen to me, William. I have the greatest respect for Mikael Blomkvist."

"You don't have to put on your politician act with me, Ove."

Levin felt like ramming something down Borg's throat.

"I'm just being open and honest," he said. "And I've always thought Blomkvist a fantastic reporter, of a different calibre from you and everyone else of his generation."

"Is that so?" Borg said, suddenly looking meek, and that made Levin feel better right away.

"That's how it is. We should be grateful to Blomkvist for the revelations he's given us, and I wish him all the best, I really do. But unfortunately it's not my job to get nostalgic and look back to the good old days. I have to concede that you have a point in suggesting that the man has gotten out of step with the times and that he could get in the way of your plans to relaunch *Millennium*."

"True, true."

"So for that reason it would be good if there weren't too many headlines about him right now."

"Positive headlines, you mean?"

"Maybe so, yes," Levin said. "That's another reason I invited you to lunch."

"Grateful for that, of course. And I do think I have something to offer. I had a call this morning from my old squash buddy," Borg said, clearly trying to regain his earlier self-confidence.

"And who's that?"

"Richard Ekström, the chief prosecutor. He's in charge of the preliminary investigation into the Balder killing. And he's not a member of the Blomkvist fan club."

"After that Zalachenko business, right?"

"Exactly. Blomkvist scuppered Ekström's entire strategy on that case and now he's worried that he's sabotaging this investigation as well."

"In what way?"

"Blomkvist isn't saying everything that he knows. He spoke to Balder just before the murder and came face-to-face with the killer. Even so he had surprisingly little to say for himself during the interviews. Ekström suspects he's saving the juiciest bits for his article."

"Interesting."

"Isn't it? We're talking about a man who was ridiculed in the media and is now so desperate for a scoop that he's prepared to let someone get away with murder. An old star reporter willing to cast social responsibility to the winds when his magazine finds itself in a financial crisis. And who has just learned that Serner Media wants to kick him off the editorial team. Hardly surprising that he's gone a step or two too far."

"I see your point. Is it anything you'd like to write about?"

"I don't think that would be productive, to be honest. Too many people know that Blomkvist and I have it in for each other. You'd be better off leaking to a news reporter and then supporting the story on your editorial pages. You'll get some good quotes from Ekström."

Levin was looking out onto Stureplan, where he spotted a beautiful woman in a bright red coat, with long strawberry-blond hair. For the first time that day he gave a big smile.

"Maybe that isn't such a bad idea," he added, ordering some more wine.

Blomkvist came walking down Hornsgatan towards Maria-torget. Further away, by Maria Magdalena kyrka, there was a white van with an ugly dent in its front wing, and next to it two men were waving their arms around and shouting at each other. But although the scene had attracted a crowd of onlookers, Blomkvist hardly noticed it.

He was thinking about how Balder's son had sat on the floor of the large house in Saltsjöbaden, reaching out over the Persian rug. The boy's hand had stains on the back of it and on the fingers, as if from crayons or pens, and that movement he was making looked as if he were drawing something complicated in midair, didn't it? Blomkvist was starting to see the whole scene in a new light.

Maybe it was not Frans Balder who had drawn the traffic light after all. Perhaps the boy had a gift. For some reason that did not surprise him as much as he might have expected. The first time he had met August Balder, sitting by his dead father, and seen him throwing himself against the headboard, he had already understood there was something exceptional about him. Now, as he cut across Mariatorget, a strange thought occurred to him and would not let him go. Up by Götgatsbacken he came to a stop.

He must at the very least follow it up, so he got out his mobile and looked up Hanna Balder. The number was unlisted, and unlikely to be one which he would find in *Millennium*'s contacts. He thought of Freja Granliden, a society reporter at *Expressen* whose columns did not do much to enhance the prestige of the profession. She wrote about divorces and romances and royalty. But she had a quick brain and a sharp wit, and whenever they met they had a good time together. He rang her number but it was engaged, of course.

These days, reporters on the evening papers were forever on the telephone, under such deadline pressure that they never left their desks to take a look at what real life was like. But he got her in the end and was not in the least surprised that she let out a yelp of delight.

"Mikael," she said. "What an honour. Are you finally going to give me a scoop? I've been waiting for so long."

"Sorry. This time *you* have to help *me*. I need an address and a phone number."

"What do I get in return? Maybe a wicked little quote about what you got up to last night."

"I could give you some career advice."

"And what might that be?"

"Stop writing crap."

"Right, then who's going to keep track of all the telephone numbers the classy reporters need? Who are you looking for?"

"Hanna Balder."

"I can imagine why. Did you meet her drunken boyfriend out there?"

"Don't you start fishing, now. Do you know where she lives?"

"Torsgatan 40."

"You know it just like that?"

"I have a brilliant memory for trivia. If you hang on, I'll give you the front-door code and the phone number as well."

"That's really kind."

"But you know . . ."

"Yes?"

"You're not the only one looking for her. Our own bloodhounds are on the hunt too, and from what I hear she hasn't answered her telephone all day."

"Wise woman."

Afterwards Blomkvist stood in the street, unsure what to do. Chasing down unhappy mothers in competition with crime reporters from the evening papers was not quite what he had hoped his day would bring. But he hailed a taxi and was driven off in the direction of Vasastan.

Hanna Balder had accompanied August and Forsberg to Oden's Medical Centre for Children and Adolescents, opposite Observatorielunden on Sveavägen. The medical centre consisted of two apartments which had been knocked together, but even though the furnishings and the courtyard had a private and sheltered feel to them, there was nonetheless something institutional about it all. Probably that had less to do with the long corridors and closed doors than the grim and watchful expressions on the faces of the staff. They seemed to have developed a certain distrust of the children for whom they were responsible.

The director, Torkel Lindén, was a vain little man who claimed to have a wide experience of children with autism. But Hanna did not like the way he looked at August. It was also troubling that there seemed to be no separation between teenagers and small children. But it felt too late to be having doubts now so on the way home she consoled herself with the thought that it would only be for a short time. Maybe she would pick August up as soon as this evening?

Then she thought about Lasse and his bouts of drunkenness and she told herself yet again that she needed to leave him and get a grip on her life. As she stepped out of the lift at her apartment she gave a start. An attractive man was sitting there on the landing, writing in a notebook. As he got to his feet and greeted her she saw that it was Mikael Blomkvist. She was terrified, so guilt-ridden that she supposed he was going to write some kind of exposé. That was absurd. He just gave an embarrassed smile and twice apologized for disturbing her. She could not help but feel a huge sense of relief. She had admired him for a long time.

"I have no comment to make," she said, in a voice which actually suggested the opposite.

"I'm not after a quote, either," he said. She remembered hearing that he and Lasse had arrived together—or at least at the same time—at Frans's the previous night, although she could not imagine what the two of them might have in common.

"Are you looking for Lasse?" she said.

"I'd like to hear about August's drawings," he replied, and at that she felt a stab of panic.

Yet she allowed him in. It was probably careless of her. Lasse had gone off to cure his hangover in some local dive and could be back at any time. He would go crazy if he found a journalist in their home. But Blomkvist had not only worried Hanna, he had also made her curious. How on earth did he know about the drawings? She invited him to sit on the grey sofa in the living room while she went to the kitchen to get some tea and biscuits. When she came back with a tray he said:

"I wouldn't be bothering you if it wasn't absolutely necessary."

"You're not bothering me," she said.

"You see, I met August last night, and I haven't been able to stop thinking about him."

"Oh?"

"I didn't understand it then," he said. "But I had the feeling he was trying to tell us something. Now I'm convinced he wanted to draw. He was making these determined movements with his hand over the floor."

"He's become obsessed with drawing."

"So he continued here at home?"

"And how! He started the minute we got here. He was

manic and what he drew was amazing, but his face became flushed and he was breathing heavily, so the psychologist said he had to stop. It was compulsive and destructive, was his opinion."

"What did he draw?"

"Nothing special, really, I'd guess it was inspired by his puzzles. But it was very cleverly done, with shadows and perspective and everything."

"But what was it?"

"Squares."

"What kind of squares?"

"Chessboard squares, I think you would call them," she said. Maybe she was imagining things, but she detected a trace of excitement in Blomkvist's eyes.

"Only chess squares?" he said. "Nothing more?"

"Mirrors too," she said. "Chessboard squares reflected in mirrors."

"Have you been to Frans's place?" he said, a new sharpness in his voice.

"Why do you ask?"

"Because the design of the floor in the bedroom—where he was killed—looks just like chessboard squares, and they're reflected in the mirrors of the wardrobe."

"Oh my God!"

"What's the matter?"

"Because . . ."

A wave of shame washed over her.

"Because the last thing I saw before I snatched the drawing away from him was a menacing shadow emerging out of those squares," she continued.

"Do you have the drawing here?"

"No, or rather yes."

"Yes?"

"I'm afraid I threw it away. But maybe it's still in the bin."

Blomkvist had coffee grounds and yoghurt all over his hands as he pulled a crumpled piece of paper out of the trash can and smoothed it out on the draining board. He brushed it with the back of his hand and looked at it in the glare of the kitchen lights. The drawing was not finished, not by any means, and it consisted mostly of chessboard squares, just as Hanna had said, seen from above or from the side. Without having been in Balder's bedroom, it would not be obvious that the squares represented a floor, but Blomkvist immediately recognized the mirrors on the wardrobe to the right of the bed. He also recognized the darkness, that special darkness that had met him during the night.

He felt transported back to the moment when he had walked in through the broken window—apart from one small important detail. The room he had entered had been almost dark, whereas the drawing showed a thin source of light falling diagonally from above, extending out over the squares. It gave contours to a shadow which was not distinct or meaningful, but which felt eerie, perhaps for that very reason.

The shadow was stretching out an arm and Blomkvist, who saw the drawing in a different light from Hanna, had no trouble interpreting what that signified. The figure meant to kill. Above the chessboard squares and the shadow there was a face which had not yet materialized.

"Where is August now?" he said. "Is he sleeping?"

"No. He . . . I've left him with someone else for a while. I couldn't handle him, to be honest."

"Where is he?"

"At Oden's Medical Centre for Children and Adolescents. On Sveavägen."

"Who knows that he's there?"

"No-one."

"Just you and the staff?"

Hanna nodded.

"Then it has to stay that way. Will you excuse me for a moment?"

Blomkvist took out his mobile and called Bublanski. In his mind he had already drafted yet another question for [*Lisbeth stuff*].

Bublanski felt frustrated—the investigation was going nowhere. Neither Balder's Blackphone nor his laptop had been found, so they had not been able to map his contacts with the outside world despite having had detailed discussions with the service provider.

For the time being they had little more than smoke screens and clichés to go on, Bublanski thought: a ninja warrior had materialized swiftly and effectively and then vanished into the darkness. In fact the attack had something far too perfect about it, as if it had been carried out by a person free of all the usual human failings and contradictions which as a rule feature in a murder. This was too clean, too clinical, and Bublanski could not help thinking that it had been just another day at the office for the killer. He was pondering this and more besides when Blomkvist rang.

"Oh, it's you," Bublanski said. "We were just talking about you. We'd like to have another word with you as soon as possible."

"Of course, not a problem. But right now I've got something much more important to tell you. The witness, August Balder, is a savant," Blomkvist said.

"A what?"

"A boy who may be severely handicapped but nonetheless has a special gift. He draws like a master, with a remarkable, mathematical sharpness. Did you see the drawings of the traffic light which were lying on the kitchen table in Saltsjöbaden?"

"Yes, briefly. Are you saying it wasn't Balder who drew them?"

"It was the boy."

"They looked like astonishingly mature pieces of work."

"But they were drawn by August. This morning he sat down and drew the chessboard squares on the floor in his father's bedroom, and he didn't stop at that. He sketched a shaft of light and a shadow. My theory is that it's the killer's shadow and the light from his headlamp, but of course we can't yet say for certain. The boy was interrupted in his work."

"Are you pulling my leg?"

"This is hardly the moment."

"How do you know all this?"

"I'm at the home of the boy's mother, Hanna Balder, and I'm looking at the drawing. The boy is no longer here. He's at . . ." The journalist hesitated. "I don't want to say more than that over the phone."

"You say that the boy was interrupted in the middle of his drawing?"

"A psychologist stopped him."

"How could one do something like that?"

"He probably didn't realize what the drawings represented, he just saw them as something compulsive. I suggest you send some people over right away. You've got your witness."

"We'll be there as soon as we can."

Jan Bublanski ended the call and went to share Blomkvist's news with the team, though soon after he wondered whether this had been wise.

CHAPTER 15

NOVEMBER 21

Salander was at the Raucher Chess Club on Hälsingegatan. She did not really feel like playing. Her head was aching—she had been on the hunt all day long. But the hunt had taken her here. When she realized that Frans Balder had been betrayed by one of his own, she had promised him she would leave the traitor alone. She had not approved of the strategy, but she had kept her word, and only when Balder had been killed did she feel absolved of her promise.

Now she was going to proceed on her own terms. But it was not all that easy. Arvid Wrange had not been at home, and instead of calling him she wanted to strike down on his life like a bolt of lightning and had therefore been out searching for him, her hoodie pulled over her head. Wrange lived the life of a drone. But as with so many other drones, he had a routine, and Salander had been able to find a number of signposts through the trail of pictures he posted on Instagram and Facebook: Riche on Birger Jarlsgatan and the Theatre Grill on Nybrogatan, the Raucher Chess Club and Café Ritorno on Odengatan, and a number of others, including a shooting club on Fridhelmsgatan, plus the addresses of two girlfriends.

Wrange had changed since the last time she had him on her radar. Not only had he gotten rid of his nerdy look. His morals were also at an ebb. Salander was not big on psychological theory, but she could see for herself that his first major transgression had led to a succession of others. Wrange was no longer an ambitious student, eager to learn. Now he was addicted to porn and bought sex online, violent sex. Two of the women had afterwards threatened to report him.

The man had a fair amount of money. He also had a load of problems. As recently as that morning he had Googled "witness protection Sweden," which was careless of him. Even though he was no longer in contact with Solifon, at least not from his computer, *they* were probably still keeping an eye on *him*. It would be unprofessional not to. Maybe he was beginning to crack up beneath the new urbane exterior, which served her purpose. When she once again rang the chess club—chess being the only connection with his former life—she was pleasantly surprised to hear that Wrange had just arrived there.

So now she walked down the small flight of steps on Hälsingegatan and along a corridor to some shabby premises where a motley crowd of mostly older men were sitting hunched over their chessboards. The atmosphere was somnolent, and nobody seemed to even notice her, let alone question her presence. They were all busy with what they were doing, and the only sound was the click of the chess clocks and the occasional swear word. There were framed photographs of Kasparov, Magnus Carlsen, and Bobby Fischer on the walls and even one of a pimply, teenaged Arvid Wrange playing the chess star Judit Polgár.

A different, older version of him was sitting at a table fur-

ther in and to the right, and he seemed to be trying out some
new opening. Next to him were a couple of shopping bags.
He was wearing a yellow lambswool sweater with a freshly
ironed white shirt and a pair of shiny English shoes, a little
too stylish for the surroundings. Salander approached him
with careful, hesitant steps and asked if he would like a game.
He responded by looking her up and down, then he said:
"OK."

"Nice of you," she replied, like a well-mannered young
girl, and sat down. She opened with e4, he answered with b5,
the Polish gambit, and then she closed her eyes and let him
play on.

Wrange tried to concentrate on the game, but he was not
managing too well. Fortunately this punk girl was going to
be easy pickings. She wasn't bad, as it turned out—she probably spent a lot of time playing—but what good was that? He
toyed with her a little, and she was bound to be impressed.
Who knows, maybe he could even get her to come home
with him afterwards. True, she looked stroppy, and Wrange
did not go in for stroppy girls, but she had nice tits and he
might be able to take out his frustrations on her. It had been
a disaster of a morning. The news that Balder had been murdered had floored him.

It wasn't grief that he felt: it was fear. Wrange really did
try hard to convince himself that he had done the right thing.
What did the goddamn professor expect when he treated him
as if he didn't exist? But of course it wouldn't look good that
Wrange had sold him down the river. He consoled himself
with the thought that an idiot like Balder must have made

thousands of enemies, but deep down he knew: the one event was linked to the other, and that scared him to death.

Ever since Balder had started working at Solifon, Wrange had been afraid that the drama would take a frightening new turn, and here he was now, wishing that it would all go away. That must have been why he went into town this morning on a compulsive spree to buy a load of designer clothes, and had ended up here at the chess club. Chess still managed to distract him, and the fact was that he was feeling better already. He felt like he was in control and smart enough to keep on fooling them all. Look at how he was playing.

This girl was not half bad. In fact there was something unorthodox and creative in her play, and she would probably be able to teach most people in here a thing or two. It was just that he, Arvid Wrange, was crushing her. His play was so brilliant and sophisticated that she had not even noticed he was on the brink of trapping her queen. Stealthily he moved his positions forward and snapped it up without sacrificing more than a knight. In a flirty, casual tone bound to impress her he said, "Sorry, baby. Your queen is down."

But he got nothing in return, no smile, not a word, nothing. The girl upped the tempo, as if she wanted to put a quick end to her humiliation, and why not? He'd be happy to keep the process short and take her out for two or three drinks before he pulled her. Maybe he would not be very nice to her in bed. The chances were that she would still thank him afterwards. A miserable cunt like her would be unlikely to have had a fuck for a long time and would be totally unused to guys like him, cool guys who played at this level. He decided to show off a bit and explain some higher chess theory. But he never got the chance. Something on the board did not feel quite right. His game began to run into some sort of resistance he could not understand. For a while he persuaded himself that it was only his imagination, perhaps the result of a few careless moves. If only he concentrated he would be able to put things right, and so he mobilized his killer instinct.

But the situation just got worse.

He felt trapped—however hard he tried to regain the initiative she hit back—and in the end he had no choice but to acknowledge that the balance of power had shifted, and shifted irreversibly. How crazy was that? He had taken her queen, but instead of building on that advantage he had landed in a fatally weak position. Surely she had not deliberately sacrificed her queen so early in the game? That would be impossible—the sort of thing you read about in books, it doesn't happen in your local chess club in Vasastan, and it's definitely not something that pierced punk chicks with attitude problems do, especially not to great players like him. Yet there was no escape.

In four or five moves he would be beaten and so he saw no alternative but to knock over his king with his index finger and mumble congratulations. Even though he would have liked to serve up some excuses, something told him that that would make matters worse. He had a sneaking feeling that his defeat was not just down to bad luck, and almost against his will he began to feel frightened again. Who the hell was she?

Cautiously he looked her in the eye and now she no longer looked like a stroppy, insecure nobody. Now she seemed cold—like a predator eyeing its prey. He felt deeply ill at ease, as if the defeat on the chessboard were but a prelude to something much, much worse. He glanced towards the door.

"You're not going anywhere," she said.

"Who are you?" he said.

"Nobody special."

"So we haven't met before?"

"Not exactly."

"But nearly, is that it?"

"We've met in your nightmares, Arvid."

"Is this some kind of joke?"

"Not really."

"What do you mean?"

"What do you think I mean?"

"How should I know?"

He could not understand why he was so scared.

"Frans Balder was murdered last night," she said in a monotone.

"Well . . . yes . . . I read that," he stammered.

"Terrible, isn't it?"

"Awful."

"Especially for you, right?"

"Why especially for me?"

"Because you betrayed him, Arvid. Because you gave him the kiss of Judas."

His body froze.

"That's bullshit," he spat out.

"As a matter of fact it's not. I hacked your computer, cracked your encryption, and saw very clearly that you sold his technology to Solifon. And you know what?"

He was finding it hard to breathe.

"I'm sure you woke up this morning and wondered if his death was your fault. I can help you there: it *was* your fault. If you hadn't been so greedy and bitter and pathetic, Frans

Balder would be alive now. I should warn you that's making me pretty fucking angry, Arvid. I'm going to hurt you badly. First of all by making you suffer the same sort of treatment you inflict on the women you find online."

"Are you insane?"

"Probably, yes," she said. "Empathy deficit disorder. Excessive violence. Something along those lines."

She gripped his hand with a force which scared him out of his wits.

"Arvid, do you know what I'm doing right now?"

"No."

"I'm sitting here trying to decide what to do with you. I'm thinking in terms of suffering of biblical proportions. That's why I might seem a bit distracted."

"What do you want?"

"I want revenge—haven't I made that clear?"

"You're talking crap."

"Definitely not, and I think you know it too. But there is a way out."

"What do I have to do?"

He could not understand why he said it. *What do I have to do?* It was an admission, a capitulation, and he considered taking it back, putting pressure on her instead, to see if she had any proof or if she was bluffing. But he could not bring himself to do it.

Only later did he realize that it was not just the threats she tossed out or the uncanny strength of her hands. It was the game of chess, the queen sacrifice. He was in shock, and something in his subconscious told him that a woman who plays like that must also know his secrets.

"What do I have to do?" he said again.

"You're going to follow me out of here and you're going to tell me everything, Arvid. You're going to tell me exactly what happened when you sold out Frans Balder."

"It's a miracle," Bublanski said as he stood in Hanna Balder's kitchen looking at the crumpled drawing which Blomkvist had plucked out of the rubbish.

"Let's not exaggerate," said Modig, who was standing right next to him. She was right. It was not much more than some chess squares on a piece of paper, after all, and as Mikael Blomkvist had pointed out over the telephone there was something strangely mathematical about the work, as if the boy were more interested in the geometry than in the threatening shadow above. But Bublanski was excited all the same. He had been told over and over how mentally impaired the Balder boy was, and how little he would be able to help them. Now the boy had produced a drawing which gave Bublanski more hope than anything else in the investigation. It strengthened his long-held conviction that one must never underestimate anyone or cling to preconceived ideas.

They could not be certain that what August was illustrating was the moment of the murder. The shadow could, at least in theory, be associated with some other occasion, and there was no guarantee that the boy had seen the killer's face or that he would be able to draw it. And yet deep down that is what Bublanski believed. Not just because the drawing, even in its present state, was masterful. He had studied the other drawings too, in which you could see, beyond the street crossing and the traffic light, a shabby man with thin lips who had been caught red-handed jaywalking, if you looked at it purely from a law-enforcement point of view. He was crossing the street on a red, and Amanda Flod, another officer on the team, had recognized him straightaway as the out-of-work actor Roger Winter, who had convictions for drunk driving and assault.

The photographic precision of August's eye ought to be a dream for any murder investigator. But Bublanski did realize that it would be unprofessional to set his hopes too high. Maybe the murderer had been masked at the time of the killing or his face had already faded from the child's memory. There were many possible scenarios and Bublanski cast a glum look in the direction of Modig.

"You think it's wishful thinking on my part," he said.

"For a man who's beginning to doubt the existence of God, you are surprisingly willing to hope for a miracle."

"Well, maybe."

"But it's worth getting to the bottom of. I agree with that," Modig said.

"Good, in that case let's see the boy."

Bublanski went out of the kitchen and nodded at Hanna Balder, who was sunk in the living-room sofa, fumbling with some tablets.

Lisbeth Salander and Arvid Wrange came out into Vasaparken arm in arm, like a pair of old friends out for a stroll. Appearances can be deceptive: Wrange was terrified as Salander steered them towards a park bench. The wind was getting up again and the temperature creeping down—it was hardly a day for feeding the pigeons—and Wrange was cold. But Salander decided that the bench would do and forced him to sit down, holding his arm in a vise-like grip.

"Right," she said. "Let's make this quick."

"Will you keep my name out of it?"

"I'm promising nothing, Arvid. But your chances of being able to go back to your miserable life will increase significantly if you tell me every detail of what happened."

"OK," he said. "Do you know Darknet?"

"I know it," she said.

No-one knew Darknet like Lisbeth Salander. Darknet was the lawless undergrowth of the Internet. The only way to access it was with specially encrypted software and the user's anonymity was guaranteed. No-one could Google your details or trace your activities online. So Darknet was full of drug dealers, terrorists, con men, gangsters, illegal arms dealers, pimps, and black hats. If there was an Internet hell, then this was it.

But Darknet was not in itself evil. Salander understood that better than anyone. These days, when spy agencies and the big software companies follow every step we take online, even honest people need a hiding place. Darknet was also a hub for dissidents, whistle-blowers, and informants. Opposition forces could protest on Darknet out of reach of their government, and Salander had used it for her own more discreet investigations and attacks. She knew its sites and search engines and its old-fashioned workings far away from the known, visible Net.

"Did you put Balder's technology up for sale on Darknet?" she said.

"No, I was just casting about. I was pissed off. You know, Frans hardly even said hello to me. He treated me like dirt, and he didn't care about that technology of his, either. It has the potential to make all of us rich, but he only wanted to play and experiment with it like a little kid. One evening when I'd had a few drinks I just chucked out a question on a geek site: 'Who can pay good money for some revolutionary AI technology?'"

"And did you get an answer?"

"It took a while. I had time to forget that I'd even asked. But in the end someone calling himself Bogey wrote back with some well-informed questions. At first my answers were ridiculously unguarded, but soon I realized what a mess I'd gotten myself into, and I became terrified that Bogey would steal the technology."

"Without you getting anything for it."

"It was a dangerous game. To be able to sell Frans's technology I had to tell people about it. But if I said too much then I would already have lost it. Bogey flattered me rotten—in the end he knew exactly where we were and what sort of software we were working on."

"He meant to hack you."

"Presumably. He somehow managed to get hold of my name, and that floored me. I became totally paranoid and announced that I wanted to pull out. But by then it was too late. Not that Bogey threatened me, at least not directly. He just went on and on about how he and I were going to do great things together and earn masses of money. In the end I agreed to meet him in Stockholm at a Chinese boat restaurant on Söder Mälarstrand. It was a windy day, I remember, and I stood there freezing. I waited more than half an hour, and afterwards I wondered if he had been checking me out in some way."

"But then he showed up?"

"Yes. At first I didn't believe it was him. He looked like a junkie, or a beggar, and if I hadn't seen that Patek Philippe watch on his wrist I probably would have tossed him twenty kronor. He had amateur tattoos and dodgy-looking scars on his arms, which he waved about as he walked. He was carrying this awful-looking trench coat and he seemed to have been more or less living on the streets. The strangest thing of all was that he was proud of it. It was only the watch and the handmade shoes which showed that he had at some point managed to raise himself out of the gutter. Other than that, he seemed keen to stick to his roots. Later on, when I'd given him everything and we were celebrating our deal over a few bottles of wine, I asked about his background."

"I hope for your sake that he gave you some details."

"If you want to track him down, I have to warn you . . ."

"I don't want advice, Arvid. I want facts."

"Fine. He was careful," he said. "But I still got a few things. He probably couldn't help himself. He grew up in a big city in Russia, though he didn't name it. He'd had everything stacked against him, he said. His mother was a whore and a heroin addict and his father could have been anybody. As a small boy he had ended up in the orphanage from hell. There was some lunatic there, he told me, who used to make him lie on a butcher's slab in the kitchen and whipped him with a broken cane. When he was eleven he ran away and lived on the street. He stole, broke into cellars and stairwells to get a little warmth, got drunk on cheap vodka, sniffed glue, and was abused and beaten. But he also discovered one thing."

"What?"

"That he had talent. He was an expert at breaking and entering, which became his first source of pride, his first identity. He was capable of doing in just a few seconds what took others hours. Before that he had been a homeless brat, everyone had despised him and spat at him. Now he was the boy who could get himself in wherever he wanted. It became an obsession. All day long he dreamed of being some sort of Houdini in reverse: he didn't want to break out, he wanted to break in. He practised for ten, twelve, fourteen hours a day, and in the end he was a legend on the streets—or so he said. He started to carry out bigger operations, using computers he stole and reconfigured to hack in everywhere. He made a heap of money which he blew on drugs and often he was robbed or taken advantage of. He could be clear as a bell when he was on one of his jobs but afterwards he would lie around in a narcotic haze and someone would walk all over him. He was a genius and a total idiot at the same time, he said. But one day everything changed. He was saved, raised up out of his hell."

"How?"

"He had been asleep in some dump of a place that was due to be pulled down and when he opened his eyes and looked around in the yellowish light there was an angel standing before him."

"An angel?"

"That's what he said, an angel, and maybe it was partly the contrast with everything else in there, the syringes, the leftover food, the cockroaches. He said she was the most beautiful woman he had ever seen. He could scarcely look at her, and he got this idea that he was going to die. It was an ominous, solemn feeling. But the woman explained, as if it were the most natural thing in the world, that she would make him rich and happy. If I've understood it right, she kept her promise. She gave him new teeth, got him into rehab. She arranged for him to train as a computer engineer."

"So ever since he's been hacking computers and stealing for this woman and her network."

"That's right. He became a new person, or maybe not completely new—in many ways he's still the same old thief and bum. But he no longer takes drugs, he says, and he spends all his free time keeping up to date with new technology. He finds a lot on Darknet and he claims to be stinking rich."

"And the woman—did he say anything more about her?"

"No, he was extremely careful about that. He spoke in such evasive and respectful terms that I wondered for a while if she wasn't a fantasy or hallucination. But I reckon she really does exist. I could sense sheer physical fear when he was talking about her—he said that he would rather die than let her down, and then he showed me a Russian patriarchal cross made of gold, which she had given him. One of those crosses, you know, which has a slanted beam down by the foot, one end pointing up and the other down. He told me this was a reference to the Gospel according to St. Luke and the two thieves who were hanged next to Jesus on the cross. The one thief believes in Jesus and goes to heaven. The other mocks him and is thrust down into hell."

"That's what awaits you if you fail her."

"That's about it, yes."

"So she sees herself as Jesus?"

"In this context the cross probably has nothing to do with Christianity. It's the message she wants to pass on."

"Loyalty or the torments of hell."

"Something along those lines."

"Yet you're sitting here, Arvid, spilling the beans."

"I didn't see an alternative."

"I hope you got paid a lot."

"Well, yes . . ."

"And then Balder's technology was sold to Solifon and Truegames."

"Yes, but I don't get it . . . not when I think of it now."

"What don't you get?"

"How could you know all this?"

"Because you were dumb enough to send an e-mail to Eckerwald at Solifon, don't you remember?"

"But I wrote nothing to suggest that I'd sold the technology. I was very careful about that."

"What you said was enough for me," she said. She got to her feet, and it was as if his entire being collapsed.

"Wait, what's going to happen now? Will you keep me out of it?"

"You can always hope," she said, and walked off towards Odenplan with purposeful steps.

Bublanski's mobile rang as he was on his way down to the front entrance on Torsgatan. It was Professor Edelman. Bublanski had been trying to reach him ever since he realized that the boy was a savant. Bublanski had found out online that two Swedish authorities were regularly quoted on this subject: Lena Ek at Lund University and Charles Edelman at the Karolinska Institute. But he had not been able to get hold of either, so he had postponed the search and gone off to see Hanna Balder. Now Edelman was ringing back, and he sounded shaken. He was in Budapest, he said, at a conference on heightened memory capacity. He had just arrived there and seen the news about the murder a moment ago, on CNN.

"Otherwise I would have gotten in touch right away," he said.

"What do you mean?"

"Professor Balder rang me yesterday evening."

That made Bublanski jump. "What did he want?"

"He wanted to talk about his son and his son's talent."

"Did you know each other?"

"Not in the slightest. He contacted me because he was worried about his boy and I was stunned to hear from him."

"Why?"

"Because it was Frans Balder. He's a household name to us neurologists. We tend to say he's just like us in wanting to understand the brain. The only difference is that he also wants to build one."

"I've heard something about that."

"I'd been told that he was an introverted and difficult man. A bit like a machine himself, people sometimes used to joke: nothing but logic circuits. But with me he was incredibly emotional, and it shocked me, to be honest. It was . . . I don't know, as if you were to hear your toughest policeman cry. I remember thinking that something must have happened, something other than what we were talking about."

"That sounds right. He had finally accepted that he was under a serious threat," Bublanski said.

"But he also had reason to be excited. His son's drawings were apparently exceptionally good, and that's not common at all at that age, not even with savants, and especially not in combination with proficiency in mathematics."

"Mathematics?"

"Yes. According to Balder his son had mathematical skills too. I could spend a long time talking about that."

"What do you mean?"

"Because I was utterly amazed, and at the same time maybe not so amazed after all. We now know that there's a hereditary factor in savants, and here we have a father who is a legend, thanks to his advanced algorithms. But still ... artistic and numerical talents do not usually present themselves together in these children."

"Surely the great thing about life is that every now and then it springs a surprise on us," Bublanski said.

"True, Chief Inspector. So what can I do for you?"

Bublanski thought through everything that had happened in Saltsjöbaden and it struck him that it would do no harm to be cautious.

"All I can say is that we need your help and expert knowledge as a matter of urgency."

"The boy was a witness to the murder, was he not?"

"Yes."

"And you want me to try to get him to draw what he saw?"

"I'd prefer not to comment."

Charles Edelman was standing in the lobby of the Hotel Boscolo in Budapest, a conference centre not far from the glittering Danube. The place looked like an opera house, with magnificent high ceilings, old-fashioned cupolas and pillars. He had been looking forward to the week here, the dinners and the presentations. Yet he was agitated and ran his fingers through his hair.

"Unfortunately I'm not in a position to help you. I have

to give an important lecture tomorrow morning," he had said to Bublanski, and that was true. He had been preparing the talk for some weeks and he was going to take a controversial line with several eminent memory experts. He recommended a young associate professor, Martin Wolgers, to Bublanski.

But as soon as he hung up and exchanged looks with a colleague who had paused next to him, holding a sandwich—he began to have regrets. He even began to envy young Martin Wolgers, who was not yet thirty-five, always looked far too good in photographs, and on top of it all was beginning to make a name for himself.

It was true that Edelman did not fully understand what had happened. The police inspector had been cryptic and was probably worried that someone might be listening in on the call. Yet the professor still managed to grasp the bigger picture. The boy was good at drawing and was a witness to a murder. That could mean only one thing, and the longer Edelman thought about it, the more he fretted. He would be giving many more important lectures in his life, but he would never get another chance to play a part in a murder investigation at this level. However he looked at the assignment he had so casually passed on to Wolgers, it was bound to be much more interesting than anything he might be involved in here in Budapest. Who knows, it could even make him some sort of celebrity.

He visualized the headline: PROMINENT NEUROLOGIST HELPS POLICE SOLVE MURDER, or better still: EDELMAN'S RESEARCH LEADS TO BREAKTHROUGH IN MURDER HUNT. How could he be so stupid as to turn it down? He picked up his mobile and called Chief Inspector Bublanski again.

. . .

Bublanski hung up. He and Modig had managed to park not far from the Stockholm Public Library and had just crossed the street. Once again the weather was dreadful, and Bublanski's hands were freezing.

"Did he change his mind?" Modig said.

"Yes. He's going to shelve his lecture."

"When can he be here?"

"He's looking into it. Tomorrow morning at the latest."

They were on their way to Oden's Medical Centre on Sveavägen to meet the director, Torkel Lindén. The meeting was only meant to settle the practical arrangements for August Balder's testimony—at least as far as Bublanski was concerned. But even though Torkel Lindén did not yet know the true purpose of their visit, he had been strangely discouraging over the telephone and said that right now the boy was not to be disturbed "in any way." Bublanski had sensed an instinctive hostility and was not particularly pleasant in return. It had not been a promising start.

Lindén turned out not to be the hefty figure Bublanski had expected. He was hardly more than five feet tall and had short, possibly dyed black hair and pinched lips. He wore black jeans, a black polo sweater, and a small cross on a ribbon around his neck. There was something ecclesiastical about him, and his hostility was genuine.

He had a haughty look and Bublanski became aware of his own Jewishness—which happened whenever he encountered this sort of malevolence and air of moral superiority. Lindén wanted to show that he was better, because he put the boy's physical well-being first rather than offering him up for police purposes. Bublanski saw no choice but to be as amiable as possible.

"Pleased to meet you," he said.

"Is that so?" Lindén said.

"Oh yes, and it's kind of you to see us at such short notice. We really wouldn't come barging in like this if we didn't think this matter was of the utmost importance."

"I imagine you want to interview the boy in some way."

"Not exactly," Bublanski said, not quite so amiably. "I have to emphasize first of all that what I'm saying now must remain between us. It's a question of security."

"Confidentiality is a given for us. We have no loose lips here," Lindén said, in such a way as to suggest that it was the opposite with the police.

"My only concern is for the boy's safety," Bublanski said sharply.

"So that's your priority?"

"As a matter of fact, yes," the policeman said with even greater severity, "and that is why none of what I'm about to tell you must be passed on in any way—least of all by e-mail or by telephone. Can we sit somewhere private?"

Sonja Modig did not think much of the place. But then she was probably affected by the crying. Somewhere nearby a little girl was sobbing relentlessly. They were sitting in a room which smelled of detergent and also of something else, maybe a lingering trace of incense. A cross hung on the wall and there was a worn teddy bear lying on the floor. Not much else made the place cozy or attractive and since Bublanski, usually so good-natured, was about to lose his temper, she took matters into her own hands and gave a calm, factual account of what had happened.

"We are given to understand," she said, "that your colleague Einar Forsberg said that August should not be allowed to draw."

"That was his professional judgment and I agree with it. It doesn't do the boy any good," Lindén said.

"Well, I don't see how anything could do him much good under these circumstances. He saw his father being killed."

"We don't want to make things any worse, do we?"

"True. But this drawing August was not allowed to finish could lead to a breakthrough in the investigation and therefore I'm afraid we must insist. We'll make sure there are people present with the necessary expertise."

"I still have to say no."

Modig could hardly believe her ears.

"With all due respect for your work," Lindén went on, doggedly, "here at Oden's we help vulnerable children. That's our job and our calling. We're not an extension of the police force. That's how it is, and we're proud of it. For as long as the children are here, they should feel confident that we put their interests first."

Modig laid a restraining hand on Bublanski's thigh.

"We can easily get a court order," she said. "But we'd prefer not to go that route."

"Wise of you."

"Let me ask you something," she said. "Are you and Forsberg so absolutely sure what's best for August, or for the girl crying over there, for that matter? Couldn't it be that we all need to express ourselves? You and I can talk or write, or even go out and get a lawyer. August doesn't have those means of expression. But he can draw, and he seems to want to tell us something. Shouldn't we let August give form to something which must be tormenting him?"

"In our judgment . . ."

"No," she cut him off. "Don't tell us about your judgment. We're in contact with the person who knows more than anyone else in this country about this particular condition. His name is Charles Edelman, he's a professor of neurology, and he's on his way here from Hungary to meet the boy."

"We can of course listen to him," Lindén said reluctantly.

"Not just listen. We let him decide."

"I promise to engage in a constructive dialogue, between experts."

"Fine. What's August doing now?"

"He's sleeping. He was exhausted when he came to us."

Modig could tell that nothing good would come of it were she to suggest that the boy be woken up.

"In that case we'll come back tomorrow morning with Professor Edelman, and I hope that we can all work together on this matter."

CHAPTER 16

NOVEMBER 21–22

Gabriella Grane buried her face in her hands. She had not been to bed for forty hours and she was racked by a deep sense of guilt, only made worse by the lack of sleep. Yet she had been working hard all day long. Since this morning she had been part of a team at Säpo—a sort of shadow unit—which was investigating in secret every detail of the Frans Balder murder under cover of looking into broader domestic policy implications.

Superintendent Mårten Nielsen was formally leading the team and had recently returned from a year of study at the University of Maryland in the United States. He was undoubtedly intelligent and well informed, but too right-wing for Grane's tastes. It was rare to find a well-educated Swede who was also a wholehearted supporter of the American Republican Party—he even expressed some sympathy for the Tea Party movement. He was passionate about military history and lectured at the Military Academy Karlberg. Although still young—thirty-nine—he was believed to have extensive international contacts.

He often had trouble, however, asserting himself in the group and in practice the real leader was Ragnar Olofsson, who was older and cockier and could silence Nielsen with one peevish little sigh or a displeased wrinkle above his bushy eyebrows. Nor was Nielsen's life made any easier by the fact that Detective Inspector Lars Åke Grankvist was also on the team.

Before joining the Security Police, Grankvist had been a semi-legendary investigator in the Swedish police's National Murder Squad, at least in the sense that he was said to be able to drink anybody else under the table and to manage, with a sort of boisterous charm, to keep a lover in every town. It was not an easy group in which to hold one's own, and Grane kept an ever lower profile as the afternoon wore on. But this was due less to the men and their macho rivalry than to a growing sense of uncertainty.

Sometimes she wondered if she knew even less now than before. She realized, for example, that there was little or no proof to support the theory of the suspected data breach. All they had was a statement from Stefan Molde at the NDRE, and not even he had been sure of what he was saying. In her view his analysis was more or less rubbish. Balder seems to have relied primarily on the female hacker he had turned to for help, the woman not even named in the investigation, but whom his assistant, Linus Brandell, had described in such vivid terms. It was likely that Balder had been withholding a lot from Grane before he left for America.

For example, was it a coincidence that he had found a job at Solifon?

The uncertainty gnawed at her and she was indignant that no help was coming from Fort Meade. She could not get hold of Alona Casales, and the NSA was once again a closed door, so she in turn no longer passed on any news. Just like

Nielsen and Grankvist, she found herself overshadowed by Olofsson. He kept getting information from his source at the Violent Crimes Division and immediately passing it on to the head of Säpo, Helena Kraft.

Grane did not like it, and in vain she had pointed out that this traffic not only increased the risk of a leak but also seemed to be costing them their independence. Instead of searching their own channels, they were slavishly relying on the information which flowed in from Bublanski's team.

"We're like people cheating on an exam, waiting for someone to whisper the answer instead of thinking for ourselves," she had said to the team, and this had not made her popular.

Now she was alone in her office, determined to move ahead on her own, trying to see the bigger picture. It might get her nowhere, but on the other hand it would do no harm. She heard steps outside in the corridor, the click-clack of determined high heels which Grane by now recognized only too well. It was Kraft, who came in wearing a grey Armani jacket, her hair pulled into a tight bun. Kraft gave her an affectionate look. But there were times when Grane resented this favouritism.

"How's it going?" Kraft asked. "Are you surviving?"

"Just about."

"I'm going to send you home after this conversation. You have to get some sleep. We need an analyst with a clear head."

"Sounds sensible."

"Do you know what Erich Maria Remarque said?"

"That it's not much fun in the trenches, or something."

"Ha, no, that it's always the wrong people who have the guilty conscience. Those who are really responsible for suffering in the world couldn't care less. It's the ones fighting for good who are consumed by remorse. You've got nothing to be ashamed of, Gabriella. You did what you could."

"I'm not so sure about that. But thanks anyway."

"Have you heard about Balder's son?"

"Just very quickly from Ragnar."

"At ten o'clock tomorrow morning Chief Inspector Bublanski, Detective Sergeant Modig, and a Professor Edelman will be seeing the boy at Oden's Medical Centre for Children and Adolescents, on Sveavägen. They're going to try and get him to draw some more."

"I'll keep my fingers crossed. But I'm not too happy to know about it."

"Relax, leave the paranoia to me. The only ones who know about this are people who can keep their traps shut."

"I suppose you're right."

"I want to show you something: photographs of the man who hacked Balder's burglar alarm."

"I've seen them already. I've even studied them in detail."

"Have you?" Kraft said, handing over an enlarged and blurred picture of a wrist.

"What about it?"

"Take another look. What do you see?"

Grane looked and saw two things: the luxury watch she had noted before and, beneath it, barely distinguishable between the glove and the jacket cuff, a couple of lines which looked like amateur tattoos.

"Contrasts," she said. "Some cheap tattoos and a very expensive watch."

"More than that," Kraft said. "That's a 1951 Patek Philippe, model 2499, first series, or just possibly second series."

"Means nothing to me."

"It's one of the finest wristwatches in the world. A few years ago a watch like this sold at auction at Christie's in Geneva for more than two million dollars."

"Are you kidding?"

"No, and it wasn't just anyone who bought it. It was Jan van der Waal, a lawyer at Dackstone & Partner. He bid for it on behalf of a client."

"Dackstone & Partner, don't they represent Solifon?"

"Correct. We don't know whether the watch on the surveillance photo is the one that was sold in Geneva, and we haven't been able to find out who that client was. But it's a start, Gabriella. A scrawny type who looks like a junkie and who wears a watch of this calibre—that should narrow the field."

"Does Bublanski know this?"

"It was his technical expert Jerker Holmberg who discovered it. Now I want you and your analytical brain to take it further. Go home, get some sleep, and get started on it in the morning."

The man who called himself Jan Holtser was sitting at home in his apartment on Högbergsgatan in Helsinki, not far from Esplanaden park, looking through an album of photographs of his daughter, Olga, who was now twenty-two and studying medicine in Gdansk.

Olga was tall and dark and intense and, as he had a habit of saying, the best thing that ever happened to him. Not just because it sounded good—he believed it. But now Olga had come to suspect what he was actually doing.

"Are you protecting evil people?" she had asked him one day, before embarking on a manic pursuit of what she called her commitment to the "weak and vulnerable."

It was pure pinko left-wing lunacy, in Holtser's opinion, not at all in keeping with Olga's character. He saw it as her attempt to stake out her independence. Behind all the talk about beggars, he thought she was still quite like him. Once upon a time Olga had been a promising 100-metre runner. She was six feet tall, muscular, and explosive, and in the old days she had loved watching action films and listening to him reminisce about the war in Chechnya. Everyone at school had known better than to pick a fight with her. She hit back, like a warrior. Olga was definitely not cut out to minister to the sick and degenerate.

Yet she claimed to want to work for Médecins Sans Frontières or go off to Calcutta like some Mother Teresa. Holtser could not bear the thought. The world belongs to the strong, he felt. But he loved his daughter, however daft some of her ideas, and tomorrow she was coming home for the first time in six months for a few days' leave. He solemnly resolved that he would be a better listener this time, and not pontificate about Stalin and great leaders and everything that she hated.

He would instead try to bring them closer again. He was certain that she needed him. At least he was pretty sure that he needed her. It was 8:00 in the evening and he went into the kitchen and pressed three oranges and poured Smirnoff into a glass. It was his third screwdriver of the day. Once he had finished a job he could put away six or seven of them, and maybe he would do that now. He was tired, weighed down by all the responsibility on his shoulders, and he needed to relax. For a few minutes he stood with his drink in his hand and dreamed about a different sort of life. But the man who called himself Jan Holtser had set his hopes too high.

The tranquility came to an abrupt end as Bogdanov rang on his secure mobile. At first Holtser hoped that Bogdanov just wanted to chat, to release some of the excitement that came with every assignment. But his colleague was calling about a very specific matter and sounded less than happy.

"I've spoken to T.," he said. Holtser felt a number of things all at once, perhaps jealousy most of all.

Why did Kira ring Bogdanov and not him? Even if it was Bogdanov who brought in the big money, and was rewarded accordingly, Holtser had always been convinced that he was the one closer to Kira. But Holtser was also worried. Had something gone wrong, after all?

"Is there a problem?" he said.

"The job isn't finished."

"Where are you?"

"In town."

"Come on up in that case and explain what the hell you mean."

"I've booked a table at Postres."

"I don't feel like going to some posh restaurant. Get yourself over here."

"I haven't eaten."

"I'll fry something up."

"Sounds good. We've got a long night ahead of us."

Holtser did not want another long night. Still less did he feel like telling his daughter that he would not be at home the next day. But he had no choice. He knew as surely as he knew that he loved Olga: You could not say no to Kira.

She wielded some invisible power and, however hard he tried, he could never be as dignified in her presence as he wanted. She reduced him to a little boy and often he turned himself inside out just to see her smile.

Kira was staggeringly beautiful and knew how to make the most of it like no other beauty before her. She was unmatched when it came to power games. She knew all the moves. She could be weak and needy when it suited, but also indomitable, hard and cold as ice, and sometimes plain evil. Nobody brought out the sadist in him like she did.

She may not have been intelligent in the conventional sense, and many pointed that out to try to take her down a peg or two. But the same people were still stupefied in her presence. Kira played them like a violin and could reduce even the toughest of men to blushing and giggling school-children.

It was 9:00 p.m. and Bogdanov was sitting next to him shov-elling in the lamb chop Holtser had prepared. Oddly enough his table manners were almost passable. That may have been Kira's influence. In many ways Bogdanov had become quite civilized—and then again not. However he tried to put on airs, he could never entirely rid himself of the appearance of the petty thief and speed addict. He had been off drugs for ages and was a computer engineer with university qualifica-tions, but still looked ravaged by street life.

"Where's your bling watch?" Holtser said. "Are you in the doghouse?"

"We both are."

"It's that bad?"

"Maybe not."

"The job isn't finished, you said?"

"No, it's that boy."

"Which boy?" Holtser pretended not to understand.

"The one you so nobly spared."

"What about him? He's a retard, you know."

"Maybe so, but he can draw."

"What do you mean, draw?"

"He's a savant."

"A *what*?"

"You should try reading something other than your fucking gun magazines for once."

"What are you talking about?"

"It's someone who's autistic or handicapped in some other way, but who has a special gift. This boy may not be able to talk or think like a normal person, but he has a photographic memory. The police think the little bastard is going to be able to draw your face, and then they're going to run it through their facial-recognition software, and then you're screwed, aren't you? You must be there somewhere in Interpol's records?"

"Yes, but Kira can't expect us to . . ."

"That's exactly what she expects. We have to fix the boy."

A wave of emotion and confusion washed over Holtser and once again he saw before him that empty, glassy look from the double bed which had made him so uncomfortable.

"The hell I will," he said, without really believing it.

"I know you've got problems with children. I don't like

it either. But we can't avoid this one. Besides, you should be grateful. Kira could just as easily have sacrificed you."

"I suppose so."

"Then it's settled. I've got the plane tickets in my pocket. We'll take the first flight in the morning to Arlanda, at 6:30, and then we're going to some place on Sveavägen called Oden's Medical Centre for Children and Adolescents."

"So the boy's in a clinic."

"Yes, and that's why we need to do some planning. Let me just finish eating."

The man who called himself Jan Holtser closed his eyes and tried to figure out what he was going to say to Olga.

Salander was up at 5:00 the next morning and hacked into the NSF Major Research Instrumentation supercomputer at the New Jersey Institute of Technology—she needed all the mathematical skills she could muster. Then she got out her own programme for elliptic curve factorization and set about cracking the file she had downloaded from the NSA.

But however hard she tried, she could not manage it. She had not really been expecting to do so. It was a sophisticated RSA encryption, named after the originators Rivest, Shamir, and Adleman. RSA has two keys—one public, one secret—and is based on Euler's phi function and Fermat's little theorem, but above all on the simple fact that it is easy to multiply two large prime numbers. A calculator will give you the answer in the blink of an eye. Yet it is all but impossible to work backwards and, on the basis of the answer, calculate the prime numbers you started out with. Computers are not yet efficient at prime number factorization, something which had exasperated Lisbeth Salander and the world's intelligence organizations many times in the past.

For about a year now Salander had been thinking that ECM, the Elliptic Curve Method, would be more promising than previous algorithms, and she had spent long nights writing her own factorization programme. But now, in the early hours of the morning, she realized it would need more refinement to have even the slightest chance of success. After three hours of work, she took a break and went to the kitchen, drank some orange juice straight from the carton, and ate two microwaved piroshki.

Back at her desk she hacked into Blomkvist's computer to see if he had come up with anything new. He had posted two more questions for her and she realized he wasn't so hopeless after all.

<Which of Frans Balder's assistants betrayed him?>, he wrote, which was a reasonable question.

She did not answer. She could not care less about Arvid Wrange. But she had made progress and worked out who the hollow-eyed junkie was, the man Wrange had been in touch with, who had called himself Bogey. Trinity in Hacker Republic remembered somebody with that same handle from a number of hacker sites some years previously. That did not necessarily mean anything—Bogey was not the most original alias. But Salander had traced the posts and thought she could be onto something, especially when he carelessly dropped that he was a computer engineer from Moscow University.

Salander was unable to find out when he graduated, or any other dates for that matter, but she got hold of a couple of nerdy details about how Bogey was hooked on fine watches and crazy for the Arsène Lupin films from the '70s, about the gentleman thief of that name.

Then Salander posted questions on every conceivable website for former and current students at Moscow University, asking if anybody knew a scrawny, hollow-eyed ex-junkie who had been a street urchin and master thief and loved Arsène Lupin films. It was not long before she got a reply.

"That sounds like Jurij Bogdanov," wrote someone who introduced herself as Galina.

According to this Galina, Bogdanov was a legend at the university. Not just because he had hacked into all the lecturers' computers and had dirt on every one of them. He liked to ask people: Will you bet me one hundred roubles I can't break into that house over there?

Many who did not know him thought this was easy money. But Jurij could pick any door lock, and if for some reason he failed then he would shin up the façade or the walls. He was known for his daring, and for his evil. He was said once to have kicked a dog to death when it disturbed him in his work and he was always stealing things, just for the hell of it. Galina thought he might have been a kleptomaniac. But he was also a genius hacker and a talented analyst, and after he graduated the world was his oyster. He did not want a job, he wanted to go his own way, he said, and it did not take Salander long to work out what he got up to after university—at least according to the official version.

Jurij Bogdanov was now thirty-four years old. He had left Russia and lived in Berlin at Budapester Strasse 8, not far from the Michelin-starred restaurant Hugo's. He ran a white

hat computer security business, Outcast Security, with seven
employees and a turnover in the last financial year of twenty-
two million euros. It was ironic yet somehow entirely logical that his front was a company which protected industrial
groups from people like himself. He had not had any criminal convictions since he took his exams and managed a wide
network of contacts—one of the members of his board of
directors was Ivan Gribanov, member of the Russian Duma
and a major shareholder in the oil company Gazprom—but
she could find nothing to get her further.

Blomkvist's second question was:

```
<Oden's Medical Centre on Sveavägen: Is
it safe? (Delete this as soon as you read
it)>
```

He did not explain why he was interested in the place.
But she knew that Blomkvist was not someone who threw
questions out at random. Nor did he make a habit of being
unclear.

If he was being cryptic, then he had a reason to be, and
the information must be sensitive. There was evidently something significant about this medical centre. Salander soon
discovered that it had attracted a number of complaints—
children had been forgotten or ignored and had been able
to self-harm. Oden's was managed privately by its director,
Torkel Lindén, and his company Care Me and, if one was to
believe past employees, Lindén's word was law. The profit
margin was always high because nothing was bought unless
absolutely necessary.

Lindén himself was a former star gymnast, among other

things a one-time Swedish horizontal bar champion. Nowadays he was a passionate hunter and member of a Christian congregation that took an uncompromising line on homosexuality. Salander went onto the websites of the Swedish Association for Hunting and Wildlife Management and the Friends of Christ to see what kinds of tempting activities were going on there. Then she sent Lindén two fake but enticing e-mails which looked as if they had come from the organizations. Attached were PDF files with sophisticated malware which would open automatically if Lindén clicked on the messages.

By 8:23 she had gotten onto the server and immediately confirmed her suspicions. August Balder had been admitted to the clinic the previous afternoon. In the medical file, underneath a description of the circumstances which had resulted in his admittance, it said:

> Infantile autism, severe mental impairment. Restless. Severely traumatized by death of father. Constant observation required. Difficult to handle. Brought jigsaw puzzles. Not allowed to draw! Observed to be compulsive and destructive. Diagnosis by psychologist Forsberg, confirmed by T.L.

And the following had been added underneath, clearly somewhat later:

> Professor Charles Edelman, Chief Inspector Bublanski, and Detective Sergeant Modig will visit A. Balder at 10:00 a.m. on Wednesday, November 22. T.L. will be present. Drawing under supervision.

Further down still it said:

> Change of venue. A. Balder to be taken by T.L.
> and Professor Edelman to his mother Hanna Balder
> on Torsgatan, Bublanski and Modig will join. A.B. is
> thought likely to draw better in his home environment.

Salander quickly checked who Edelman was, and when
she saw that his specialty was savant skills she understood
straightaway what was going on. They seemed to be working
towards some sort of testimony in the form of a sketch. Why
else would Bublanski and Sonja Modig be interested in the
boy's drawing, and why else would Blomkvist have been so
cautious in framing his question?

None of this must be allowed to get out. No killer must
be able to find out that the boy might draw a picture of him.
Salander decided to see for herself how careful Lindén had
been in his correspondence. Luckily he had not written
anything more about the boy's drawing ability. He had on
the other hand received an e-mail from Edelman at 11:10
last night, copied to Modig and Bublanski. That e-mail was
clearly the reason why the meeting place had been changed.
Edelman wrote:

```
<Hi Torkel, How good of you to see me at
your medical centre. I really appreci-
ate it. But I'm afraid I have to be a bit
awkward. I think we stand the best chance
of getting a good result if we arrange for
the boy to draw in an environment where
he feels secure. That's not in any way to
```

```
criticize your medical centre. I've heard
a lot of good things about it.>
```

The hell you have, Salander thought, and read on:

```
<Therefore I'd like us to move the boy
to his mother Hanna Balder on Torsgatan,
tomorrow morning. The reason being that it
is recognized in literature on the sub-
ject that the presence of the mother has
a positive effect on children with savant
skills. If you and the boy can wait out-
side the entrance on Sveavägen at 9:15
a.m., then I can pick you up as I go by.
That would give us the opportunity for a
bit of a chat between colleagues.
Best regards
Charles Edelman>
```

Bublanski and Modig had replied at 7:01 and 7:14 a.m. respectively. There was good reason, they wrote, to rely on Edelman's expertise and follow his advice. Lindén had, at 7:57, confirmed that he and the boy would await Charles Edelman outside the entrance on Sveavägen. Salander sat for a while, lost in thought. Then she went to the kitchen and picked up a few old biscuits from the larder while she looked out towards Slussen and Riddarfjärden. *So,* she thought, *the venue for the meeting has been changed.* Instead of doing his drawing at the medical centre, the boy would be driven home to his mother.

The presence of the mother has a positive effect, Edelman wrote. There was something about that phrase Salander did not like. It felt old-fashioned, didn't it? And the introduction itself was not much better: "The reason being that it is recognized in literature on the subject . . ." It was stilted. Although it was true that many academics could not write to save their lives, and she knew nothing about the way in which this professor normally expressed himself, would one of the world's leading neurologists really feel the need to lean on what is recognized in the literature? Wouldn't he be more self-assured?

Salander went to her computer and skimmed through some of Edelman's papers online; she may have found the odd little touch of vanity, even in the most factual passages, but there was nothing clumsy or psychologically naïve in what he had written. On the contrary, the man was sharp. So she went back to the e-mails and checked to find out which SMTP server they had been transmitted through, and that made her jump right away. The server, Birdino, was not familiar, which it should have been, so she sent it a series of commands to see exactly what it was. In a matter of seconds she had the evidence in black and white: the server supported open mail relay, and the sender could therefore transmit messages from any address he wanted.

In other words, the e-mail from Edelman was a fake, and the copies to Bublanski and Modig were a smoke screen. She hardly even needed to check, she already knew what had happened: the police replies and the approval of the altered arrangements were also a bluff. It didn't just mean that someone was pretending to be Edelman. There also had to be a leak, and above all, somebody wanted the boy outside on Sveavägen.

Somebody wanted him defenceless in the street so that . . . what? They could kidnap or get rid of him? Salander looked at her watch, it was already 8:55. In just twenty minutes Torkel Lindén and August Balder would be outside waiting for someone who was not Professor Edelman, and who had anything but good intentions towards them.

What should she do? Call the police? That was never her first choice. She was especially reluctant when there was a risk of leaks. Instead, she went onto Oden's website and got hold of Lindén's office number. But she only made it as far as the switchboard. Lindén was in a meeting. So she found his mobile. After ending up in his voicemail, she swore out loud, and sent him both a text and an e-mail telling him on no account to go out into the street with the boy, not under any circumstances. She signed herself "Wasp" for lack of a better idea.

Then she threw on her leather jacket and rushed out. After a second, she turned, ran back into the apartment, and packed her laptop with the encrypted file and her pistol, a Beretta 92, into a black sports bag. Then she hurried out again. She wondered if she should take her car, the BMW M6 Convertible gathering dust in the garage. But she decided a taxi would be quicker. She soon regretted it.

When a taxi finally appeared, it was clear that rush hour had not subsided. Traffic inched forward and Centralbron was almost at a standstill. Had there been an accident? Everything went slowly, everything but the time, which flew. Soon it was 9:05, then 9:10. She was in a tearing hurry and in the worst case it was already too late. Most likely Lindén and the boy went out onto the street ahead of time and the killer, or whoever it was, had already struck.

She dialled Lindén's number again. This time the call went through, but there was no answer, so she swore again and thought of Mikael Blomkvist. She had not actually spoken to him in ages. But now she called him and he answered, sounding irritated. Only when he realized who it was did he brighten up:

"Lisbeth, is that you?"

"Shut up and listen," she said.

Blomkvist was in the *Millennium* offices on Götgatan, in a foul mood. It was not just because he had had another bad night. It was TT. Usually a serious and decent news agency, TT had put out a bulletin claiming that Mikael Blomkvist was sabotaging the murder enquiry by withholding crucial information, which he intended to publish first in *Millennium.*

Allegedly his aim was to save the magazine from financial disaster and rebuild his own "ruined reputation." Blomkvist had known that the story was in the offing. He had had a long conversation with its author, Harald Wallin, the evening before. But he could not have imagined such a devastating result.

It was made up of idiotic insinuations and unsubstantiated accusations, but Wallin had nonetheless managed to produce something which sounded almost objective, almost credible. The man obviously had good sources both within the Serner Group and the police. Admittedly the headline was innocuous—PROSECUTOR CRITICAL OF MIKAEL BLOMKVIST—and there was plenty of room in the story for Blomkvist to defend himself. But whichever one of his enemies was responsible understood media logic: if a news bureau as serious as TT publishes a story like this one, not only does that make it legitimate for everybody else to jump on the bandwagon, it just about requires them to take a tougher line. It explains why Blomkvist woke up to the online papers saying BLOMKVIST SABOTAGES MURDER INVESTIGATION and BLOMKVIST ATTEMPTS TO SAVE MAGAZINE. MURDERER RUNS FREE. The print media were good enough to put quotation marks around the headlines. But the overall impression was nevertheless that a new truth was being served up with the breakfast coffee. A columnist by the name of Gustav Lund, who claimed to be fed up with all the hypocrisy, began his piece by writing: "Mikael Blomkvist, who has always thought of himself as a cut above the rest, has now been unmasked as the biggest cynic of us all."

"Let's hope they don't start waving subpoenas at us," said Malm, designer and part owner of the magazine, as he stood next to Blomkvist, nervously chewing gum.

"Let's hope they don't call in the Marines," Blomkvist said.

"What?"

"It was meant to be a joke."

"I get it. I don't like the tone," Malm said.

"Nobody likes it. But the best we can do is grit our teeth and keep working as usual."

"Your phone's buzzing."

"It's always buzzing."

"How about answering it, before they come up with anything worse?"

"Yes, yes," Blomkvist muttered, and answered gruffly.

It was a girl. He thought he recognized the voice but, caught off guard, he could not at first place it.

"Who's that?" he said.

"Salander," said the voice, and at that he gave a big smile.

"Lisbeth, is that you?"

"Shut up and listen," she said. And so he did.

The traffic had eased and Salander and the taxi driver, a young man from Iraq named Ahmed who had lost his mother and two brothers in terrorist attacks, had emerged onto Sveavägen and passed the Stockholm Konserthuset on their left. Salander, who was a terrible passenger, sent off yet another text message to Lindén and tried to call some other member of the staff at Oden's, anybody who could run out and warn him. No reply. She swore aloud, hoping that Blomkvist would do better.

"Is it an emergency?" Ahmed said from the driver's seat.

When Salander replied "Yes," Ahmed shot the light and got a fleeting smile out of her.

After that she focused on every foot they covered. Away to the left she caught a glimpse of the School of Economics and the Public Library—it was not far to go now. She scanned for the street numbers on the right-hand side, and at last saw the address. Thankfully there was no-one lying dead on the sidewalk. Salander pulled out some hundred-kronor notes for Ahmed. It was an ordinary, dreary November day, no more than that, and people were on their way to work. But wait . . . She looked over towards the low, green-speckled wall on the other side of the street.

A powerfully built man in a woollen hat and dark glasses was standing there, staring intently at the entrance on Sveavägen. There was something about his body language—his right hand was not visible but the arm was tensed and ready. Salander looked again at the entrance to Oden's, to the extent that she could see anything from her oblique angle, and she noticed the door opening.

It opened slowly, as if the person about to come out were hesitant or finding the door heavy, and all of a sudden Salander shouted to Ahmed to stop. She jumped out of the moving car, just as the man across the street raised his right hand and aimed a pistol with a telescopic sight at the door as it slid open.

CHAPTER 17

NOVEMBER 22

The man who called himself Jan Holtser was not happy with the situation. The place was wide open and it was the wrong time of day. The street was too busy, and although he had done his best to cover his face, he was uncomfortable in daylight, and so near the park. More than ever he felt that he hated killing children.

But that's the way it was and he had to accept that the situation was of his own making.

He had underestimated the boy and now he had to correct his mistake. He must not let wishful thinking or his own demons get in the way. He would keep his mind on the job, be the professional he always was, and above all not think about Olga, still less recall that glassy stare which had confronted him in Balder's bedroom.

He had to concentrate now on the doorway across the street and on his Remington pistol, which he was keeping under his windbreaker. But why wasn't anything happening? His mouth felt dry. The wind was biting. There was snow lying in the street and on the sidewalk and people were hurrying back and forth to work. He tightened his grip on the pistol and glanced at his watch.

It was 9:16, and then 9:17. But still no-one emerged from the doorway across the road and he cursed: Was something wrong? All he had to go by was Bogdanov's word, but that was assurance enough. The man was a wizard with computers and last night he had sat engrossed in his work, sending off fake e-mails and getting the language right with the help of his contacts in Sweden. Holtser had taken care of the rest: studying pictures of the place, selecting the weapon, and above all organizing the getaway car—a rental which Dennis Wilton of the Svavelsjö Motorcycle Club had fixed for them under a false name, and which was now standing ready three blocks away, with Bogdanov at the wheel.

Holtser sensed a movement immediately behind him and jumped. But it was just two young men walking past a little too close to him. The street seemed to be getting busier and he did not like that. In the distance a dog was barking and there was a smell, maybe food frying at McDonald's, then . . . at long last . . . a short man in a grey overcoat and a curly-haired boy in a red quilted jacket could be seen through the glass door on the other side of the street. Holtser crossed himself with his left hand as he always did and started to squeeze the trigger on his weapon. But what was happening?

The door did not open. The man hesitated and looked down at his mobile. *Get a move on,* Holtser thought. *Here we go . . .* Slowly, slowly the door was pushed open and they were on their way out, and Holtser raised his pistol, aiming at the boy's face through the telescopic sight, and saw once more those glassy eyes. Suddenly he felt an unexpected, violent rush of excitement. Suddenly he did want to kill the boy. Suddenly he wanted to snuff out that frightening look, once and for all. But then something happened.

A young woman came running out of nowhere and threw herself over the boy as Holtser fired and hit on his target. He hit something, and shot again and again. But the boy and the woman had rolled behind a car, quick as lightning. Holtser caught his breath and looked right and left. Then he raced across the street, commando-style.

This time he was not going to fail.

Lindén had never been on satisfactory terms with telephones. His wife, Saga, leaped with anticipation at every call, hoping that it would bring a new job or a new offer; he felt uncomfortable whenever his mobile rang.

It was because of all the complaints. He and the medical centre were always taking abuse. In his view that was part of their business—Oden's was an emergency centre and so inevitably emotions tended to run high. But he also knew on some level that the complaints were justified. He may have driven his cost cutting too far. Occasionally he just ran away, went out to the woods and let the others get on with it. On the other hand, he did from time to time get recognition, most recently from no less a person than Professor Edelman.

The professor had irritated him at first. He did not like it when outsiders meddled in the way the clinic managed their procedures. But he felt more conciliatory since he had been praised in that e-mail. Who knows, he might even get the professor to support the idea of the boy staying on at Oden's for a while. That would add some spark to his life, although he could not quite understand why. As a rule he tended to keep himself apart from the children.

There was something enigmatic about this August Balder

which intrigued him. From the very first he had been irritated by the police and their demands. He wanted August to himself and hoped perhaps to capture some of the mystique surrounding the boy—or at least to be able to understand what those endless rows of numbers meant, the ones he had written on that comic in the playroom. But it was far from easy. The boy seemed to dislike any form of contact and now he was refusing to come out to the street. He was being hopelessly contrary, and Lindén was forced to drag him along.

"Come on, come *on*," he muttered.

Then his mobile buzzed. Somebody was determined to get hold of him.

He did not answer. Probably it was some trivial nonsense, yet another complaint. But as he reached the door, he decided to check his messages. There were several texts from a withheld number, and they were saying something strange, presumably some kind of a joke: they told him not to go outside. He was under no circumstances to go into the street.

Incomprehensible, and at that moment August seemed to want to run for it. Lindén took a firm grip on his arm, opened the door hesitantly, and pulled the boy out. Everything was normal. People walked by as they did every day and he wondered again about the text messages, but before he had time to complete the thought, a figure came rushing in from the left and threw itself over the boy. In that instant he heard a shot.

Obviously he was in danger. He looked around wildly and saw a tall, powerful man running towards him across Sveavägen. What the hell did he have in his hand? Was that a pistol?

Without a thought for August, Lindén turned to go back

through the door and for a second or two he thought he was going to make it to safety. But he never did.

Salander's reaction had been instinctive as she launched herself on top of the boy. She had hurt herself when she hit the sidewalk, or at least there was pain in her shoulder and chest. But she had no time to take stock. She took hold of the child and hid behind a car and they lay there breathing heavily while shots were fired. After that it became disturbingly quiet, and when Salander peered under the car she could see the sturdy legs of their attacker racing across the street. It crossed her mind to grab the Beretta from her sports bag and return fire, but she realized she would not have time. On the other hand . . . a large Volvo came crawling past, so she jumped to her feet and in one confused rush lifted the boy and ran towards the car. She wrenched open the back door and threw herself in with him.

"Drive!" she yelled as she saw blood spreading onto the seat.

Jacob Charro was twenty-two and the proud owner of a Volvo XC60, which he had bought on credit with his father as guarantor. He was on his way to Uppsala to have lunch with his uncle and aunt and cousins, and he was looking forward to it. He was dying to tell them that he'd gotten a place on Syrian FC's first team.

The radio was playing "Wake Me Up" by Avicii and he was drumming his fingers on the steering wheel as he drove past the Concert Hall and the Stockholm School of Economics. Something was going on further down the street. People were running in all directions. A man was shouting, and the cars in front of the Volvo were driving erratically, so Charro slowed down. If there had been an accident, he might be able to help. Charro was always dreaming of being a hero.

But this time he got a fright. The man to the left of him across the road ran into the traffic, looking like a soldier on an offensive. There was something brutal in his movements and Charro was about to floor the accelerator when he heard his rear door being yanked open. Someone had thrown themselves in. Charro started shouting, had no idea what. Maybe it was not even in Swedish. But the person—it was a girl with a child—yelled back.

"Drive!"

He hesitated for a second. Who *were* these people? Maybe they meant to rob him, or steal the car. He could not think straight, the whole situation was crazy. Then he had no choice but to act. His rear window was shattered because someone was shooting at them, so he accelerated wildly and with a pounding heart drove through a red light at the intersection with Odengatan.

"What's all this about?" he shouted. "What's going on?"

"Shut it!" the girl snapped back. In the rearview mirror he could see her examining the small boy with large terrified eyes, checking him over with practised movements, like a hospital nurse. Then he noticed for the first time that there was not just broken glass all over the backseat. There was blood too.

"Has he been shot?"

"I don't know. Just keep driving. Go left there . . . Now!"

"OK, OK," he said, terrified, and he took a hard left up

along Vanadisvägen and drove at high speed towards Vasastan, wondering if they were being followed and if anyone
would shoot at them again.

He lowered his head towards the steering wheel and felt
the draft through the broken rear window. What the hell had
he been dragged into, and who *was* this girl? He looked at
her again in the mirror. Black hair and piercings and a glowering look, and for a moment he felt that as far as she was
concerned he simply did not exist. But then she muttered
something which sounded almost cheerful.

"Good news?" he asked.

She did not answer. Instead she pulled off her leather
jacket, took hold of her white T-shirt, and then . . . Jesus! She
ripped it apart with a sudden jerk and was sitting there naked
from the waist up, not wearing a bra or anything, and he
glanced in bewilderment at her breasts, which stood straight
out, and above all at the blood that ran over them like a riv-
ulet, down towards her stomach and the waistband of her
jeans.

The girl had been hit somewhere below the shoulder,
not far above her heart, and was bleeding heavily. Using the
T-shirt for a bandage, she wound it tightly to staunch the
flow of blood and put her leather jacket back on. She looked
ridiculously pleased with herself, especially since some of the
blood had splashed onto her cheek and forehead, like war
paint.

"So the good news is that you got shot and not the boy,"
he said.

"Something like that," she said.

"Should I take you to the Karolinska hospital?"

"No."

. . .

Salander had found both the entry and exit holes. The bullet must have gone straight through the front of her shoulder, which was bleeding profusely—she could feel her heart pounding all the way up to her temples. But she did not think any artery had been severed, or at least so she hoped. She looked back. The attacker must have had a getaway car somewhere close by but nobody seemed to be following them. With any luck they had managed to escape fast enough.

She quickly looked down at the boy—August—who was sitting with his hands crossed over his chest, rocking backwards and forwards. It struck Salander that she ought to do something, so she brushed the glass fragments from the boy's hair and legs, and that made him sit still for a moment. Salander was not sure that was a good sign. The look in his eyes was rigid and blank. She nodded at him and tried to look as if she had the situation under control. She was feeling sick and dizzy and the T-shirt she had wound around her shoulder was by now soaked in blood. She was afraid that she might be losing consciousness and tried to come up with some sort of plan. One thing was crystal clear: the police were not an option. They had led the boy right into the path of the assailant and were plainly not on top of the situation. So what should she do?

She could not stay in this car. It had been seen at the shooting and the shattered rear window was bound to attract attention. She should get the man to drive her home to Fiskargatan. Then she could take her BMW, registered to Irene Nesser, if only she had the strength to drive it.

"Head towards Västerbron!" she ordered.

"OK, OK," said the man driving.

"Do you have anything to drink?"

"A bottle of whisky; I was going to give it to my uncle."

"Pass it back here," she said, and was handed a bottle of Grant's, which she opened with difficulty.

She tore off her makeshift bandage and poured whisky onto the bullet wound. She took one, two, three big mouthfuls, and was just offering some to August when it dawned on her that that was perhaps not such a good idea. Children don't drink whisky. Not even children in shock. Her thoughts were getting confused, was that what was happening?

"You'll have to give me your shirt," she said to the man up front.

"What?"

"I need something else to bandage my shoulder with."

"OK, but—"

"No buts."

"If you want me to help you, you could at least tell me why you were being shot at. Are you criminals?"

"I'm trying to protect the boy, it's that simple. Those bastards were after him."

"Why?"

"None of your business."

"So he's not your son."

"I don't even know him."

"So why are you helping him?"

Salander hesitated.

"We have the same enemies," she said. At that the young man pulled off his V-necked pullover—with a certain amount of reluctance and difficulty—as he steered the car with his other hand. Then he unbuttoned his shirt, took it off, and handed it back to Salander, who wound it gingerly around her shoulder. August, who was worryingly immobile now, looked down at his skinny legs with a frozen expression, and once again Salander asked herself what she ought to do.

They could hide out at her place on Fiskargatan. Blomkvist was the only person who knew the address, and the apartment could not be traced through her name on any public register. But it was still a risk. There had been a time when she was known up and down the country as a complete lunatic, and this enemy was certainly skilled at digging up information.

Someone on Sveavägen might have recognized her, the police might already be turning everything upside down to find her. She needed a new hiding place, not linked to any of her identities, and so she needed help. But from whom? Holger?

Her former guardian Holger Palmgren had almost recovered from his stroke and was living in a two-room apartment on Liljeholmstorget. Holger was the only person who really knew her. He was loyal to a fault and would do everything in his power to help. But he was elderly and anxious and she did not want to drag him into this if she could help it.

There was Blomkvist, of course, and in fact there was nothing wrong with him. Still, she was reluctant to contact him again—perhaps *precisely* because there was nothing wrong with him. He was such a damn good person. But what the hell . . . you could hardly hold that against him, or at least not too much. She called his mobile. He picked up after just one ring, sounding alarmed.

"It's such a relief to hear your voice! What the hell happened?"

"I can't tell you now."

"It looks like one of you's been shot. There's blood here."

"The boy's OK."

"And you?"

"I'm OK."

"You've been shot."

"You'll have to wait, Blomkvist."

She looked out at the town and saw that they were close to Västerbron already. She turned to the driver:

"Pull up there, by the bus stop."

"Are you getting out?"

"*You're* getting out. You're going to give me your mobile and wait outside while I talk. Is that clear?"

He glanced at her, terrified, then passed back his mobile, stopped the car, and got out. Salander continued her conversation.

"What's going on?" Blomkvist said.

"Don't you worry about that," she said. "From now on I want you to carry an Android phone with you, a Samsung or something. You must have one at the office?"

"Yes, I think there are a couple."

"Good. So go straight into Google Play and download the RedPhone app and also the Threema app for text messaging. We need a secure line of communication."

"Right."

"If you're as much of an idiot as I think you are, whoever helps you do it has to remain anonymous. I don't want any weak points."

"Of course."

"And then . . ."

"Yes?"

"Only use it in an emergency. All other communication should be through a special link on your computer. You or the person who isn't an idiot needs to go into www.pgpi.org and download an encryption programme for your e-mails. I want you to do that right now, then I want you to find a safe hiding place for the boy and me—somewhere not connected to you or *Millennium,* and let me have the address in an encrypted e-mail."

"It's not your job to keep the boy safe, Lisbeth."

"I don't trust the police."

"Then we'll have to find someone else you *do* trust. The boy is autistic, he has special needs, I don't think you should be responsible for him, especially not if you're wounded . . ."

"Are you going to keep talking crap or do you want to help me?"

"Help you, of course."

"Good. Check [*Lisbeth stuff*] in five minutes. I'll give you more information there. Then delete it."

"Lisbeth, listen to me, you need to get to a hospital. You need to be fixed up. I can tell by your voice . . ."

She hung up, waved the young man back in from the bus stop, got out her laptop, and through her mobile hacked into Blomkvist's computer. She wrote out instructions on how to download and install the encryption programme.

She then told the man to drive her to Mosebacke torg. It was a risk, but she had no choice. The city was beginning to look more and more blurred.

Blomkvist swore under his breath. He was standing on Sveavägen, not far from the body of Torkel Lindén and the cordon which the police who had been first on the scene were putting in place. Ever since Salander's original call he had been engaged in a frenzy of activity. He had thrown himself into a taxi to get here and had done everything he could during the trip to stop the boy and the director from stepping out onto the street.

The only other member of the staff he had managed to get hold of at Oden's Medical Centre was Birgitta Lindgren, who had rushed into the hallway only to see her colleague fall against the door with a fatal bullet wound to his head. When Blomkvist arrived ten minutes later she was beside herself, but she and another woman by the name of Ulrika Franzén, who had been on her way to the offices of Albert Bonniers, the publishers further up the street, had still been able to give Blomkvist a pretty coherent account of what had happened.

Which was why Blomkvist knew, even before his mobile rang again, that Salander had saved August Balder's life. She and the boy were now in some car with a driver who had no reason to be enthusiastic about helping them after getting shot at. Blomkvist had seen the blood on the sidewalk and on the street and, even though the call reassured him somewhat, he was still extremely concerned. Salander had sounded in a bad way and yet—not that it surprised him—she had been as pig-headed as ever.

She had a gunshot wound, but she was determined to hide the boy herself. That was understandable, given her history, but should he and the magazine get involved? However heroic her actions on Sveavägen, what she had done might from a legal point of view be seen as kidnapping. He could not help her with that. He was already in trouble with the media as well as the public prosecutor.

But this was Salander, after all, and he had given his word. He would damn well help her, even if Berger threw a fit. He took a deep breath and pulled out his mobile. But a familiar voice was calling out behind him. It was Jan Bublanski. Bublanski came running along the sidewalk close to physical collapse, and with him were Detective Sergeant Modig and a tall, athletic man in his fifties, presumably the professor Salander had mentioned.

"Where's the boy?" Bublanski panted.

"He was whisked away in a big red Volvo, somebody rescued him."

"Who?"

"I'll tell you what I know," Blomkvist said, not sure what he would or should say. "But first I have to make a call."

"Oh no, first you're going to talk to us. We have to send out a nationwide alert."

"Talk to that lady over there. Her name is Ulrika Franzén. She knows more than I do. She saw it happen; she's even got some sort of description of the assailant. I arrived after it happened."

"And the man who saved the boy?"

"The *woman* who saved him. Fru Franzén has a description of her as well. But just give me a minute here . . ."

"How did you know something was going to happen in the first place?" Modig spat, with unexpected anger. "They said on the radio that you had called the emergency services before any shots were fired."

"I had a tip-off."

"From whom?"

Blomkvist took another deep breath and looked Modig straight in the eye, unmoveable as ever.

"Whatever may have been written in today's papers, I hope you realize that I want to cooperate with you in every way I can."

"I've always trusted you, Mikael. But I'm beginning to have my doubts," Modig said.

"OK, I understand that. But you have to understand that *I* don't trust *you* either. There's been a serious leak; you've grasped that much, haven't you? Otherwise this wouldn't have happened," he said, pointing at the prone body inside the cordon.

"That's true, and it's absolutely terrible," Bublanski said.

"I'm going to make my call now," Blomkvist said, and he walked up the street so he could talk undisturbed.

But he never made the call. He realized that the time had come to get serious about security, so he walked back and informed Bublanski and Modig that he had to go to his office immediately, but he was at their disposal whenever they needed him. At that moment, to her own surprise, Modig took hold of his arm.

"First you have to tell us how you knew that something was going to happen," she said sharply.

"I'm afraid I have to invoke my right to protect my sources," Blomkvist answered, with a pained smile.

Then he waved down a taxi and took off for the office, deep in thought. *Millennium* used Tech Source, a consultancy firm with a team of young women who gave the magazine quick and efficient help, whenever they had more complex IT issues. But he did not want to bring them in. Nor did he feel like turning to Christer Malm, even though he knew more about IT than anyone on the editorial team. Instead he thought of Zander, who was already involved in the story and was also great with computers. Blomkvist decided to ask for his help, and promised himself that he would fight to get the boy a permanent job—provided that he and Berger managed to sort out this mess.

Berger's morning had been a nightmare even before shots were fired on Sveavägen, and that was due to the sickening TT bulletin. To some extent it was a continuation of the old campaign against Blomkvist—all the jealous, twisted souls came crawling out of the woodwork again, spewing their bile on Twitter and online forums and in e-mails. This time the racist mob joined in, because *Millennium* had been in the forefront of the battles against xenophobia and racism for many years.

The worst part was surely that this hate campaign made it so much more difficult for everyone to do their jobs. All of a sudden people were less inclined to share information with the magazine. On top of that there was a rumour that Chief Prosecutor Ekström was planning to issue a search warrant for the magazine's offices. Berger did not really believe it. That kind of warrant was a serious matter, given the right to source protection.

But she did agree with Christer Malm that the toxic atmosphere would even give lawyers ludicrous ideas about how they should act. She was standing there thinking about how to retaliate when Blomkvist stepped into the offices. To her surprise, he did not want to talk to her. Instead he went straight to Zander and ushered him into her room.

After a while she followed. She found the young man looking tense. She heard Blomkvist mention "PGP." She had taken an IT security course so she knew what that meant, and she saw Zander making notes before; without so much as a glance in her direction, he made a beeline for Blomkvist's laptop in the open-plan office.

"What was all that about?" she said.

Blomkvist told her in a whisper. She could barely take it in, and he had to repeat himself.

"So you want me to find a hiding place for them?"

"Sorry to drag you into this, Erika," he said. "But I don't know anyone who has as many friends with summer houses as you do."

"I don't know, Mikael. I really don't know."

"We can't let them down. Salander has been shot. The situation is desperate."

"If she's been shot, she should go to a hospital."

"She won't. She wants to protect the boy at all costs."

"To give him the calm he needs to draw the murderer."

"Yes."

"It's too great a responsibility, Mikael, too great a risk. If something happens, the fallout would destroy the magazine. Witness protection is not our job. This is something for the police—just think of all the questions that will be thrown up by those drawings, both for the investigation and on a psychological level. There has to be another solution."

"Maybe—if we were dealing with someone other than Lisbeth Salander."

"You know what? I get really pissed off with the way you always defend her."

"I'm only trying to be realistic. The authorities have let the Balder boy down and put his life in danger—I know that infuriates Salander."

"So we just have to go along with it, is that it?"

"We don't have a choice. She's out there somewhere, hopping mad, and has nowhere to go."

"Take them to Sandhamn, then."

"There's too much of a connection between Lisbeth and me. If it comes out that it's her, they would search my addresses straightaway."

"OK then."

"OK then, what?"

"OK, I'll find something."

She could hardly believe she was saying it. That is how it was with Blomkvist—she was incapable of saying no—but there was no limit to what he would do for her either.

"Great, Ricky. Where?"

She tried to think, but her mind was a blank. She could not come up with a single name.

"I'm racking my brains," she said.

"Well, do it quickly, then give the address and directions to Andrei. He knows what to do."

Berger needed some air and so she went down onto Götgatan and walked in the direction of Medborgarplatsen, running through one name after another in her mind. But not one of them felt right. There was too much at stake. Everyone she thought of had some drawback or, even if not, she was reluctant to expose them to the risk or put them to the trouble by asking, perhaps because she herself was so upset by the situation. On the other hand . . . here was a small boy and people were trying to kill him and she had promised. She had to come up with something.

A police siren wailed in the distance and she looked over towards the park and the tunnelbana station and at the mosque on the hill. A young man went by, surreptitiously shuffling some papers, and then suddenly—*Gabriella Grane*. At first the name surprised her. Grane was not a close friend and she worked at a place where it was unwise to flout any laws. Grane would risk losing her job if she so much as got near this, and yet . . . Berger could not get the idea out of her head.

It was not just that Grane was an exceptionally good and responsible person. A memory also kept intruding. It was from the summer, in the early hours of the morning or maybe even at daybreak after a crayfish party out at Grane's summer house on Ingarö island, when the two had been sitting in a garden swing on the terrace looking down at the water through a gap in the trees.

"This is where I'd run to if the hyenas were after me," Berger had said without really knowing what she meant. She had been feeling tired and vulnerable at work, and there was something about that house which she thought would make it an ideal place of refuge.

It stood on a rock promontory with steep, smooth sides, and was shielded from onlookers by the surrounding trees and elevation. She remembered Grane replying, "If the hyenas come after you, you're welcome to hide here, Erika."

Maybe it was asking too much, but she decided to give it a try. She went back to the office to call from the encrypted Red-Phone app, which Zander had by then installed for her too.

CHAPTER 18

NOVEMBER 22

Gabriella Grane was on her way to a meeting at Säpo when her personal mobile buzzed. The meeting had been called at very short notice to discuss the incident at Sveavägen. She answered tersely:

"Yes?"

"It's Erika."

"Hi there. Can't talk now. We'll speak later."

"I have a . . ." Berger said.

But Grane had already hung up—this was no time for personal calls. She walked into the meeting room wearing an expression that suggested she meant to start a minor war. Crucial information had been leaked and now a second person was dead and one more apparently seriously wounded. She had never felt more like telling the whole lot of them to go to hell. They had been so eager to get hold of new information that they had lost their heads. For half a minute she did not hear one word her colleagues were saying. She just sat there, seething. But then she pricked up her ears.

Someone was saying that Mikael Blomkvist, the journalist, had called the emergency services before shots were fired

on Sveavägen. That was strange, and now Erika Berger had
called, and she was not the type to make casual calls, certainly
not during working hours. She may have had something
important or even critical to say. Grane got up and made an
excuse.

"Gabriella, you need to listen to this," Kraft said in an
unusually sharp tone.

"I have to take a call," she replied, and suddenly she was
not in the least interested in what the head of the Security
Police thought of her.

"What sort of call?"

"A call," she said, and left them to go into her office.

Berger at once asked Grane to call her instead on the Samsung. The minute she had her friend on the line again, she
could tell that something was going on. There was none of
the usual warm enthusiasm in her voice. On the contrary,
Grane sounded worried and tense, as if she knew from the
start that the conversation was important.

"Hi," she said simply. "I'm still really pushed. But is it
about August Balder?"

Berger felt acutely uncomfortable.

"How did you know?"

"I'm on the investigation and I've just heard that Mikael
Blomkvist was tipped off about what was going to happen
on Sveavägen."

"You've already heard that?"

"Yes, and now of course we're eager to know how that
came about."

"Sorry. I can't tell you."

"OK. Understood. But why did you call?"

Berger closed her eyes. How could she have been such an idiot?

"I'm so sorry. I'll have to ask somebody else," she said. "You have a conflict of interest."

"I'm happy to take on almost any conflict of interest, Erika. But I can't stand your withholding information. This investigation means more to me than you can imagine."

"Really?"

"Yes, it does. I knew that Balder was under serious threat, yet I still couldn't prevent the murder, and I'm going to have to live with that for the rest of my life. So please, don't hide anything from me."

"I'm going to have to, Gabriella. I'm sorry. I don't want you to get into trouble because of us."

"I saw Mikael in Saltsjöbaden the night before last, the night of the murder."

"He didn't mention that."

"It wouldn't have made sense to identify myself."

"I understand."

"We could help each other out in this mess."

"That sounds like a good idea. I can ask Mikael to call you later. But now I have to get on with this."

"I know just as well as you do that there's a leak in the police team. At this stage we could benefit from unlikely alliances."

"Absolutely. But I'm sorry, I have to press on."

"OK," Grane said, obviously disappointed. "I'll pretend this call never happened. Good luck now."

"Thanks," Berger said, and went back to searching through her contacts.

· · ·

Grane went back to the meeting room, her mind whirling. What was it that Erika had wanted? She did not fully understand and yet she had a vague idea. As she came back into the room the conversation died and everyone looked at her.

"What was that about?" Kraft said.

"Something private."

"That you had to deal with now?"

"That I had to deal with. How far have you gotten?"

"We were talking about what happened on Sveavägen," said Ragnar Olofsson, the head of the division. "But as I was saying, we don't yet have enough information. The situation is chaotic, and it looks as if we're losing our source in Bublanski's group. The detective inspector has become paranoid."

"You can't blame him," Grane said.

"Well . . . perhaps not. We've talked about that too. We'll leave no stone unturned until we know how the attacker figured out that the boy was at the medical centre and that he was going to go out by the front door when he did. No effort will be spared, I need hardly say. But I must emphasize that the leak did not necessarily come from within the police. The information was quite widely known—at the medical centre of course, by the mother and her unreliable partner, Lasse Westman, and in the offices of *Millennium*. And we can't rule out hacker attacks. I'll come back to that. If I might continue with my report?"

"Please."

"We've been discussing how Mikael Blomkvist comes into all this, and this is where we're worried. How could he know about a shooting before it happens? In my opinion, he's got some source close to the criminals themselves, and I see no reason for us to tiptoe around his efforts to protect those sources. We have to find out where he got his information from."

"The more so since he seems desperate and will do anything for a scoop," Superintendent Mårten Nielsen added.

"It would appear that Mårten has some excellent sources too. He reads the evening papers," Grane said acidly.

"Not the evening papers, sweetie. TT—a source which even we at Säpo regard as fairly reliable."

"That was defamatory, and you know it as well as I do," Grane hissed.

"I had no idea you were so besotted with Blomkvist."

"Idiot!"

"Stop it at once," Kraft said. "This is ridiculous behaviour! Carry on, Ragnar. What do we know about what happened?"

"The first people on the scene were two regular police officers, Erik Sandström and Tord Landgren," Olofsson said. "My information comes from them. They were there on the dot of 9:24, and by then it was all over. Torkel Lindén was dead, shot in the back of the head, and the boy, well, we don't know. According to witnesses, he was hit too. We have blood in the street. But nothing is confirmed. The boy was driven away in a red Volvo—we do at least have parts of the registration number plus the model of the vehicle. I anticipate that we'll get the name of its owner pretty soon."

Grane noticed that Kraft was writing everything down, just as she had done at their earlier meetings.

"But what actually happened?" she asked.

"According to two students from the School of Economics who were standing on the opposite side of Sveavägen, it looked like a settling of scores between two criminal gangs who were both after the boy."

"Sounds far-fetched."

"I'm not so sure," Olofsson said.

"What makes you say that?" Kraft said.

"There were professionals on both sides. The assailant seems to have been standing and watching the door from a low green wall on the other side of Sveavägen, in front of the park. There's a lot to suggest that he's the man who shot Frans Balder. Not that anyone has seen his face; it's possible he was wearing some sort of mask. But he seems to have moved with the same remarkable efficiency and speed. And in the opposite camp there was this woman."

"What do we know about her?"

"Not much. She was wearing a black leather jacket, we think, and dark jeans. She was young with black hair and piercings, a punk according to one witness, also short, but fierce. She appeared out of nowhere and shielded the boy with her body. The witnesses all agree that she was not some ordinary member of the public. She seemed to have training, or had at least found herself in similar situations before. Then there's the car—we have conflicting reports. One witness says it just happened to be driving by, and the woman and the boy threw themselves in more or less while it was moving. Others—especially those guys from the School of Economics—think the car was part of the operation. Either way, I'm afraid we have a kidnapping on our hands."

"It doesn't make sense. This woman saved the boy only to abscond with him?" Grane said.

"That's what it looks like. Otherwise we would have heard from her by now, wouldn't we?"

"How did she get to Sveavägen?"

"We don't know yet. But a witness, a former editor-in-chief of a trade union paper, says the woman looked somehow familiar," Olofsson said.

He went on to say something else, but by then Grane had stopped listening. She was thinking: "Zalachenko's daughter, it has to be Zalachenko's daughter," knowing full well how unfair it was to call her that. The daughter had nothing to do with the father. On the contrary, she had hated him. But Grane had known her by that name ever since, years earlier, she had read everything she could lay her hands on about the Zalachenko affair.

While Olofsson continued speculating she began to feel the pieces falling into place. Already the day before she had identified some commonalities between Zalachenko's old network and the group which called itself the Spiders, but had dismissed them. She had believed there was a limit to how far thuggish criminals could develop their skills; it seemed entirely unreasonable to suppose that they could go from seedy-looking biker types in leather vests to cutting-edge hackers. Yet the thought had occurred to her. Grane had even wondered if the girl who helped Linus Brandell trace the break-in on Balder's computers might have been Zalachenko's daughter. There was a Säpo file on the woman, with a note that said "Hacker? Computer savvy?" and even though it seemed prompted by the surprisingly favourable reference she had received for her work at Milton Security, it was clear from the document that she had devoted a great deal of time to research into her father's criminal organization.

Most striking of all was that there was a known connection between the woman and Mikael Blomkvist. It was unclear what exactly that connection was—Grane did not for one moment believe the malicious rumours that it was sado-masochistic sex—but the connection was there. Both Blomkvist and the woman who matched the description of Zalachenko's daughter appeared to have known something about the shooting on Sveavägen beforehand, and afterwards Erika Berger had rung to discuss something important. Wasn't it all pointing in the same direction?

"I was wondering," Grane said, perhaps too loudly, interrupting Olofsson.

"Yes?" he said testily.

She was about to present her theory when she noticed something which made her hesitate.

It was nothing remarkable, just that Kraft was once again meticulously writing down what Olofsson had said. It was probably good to have a senior boss who was so committed, but there was something rather too zealous about that scratching pen, and it made Grane wonder why that senior boss, whose job it was to see the bigger picture, should be preoccupied with every tiny detail.

Without really knowing why, Grane began to feel very uneasy. It may have been because she was formulating suspicion on flimsy grounds. Then Kraft realized that she was being observed and looked away in embarrassment. It looked like she was blushing. Grane decided not to finish the sentence she had begun. "Or rather . . ."

"Yes, Gabriella?" Olofsson prompted.

"Oh, nothing," she said, feeling a sudden need to get away. Even though she knew it would not look good, she left the meeting room once more and went to the toilet.

Later she would remember how she stared at herself in the mirror and tried to understand what she had seen. Had Kraft blushed, and if so what did that mean? Maybe nothing, she decided, absolutely nothing, and even if it really was shame or guilt that Grane had read in her face it could have been about almost anything. It occurred to her that she did not know her boss all that well. But she knew enough to realize that Kraft would not send a child to his death for financial or any other gain, no, that was out of the question.

Grane had simply become paranoid, a typically suspicious spy who saw moles everywhere, even in her own reflection. "Idiot," she muttered, and smiled at herself despondently, as if to dismiss the idea and come back down to earth. But that didn't solve anything. In that instant she thought she saw a new kind of truth in her own eyes.

She suspected that she was quite like Helena Kraft in that she was capable and ambitious and wanted to get a pat on the back from her superiors. That was not necessarily always a good thing. With that tendency, if you operate in an unhealthy culture you risk becoming just as unhealthy yourself. Who knows, perhaps the will to please leads people to crime as often as evil or greed does. People want to fit in and do well, and they do indescribably stupid things because of it. Is that what happened here?

Hans Faste—because surely he was their source in Bublanski's group—had been leaking to them because that was what he was expected to do and because he wanted to score points with Säpo. Olofsson had seen to it that Kraft was kept informed of every little detail; she was his boss and he wanted to be in her good books. And then—well, maybe Kraft in turn had passed on some information because she wanted to be seen as doing a good job. But, if so, by whom? The head of the national police, the government, foreign intelligence, in that case most likely American or English, who perhaps then . . .

Grane did not take this thought any further. She asked herself again if she was letting her imagination run away with her. Even if she was, she still could not trust her team. She wanted to be good at her job, but not necessarily by doing her duty to Säpo. She just wanted the Balder boy to be all right. Instead of Kraft's face she now saw Berger's, so she went to her office and got out her Blackphone, the same one she had been using to call Frans Balder.

Berger had left the office to have an undisturbed conversation and was now standing in front of Söderbokhandeln, the bookstore on Götgatan, wondering if she had done something stupid. Grane had argued her case in such a way that Berger could not defend herself. That is no doubt the disadvantage of having intelligent friends. They see straight through you.

Not only had Grane worked out what Berger wanted to talk to her about, she had also persuaded her that she felt a moral responsibility and would never reveal the hiding place, however much that might appear to conflict with her professional ethics. She said she had a debt to repay and insisted on helping. She was going to courier over the keys to her summer house on Ingarö and arrange for directions to be sent via the encrypted link which Andrei Zander had set up.

Further up Götgatan a beggar collapsed, scattering two

carrier bags full of plastic bottles across the sidewalk. Berger hurried over, but the man, who was soon on his feet again, declined her help so she gave him a sad smile and went back up to the *Millennium* offices.

Blomkvist was looking upset and exhausted. His hair stood on end and his shirt hung outside his trousers. She had not seen him looking so worn out in a long time. Yet when his eyes shone like that, there was no stopping him. It meant he had entered into that absolute concentration from which he would not emerge until he had gotten to the heart of the story.

"Have you found a hiding place?" he said.

She nodded.

"It might be best if you say nothing more. We have to keep this to as small a circle of people as possible."

"That sounds sensible. But let's hope it's a short-term solution. I don't like the idea of Lisbeth Salander being responsible for the boy."

"Who knows, maybe they're good for each other."

"What did you tell the police?"

"Almost nothing."

"Not a good time to be keeping things under wraps."

"Not really, no."

"Maybe Salander is prepared to make a statement, so you can get some peace and quiet."

"I don't want to put any pressure on her. She's in bad shape. Can you get Zander to ask her if we can send a doctor out there?"

"I will. But you know . . ."

"What?"

"I'm actually coming round to the idea that she's doing the right thing," Berger said.

"Why do you say that, all of a sudden?"

"Because I too have my sources. Police headquarters isn't a secure place right now," she said, and walked over to Andrei Zander with a determined stride.

CHAPTER 19

NOVEMBER 22—EVENING

Bublanski was standing alone in his office. In the end Hans Faste had admitted to keeping Säpo informed, and without even listening to his justification Bublanski removed him from the investigation. But even if that had provided further evidence that Faste was an unscrupulous opportunist, he could not bring himself to believe that the man had also been leaking to criminals.

Inevitably there were corrupt and depraved people in the force. But to deliver a small, mentally disabled boy into the hands of a cold-blooded murderer was beyond the pale, and he refused to believe that any policeman would be capable of that. Perhaps the information had seeped out by some other route. Their phones might be tapped or they could have been hacked, though he could not remember notes about August's abilities being entered in any police computer. He had been trying to reach the Säpo head, Helena Kraft, to discuss the matter. He had stressed that it was important, but she had not returned his call.

The Swedish Trade Council and the Ministry of Enterprise had called him, which was worrisome. Even if it was not said in so many words, their main concern was not for the boy or the shooting on Sveavägen, but rather for the research programme which Frans Balder had been working on, which appeared to have been stolen on the night of his murder.

Several of the most skilled computer technicians in the force and three IT experts from Linköping University and the Royal Institute of Technology had been to the house in Saltsjöbaden, but they had found no trace of this research, either on his computers or among the papers which he had left behind.

"So now, on top of everything else, we have an Artificial Intelligence on the loose," Bublanski muttered to himself. He was reminded of an old riddle his mischievous cousin Samuel liked to put to his friends in synagogue. It was a paradox: If God is indeed omnipotent, is he then capable of creating something more intelligent than himself? The riddle was considered disrespectful, he recalled, even blasphemous. It had that evasive quality which meant that, however you answered, you were wrong. There was a knock at the door, and Bublanski was brought back to the questions at hand. It was Modig, ceremoniously handing over another piece of Swiss orange chocolate.

"Thank you," he said. "Have you got anything new?"

"We think we know how the killers got Lindén and the boy out of the building. They sent fake e-mails from our and Professor Edelman's addresses and arranged a pickup on the street."

"Is that possible?"

"Sure, it's not even very difficult."

"Terrifying."

"True, but that still doesn't explain how they knew to access the Oden's Medical Centre computer, or how they found out that Edelman was involved."

"I suppose we'd better have our own computers checked out," Bublanski said gloomily.

"Already in hand."

"Is this how it was meant to be, that we won't dare to write or say anything for fear of being overheard?"

"I don't know. I hope not. Meanwhile we have a Jacob Charro out there waiting to be interviewed."

"Who's he?"

"A footballer, plays for Syrian F.C. He's the one who drove the woman and August Balder away from Sveavägen."

A muscular young man with short dark hair and high cheek-bones was sitting in the interview room. He was wearing a mustard-coloured V-necked pullover without a shirt and seemed at once agitated and a little proud.

Modig opened with "6:35 p.m. on November 22. Interview with witness Jacob Charro, twenty-two years old, resident in Norborg. Tell us what happened this morning."

"Well . . ." Charro said. "I was driving along Sveavägen and noticed some commotion in the street ahead of me. I thought there'd been an accident, so I slowed down. But then I saw a man come from the left and run across the road. He ran out without even looking at the traffic and I remember thinking he must be a terrorist."

"Why is that?"

"He seemed to be bursting with this sacred fury."

"Were you able to see what he looked like?"

"Not really, but since then it's struck me that there was something unnatural about his face."

"What do you mean?"

"Like it wasn't his real face. He was wearing sunglasses, which must have been secured around his ears, but his cheeks, it looked as if he had something in his mouth, I don't know. Then there was his moustache and eyebrows, and the colour of his skin."

"Do you think he was wearing a mask?"

"Something like that. But I didn't have time to think too much about it. Before I knew it the rear door of the car was yanked open and then . . . what can I say? It was one of those moments when everything happens all at once, the whole world comes down on your head. Suddenly there were strangers in my car and the rear windscreen shattered. I was in shock."

"What did you do?"

"I accelerated like crazy. The girl who jumped in was shouting at me to drive, and I was so scared I hardly knew what I was doing. I just followed orders."

"Orders?"

"That's how it seemed. I reckoned we were being chased, and I didn't see any other way out. I kept swerving just like the girl told me to, and besides . . ."

"Go on."

"There was something about her voice. It was so cold and intense, I found myself hanging on to it, as if it were the only thing that was under control in the mayhem."

"You said you thought you recognized the woman?"

"Yes, but not at the time, definitely not. I was scared to death and was busy concentrating on all the weird things that were happening. There was blood all over the place."

"Coming from the boy or the woman?"

"I wasn't sure at first, and neither of them seemed to know. But then I heard her say 'Yes!,' like something good had happened."

"What was that about?"

"The girl realized she was the one bleeding and not the boy, and that really struck me. It was like, 'Hurray, I've been shot,' and I tell you, it wasn't some little graze. However she tried to bandage it, she couldn't staunch the blood. It just kept oozing out, and the girl kept getting paler and paler. She must have felt like shit."

"And still she was happy that it wasn't the boy who'd been hit."

"Exactly. Like a mother."

"But she wasn't the child's mother."

"No. They didn't even know each other, she said, and that became more and more obvious. She didn't have a clue about children."

"On the whole," Modig said, "how did you think she treated the boy?"

"Not sure how to answer that, to be honest. I wouldn't say she had the world's best social skills. She treated me like a damn servant, but even so . . ."

"Yes?"

"I reckon she was a good person. I wouldn't have liked her to babysit, if you see what I mean. But she was OK."

"So you think the child is safe with her?"

"She's obviously fucking crazy. But the little boy . . . he's called August, right?"

"That's right."

"She'll guard August with her life, if it came to it. That was my impression."

"How did you part company?"

"She asked me to drive them to Mosebacke torg."

"Is that where she lives, on the square?"

"I have no idea. She gave me no explanation whatsoever. I got the feeling she had some other kind of transport from there, but she didn't say more than was necessary. She just asked me to write down my details. She was going to pay for the damage to the car, she said, plus a little extra."

"Did she look as though she had money?"

"Going by her appearance alone, I'd say she lived in a dump. But the way she behaved . . . I don't know. It wouldn't surprise me if she was loaded. You could tell she was used to getting her own way."

"What happened then?"

"She told the boy to get out of the car."

"And did he?"

"He just rocked backwards and forwards and didn't move. But then her tone hardened. She said it was a matter of life and death or something like that, and he tottered out of the car with his arms stiff, as if he was sleepwalking."

"Did you see where they went?"

"Only that it was to the left—towards Slussen. But the girl . . ."

"Yes?"

"Well, she was obviously still feeling like shit. She was weaving about and seemed on the point of collapse."

"Doesn't sound good. And the boy?"

"Probably wasn't in great shape either. He was looking really odd. The whole time in the car I worried he was going to have some sort of fit. But when he got out he seemed to have come to terms with the situation. In any case he kept asking 'Where?' over and over, 'Where?'"

Modig and Bublanski looked at each other.

"Are you sure about that?" Modig said.

"Why shouldn't I be?"

"Well, you might have thought you heard him saying that because he had a questioning look on his face."

"Why would I have thought that?"

"Because the boy's mother says he doesn't speak at all, never has," Modig continued.

"Are you joking?"

"No, and it would be odd for him to suddenly start speaking under these very circumstances."

"I heard what I heard."

"OK, and what did the woman answer?"

"'Away,' I think. 'Away from here.' Something like that. Then she almost collapsed, like I said. And she told me to drive off."

"And you did?"

"Like a bat out of hell."

"And then you realized who you'd had in your car?"

"I'd already worked out that the boy was the son of that genius who'd been murdered. But the girl ... She vaguely reminded me of someone. I was shaking like a leaf and in the end I couldn't drive anymore. I stopped on Ringvägen, by Skanstull, got myself a beer at the Clarion Hotel and tried to calm down. And that's when it hit me. It was the girl who was wanted for murder a few years ago but then the charges were dropped, and it came out that she'd been through some terrible things in a mental hospital when she was a child. I remember it well; the father of a friend of mine had been tortured in Syria, and he was having more or less the same stuff done to him at the time, electroshock therapy and that sort of shit, because he couldn't deal with his memories. It was like he was being tortured all over again."

"Are you sure about that?"

"That he was tortured?"

"No, that it was her, Lisbeth Salander."

"I looked at all the pictures online and there's no doubt about it. There were other things that fit too, you know . . ."

Charro hesitated, as if embarrassed.

"She took off her T-shirt because she needed to use it as a bandage and when she turned to wrap it around her shoulder I saw that she had a large tattoo of a dragon all the way up her back. That same tattoo was mentioned in one of the old newspaper articles."

Berger arrived at Grane's summer house with several shopping bags filled with food, crayons and paper, a couple of difficult puzzles, and a few other things. But there was no sign of August or Salander. Salander had not responded, either on her RedPhone app or on the encrypted link. Berger was sick with anxiety.

Whichever way she looked at it, this did not bode well. Admittedly Salander was not known for unnecessary communication or reassurance, but it was she who had asked for a safe house. Also she had responsibility for a child, and if she was not answering their calls under those circumstances, she must be in a bad way.

Berger swore and walked out onto the terrace, to where she and Grane had been sitting and talking about escaping from the world. That was only a few months ago, but it felt like an age. There was no table now, no chairs, no bottles, no hubbub behind them, only snow, branches, and debris flung there by the storm. It was as if life itself had abandoned the place. Somehow the memory of that crayfish party increased the sense of desolation, as if the festivities were draped like a ghost over its walls.

Berger went back into the kitchen and put some microwaveable food into the refrigerator: meatballs, packets of spaghetti with meat sauce, sausage stroganoff, fish pie, potato cakes, and a whole lot of even worse junk food Blomkvist had advised her to buy: Billy's Pan Pizza, piroshki, chips, Coca-Cola, a bottle of Tullamore D.E.W., a carton of cigarettes, three bags of crisps, three bars of chocolate, and some sticks of fresh liquorice. She set out drawing paper, crayons, pencils, an eraser, and a ruler and compass on the large round table. On the top sheet of paper she drew a sun and a flower and wrote the word *WELCOME* in four warm colours.

The house was near Ingarö beach, but you could not see it from there. It lay high up on the rock promontory, concealed behind pine trees, and consisted of four rooms. The kitchen with glass doors onto the terrace was the largest and also the heart of the house. In addition to the round table there was an old rocking chair and two worn, sagging sofas which nonetheless managed to look inviting thanks to a pair of red tartan rugs. It was a cozy home.

It was also a good safe house. Berger left the door open,

put the keys in the top drawer of the hall closet, as agreed, and wandered down the long flight of wooden stairs flanking the steep, smooth rock slope—the only way to the house for anyone arriving by car.

The sky was dark and turbulent, the wind blowing hard again. Her spirits were low and did not improve during the drive home. Her thoughts turned to Hanna Balder. Berger had not exactly been a member of the fan club—Hanna often played the parts of women who were both sexy and dim-witted, whom all men thought they could seduce, and Berger was disgusted by the film industry's devotion to that type of character. But none of that was true any longer and Berger regretted that she had been so ungracious at the time. She had been too hard on the woman; it was only too easy to criticize a pretty girl who gets a big break early in her career.

Nowadays, on the rare occasions Hanna Balder appeared in a major production, her eyes tended to reflect a restrained sorrow, which gave depth to the parts she played, and—what did Berger know?—that may have been genuine. She had been through some difficult times, not least the past twenty-four hours.

Since morning Berger had been insisting that Hanna be taken to August. This was surely a situation in which a child needed his mother more than ever. But Salander, who was still communicating with them at the time, had been against the idea. No-one yet knew where the leak had come from, she had written, and they could not rule out the mother's immediate circle. Lasse Westman for one, whom nobody trusted, seemed to be staying in the house all day to avoid the journalists camped outside.

They were in a bind, and Berger did not like it. She hoped *Millennium* would still be able to tell the story with dignity and depth, without the magazine or anyone else coming to harm. She had no doubt that Blomkvist would be up to it, given the way he looked right now. Besides, he had Zander to help him.

Berger had a soft spot for Zander. Not long ago, over dinner at her and Greger's home in Saltsjöbaden, he had told them his life story, which had only increased her sympathy.

When Zander was eleven he lost both his parents in a bomb blast in Sarajevo. After that he came to live in Tensta outside Stockholm with an aunt who altogether failed to notice either his intellectual disposition or the psychological wounds he bore. He had not been there when his parents were killed, but his body reacted as if he were suffering from post-traumatic stress. To this day he detested loud noises and sudden movements. He hated seeing unattended bags in public places, and loathed violence with a passion Berger had never encountered before.

As a child he sought refuge in his own worlds. He immersed himself in fantasy literature, read poetry and biographies, adored Sylvia Plath, Borges and Tolkien, and learned everything there was to know about computers. He dreamed of writing heart-rending novels about love and human tragedy, and was an incurable romantic who hoped that great passion would heal his wounds. He was not in the least bit interested in the outside world. One evening in his late teens, however, he attended a public lecture given by Mikael Blomkvist at the Institute for Media Studies at Stockholm University, and it changed his life.

Blomkvist's fervour inspired him to bear witness to a world which was bleeding with injustice and intolerance and petty corruption. He started to imagine himself writing articles critical of society instead of tear-jerking romances. Not long after that he knocked on *Millennium*'s door and asked if there was anything they would let him do—make coffee, proofread, run errands. Berger, who had seen the fire in his eyes right from the start, assigned him some minor editorial tasks: public notices, research, and brief portraits. But most of all she told him to study, and he did so with the same energy he put into everything else. He read political science, mass media communications, finance, and international conflict resolution, and at the same time he helped out on temporary assignments at *Millennium*.

He wanted to become a heavyweight investigative journalist, like Blomkvist. But unlike so many other investigative journalists he was no tough guy. He remained a romantic. Blomkvist and Berger had both spent time trying to sort out his relationship problems. He was too open and transparent. Too good, as Blomkvist would say.

But Berger believed that Zander was in the process of shedding that youthful vulnerability. She had been seeing the change in his journalism. That ferocious ambition to reach out and touch people, which had made his writing heavy-handed at first, had been replaced by a more effective, matter-of-fact style. She knew he would pull out all the stops now that he had been given the chance to help Blomkvist with the Balder story. The plan was for Blomkvist to write the big, central narrative, and for Zander to help with the research as well as writing some explanatory sidebars. Berger thought they made a great team.

After parking on Hökens gata she walked into the offices and found Blomkvist and Zander sitting there, deep in concentration, just as she expected. Every now and then, Blomkvist muttered to himself and she saw that sense of purpose in his eyes, but there was also suffering. He had hardly slept all night. The media campaign against him had not let up and in his police interviews he had to do the very thing the press accused him of—withhold information. Blomkvist did not like it one bit.

He was in many ways a model, law-abiding citizen. But if there was anyone who could get him to cross the line, it was Lisbeth Salander. Blomkvist would rather dishonour himself than betray her, which is why he kept repeating to the police: "I assert my right to protect my sources." No wonder he was unhappy and worried about the consequences. But, like Berger, he had far greater fears for Salander and the boy than for their own situation.

"How's it going?" she asked, after watching him for a while.

"What? . . . Well . . . OK. How was it out there?"

"I made up the beds and put food in the fridge."

"Good. And the neighbours didn't see you?"

"There wasn't a soul out."

"Why are they taking so long?" he said.

"I don't know, but I'm worried sick."

"Let's hope they're resting at Lisbeth's."

"Let's hope so. What else did you find out?"

"Quite a bit. But . . ." Blomkvist trailed off.

"Yes?"

"It's just that . . . it feels as if I'm being thrown back in time, or going back to places I've been to before."

"You'll have to explain better," she said.

"I will . . ."

Blomkvist glanced at his computer screen.

"But first I have to keep on digging. Let's speak later," he said, and so she left him and got her things to drive home, although she would be ready to join him at a second's notice.

CHAPTER 20

NOVEMBER 23

The night had turned out to be calm, alarmingly calm, and at eight in the morning a brooding Bublanski stood facing his team in the meeting room. Having kicked out Faste, he felt reasonably sure that he could talk freely again. At least he felt safer in here with his colleagues than at his computer, or with his mobile.

"You all appreciate how serious the situation is," he said. "Confidential information has been leaked. One person is dead as a result. A small boy's life is in danger. In spite of immense efforts we still don't know how this happened. The leak could have been at our end, or at Säpo, or at Oden's Medical Centre, or in the group around Professor Edelman, or from the boy's mother and her partner, Lasse Westman. We know nothing for certain, and therefore we have to be *extremely* circumspect, paranoid even."

"We may also have been hacked or phone tapped," Modig said. "We seem to be dealing with criminals whose command of new technologies is far beyond anything we've seen before."

"Very true," Bublanski said. "We need to take precautions at every level, not say anything significant relating to this investigation—or to any other—over the telephone, no matter how highly our superiors rate our new mobile phone system."

"They think it's great because it cost so much to install," Holmberg said.

"Maybe we should also be reflecting a little on our own role," Bublanski said, ignoring him. "I was just talking to a gifted young analyst at Säpo, Gabriella Grane—you may have heard of her. She pointed out that the concept of loyalty is not as straightforward as one might think for us policemen. We have many different loyalties, don't we? There's the obvious one, to the law. There's a loyalty to the public, and to one's colleagues, but also to our bosses, and to ourselves and our careers. Sometimes, as you all know, these interests end up competing with each other. We might choose to protect a colleague at work and thereby fail in our duty to the public, or we might be given orders from higher up, like Hans Faste was, and then that conflicts with the loyalty he should have had to us. But from now on—and I'm deadly serious—there's only one loyalty I want to hear of, and that is to the investigation itself. We're going to catch the murderers and we're going to make sure that no-one else falls victim to them. Agreed? Even if the prime minister himself or the head of the CIA calls and goes on about patriotism and huge career opportunities, you still won't utter a peep, will you?"

"No," they all said in unison.

"Excellent. As we all know, the person who intervened on Sveavägen was none other than Lisbeth Salander, and we're doing everything in our power to locate her."

"Which is why we've got to release her name to the media!" Svensson called out, somewhat heatedly. "We need help from the public."

"We don't all agree on this, I know, so I'd like to raise the question again. Let's remember that in the past Lisbeth Salander has had some very shabby treatment, from us and from the media."

"At this point that doesn't matter," Svensson said.

"And it's conceivable that people recognized her on Sveavägen and her name will come out at any moment anyway. In which case this would no longer be an issue. But before that happens, keep in mind she saved the boy's life."

"No doubt about that," Svensson said. "But then she more or less kidnapped him."

"Our information suggests that she was determined to protect the boy at all costs," Modig said. "Salander's experience of public institutions has been anything but positive—her entire childhood was marred by the injustices inflicted on her by Swedish officialdom. If she suspects, as we do, that there's a leak inside the police force then there's no chance she's going to contact us. Fact."

"That's irrelevant," Svensson insisted.

"Maybe," Modig said. "Jan and I share your view that the most important thing here is whether it's in the interests of the investigation to release her name. And as to the investigation, our priority is the boy's safety, and that's where we have a big element of uncertainty."

"I follow your reasoning," Holmberg said in a low, thoughtful tone which immediately commanded everyone's attention. "If people know of Salander's involvement then the boy will be at risk. But that still leaves a number of questions—first: What's the ethical thing to do? And I have to say, even if there's been a leak here we cannot accept that Salander should keep the boy hidden away. He's a crucial part of the investigation and, leak or no leak, we're better at protecting a child than an emotionally disturbed young woman could ever be."

"Absolutely. Of course," Bublanski muttered.

"And even if this isn't a kidnapping in the ordinary sense—yes, even if it's been carried out with the best of intentions—the potential harm to the child could be just as great. Psychologically it must be hugely damaging for him to be, as it were, on the run after everything he's been through."

"True," Bublanski said. "But the question still remains: How do we handle the information we have?"

"There I agree with Curt. We have to release her name and photo right away. It could produce invaluable leads."

"Probably," Bublanski said. "But it could at the same time give the killers invaluable leads. We have to assume that they haven't given up looking for the boy—quite the opposite, in fact—and since we have no idea what the connection is between the boy and Salander, we don't know what sort of clues her name would provide them with. I'm not persuaded that we would be protecting the boy by giving the media these details."

"But neither do we know if we're protecting him by holding them back," Holmberg said. "There are too many pieces of the puzzle missing for us to draw any conclusions. Is Salander doing this for someone else, for example? Does she have her own agenda for the child, other than to protect him?"

"And how could she have known that the boy and Torkel Lindén would come out onto Sveavägen at that exact moment?" Svensson said.

"Maybe she just happened to be there."

"Doesn't seem likely."

"The truth is often unlikely," Bublanski said. "That's the nature of truth. But I agree, it doesn't feel like a coincidence, not under the circumstances."

"What about the fact that Mikael Blomkvist also knew something was going to happen?" Amanda Flod said.

"There's some sort of connection between Blomkvist and Salander," Holmberg said.

"True."

"Blomkvist knew that the boy was at Oden's Medical Centre, didn't he?"

"The mother told him," Bublanski said. "As you might imagine, she's feeling desperate right now. I've just had a long conversation with her. But there was no reason on earth why Blomkvist should have known that the boy and Lindén would be tricked into going out onto the street."

"Could he have had access to a computer at Oden's?" Flod said pensively.

"I can't imagine Mikael Blomkvist getting involved in hacking," Modig said.

"But what about Salander?" Holmberg said. "What do we actually know about her? We have a massive file on the girl. Yet the last time we had anything to do with her, she surprised us on every count. Maybe appearances are just as deceptive this time around."

"I agree," Svensson said. "We have far too many question marks."

"Question marks are about all we have. And that's exactly why we ought to stick to the rules," Holmberg said.

"I didn't realize the rule book covered quite so much," Bublanski said, with a sarcasm even he did not like.

"I only mean that we should take this for what it is—the

kidnapping of a child. They disappeared almost twenty-four hours ago. We haven't heard a word from them. We should put out Salander's name and picture and then look carefully at all the tip-offs that come in," Holmberg said with authority. He seemed to have the backing of the whole group, and at that Bublanski closed his eyes and reflected that he loved them all. He felt a greater affinity with his team than he did for his own brothers and sisters, or even his parents. But right now he felt compelled to disagree with them.

"We'll do everything we can to try to find them. But for the time being we will not release the name and picture. That would only make the situation more fraught, and I don't want to risk giving the killers any leads at all."

"And you feel guilty," Holmberg said, without warmth.

"I feel very guilty," Bublanski said, thinking again of his rabbi.

Blomkvist was so worried about the boy and Salander that he had hardly slept. Time and again he had tried to reach Salander on her RedPhone app, but she had not answered. He had not heard a word from her since yesterday afternoon. Now he was sitting in the office, trying to immerse himself in his work and figure out what it was that had escaped him. For some time already he had had a sense—impossible to put his finger on—that there was a key piece missing, something which could shed light on the whole story. Perhaps he was fooling himself. Maybe it was just wishful thinking, a need to see a grand design. The last message from Salander on the encrypted link was:

```
<Jurij Bogdanov. Check him out. He's the
one who sold Balder's technology to Ecker-
wald at Solifon.>
```

There were some images of Bogdanov online. They showed him wearing pin-striped suits which fit perfectly but still managed to look wrong on him, as if he had stolen them on the way to the photographer's. Bogdanov had long, lank hair, a pockmarked face, and large rings under his eyes, and you could just about make out some amateurish tattoos beneath his shirt cuffs. His look was dark, intense, and piercing. He was tall but cannot have weighed more than 130 pounds.

He looked like an old jailbird, but most striking: there was something about his body language which Blomkvist recognized from the images on the surveillance cameras at Balder's place. The man gave the same tattered, rough-edged impression.

There were also interviews he had given as a businessman in Berlin in which he vouchsafed that he had been born more or less on the streets. "I was doomed to end up dead in an alleyway with a needle stuck in my arm. But I managed to pull myself out of the muck. I'm intelligent and I'm one hell of a fighter," he said. There was nothing in the details of his life to contradict these claims, save for the suspicion that he may not have been raised exclusively through his own efforts. There were clues to suggest he had been given a helping hand by powerful people who had spotted his talent. In a German technology magazine, a security chief at the Horst credit institution was quoted as saying, "Bogdanov has magic in his eyes. He can detect vulnerabilities in security systems like no-one else. He's a genius."

So Bogdanov was a star hacker, although the official version had him acting only as a "white hat," someone who served the good, legal side, who helped companies identify flaws in their IT security in exchange for decent compensation. There was nothing in the least suspicious about his company, Outcast Security. The board members were all respectable, well-educated people. But Blomkvist did not leave it at that. He and Zander scrutinized every individual who had had any contact with the company, even partners of partners, and they noticed that somebody called Orlov had been a deputy board member only for a short time, which seemed strange. Vladimir Orlov was no IT man, but a minor player in the construction sector. He had once been a promising heavyweight boxer in the Crimea and, judging by the few pictures Blomkvist found online, he looked ravaged and brutal.

There were rumours that he had been convicted of assault and procuring. He had been married twice—both wives were dead, and Blomkvist had not been able to find a cause of death in either case. But the most interesting discovery he made was that the man had served as a substitute board member of a company—minor and long since defunct—by the name of Bodin Construction & Export, which had dealt in "sales of construction materials."

The owner of the company had been Karl Axel Bodin, the alias of Alexander Zalachenko, a name that revived memories of the evil conspiracy which became the subject of *Millennium*'s greatest scoop. Zalachenko, who was Salander's father, and her dark shadow, the black heart behind her throbbing determination to exact revenge.

Was it a coincidence that his name cropped up? Blomkvist knew better than anyone that if you dig deep enough into a story, you will always find links. Life is constantly treating us to illusory connections. It was just that when it came to Lisbeth Salander, he stopped believing in coincidence.

If she broke a surgeon's fingers or delved into the theft of some advanced AI technology, you could be sure that she had not only thought it through to the last particle, she would also have a reason. Salander was not one to forget an injustice. She retaliated and she righted wrongs. Could her involvement in this story be connected to her own background? It was by no means inconceivable.

Blomkvist looked up from his computer and glanced at Zander. Zander nodded back at him. The faint smell of something cooking was coming from the kitchen. Thudding rock music could be heard from Götgatan. Outside the storm was howling, and the sky was still dark and wild. Blomkvist went into the encrypted link out of habit, not expecting to find anything. But then his face lit up. He even let out a small whoop of joy.

It said:

```
<OK now. We'll be going to the safe house
shortly.>
```

He wrote:

```
<Great news. Drive carefully.>
```

Then he could not resist adding:

<Who are we actually after?>

She answered at once:

<You'll soon work it out, smartarse!>

"OK" was an exaggeration. Salander was better, but still in bad shape. For half of yesterday, in her apartment, she had been barely conscious and only managed with the greatest difficulty to drag herself out of bed to see that August had something to eat and drink and make sure he had pencils, crayons, and paper. But as she approached him now she could see even from a distance that he had drawn nothing.

There was paper scattered all over the coffee table in front of him, but no drawings. Instead she saw rows of scribbles. More absentmindedly than out of curiosity she tried to make out what they were—he had written numbers, endless series of numbers, and even if at first they made no sense to her, she was intrigued. Suddenly she gave a whistle.

"Oh my God," she muttered.

They were staggeringly large numbers, which formed a familiar pattern alongside the numbers next to them. As she looked through the papers and came across the simple sequence 641, 647, 653, and 659, there was no longer any doubt: they were sexy prime quadruplets, sexy in the sense that they differed from each other by six.

There were also twin primes, and every other imaginable combination of prime numbers. She could not help but smile. "Wicked."

But August neither responded nor looked up at her. He just kept kneeling by the coffee table, as if he wanted nothing more than to go on writing his numbers. It occurred to her that she had read something about savants and prime numbers, but she put it out of her mind. She was far too unwell for any kind of advanced thinking. Instead she went into the bathroom and took two more Vibramycin antibiotics which had been lying around in her apartment for years.

She packed her pistol and her computer, a few changes of clothes, and to be on the safe side she put on a wig and a pair of dark glasses. When she was ready she asked the boy to get up. He did not respond, just held his pencil in a tight grip. For a moment she stood in front of him, stumped. Then she said sternly, "Get up!," and he did.

They put on their outer layers, took the lift down to the garage, and set off in her BMW for the safe house on Ingarö. Her left shoulder was tightly strapped and it ached, so she steered with her right hand. The top of her chest was hurting, she had a fever and had to stop a couple of times at the side of the road to rest. When finally they got to the beach and the jetty by Stora Barnvik on Ingarö, and followed the directions to climb the wooden stairs alongside the slope to the house, she collapsed exhausted on the first bed she saw. She was shivering and freezing cold.

Soon after, breathing laboriously, she got up and sat at the kitchen table with her laptop, trying once more to crack the file she had downloaded from the NSA. But she did not even come close. August sat next to her, looking stiffly at the pile of paper and crayons Berger had left for him, no longer interested in prime numbers, still less in drawing pictures. Perhaps he was in shock.

The man who called himself Jan Holtser was sitting in a room at the Clarion Hotel Arlanda talking on the telephone with his daughter. As he had expected, she did not believe him.

"Are you scared of me?" she said. "Are you afraid I'm going to cross-examine you?"

"No, Olga, absolutely not," he said. "It's just that . . ."

He could not find the words. He knew Olga could tell he was hiding something, and ended the conversation sooner than he wanted to. Bogdanov was sitting next to him on the hotel bed, swearing. He had been through Balder's computer at least a hundred times and found "fuck all," as he put it. "Not a single fucking thing!"

"I stole a computer with nothing on it," Holtser said.

"Right."

"So what was the professor using it for?"

"For something very important, clearly. I can see that a large file, presumably connected to other computers, was deleted recently. But I can't recover it. He knew his stuff, that guy."

"Useless," Holtser said.

"Completely fucking useless."

"And the Blackphone?"

"There are a couple of calls I haven't been able to trace, presumably from the Swedish security services or the NDRE. But there's something bothering me much more."

"What?"

"A long conversation the professor had just before you stormed in—he was talking to someone at the MIRI, Machine Intelligence Research Institute."

"What's the problem with that?"

"The timing. I get the feeling he was having some sort of crisis. Also this Institute works to ensure that intelligent computers don't become a threat to mankind—it doesn't look good. Balder could have given the MIRI his research or . . ."

"Or what?"

"Or he could have spilled the beans on us, at least what he knew."

"That would be bad."

Bogdanov nodded and Holtser swore quietly. Nothing had gone as planned and neither of them was used to failing. But here were two major mistakes in a row, and all because of a child, a retarded child.

That was bad enough. But the worst of it was that Kira was on her way, unhinged on top of everything else. Neither of them was used to that either. On the contrary, they had grown accustomed to her cool elegance, the air of invincibility it gave their operations. Now she was furious, completely off the wall, screaming at them that they were useless, incompetent cretins. It was not so much that those shots may have missed Balder's son. It was because of the woman who had appeared out of nowhere and rescued the boy. That woman sent Kira around the bend.

When Holtser had begun to describe her—the little he had seen—Kira bombarded him with questions. Every answer he gave was wrong, according to Kira. She went berserk, yelling that they should have killed her and that this was typical of them, brainless, useless. Neither of them could make sense of her violent reaction. They had never heard her yell like that before.

In fact there was a lot they did not know about her. Holtser would never forget his evening with her in a suite at the Hotel d'Angleterre in Copenhagen—they had had sex for the third or fourth time, and afterwards had been lying in bed drinking champagne and chatting about his wars and his murders, as they so often did. While stroking her arm he had discovered three scars side by side on her wrist.

"How did you get those, gorgeous?" he had said, and got a look of pure loathing in return.

He had never been allowed to sleep with her again. He took it to be a punishment for having asked. Kira looked after the group and gave them a lot of money. But neither he nor Bogdanov, nor anyone else, was allowed to ask about her past. That was one of the unspoken rules and none of them would even dream of trying. For better or for worse she was their benefactress, mostly for better, they thought, and they went along with her whims, living in constant uncertainty as to whether she would be affectionate or cold, or even give them a brutal, stinging slap.

Bogdanov closed the computer and took a swallow of his drink. They were trying to limit their drinking, so that Kira would not use that against them. But it was nearly impossible. The frustration and adrenaline drove them to it. Holtser fingered his mobile nervously.

"Didn't Olga believe you?" Bogdanov said.

"Not a word. Soon she'll see a child's drawing of me on every billboard."

"I don't buy that drawing thing. Probably wishful thinking on the part of the police."

"So we're supposed to kill a child for no reason?"

"It wouldn't surprise me. Shouldn't Kira be here by now?"

"Any minute."

"Who do you think it was?"

"Who?"

"The girl who appeared from nowhere."

"No idea," Holtser said. "Not sure Kira knows either. But she's worried about something."

"We'll probably end up having to kill them both."

"That might be the least of it."

August was not feeling well. That was obvious. Red patches flared on his throat and he was clenching his fists. Salander, sitting next to him at the round table, working on her RSA encryption, was afraid he was on the verge of some sort of fit. But August only picked up a crayon, a black one.

At the same moment a gust of wind shook the large windowpanes in front of them. August hesitated and moved his hand back and forth across the table. But then he started to draw, a line here, a line there, followed by some small circles, buttons, Salander thought, then a hand, details of a chin, an unbuttoned shirt front. It began to go more quickly and the tension in the boy's back and shoulders subsided—as if a wound had burst open and begun to heal.

There was a searing, tortured look in his eyes, and every now and then he shivered. But there was no doubt that something within him had eased. He picked up some new crayons and started to draw an oak-coloured floor, on which appeared pieces of a puzzle that seemed to represent a glittering town at night-time. It was clear at this stage that the drawing would be anything but a pleasant one.

The hand and the unbuttoned shirt front became part of a large man with a protruding belly. The man was standing, bent like a jackknife, beating a small person on the floor, a person who was not in the drawing for the simple reason that he was observing the scene, and on the receiving end of the blows.

It was an ugly scene, no doubt about that. But even though the picture revealed an assailant, it did not seem to have anything to do with the murder. Right in the middle, at the epicentre of the drawing, a furious, sweaty face appeared, every foul and bitter furrow captured with precision. Salander recognized it. She rarely watched TV or went to the cinema, but she knew it was the face of the actor Lasse Westman, August's mother's partner. She leaned forward to the boy and said, with a holy, quivering rage:

"We'll never let him do that to you again. Never."

CHAPTER 21

NOVEMBER 23

Casales knew at once that something was wrong when she saw Commander Ingram's lanky figure approach Needham's desk. You could tell from his hesitant manner that the news was not good.

Ingram usually had a malicious grin on his face when he stuck a knife in someone's back, but with Needham it was different. Even the most senior bosses were scared of Needham—he would raise all hell if anyone tried to mess with him. Ingram did not like scenes, still less humiliation, and that was what awaited him if he picked a fight with Needham.

While Needham was brash and explosive, Ingram was a refined upper-class type with spindly legs and an affected manner. Ingram was a serious power player and had influence where it mattered, be it in Washington or in the world of business. As a member of the NSA management, he ranked just below Admiral Charles O'Connor. He might be quick to smile and adept at handing out compliments, but his smile never reached his eyes.

He had leverage over people and was, among other things, in charge of "monitoring strategic technologies"—

more cynically known as industrial espionage, that part of the NSA which gives the American tech industry a helping hand in global competition. He was feared as few others were.

But now as he stood in front of Needham in his fancy suit, his body seemed to shrink even from one hundred feet away. Casales knew exactly what was about to happen: Needham was on the brink of exploding. His pale, exhausted face was going red. Without waiting he got to his feet, his back crooked and bent, his belly sticking out, and roared in a furious voice.

"You sleazy bastard!"

No-one but Needham would call Jonny Ingram a "sleazy bastard," and Casales loved him for it.

August started on a new drawing.

He sketched a few lines. He was pressing so hard on the paper that the black crayon broke and, just like the last time, he drew rapidly, one detail here and another one there, disparate bits which ultimately came together and formed a whole. It was the same room, but there was a different puzzle on the floor, easier to make out: it represented a red sports car racing by a sea of shouting spectators in a stand. Above the puzzle not one but two men could be seen standing.

One of them was Westman again. This time he was wearing a T-shirt and shorts and he had bloodshot, squinting eyes. He looked unsteady and drunk, but no less furious. He was drooling. Yet he was not the most frightening figure in the drawing. That was the other man, whose watery eyes shone with pure sadism. He too was unshaven and drunk, and he had thin, almost nonexistent lips. He seemed to be kicking August, although again the boy could not be seen in the picture, his very absence making him extremely present.

"Who's the other one?" Salander said.

August said nothing. But his shoulders shook, and his legs twisted into a knot under the table.

"Who's the other one?" Salander said again, in a more forceful tone, and August wrote on the drawing in a shaky, childish hand:

R O G E R

Roger—the name meant nothing to Salander.

A couple of hours later in Fort Meade, once his hacker boys had cleaned up after themselves and shuffled off, Needham walked over to Casales. The odd thing was, he no longer looked at all angry or upset. He was radiant with defiance and carrying a notebook. His shirt was disheveled.

"Hey, bud," she said. "Tell me, what's going on?"

"I got some vacation time," he said. "I'm off to Stockholm."

"Of all places. Isn't it cold this time of year?"

"Freezing, by all accounts."

"So you're not really going there on vacation."

"Strictly between us?"

"Go on."

"Ingram ordered us to halt our investigation. The hacker goes free, and we're supposed to be satisfied with stopping up a few leaks. Then the whole thing gets swept under the carpet."

"How the hell can he lay down something like that?"

"They don't want to awaken any sleeping dogs, he says, and run the risk of anyone finding out about the attack. It would be devastating if it ever got out. Just think of all the malicious glee, and all the people whose heads would roll, starting with yours truly."

"He threatened *you*?"

"Did he ever! Went on about how I would be publicly humiliated, even sued."

"You don't seem worried."

"I'm going to break him."

"How? Our glamour boy has powerful connections everywhere, you know that."

"I have a few of my own. Besides, Ingram isn't the only one with dirt on people. That damn hacker was gracious enough to link and match our computer files and show us some of our own dirty laundry."

"That's ironic, isn't it?"

"It takes a crook to know one. At first the data didn't look all that spectacular, not compared to the other stuff we're doing. But when we started to really get into it . . ."

"Yes?"

"It turned out to be dynamite."

"In what way?"

"Ingram's closest colleagues not only *collect* trade secrets to help our own major companies. Sometimes they also *sell* the information for a lot of money. And that money, Alona, doesn't always find its way into the coffers of the organization . . ."

"But into their own pockets."

"Ex*act*ly. I already have enough evidence on that to put two of our top industrial espionage executives behind bars."

"Jesus."

"Unfortunately it's less straightforward with Ingram. I'm convinced he's the brains behind the whole thing. Otherwise all of this doesn't add up. But I don't have a smoking gun, not yet, which makes the whole operation risky. There's always a chance—though I wouldn't bet on it—that the file the hacker downloaded has something specific on him. But it's impossible to crack—a goddamn RSA encryption."

"So what are you going to do?"

"Tighten the net. Show the world that our own co-workers are in cahoots with criminal organizations."

"Like the Spiders."

"Like the Spiders. And plenty of other bad guys. It wouldn't surprise me if they were involved in the killing of your professor in Stockholm. They had a clear interest in seeing him dead."

"You've got to be joking."

"I'm completely serious. Your professor knew things that could have blown up in their faces."

"Holy shit. And you're off to Stockholm like some private detective to investigate?"

"Not like a private detective, Alona. I'm going to be official, and while I'm there I'm going to give our hacker such a pummelling she won't be able to stand."

"Wait, Ed. Did you say she?"

"You better believe it. Our hacker's a she!"

August's drawings took Salander back in time. She thought of that fist beating rhythmically and relentlessly on the mattress. She remembered the thuds and the grunting and the crying from inside the bedroom next door. She remembered the times at Lundagatan when her comics and fantasies of revenge were her only refuge.

But she shook off the memories. She changed the dressing on her shoulder. Then she checked her pistol, made sure that it was loaded. She went onto the PGP link. Andrei Zander was asking how they were, and she gave a short reply.

Outside, the storm was shaking the trees and bushes. She helped herself to some whisky and a piece of chocolate, then went out onto the terrace and from there to the rock slope where she carefully reconnoitred the terrain, noticing a small cleft some way down. She counted her steps and memorized the lay of the land.

By the time she got back, August had made another drawing of Westman and the Roger person. She supposed he needed to get it out of his system. But still he had not drawn anything from the night of the murder. Perhaps the experience was blocked in his mind.

Salander was overcome by a feeling of time running away from them and she cast a worried look at August. For a minute or so she focused on the mind-boggling numbers he had put down on paper. She studied their structure until suddenly she spotted a sequence which did not fit in with the others.

It was relatively short: 2305843008139952128. She got it immediately. It was not a prime number, it was—and here her spirits lifted—a number which, according to a perfect harmony, is made up of the sum of all its positive divisors. It was, in other words, a perfect number, just as 6 is because it can be divided evenly by 3, 2, and 1, and 3 + 2 + 1 happen to add up to 6. She smiled. And then she had an exhilarating thought.

"Now you're going to have to explain yourself," Casales said.

"I will," Needham said. "But first, even though I trust you, I need you to give me a solemn promise that you won't say any of this to anybody."

"I promise, you jerk."

"Good. Here's the story: After I yelled at Ingram, mostly for the sake of appearances, I told him he was right. I even pretended to be grateful to him for putting a stop to our investigation. We wouldn't have gotten any further anyway, I said, and it was partly true. From a purely technical point of view we were out of options. We'd done everything and then some, but it was pointless. The hacker put red herrings all over the place and kept leading us into new mazes and labyrinths. One of my guys said that even if we got to the end, against all odds, we wouldn't believe we'd made it. We'd kid ourselves that it was a new trap. We were prepared for just about anything from this hacker, anything but flaws and weaknesses. So if we kept going the usual way, we'd had it."

"You don't tend to go the usual way."

"No, I prefer the roundabout way. The truth is, we hadn't given up at all. We'd been talking to our hacker contacts out there and our friends in the software companies. We did advanced searches, surveillance, and our own computer breaches. You see, when an attack is as complex as this one, you can always be sure there's been some research up front. Certain specific questions have been asked. Certain specific sites have been visited and inevitably some of that becomes known to us. But there was one factor above all that played into our hands, Alona: the hacker's skill. It was so incredible that it limited the number of suspects. Like a criminal suddenly running a hundred metres in 9.7 seconds at a crime scene—you'd be pretty sure the guy is a certain Mr. Bolt or one of his close rivals, right?"

"So it's at that level?"

"Well, there are parts of this attack that just made my jaw drop, and I've seen a fair amount in my day. That's why we spent a hell of a lot of time talking to hackers and insiders in this industry and asking them: Who is capable of something really, really big? Who are the *seriously* big players these days? We had to be pretty smart about how we framed our questions, so that nobody would guess what actually happened. For a long time we got nowhere. It was like shooting in the dark—like calling out into the dead of night. Nobody knew anything, or they claimed they didn't. A few names were mentioned, but none of them felt right. For a while we chased down some Russian, a Jurij Bogdanov—an ex-druggie and thief who apparently can hack into anything he damn well likes. The security companies were already trying to recruit him when he was living on the street in St. Petersburg, hot-wiring cars, weighing in at 90 pounds of skin and bone. Even the people from the police and intelligence services wanted him on their side. They lost that battle, needless to say. These days Bogdanov looks clean and successful and has ballooned to 130 pounds of skin and bone, but we're pretty sure he's one of the crooks in your organization, Alona. That was another reason he interested us. There had to be a connection to the Spiders, because of the searches that got carried out, but then . . ."

"You couldn't understand why one of their own would be giving us new leads and associations?"

"Exactly, and so we looked further. After a while another outfit cropped up in the conversations."

"Which one?"

"They call themselves Hacker Republic. They have a big reputation out there. A bunch of talents at the top of their game and rigorous about their encryptions. And for good reason. We're constantly trying to infiltrate these groups, and we're not the only ones. We don't just want to find out what they're up to, we also want to recruit people. These days there's big competition for the sharpest hackers."

"Now that we've all become criminals."

"Ha, yes, maybe. Whatever, Hacker Republic has major talent. Lots of the guys we talked to backed that up. And it wasn't just that. There were also rumours that they had something big going on, and then a hacker with the handle Bob the Dog, who we think is linked to the gang, was running searches and asking questions about one of our guys, Richard Fuller. Do you know him?"

"No."

"A manic-depressive, self-righteous prick who's been bugging me for a while. The archetypal security risk who gets arrogant and sloppy when he's in a manic phase. He's just the kind of person a bunch of hackers *should* be targeting, and you'd need classified information to know that. His mental health issues aren't exactly common knowledge, his own mother hardly knows. But I'm pretty confident that in the end they didn't get in via Fuller. We've examined every file he's received recently and there's nothing there. We've scrutinized him from top to bottom. But I bet Fuller was part of Hacker Republic's original plan and then they changed strategies. I can't claim to have any hard evidence against them, not at all, but my gut feeling is still that these guys are behind the break-in."

"You said the hacker was a girl."

"Right. Once we'd homed in on this group we found out as much as possible about them. It wasn't easy to separate rumour from myth and from fact. But one thing came up so often that in the end I saw no reason to question it."

"And what's that?"

"Hacker Republic's big star is someone who uses the alias Wasp."

"Wasp?"

"I won't bore you with technical details, but Wasp is something of a legend in certain circles, one of the reasons being her ability to turn accepted methods on their heads. Someone said you can sense Wasp's involvement in a hacker attack the same way you can recognize Mozart in a melodic loop. Wasp has her own unmistakable style and that was the first thing one of my guys said after he'd studied the breach: this is different from anything we've come across, it's got a completely new threshold of originality."

"A genius, in short."

"Without a doubt. So we started to search everything we could find about this Wasp, to try to crack the handle. No-one was particularly surprised when that didn't work. This person wouldn't leave openings. But you know what I did then?" Needham said proudly.

"Tell me."

"I looked up what the word stood for."

"Beyond its literal meaning, you mean?"

"Right, but not because I or anyone else thought it would get us anywhere. Like I said, if you can't get there on the main road, you take the side roads; you never know what you might find. It turns out Wasp could mean all sorts of things. Wasp is a British fighter plane from World War Two, a comedy by Aristophanes, a famous short film from 1915, a satirical magazine from nineteenth-century San Francisco, and there's also of course White Anglo-Saxon Protestant, plus a whole lot more. But those references are all a little too sophisticated for a hacker genius; they don't go with the culture. You know what did fit? The superhero in Marvel Comics: Wasp is one of the founding members of the Avengers."

"Like the movie?"

"Exactly, with Thor, Iron Man, Captain America. In the original comics she was even their leader for a while. I have to say, Wasp is a pretty badass superhero, kind of rock-and-roll, a rebel who wears black and yellow with insect's wings and short black hair. She's got attitude, the underdog who hits back and can grow or shrink. All the sources we've been talking to think that's the Wasp we're looking for. It doesn't necessarily mean the person behind the handle is some Marvel Comics geek. That handle has been around for a while, so maybe it's a childhood thing that stuck, or an attempt at irony. Like the fact that I named my cat Peter Pan even though I never liked that self-righteous asshole who doesn't want to grow up. Anyway . . ."

"Yes?"

"I couldn't help noticing that this criminal network Wasp

was looking into also uses names from Marvel Comics. They sometimes call themselves the Spider Society, right?"

"Yes, but I think that's just a game, as I see it, sticking it to those of us who monitor them."

"Sure, I get that, but even jokes can give you leads, or cover up something serious. Do you know what the Spider Society in Marvel Comics does?"

"No."

"They wage war against the 'Sisterhood of the Wasp.'"

"OK, fine, it's an interesting detail, but I don't understand how that could be your lead."

"Just wait. Will you come downstairs with me? I have to head to the airport soon."

It was not late, but Blomkvist knew that he could not keep going much longer. He had to go home and get a few hours' sleep and then start working again tonight or tomorrow morning. It might help too if he had a few beers on the way. The lack of sleep was pounding in his forehead and he needed to chase away a few memories and fears. Perhaps he could get Zander to join him. He looked over at his colleague.

Zander had youth and energy to spare. He was banging away at his keyboard as if he had just started work for the day and every now and then he flicked excitedly through his notes. Yet he had been in the office since five o'clock in the morning. It was now a quarter to six in the evening and he had hardly taken a break.

"What do you say, Andrei? How about we get a beer and a bite to eat and discuss the story?"

At first Zander did not seem to understand. Then he

raised his head and suddenly no longer looked quite so energetic. He gave a little grimace as he massaged his shoulder.

"What . . . well . . . maybe," he said hesitantly.

"I'll take that as a yes," said Blomkvist. "How about Folksoperan?"

Folksoperan was a bar and restaurant on Hornsgatan, not far away, which attracted journalists and the arty crowd.

"It's just that . . ." Zander said.

"Just that what?"

"I've got this portrait to do, of an art dealer working at Bukowski's who got onto a train at Malmö Central and was never seen again. Erika thought it would fit into the mix."

"Jesus, the things she makes you do, that woman."

"I honestly don't mind. But I'm having trouble pulling it together. It feels so messy and contrived."

"Do you want me to have a look at it?"

"I'd love that, but let me do some more work on it first. I would die of embarrassment if you saw it in its present state."

"In that case deal with it later. But come on now, Andrei, let's go and at least get something to eat. You can come back and work afterwards if you must," Blomkvist said. He looked over at Zander.

That memory would stay with him for a long time. Zander was wearing a brown checked jacket and a white shirt buttoned up all the way. He looked like a film star, at any rate even more like a young Antonio Banderas than usual.

"I think I'd better stay and keep plugging away," he said. "I have something in the fridge which I can microwave."

Blomkvist wondered if he should pull rank, order him to come out and have a beer. Instead he said:

"OK, we'll see each other in the morning. How are they

doing out there meanwhile? No drawing of the murderer yet?"

"Seems not."

"We'll have to find another solution tomorrow. Take care," Blomkvist said, getting up and putting on his overcoat.

Salander remembered something she had read about savants a long time ago in *Science* magazine. It was an article by Enrico Bombieri, an expert in number theory, referring to an episode in Oliver Sacks's *The Man Who Mistook His Wife for a Hat* in which a pair of autistic and mentally disabled twins recite staggeringly high prime numbers to each other, as if they could see them before their eyes in some sort of inner mathematical landscape.

What these twins were able to do and what Salander now wanted to achieve were two different things. But there was still a similarity, she thought, and decided to try, however sceptical she might be. So she brought up the encrypted NSA file and her programme for elliptic curve factorization. Then she turned to August. He responded by rocking back and forth.

"Prime numbers. You like prime numbers," she said.

August did not look at her, or stop his rocking.

"I like them too. And there's one thing I'm particularly interested in just now. It's called factorization. Do you know what that is?"

August stared at the table as he continued rocking and did not look as if he understood anything at all.

"Prime number factorization is when we rewrite a number as the product of prime numbers. By product in this context I mean the result of a multiplication. Do you follow me?"

August's expression did not change, and Salander wondered if she should just shut up.

"According to the fundamental principles of arithmetic, every whole number has a unique prime number factorization. It's pretty cool. We can produce a number as simple as 24 in all sorts of ways, for example by multiplying 12 by 2 or 3 by 8, or 4 by 6. Yet there's only one way to factorize it with prime numbers and that's $2 \times 2 \times 2 \times 3$. Are you with me? The problem is even though it's easy to multiply prime numbers to produce large numbers, it's often impossible to go the other way, from the answer back to the prime numbers. A really bad person has used this to code a secret message. Do you understand? It's a bit like mixing a drink: easy to do but harder to unmix again."

August neither nodded nor said a word. But at least his body was no longer rocking.

"Shall we see if you're any good at prime number factorization, August? Shall we?"

August did not budge.

"I'll take that as a yes. Let's start with the number 456."

August's eyes were bright but distant, and Salander had the feeling that this idea of hers really was absurd.

It was cold and windy and there were few people out. But Blomkvist thought the cold was doing him good—he was perking up a bit. He thought of his daughter, Pernilla, and what she said about writing "for real," and of Salander of course, and the boy. What were they doing right now?

On the way up towards Hornsgatspuckeln he stared for a while at a painting hanging in a gallery window which showed cheerful, carefree people at a cocktail party. At that moment it felt, perhaps wrongly, as if it had been ages since he had last stood like that, drink in hand and without a care in the world. Briefly he longed to be somewhere far away. Then he shivered, struck by the feeling that he was being followed. Perhaps it was a consequence of everything he had been through in the last few days. He turned round, but the only person near him was an enchantingly beautiful woman in a bright red coat with flowing dark-blond hair. She smiled at him a little uncertainly. He gave her a tentative smile back and was about to continue on his way. Yet his gaze lingered, as if he were expecting the woman to turn into something more run-of-the-mill at any moment.

Instead she became more dazzling with each passing second, almost like royalty, a star who had accidentally wandered in among ordinary people, a gorgeous spread in a fashion magazine. The fact was that right then, in that first moment of astonishment, Blomkvist would not have been able to describe her, or provide even one single detail about her appearance.

"Can I help you?" he said.

"No, no," she said, apparently shy, and there was no getting away from it: her hesitancy was beguiling. She was not a woman you would have thought to be shy. She looked as if she might own the world.

"Well then, have a nice evening," he said, and turned again, but he heard her nervously clear her throat.

"Aren't you Mikael Blomkvist?" she said, even more uncertain now, looking down at the cobbles in the street.

"Yes, I am," he said, and smiled politely, as he would have done for anybody.

"Well, I just want to say that I've always admired you," she said, raising her head and gazing into his eyes with a long look.

"I'm flattered. But it's been a long time since I wrote anything decent. Who are you?"

"My name is Rebecka Mattson," she said. "I've been living in Switzerland."

"And now you're home for a visit?"

"Only for a short time, unfortunately. I miss Sweden. I even miss November in Stockholm. But I guess that's how it is when you're homesick, isn't it?"

"What do you mean?"

"That you miss even the bad bits."

"True."

"Do you know how I cure it all? I follow the Swedish press. I don't think I've missed a single issue of *Millennium* in the last few years," she said.

He looked at her again, and noticed that every piece of clothing, from the black high-heeled shoes to the checked blue cashmere shawl, was expensive and elegant. Rebecka Mattson did not look like your typical *Millennium* reader. But there was no reason to be prejudiced, even against rich expatriate Swedes.

"Do you work there?" he said.

"I'm a widow."

"I see."

"Sometimes I get so bored. Were you going somewhere?"

"I was thinking of having a drink and a bite to eat," he said, at once regretting his reply. It was too inviting, too predictable. But it was at least true.

"May I keep you company?" she asked.

"That would be nice," he said, sounding unsure. Then she touched his hand—unintentionally, at least that is what he wanted to believe. She still seemed bashful. They walked slowly up Hornsgatspuckeln, past a row of galleries.

"How nice to be strolling here with you," she said.

"It's a bit unexpected."

"So true. It's not what I was thinking when I woke up this morning."

"What were you thinking?"

"That the day would be as dreary as ever."

"I don't know if I'll be such good company," he said. "I'm pretty much immersed in a story."

"Are you working too hard?"

"Maybe so."

"Then you need a little break," she said, giving him a bewitching smile, filled with longing or some sort of promise. At that moment he thought she seemed familiar, as if he had seen that smile before, but in another form, distorted somehow.

"Have we met before?" he said.

"I don't think so. Except that I've seen you a thousand times in pictures, and on TV."

"So you've never lived in Stockholm?"

"When I was a little girl."

"Where did you live then?"

She pointed vaguely up Hornsgatan.

"Those were good times," she said. "Our father took care of us. I often think about him. I miss him."

"Is he no longer alive?"

"He died much too young."

"I'm sorry."

"Thank you. Where are we headed?"

"Well," he said. "There's a pub just up Bellmansgatan, the Bishops Arms. I know the owner. It's quite a nice place."

"I'm sure . . ."

Once again she had that diffident, shy look on her face, and once again her hand happened to brush against his fingers—this time he wasn't so sure it was accidental.

"Perhaps it isn't fancy enough?"

"Oh, I'm sure it's fine," she said apologetically. "It's just that people tend to stare at me. I've come across so many bastards in pubs."

"I can believe it."

"Wouldn't you . . . ?"

"What?"

She looked down at the ground again and blushed. At first he thought he was seeing things. Surely adults don't blush that way? But Rebecka Mattson from Switzerland, who looked like seven million dollars, went red like a little school-girl.

"Wouldn't you like to invite me to your place instead, for a glass of wine or two?" she said. "That would be nicer."

"Well . . ."

He hesitated.

He badly needed some sleep, to be in good shape tomorrow. Yet he said:

"Of course. I've got a bottle of Barolo in the wine rack," and for a second he thought something exciting might be about to happen after all, as if he were about to embark on an adventure.

But his doubt would not subside. At first he could not understand why. He did not normally have a problem with this kind of situation—he had more success than most when it came to women flirting with him. This particular encounter had developed very quickly, but he was not unused to that either. So it was something about the woman herself, wasn't it?

Not only was she young and exceptionally beautiful and should have had better things to do than chase after burned-out middle-aged journalists. It was something in her expression, the way she switched between bold and shy, and the physical contact. Everything he had at first found spontaneous increasingly seemed to him to be contrived.

"How lovely. I won't stay long; I don't want to spoil your story," she said.

"I'll take full responsibility for any spoiled stories," he said, and tried to smile back.

It was a forced smile and in that instant he caught a strange twitch in her eyes, a sudden icy chill which in a second turned into its very opposite, full of affection and warmth, like an acting exercise. He became more convinced that there was something wrong. But he had no idea what, and did not want his suspicions to show, at least not yet. What was going on? He wanted to understand.

They continued on up Bellmansgatan. He was not thinking of taking her back to his place any longer, but he needed time to figure her out. He looked at her again. She really was gorgeous. Yet it occurred to him that it was not her beauty which had first captivated him. It was something else, something more elusive. Just then he saw Rebecka Mattson as a riddle to which he ought to have the answer.

"A nice part of town, this," she said.

"It's not bad." He looked up towards the Bishops Arms.

Diagonally across from the pub, just a bit higher up by the intersection with Tavastgatan, a scrawny, lanky man in a black cap was standing studying a map. He looked like a tourist. He had a brown suitcase in his other hand and white sneakers and a black leather jacket with its fur collar turned up, and under normal circumstances Blomkvist would not have given him a second glance.

But now he observed that the man's movements were nervous and unnatural. Perhaps Blomkvist was suspicious to begin with, but the distracted way he was handling the map seemed more and more put on. Now he raised his head and stared straight at Blomkvist and the woman, studying them for a brief second. Then he looked down at his map again, seeming ill at ease, almost trying to hide his face under the cap. The bowed, almost timid head reminded Blomkvist of something, and again he looked into his companion's dark eyes.

His look was persistent and intense. She gazed at him with affection, but he did not reciprocate; instead he scrutinized her. Then her expression froze. Only in that moment did Blomkvist smile back at her.

He smiled because suddenly the penny had dropped.

CHAPTER 22

NOVEMBER 23—EVENING

Salander got up from the table. She did not want to pester August any longer. The boy was under enough pressure as it was and her idea had been crazy from the start.

One always expects too much of these poor savants, and what August had done was already impressive. She went out onto the terrace again and gingerly felt the area around the bullet wound, which was still aching. She heard a sound behind her, a hasty scratching on paper, so she turned and went back inside. When she saw what August had written, she smiled:

$2^3 \times 3 \times 19$

She sat down and said, without looking at him this time, "OK. I'm impressed. But let's make this a little harder. Have a go at 18,206,927."

August was hunched over the table and Salander thought it might have been unkind to throw an eight-digit figure at him right away. But if they were to stand any chance of getting what she needed they would need to go much higher than that. She was not surprised to see August begin to sway nervously back and forth. After a few seconds he leaned forward and wrote on his paper: 9419×1933.

"Good. How about 971,230,541?"

August wrote, 983 × 991 × 997.

"That's great," Salander said, and on they went.

Outside the black, cube-like office building in Fort Meade with its reflective glass walls, not far from the big radome with its dish aerials, Casales and Needham were standing in the packed parking lot. Needham was twirling his car keys and looking beyond the electric fence in the direction of the surrounding woods. He should be on his way to the airport, he said, he was late already. But Casales did not want to let him leave. She had her hand on his shoulder and was shaking her head.

"That's twisted."

"It's out there," he said.

"So every one of the handles we've picked up for people in the Spider Society—Thanos, Enchantress, Zemo, Alkhema, Cyclone, and the rest—what they have in common is that they're all . . ."

"Enemies of Wasp in the original comic book series, yes."

"That's insane."

"A psychologist would have fun with it."

"This kind of fixation must run deep."

"I get the feeling it's real hate," he said.

"You will be careful over there, won't you?"

"Don't forget I used to be in a gang."

"That was a long time ago, Ed, and many pounds too."

"It's not a question of weight. What is it they say? You can take the boy out of the ghetto . . ."

"Yes, yes."

"You can never get rid of it. Besides, I'll have help from the NDRE in Stockholm. They're itching as much as I am to put that hacker out of action once and for all."

"What if Ingram finds out?"

"That wouldn't be good. But as you can imagine, I've been laying the groundwork. Even exchanged a word or two with O'Connor."

"I figured as much. Is there anything I can do for you?"

"Yep."

"Shoot."

"Ingram's crew seems to have had full insight into the Swedish police investigation."

"They've been eavesdropping on the police?"

"Either that or they have a source, maybe an ambitious soul at Säpo. If I put you together with two of my best hackers, you could do some digging."

"Sounds risky."

"OK, forget it."

"That wasn't a no."

"Thanks, Alona. I'll send info."

"Have a good trip," she said, and Needham smiled defiantly and got into his car.

Looking back, Blomkvist could not explain how he had worked it out. It may have been something in the Mattson woman's expression, something unknown and yet familiar. The perfect harmony of that face may have reminded him of its opposite, and that, together with other hunches and misgivings, gave him the answer. True, he was not yet certain. But he had no doubt that something was very wrong.

The man now walking off with his map and brown suitcase was the same figure he had seen on the security camera in Saltsjöbaden, and that coincidence was too improbable not to be of some significance, so Blomkvist stood there for a few seconds and thought. Then he turned to the woman who called herself Rebecka Mattson and tried to sound confident:

"Your friend is heading off."

"My friend?" she said, genuinely surprised. "What friend?"

"Him up there," he said, pointing at the man's skeletal back as he sauntered gawkily down Tavastgatan.

"Are you joking? I don't know anyone in Stockholm."

"What do you want from me?"

"I just want to get to know you, Mikael," she said, fingering her blouse, as if she might undo a button.

"Stop that!" he said sharply, and was about to lose his temper when she looked at him with such vulnerable, piteous eyes that he was thrown. For a moment he thought he had made a mistake.

"Are you cross with me?" she said, hurt.

"No, but . . ."

"What?"

"I don't trust you," he said, more bluntly than he intended.

She smiled sadly and said: "I can't help feeling that you're not quite yourself today, are you, Mikael? We'll have to meet some other time instead."

She moved to kiss his cheek so discreetly and quickly that he had no time to stop her. She gave a flirtatious wave of her fingers and walked away up the hill on high heels, so resolutely self-assured that he wondered if he should stop her and fire some probing questions. But he could not imagine that anything would come of it. Instead he decided to follow her.

It was crazy, but he saw no alternative, so he let her disappear over the brow of the hill and then set off in pursuit. He hurried up to the intersection, sure that she could not have gone far. But there was no sign of her, or of the man either. It was as if the city had swallowed them up. The street was empty, apart from a black BMW backing into a parking space some way down the block, and a man with a goatee wearing an old-fashioned Afghan coat who came walking in his direction on the opposite sidewalk.

Where had they gone? There were no side streets for them to slip into, no alleys. Had they ducked into a doorway? He walked on down towards Torkel Knutssonsgatan, looking left and right. Nothing. He passed what had been Samir's Cauldron, once a favourite locale of his and Berger's; now called Tabbouli, it served Lebanese food. They might have stepped inside.

But he could not see how she would have had time to get there, he had been hot on her heels. Where the hell was she? Were she and the man standing somewhere nearby, watching him? Twice he spun around, certain that they were right behind him, and once he gave a start because of an icy feeling that someone was looking at him through a telescopic sight.

When eventually he gave up and wandered home it felt as though he had escaped a great danger. He had no idea how close to the truth that feeling was, yet his heart was beating fiercely and his throat was dry. He was not easily scared, but tonight he had been frightened by an empty street.

The only thing he did understand was who he needed to speak to. He had to get hold of Holger Palmgren, Salander's old guardian. But first he would do his civic duty. If the man he had seen was the person from Balder's security camera, and there was even a minimal chance that he could be found, the police had to be informed. So he rang Bublanski.

It was by no means easy to convince the chief inspector. It had not been easy to convince himself. But he still had some residual credibility to fall back on, however many liberties he had taken with the truth of late. Bublanski said that he would send out a unit.

"Why would he be in your part of town?"

"I have no idea, but it wouldn't hurt to see if you could find him, would it?"

"I suppose not."

"The best of luck to you in that case."

"It's damn unsatisfactory that the Balder boy is still out there somewhere," Bublanski said reproachfully.

"And it's damn unsatisfactory that there was a leak in your unit," Blomkvist said.

"I can tell you, we've identified *our* leak."

"You have? That's fantastic."

"It's not all that fantastic, I'm afraid. We believe there may have been several leaks, most of which did minimal damage except maybe for the last."

"Then you'll have to make sure you put a stop to it."

"We're doing everything we can, but we're beginning to suspect . . ." And then he paused.

"What?"

"Nothing."

"OK, you don't have to tell me."

"We live in a sick world, Mikael."

"We do?"

"A world in which paranoia is a requirement."

"You could be right about that. Good night, Chief Inspector."

"Good night, Mikael. Don't do anything silly now."

"I'll do my best."

Blomkvist crossed over Ringvägen and went down into the tunnelbana. He took the red line towards Norsborg and got off at Liljeholmen, where for about a year Holger Palmgren had been living in a small, modern apartment. Palmgren had sounded alarmed when he heard Blomkvist's voice on the telephone. But as soon as he had been assured that Salander was in one piece—Blomkvist hoped he wasn't wrong about this—he made him feel welcome.

Palmgren was a lawyer, long retired, who had been Salander's guardian for many years, ever since the girl was thirteen and had been locked up in St. Stefan's psychiatric clinic in Uppsala. He was elderly and not in the best of health, having suffered two strokes. For some time now he had been using a walker, and had trouble getting around even so. The left side of his face drooped and his left hand no longer functioned. But his mind was clear and his long-term memory was outstanding—especially on Salander.

No-one knew Lisbeth Salander as he did. Palmgren had succeeded where all the psychiatrists and psychologists had failed, or perhaps had not wanted to succeed. After a childhood from hell, when the girl had lost faith in all adults and in all authority, Palmgren had won her confidence and persuaded her to open up. Blomkvist saw it as a minor miracle. Salander was every therapist's nightmare, but she had told

Palmgren about the most painful parts of her past. That was why Blomkvist now keyed in the front-door code at Lilje-holmstorget 96, took the lift to the fifth floor, and rang the doorbell.

"My dear old friend," Holger said in the doorway. "It's so wonderful to see you. But you're looking pale."

"I haven't been sleeping well."

"Not surprising, when people are shooting at you. I read about it in the paper. A dreadful story."

"Appalling."

"Have there been any developments?"

"I'll tell you all about it," Blomkvist said, sitting on a yellow sofa near the balcony, waiting for Palmgren to settle with difficulty into a wheelchair next to him.

Blomkvist ran through the story in broad outline. When he came to the point of his sudden inspiration, or suspicion, on the cobblestones in Bellmansgatan, he was interrupted:

"What are you saying?"

"I think it was Camilla."

Palmgren looked stunned.

"*That* Camilla?"

"The very same."

"Jesus," Palmgren said. "What happened?"

"She vanished. But afterwards I felt as if my brain were on fire."

"I can well understand. I was sure Camilla had disappeared off the face of the earth."

"And I had almost forgotten that there were two of them."

"There were two of them all right, very much so, twin sisters who loathed each other."

"I remember that," Blomkvist said. "But I need to be

reminded of as much as you can tell me, to fill in the gaps. I've been asking myself why on earth Salander got involved in this story. Why would she, the superhacker, take an interest in a simple data breach?"

"Well, you know the background, don't you? The mother, Agneta Salander, was a cashier at Konsum Zinken and lived with her two daughters on Lundagatan. They might have had quite a nice life together. There wasn't much money and Agneta was very young and had had no opportunity to get an education. But she was loving and caring. She wanted to give her girls a good upbringing. It was just . . ."

"That the father came to visit."

"Yes, the father, Alexander Zalachenko. He came from time to time and his visits nearly always ended in the same way. He assaulted and raped Agneta while the girls sat in the next room and heard everything. One day Lisbeth found her mother unconscious on the floor."

"And that was the first time she took revenge?"

"The second time. The first was when she stabbed Zalachenko repeatedly in the shoulder."

"But now she firebombed his car."

"Yes. Zalachenko burned like a torch. Lisbeth was committed to St. Stefan's psychiatric clinic."

"And her mother was admitted to Äppelviken Nursing Home."

"For Lisbeth that was the most painful part. Her mother was just twenty-nine, and she was never herself again. She survived at the nursing home for fourteen years, with severe brain injuries and suffering a great deal of pain. Often she could not communicate at all. Lisbeth went to see her as frequently as she could, and I know she dreamed that her mother would one day recover so they could talk again and look after each other. But it never happened. That if anything is the darkest corner of Lisbeth's life. She saw her mother wither away and eventually die."

"It's terrible. But I've never understood Camilla's role in the story."

"That's more complicated, and in some ways I think one has to forgive the girl. After all, she too was only a child, and before she was even aware of it she became a pawn in the game."

"In what way?"

"They chose opposite camps in the battle, you could say. It's true that the girls are fraternal twins and not alike in appearance, but they also have completely different temperaments. Lisbeth was born first. Camilla came twenty minutes later and was apparently a joy to behold, even when she was tiny. While Lisbeth was an angry creature, Camilla had everyone exclaiming 'Oh, what a sweet girl,' and it can't have been a coincidence that Zalachenko showed more forbearance towards her from the start. I say forbearance because it was never a question of anything kinder in those first years. Since Agneta was no more than a whore to him, it followed that her children were bastards with no claim on his affections, little wretches who just got in the way. And yet . . ."

"Yes?"

"And yet even Zalachenko noticed that one of the children was beautiful. Sometimes Lisbeth would say there was a genetic defect in her family and, though it's doubtful that her claim would stand up to medical scrutiny, it cannot be denied that Zala fathered some exceptional children. You came across their half-brother, Ronald Niedermann, didn't you? He was blond, enormous, and had congenital analgesia, the inability to feel pain, so was therefore an ideal hit man and murderer, while Camilla . . . well, in her case the genetic abnormality was quite simply that she was astoundingly, ridiculously lovely to look at, and that just got worse as she grew older. I say worse because I'm pretty sure it was a misfortune. The effect may have been exaggerated by the fact that her twin sister always looked sour. Grown-ups were liable to frown when they saw her. But then they would notice Camilla, and go soft in the head. Can you imagine how that must have impacted her?"

"It must have been hard to get passed over."

"I wasn't thinking of Lisbeth, and I don't remember seeing any evidence that she resented the situation. If it was just a question of beauty, she probably would have felt her sister was welcome to it. No, I'm talking about Camilla. What must it do to a child who doesn't have much in the way of empathy to be told all the time how divine she is?"

"It goes to her head."

"It gives her a sense of power. When she smiles, we melt. When she doesn't, we feel excluded, and do absolutely anything to see her beam again. Camilla learned early on to exploit that. She became a master manipulator. She had large, expressive doe eyes."

"She still does."

"Lisbeth told me how Camilla would sit for hours in front of the mirror, practising her look. Her eyes were a fantastic weapon. They could both bewitch you and freeze you out, make children and adults alike feel special one day and rejected the next. It was an evil gift and, as you could guess, she soon became very popular at school. Everyone wanted to be with her and she took advantage in every conceivable way. She made sure that her classmates gave her presents daily: marbles, sweets, small change, pearls, brooches. And those who didn't, or generally didn't behave as she wanted, she wouldn't even look at the next day. Anyone who had ever found themselves basking in her radiance knew how painful that was. Her classmates did everything they could to be in her good graces. They fawned over her. With one exception, of course."

"Her sister."

"That's right, and so Camilla turned them against Lisbeth. She got some fierce bullying going—they pushed Lisbeth's head into the toilet and called her a freak and a weirdo and all sorts of names. This went on until one day they found out who they were picking on. But that's another story, and one you're familiar with."

"Lisbeth doesn't turn the other cheek."

"No indeed. But the interesting thing in this story from a psychological point of view is that Camilla learned how to dominate her surroundings from an early age. She worked out how to control everybody, apart from two significant people in her life, Lisbeth and her father, and that annoyed her. She put a vast amount of energy into winning those fights as well, and she needed totally different strategies for each of them. She could never win Lisbeth over, and pretty soon I think she gave up. In her eyes, Lisbeth was simply strange, a surly, stroppy girl. Her father, on the other hand . . ."

"He was evil through and through."

"He was evil, but he was also the family's centre of gravity. He was the one around whom everything revolved, even if he was rarely there. He was the absent father. In a normal family such a figure can take on a quasi-mystical status for a child, but in this case it was much more than that."

"In what way?"

"I suppose I mean that Camilla and Zalachenko were an unfortunate combination. Although Camilla hardly understood it herself, she was only interested in one thing, even then: power. And her father, well, you can say many things about him, but he was not short on power. Plenty of people can testify to that, not least that wretched lot at Säpo. No matter how firmly they tried to put their foot down, they still ended up huddled like a flock of frightened sheep when they came eyeball to eyeball with him. There was an ugly, imposing self-assurance about Zalachenko which was merely amplified by the fact that he was untouchable. It made no difference how many times he was reported to the social welfare agency—the Security Police always protected him. This is what persuaded Lisbeth to take matters into her own hands. But for Camilla, things were different."

"She wanted to be like him."

"Yes, I think so. Her father was her ideal—she wanted the same aura of immunity and strength. But most of all, perhaps, she wanted to be acknowledged by him. To be seen as a worthy daughter."

"She must have known how terribly he mistreated her mother."

"Of course she knew. Yet still she took her father's side. One could say she chose to side with strength and power. Apparently even as a little girl she often said that she despised weak people."

"She despised her mother, do you think?"

"Unfortunately I think you're right. Lisbeth once told me something which I've never been able to forget."

"What's that?"

"I've never told anyone."

"Isn't it about time, then?"

"Well, maybe, but in that case I need a strong drink. How about a good brandy?"

"That wouldn't be such a bad idea. But you stay right where you are, I'll get some glasses and the bottle," Blomkvist said, going to the mahogany drinks cabinet in the corner by the kitchen door.

He was digging around among the bottles when his iPhone rang. It was Zander, or at least his name was on the display. But when Blomkvist answered no-one was there, it must have been a pocket call, he thought. He poured out two glasses of Rémy Martin and sat down again next to Palmgren.

"So tell me," he said.

"I don't know where to begin. But one fine summer's day, as I understood it, Camilla and Lisbeth were both sitting in their bedroom. The door was locked."

CHAPTER 23

NOVEMBER 23—EVENING

August's body stiffened again. He could no longer find the answers, the numbers were too big. Instead of picking up his pencil he clenched his fists so that the backs of his hands whitened. He banged his head against the tabletop.

Salander should have tried to comfort him, or at least prevent him from hurting himself. But she was not entirely conscious of what was happening. Her mind was on her encrypted file. She realized she was not going to get any further by this route either. It was hardly surprising—how could August succeed where supercomputers had failed? Her expectations had been absurdly high from the start. But still she felt disappointed.

She went out into the darkness to survey the barren, untamed landscape before her. Below the steep rock slope lay the beach and a snow-covered field with a deserted dance pavilion.

The place probably teemed with people on a lovely summer's day. Now it was empty. The boats had been pulled up on land and not a soul could be seen, no lights were shining in the houses on the other side of the water. Salander liked it. At least she liked it as a hiding place at the end of November.

If someone arrived by car she was unlikely to pick up the sound of the engine. The only conceivable place to park was down by the beach, and to get to the house you had to climb up the wooden stairs along the steep rock slope. Under the cover of darkness, someone might be able to sneak up on them. But she would sleep tonight. She needed it. Her wound was still giving her pain—maybe that was why she had gotten her hopes up about August, against the odds. But when she went back into the house, she realized that there was something else besides.

"Normally Lisbeth isn't someone who bothers about the weather or what's going on beyond her immediate focus," Palmgren said. "She blocks out everything she considers unimportant. But on this occasion she did mention that the sun was shining on Lundagatan and in Skinnarviksparken. She could hear children laughing. On the other side of the windowpane, people were happy. Perhaps that is what she was trying to say—she wanted to point out the contrast. Ordinary people were having ice cream and playing with kites and balls. Camilla and Lisbeth sat locked in their bedroom and could hear their father assaulting their mother.

"I believe this was just before Lisbeth took her revenge on Zalachenko, but I'm not sure about the sequence of events. There were many rapes, and they followed the same pattern. Zala would appear in the afternoon or evening, very drunk. Sometimes he would ruffle Camilla's hair and say things like: 'How can such a pretty girl have such a loathsome sister?' Then he would lock his daughters in their room and settle down in the kitchen to have more to drink. He drank his vodka neat, and often he would sit quietly at first, smacking his lips like a hungry animal. Then he would mumble something like: 'And how's my little whore today?,' sounding almost affectionate. But Agneta would do something wrong, or rather, Zalachenko would decide that she had done something wrong, and then the first blow came, usually a slap followed by: 'I thought my little whore was going to behave herself today.' Then he would shove her into the bedroom and beat her. After a while slaps would turn to punches. Lisbeth could tell from the sounds. She could tell exactly what sort of blows they were, and where they landed. She felt it as clearly as if she herself were the victim of this savagery. After the punches came the kicks. Zala kicked and shoved her mother against the wall and shouted 'bitch' and 'tramp' and 'whore,' and that aroused him. He was turned on by her suffering. Only once Agneta was black-and-blue and bleeding did he rape her, and when he climaxed he would yell even fouler insults. Then it would be quiet for a while. All that could be heard was Agneta's choked sobbing and Zala's own heavy breathing. Then he would get up and have another drink and mutter and swear and spit on the floor. Sometimes he unlocked the door to the children's room, with something like 'Mummy's behaving herself again now.' And he would leave, slamming the door behind him. That was the usual pattern. But on this particular day something new happened."

"What?"

"The girls' bedroom was quite small. However hard they tried to get away from each other, the beds were still close and, while the abuse went on, each one sat on her own mattress, facing the other. They hardly ever said anything, and usually avoided eye contact. On this day Lisbeth was staring through the window at Lundagatan, that's probably why she talked about the sunlight and the children out there. But then she looked at her sister, and that's when she saw it."

"She saw what?"

"Camilla's right hand, beating against her mattress. It could have been a sign of nervous or compulsive behaviour. That's what Lisbeth thought at first. But then she noticed that the hand was beating in time with the blows from the bedroom, and at that she looked up at Camilla's face. Her sister's eyes were glowing with excitement, and the eeriest thing was: Camilla looked just like Zala himself and she was smiling. She was suppressing a smirk, and in that instant Lisbeth realized that Camilla was not only trying to ingratiate herself with her father. She was also right behind his violence. She was cheering him on."

"That's sick."

"But that's how it was. Do you know what Lisbeth did? She remained perfectly calm. She sat down next to Camilla and took her hand almost tenderly. Perhaps Camilla thought her sister was looking for some comfort or closeness. Stranger things have happened. Lisbeth rolled up her sister's shirt sleeve and dug her fingernails into Camilla's wrist—down to the bone—ripping open a terrible wound. Blood streamed onto the bed. Lisbeth dragged Camilla to the floor and swore she would kill both her and her father if the beatings and the rapes did not stop."

"Jesus!"

"You can imagine the hatred between the sisters. Both Agneta and the social services were so worried that something even more serious would happen that they were kept apart.

For a while they arranged a home elsewhere for Camilla. Sooner or later they probably would have clashed again, but in the end, as you know, things did not turn out like that. I believe the sisters only saw each other once after Lisbeth was locked up—several years later—when a disaster was narrowly averted, but I know none of the details. I haven't heard anything of Camilla for a long time now. The last people to have had contact with her are the foster family with whom she lived in Uppsala, people called Dahlgren. I can get you the number. But ever since Camilla was eighteen or nineteen and she packed a bag and left the country she hasn't been heard from. That's why I was astonished when you said that you had met her. Not even Lisbeth, with her famous ability to track people down, has been able to find her."

"So she *has* tried?"

"Oh yes. As far as I know, the last time was when her father's estate was to be apportioned."

"I didn't realize."

"Lisbeth mentioned it in passing. She didn't want a single penny from that will—to her it was blood money—but she could tell that there was something strange about it. There were assets of four million kronor: the farm in Gosseberga, some securities, a run-down industrial site in Norrtälje, a cottage somewhere, and various other bits and pieces. Not insignificant by any means, and yet . . ."

"He should have been worth much more."

"Yes, Lisbeth was aware that he ran a vast criminal empire. Four million would have been small change in that context."

"So you're saying she wondered if Camilla inherited the lion's share."

"I think that's what she's been trying to find out. The

mere thought that her father's fortune was going on doing harm after his death was torture to her. But for a long time she got nowhere."

"Camilla concealed her identity well."

"I assume so."

"Do you have any reason to think Camilla might have taken over her father's trafficking business?"

"Maybe, maybe not. She may have struck out into something altogether different."

"Such as?"

Palmgren closed his eyes and took a large sip of his brandy.

"I can't be sure of this, Mikael. But when you told me about Professor Balder, I had a thought. Do you have any idea why Lisbeth is so good with computers? Do you know how it all started?"

"I have no idea."

"Then I'll tell you. I wonder if the key to your story doesn't lie there."

When Salander came in from the terrace and saw August huddled in a stiff and unnatural position by the round table, she realized that the boy reminded her of herself as a child.

That is exactly how she had felt at Lundagatan, until one day it became clear to her that she had to grow up far too soon, to take revenge on her father. It was a burden no child should have to bear. But it had been the beginning of a real life, a more dignified life. No bastard should be allowed to do what Zalachenko or Balder's murderer had done with impunity. She went to August and said solemnly, as if giving an important order, "You're going to go to bed now. When you wake up I want you to do the drawing that will nail your father's killer. Do you get that?" The boy nodded and shuffled into his bedroom while Salander opened her laptop and started to look for information about Lasse Westman and his circle of friends.

"I don't think Zalachenko himself was much use with computers," Palmgren said. "He wasn't of that generation. But perhaps his dirty business grew to such a scale that he had to use a computer programme to keep his accounts, and to keep them away from his accomplices. One day he came to Lundagatan with an IBM machine which he installed on the desk next to the window. Nobody in the family had seen a computer before. Zalachenko promised that if anyone so much as touched the machine he would flay them alive. From a purely psychological point of view, that was telling. It increased the temptation."

"Forbidden fruit."

"Lisbeth was around eleven at the time. It was before she tore into Camilla's right arm, and before she went for her father with knives and petrol bombs. You could say it was just before she became the Lisbeth we know today. She lacked stimulation. She had no friends to speak of, partly because Camilla had made sure that nobody came anywhere near her at school, but partly because she was different. I don't know if she realized it herself yet. Her teachers and those around her didn't. But she was an extremely gifted child. Her talent alone set her apart. School was deadly boring for her. Everything was obvious and easy. She needed only to take a quick look at things to understand them, and during lessons she sat there daydreaming. I do believe, however, that by then she had managed to find some things in her free time which interested her—advanced maths books, that sort of thing. But basically she was bored stiff. She spent a lot of time reading her Marvel comics, which were way below her intellectual level but perhaps fulfilled another, therapeutic function."

"In what sense?"

"To be honest I'm reluctant to try to play the shrink with Lisbeth. She would hate it if she could hear me. But those comics are full of superheroes fighting against supervillains, taking matters into their own hands to exact revenge and see to it that justice is done. For all I know, that may have been the perfect sort of reading material. Perhaps those stories with their black-and-white view of the world helped her to gain some clarity."

"You mean she understood she had to grow up and become a superhero herself."

"In some way, maybe, in her own little world. At the time she didn't know that Zalachenko had been a Soviet spy, and that his secrets had given him a unique position in Swedish society. She wouldn't have had any idea either that there was a special section within Säpo which protected him. But like Camilla, she sensed that her father had some sort of immunity. One day a man in a grey overcoat appeared at the apartment and hinted that their father must come to no harm. Lisbeth realized early on that there was no point in reporting Zalachenko to the police or the social services. That would only result in yet another man in a grey overcoat turning up on their doorstep.

"Powerlessness, Mikael, can be a devastating force, and

before Lisbeth was old enough to do something about it she needed a place of strength, a refuge. She found that in the world of superheroes. I know better than most how important literature can be, whether it's comic books or fine old novels, and I know that Lisbeth grew particularly attached to a young heroine called Janet van Dyne."

"Van Dyne?"

"That's right, a girl whose father was a rich scientist. The father is murdered—by aliens, if I remember right—and in order to take revenge Janet van Dyne gets in touch with one of her father's old colleagues, and in his laboratory acquires superpowers. She becomes the Wasp, someone you can't push around, either literally or figuratively."

"I didn't know that. So that's where she gets her handle from?"

"Not just the handle. I knew nothing about all that sort of stuff—I was an old dinosaur who got the Phantom mixed up with Mandrake the Magician. But the first time I saw a picture of the Wasp, it gave me a start. There was so much of Lisbeth in her. There still is, in a way. I think she picked up a lot of her style from that character. I don't want to make too much of it. But I do know she thought a great deal about the transformation Janet van Dyne underwent when she became the Wasp. Somehow she understood that she herself had to undergo the same drastic metamorphosis: from child and victim to someone who could fight back against a highly trained and ruthless intelligence agent.

"Thoughts like these occupied her day and night and so the Wasp became an important figure for her during her period of transition, a source of inspiration. And Camilla found out about it. That girl had an uncanny ability to nose out other people's weaknesses—she used her tentacles to feel for their sensitive points and would then strike exactly there. So she came to make fun of the Wasp in whichever way she could. She even found out who Wasp's Marvel enemies were and began to call herself by their names, Thanos and all the others."

"Did you say Thanos?" said Blomkvist, suddenly alert.

"I think that's what he was called, a destroyer who once fell in love with Death itself. Death had appeared to him in the shape of a woman, and after that he wanted to prove himself worthy of her, or something like that. Camilla became a fan of his so as to provoke Lisbeth. She even called her gang of friends the Spider Society—in one of the comics that group are the sworn enemies of the Sisterhood of the Wasp."

"Really?" Blomkvist said, his mind racing.

"Yes, I suppose it was childish, but that didn't make it innocent. There was such hostility between the sisters even then that those names took on a nasty significance."

"Do you think that's still relevant?"

"The names, you mean?"

"Yes, I suppose so."

Blomkvist was not sure what he meant, but he had a vague feeling that he had lit upon something important.

"I don't know," Palmgren said. "They're grown women now, but we mustn't forget that those were decisive times in their lives. Looking back, it's perfectly possible that small details could turn out to be of fateful significance. It wasn't just that Lisbeth lost a mother and was then locked up. Camilla's existence too was smashed to pieces. She lost her home, and the father she admired suffered severe burns. As you know, after the petrol bomb, Zalachenko was never himself again. Camilla was put in a foster home miles from the world whose undisputed leading light she had been. It must have been bitterly hurtful for her too. I don't doubt for one second that she's hated Lisbeth with a murderous fury ever since."

"It certainly looks like it," Blomkvist said.

Palmgren took another sip of brandy.

"The sisters were in a state of out-and-out war during this period, and somehow I think they both knew that everything was about to blow up. I think they were even preparing for it."

"But in different ways."

"Oh yes. Lisbeth had a brilliant mind, and infernal plans and strategies were constantly ticking away in her head. But she was alone. Camilla was not so bright, not in the conventional sense—she never had a head for studies, and was incapable of understanding abstract reasoning. But she knew how to manipulate people to do her bidding, so unlike Lisbeth she was never alone. If Camilla discovered that Lisbeth was good at something which could be a threat to her, she never tried to acquire the same skill, for the simple reason she knew she couldn't compete with her sister."

"So what did she do instead?"

"Instead she would track down somebody—or better still, more than one person—who could do whatever it was, and strike back with their help. She always had minions. But forgive me, I'm getting ahead of myself."

"Yes, tell me, what happened with Zalachenko's computer?"

"Lisbeth was short of stimulation, as I said. And she would

lie awake at night, worrying about her mother. Agneta bled badly after the rapes but wouldn't go to a doctor. She probably felt ashamed. Periodically she sank into deep depressions and no longer had the strength to go to work or look after the girls. Camilla despised her even more. Mamma is weak, she'd say. As I told you, in her world, to be weak was worse than anything else. Lisbeth, on the other hand, saw a person she loved—the only person she had ever loved—fall victim to a dreadful injustice. She was a child in so many ways, but she was also becoming convinced that she was the only person in the world who could save her mother from being beaten to death. She got up in the middle of the night—quietly, so as not to wake Camilla—and saw the computer, on the desk by the window overlooking Lundagatan.

"At that time she didn't even know how to switch on a computer. But she figured it out. The computer seemed to be whispering to her: 'Unlock my secrets.' She didn't get far, not at first. A password was needed. Since her father was known as Zala, she tried that, and Zala666 and similar combinations, and everything else she could think of. But nothing worked. I believe this went on for two or three nights, and if she slept at all then it was at school or at home in the afternoon.

"Then one night she remembered something her father had written in German on a piece of paper in the kitchen: *Was mich nicht umbringt, macht mich stärker.* What doesn't kill me makes me stronger. At the time it meant nothing to her, but she realized that the phrase was important to her father, so she tried it. That didn't work either. There were too many letters. So she tried Nietzsche, the source of the quote, and there she was, suddenly she was in. A whole world opened up to her. Later she would describe it as a moment which changed her forever. She thrived when she overcame that barrier. She explored what was meant to stay hidden."

"And Zalachenko never knew of this?"

"It seems not. She understood nothing at first—it was all in Russian. There were various lists, and some numbers, accounts of the revenues from his trafficking operations. To this day I have no idea how much she worked out then and how much she found out later. She came to understand that her mother was not the only one made to suffer by her father. He was destroying other women's lives too, and that made her wild with rage. That is what turned her into the Lisbeth we know today, the one who hates men who . . ."

". . . hate women."

"Precisely. But it also made her stronger. She saw that there was no turning back—she had to stop her father. She went on with her searches on other computers, including at school, where she would sneak into the staff room. Sometimes she pretended to be sleeping over with the friends she didn't have while in fact she stayed overnight at school and sat at the computers until morning. She started to learn everything about hacking and programming, and I imagine that it was the same as when other child prodigies discover their niche: she was in thrall. She felt that she was born for this. Many of her contacts in the digital world began to take an interest in her even then, the way the older generation has always engaged with younger talents, whether to encourage or crush them. Many people out there were irritated by her unorthodox ways, her completely new approach. But others were impressed, and she made friends, including Plague— you know about him. She got her first real friends by way of the computer and above all, for the first time in her life, she felt free. She could fly through cyberspace, just like the Wasp. There was nothing to tie her down."

"Did Camilla realize how skilled she'd become?"

"She must have had her suspicions. I don't know, I shouldn't speculate, but sometimes I think of Camilla as Lisbeth's dark side, her shadow figure."

"The evil twin."

"A bit, though I don't like to call people evil, especially not young women. If you want to dig into it yourself I suggest you get in touch with Margareta Dahlgren, Camilla's foster mother after the havoc at Lundagatan. Margareta lives in Stockholm now, in Solna, I think. She's a widow and has had a desperately sad life."

"In what way?"

"Well, that may also be of interest. Her husband, Kjell, a computer programmer at Ericsson, hanged himself a short time before Camilla left them. A year later their nineteen-year-old daughter also committed suicide, by jumping from a Finland ferry—at least that's what the inquest concluded. The girl had emotional problems, she struggled with her self-esteem. But Margareta never believed that version, and she even hired a private detective. Margareta is obsessed by Camilla, and to be honest I've always had a bit of a problem with her. I'm embarrassed to say, Margareta got in touch with me straight after you published your Zalachenko story. As you know that's when I had just been discharged from the rehabilitation clinic and I was mentally and physically at the end of my tether. Margareta talked endlessly, she was fixated. The sight of her number on my telephone display would exhaust me, and I went to some efforts to avoid her.

But now when I think about it I understand her more. I think she would be happy to talk to you, Mikael."

"Can you let me have her details?"

"I'll get them for you. Just wait a moment."

When Palmgren came back he said: "So you're sure that Lisbeth and the boy are safely tucked away somewhere?"

"I'm sure," Blomkvist said. *At least I hope I am*, he thought. He stood up and embraced Palmgren.

Out on Liljeholmstorget the storm tore into him again. He pulled his coat close and thought of Salander and her sister, and for some reason also of Andrei Zander.

He decided to call him to find out how he was getting on with his story on the art dealer. But Zander never picked up.

CHAPTER 24

NOVEMBER 23—EVENING

Zander had called Blomkvist because he had changed his mind. Of course he wanted to go out for a beer. How could he not have taken him up on the offer? Blomkvist was his idol and the very reason he had gone in for journalism. But once he dialled the number he felt embarrassed and hung up. Maybe Blomkvist had found something better to do. Zander did not like disturbing people unnecessarily, least of all Blomkvist.

Instead he worked on. But however hard he tried, he got nowhere. The words just would not come out right. After about an hour he decided to take a walk, and so he tidied his desk and checked once again that he had deleted every word on the encrypted link. Then he said goodbye to Emil Grandén, the only other person left in the office.

Grandén was thirty-six and had worked at both TV4's *Cold Facts* and *Svenska Morgon-Posten*. Last year he had been awarded the Stora Journalist prize for Investigative Reporter of the Year. But Zander thought—even though he tried not to—that Grandén was conceited and overbearing, at least towards a young temp like him.

"Going out for a bit," Zander said.

Grandén looked at him as if there was something he had forgotten to say. Then he uttered in a bored tone:

"OK."

Zander felt miserable. It may only have been Grandén's arrogant attitude, but it was more likely because of the article about the art dealer. Why was he finding it so difficult? Presumably because all he wanted to do was help Blomkvist with the Balder story. Everything else felt secondary.

But he was also spineless, wasn't he? Why had he not let Blomkvist take a look at what he had written? No-one could raise the level of a story like Blomkvist could, with just a few light pen strokes or deletions. Never mind. Tomorrow he would see the story with fresh eyes and then Blomkvist could read it, however bad it might be.

Zander closed the door to the office and walked out towards the lift. Further down the stairs a drama was unfolding. At first he could not make out what was going on, but there was a scrawny, hollow-eyed figure molesting a beautiful young woman. Zander froze—he had always loathed violence, ever since his parents had been killed in Sarajevo. He hated fights. But his self-respect was at stake. It was one thing to run away for your own sake, but quite another to leave a fellow human being in danger, and so he rushed down the stairs yelling: "Stop, let her go!"

At first that seemed like a fatal mistake. The hollow-eyed man pulled out a knife and muttered some threat in English. Zander's legs nearly gave way, yet he managed to muster the last remnants of his courage and spat back, like something from a B movie, "Hey, get lost! If you don't, you'll regret it." After a few seconds of posturing, the man took off. Zander and the woman were left alone in the stairwell, and that too was like a scene from a film.

The woman was shaken and shy. She spoke so softly that Zander had to lean in close to hear what she was saying, and it took a while before he understood what had happened. The woman had been in a marriage from hell, she said, and even though she was now divorced and living with a protected identity her ex-husband had managed to track her down and send some stooge to harass her.

"That's the second time that foul man has thrown himself at me today," she said.

"Why were you up here?"

"I tried to get away and ran in, but it didn't help. I can't thank you enough."

"It was nothing."

"I'm so fed up with nasty men," she said.

"I'm a nice man," he said, perhaps a little too quickly, and that made him feel pathetic. He was not in the least bit surprised that the woman did not answer, but looked down at the stairs in embarrassment. He felt ashamed of such a cheap reply.

But then, just as he thought he had been rejected, she raised her head and gave him a careful smile.

"I think you really might be. My name's Linda."

"I'm Andrei."

"Nice to meet you, Andrei, and thank you again."

"Thank you too."

"What for?"

"For . . ."

He didn't finish his sentence. He could feel his heart beating, his mouth was dry. He looked down the staircase.

"Yes, Andrei?" she said.

"Would you like me to walk you home?"

He regretted saying that too.

He was afraid it would be misinterpreted. But instead she gave him another of her enchanting, hesitant smiles, and said that she would feel safe with him by her side, so they went out into the street and down towards Slussen. She told him how she had been living more or less locked up in a big house in Djursholm. He said that he understood—he had written a series of articles on violence against women.

"Are you a journalist?" she said.

"I work at *Millennium*."

"Wow," she said. "Seriously? I'm a huge fan of that magazine."

"It's done a lot of good things," he said shyly.

"It really has," she said. "A while ago I read a wonderful article about an Iraqi who had been wounded in the war and got sacked from his job as a cleaner at some restaurant in the city. He was left destitute. Today he's the owner of a whole chain of restaurants. I cried when I read it; it was so beautifully written and inspiring."

"I wrote that," he said.

"Are you joking?" she said. "It was fantastic."

Zander was not exactly spoiled when it came to praise for his journalistic efforts, especially from unknown women. Whenever *Millennium* was mentioned, people wanted to talk about Mikael Blomkvist, and Zander did not object to that. But secretly he dreamed of recognition for himself too, and now this beautiful Linda had praised him without even meaning to.

It made him so happy and proud that he plucked up the

courage to suggest a drink at Papagallo, since they were just passing. To his delight she said: "What a good idea!," so they went into the restaurant, Zander's heart pounding.

He tried to avoid looking into her eyes. Those eyes had knocked him off his feet and he could not believe this was really happening. They sat down at a table not far from the bar and Linda tentatively put out her hand. As he took it he smiled and mumbled something, hardly aware of what he was saying.

He looked down at his phone—Grandén was calling. To his own surprise he ignored it and turned off his ringer. For once the magazine would have to wait. He just wanted to gaze into Linda's face, to drown in it. She was so beautiful that it felt like a punch to the stomach, yet she seemed fragile, like a wounded bird.

"I can't imagine why anyone would want to hurt you," he said.

"It happens all the time."

Perhaps he could understand it after all. A woman like her probably attracted psychopaths. No-one else would dare ask her out. Most men would just shrivel up and feel inferior.

"It's so nice to be sitting here with you," he said.

"It's so nice to be sitting here with *you*," she repeated, gently stroking his hand. They each ordered a glass of red wine and started to talk; they had so much to say, and he didn't notice his mobile vibrating in his pocket, not once but twice, which is how he came to ignore a call from Mikael Blomkvist for the first time in his life.

Soon afterwards she took his hand and led him out into the night. He did not ask where they were going. He was prepared to follow her anywhere. She was the most wonderful creature he had ever met, and from time to time she gave him a smile that made every paving stone, every breath, sound out a promise that something wonderful and overwhelming was happening. You live an entire life for the sake of a walk like this, he thought, barely noticing the cold and the city around him.

He was intoxicated by her presence and what might await him. But maybe—he wasn't sure—there was a hint of suspicion too. At first he dismissed these thoughts, his usual scepticism at any form of happiness. And yet he could not help asking himself: Is this too good to be true?

He studied Linda with a new focus, and noticed that not everything about her was attractive. As they walked past Katarinahissen he even thought he noticed something hard in her eyes. He looked anxiously down at the choppy waters. "Where are we going?"

"I have a friend with a small apartment in Mårten Trotzigs gränd," she said. "She lets me use it sometimes. We could have another drink there." That made him smile as if it were the most wonderful idea he had ever heard.

Yet he felt more and more confused. Not long ago he had been looking after her, and now she had taken the initiative. When a quick glance at his mobile told him that Blomkvist had rung twice, he felt he had to call back immediately. Come what may, he could not let the magazine down.

"I'd like that," he said. "But first I have to make a call. I'm in the middle of a story."

"No, Andrei," she said in a surprisingly firm tone. "You're not calling anyone. Tonight it's just you and me."

They got to Järntorget. In spite of the storm there were quite a few people around and Linda stared at the ground, as if she did not want to be noticed. He looked over to the right at Österlånggatan and the statue of Evert Taube. The troubadour was standing there immobile, holding a sheet of music in his right hand, looking up at the sky in dark glasses. Should he suggest that they meet the following day?

"Maybe . . ." he started.

He got no further, because she pulled him to her and kissed him with a force which emptied his mind. Then she stepped up the pace again. She held his hand and pulled him to the left into Västerlånggatan, then right into a dark alley. Was that someone behind them? No, no, the footsteps and voices he could hear came from further away. It was just him and Linda, wasn't it? They passed a window with a red frame and black shutters and came to a grey door which Linda had some trouble opening. The key was shaking in her hand and he wondered at that. Was she still afraid of her ex-husband and his goon?

They climbed a dark stone stairway. Their footsteps echoed and there was a faint smell of something rotten. On one of the steps past the third floor he saw a playing card, the queen of spades, and he did not like that, he could not understand why, it was probably some silly superstition. He tried to ignore it, and think about how great it was that they had met. Linda was breathing heavily. Her right hand was clenched. A man's laughter could be heard in the alley. Not laughing at him, surely? He was just agitated. But it felt as if they were climbing and climbing and not getting anywhere. Could the house really be so tall? No, here they were. The friend lived in the attic apartment.

The name on the door was Orlov and again Linda took out her bunch of keys. This time her hand was not shaking.

· · ·

Blomkvist was sitting in an apartment with old-fashioned furniture on Prostvägen in Solna, next to a large churchyard. Just as Palmgren had anticipated, Margareta Dahlgren agreed to see him at once, and even though she had sounded manic over the telephone she turned out to be an elegant lady in her sixties. She was wearing a fashionable yellow sweater and neatly pressed black trousers. Perhaps she had had time to dress up for him. She was in high-heeled shoes and had it not been for her restless eyes he would have thought her to be a woman at peace with herself, despite everything.

"You want to hear about Camilla," she said.

"Especially about her life more recently—if you know anything about it," he said.

"I remember when she came to us," she said, as if she had not been listening. "My husband, Kjell, thought we could make a contribution to society at the same time as adding to our little family. We had only one child, you see, our poor Moa. She was fourteen then, and quite lonely. We thought it would do her good if we took in a foster daughter of roughly the same age."

"Did you know what had happened in the Salander family?"

"We didn't have all the details, but we knew that it had been awful and traumatic and the mother was ill and the father had suffered serious burns. We were deeply moved and were expecting to meet a girl who had fallen apart, someone who would need an incredible amount of care and affection. But do you know what arrived?"

"Tell me."

"The most adorable girl we'd ever seen. It wasn't just that she was pretty. My goodness, you should have heard her talk. She was so wise and mature, and she told such heart-rending stories about how her mentally ill sister had terrorized the family. Yes, of course I now know how far from the truth that was. But how could we have doubted her then? Her eyes were bright with conviction, and when we said, 'How dreadful, poor you,' she answered, 'It wasn't easy, but I still love my sister, she's just sick and now she's getting treatment.' It sounded so grown-up and full of empathy, and for a while it almost felt like she was the one taking care of us. Our whole family lit up, as if something glamorous had come into our lives and made everything bigger and more beautiful, and we blossomed. Moa blossomed most of all. She began to take care of her appearance, and quite soon she became more popular at school. There was nothing I wouldn't have done for Camilla right then. And Kjell, my husband, what can I say? He was a new person. He was smiling and laughing all the time, and we began to make love again, if you'll forgive my being so frank. Perhaps I should have started to worry even then. But it felt like everything had finally fallen into place for our family. For a while we were all happy, as everybody is who meets Camilla. They're happy to start with. Then . . . after some time with her you don't want to live anymore."

"Is it that bad?"

"It's horrific."

"So what happened?"

"A poison began to spread among us. Camilla slowly took control of our family. Looking back, it's impossible to tell when the party ended and the nightmare began. It had happened so gradually and imperceptibly that we woke up one day and realized everything was ruined: our trust, our sense of security, the very foundations of our life together. Moa's self-confidence plummeted. She lay awake at night weeping, saying she was ugly and horrible and didn't deserve to live. Only later did we find out that her savings account had been cleaned out. I still don't know how that happened, but I'm convinced Camilla blackmailed her. Blackmail came as naturally to her as breathing. She collected compromising information on people. For a long time I thought she was keeping a diary, but instead it was a catalogue of all the dirt she had on people close to her. And Kjell . . . the bastard . . . you know, I believed him when he said that he'd started having problems sleeping and needed to use the bed in the basement guest room. But that was an excuse to be with Camilla. Starting when she was sixteen, she would sneak in there at night and have perverted sex with him. I say perverted because I got wind of what was going on when I asked about the cuts on Kjell's chest. He didn't say anything then, of course. Just gave me some unconvincing explanation and somehow I managed to suppress my suspicions. But do you know what they did? In the end Kjell came clean: Camilla tied him up and cut him with a knife. He said she enjoyed it. Sometimes I even hoped it was true, strange though that may sound—I hoped she got something out of it and didn't only want to torture him, to destroy his life."

"Did she blackmail him too?"

"Oh yes, but I don't have the full story. He was so humiliated by Camilla that he wasn't willing to tell me the truth, even when all was lost. Kjell had been the rock in our family. If we lost our way while out driving, if there was a flood, if any of us fell ill, he was the calm, sensible one. It'll all be all right, he would say in his wonderful voice—I still fantasize about it. But after a few years with Camilla in the house he was a wreck. Hardly dared to cross the road, looked a hundred times to make sure it was safe. And he lost all motivation at work, just sat with his head hanging. One of his closest colleagues, Mats Hedlund, rang and told me in confidence that an enquiry had been set up to investigate whether Kjell had been selling company secrets. It sounded crazy. Kjell was the most honest man I've ever known. Plus if he'd sold anything, where was the money? We had less than ever. His bank account was stripped bare, same with our joint account."

"Forgive me for asking, but how did he die?"

"He hanged himself—without a word of explanation. I came home from work one day and found him swinging from the ceiling in the guest room, yes, the same room in which Camilla had had her fun with him. I was a well-paid CFO at the time, and chances are I would have had a great career to look forward to. But after that, Moa's and my world collapsed. I won't go into it any further. You want to know what happened to Camilla. But there was no end to the misery. Moa started cutting herself and practically stopped eating. One day she asked me if I thought she was scum. 'My God, darling,' I replied. 'How can you say something like that?' Then she told me it was Camilla. That Camilla had claimed every single person who had ever met Moa thought she was repulsive. I sought all the help I could: psychologists, doctors, wise friends, Prozac. But to no avail. One gloriously beautiful spring day, when the rest of Sweden was celebrating some ridiculous triumph in the Eurovision Song Contest, Moa jumped from a ferry, and my life ended with hers—that's how it felt. I no longer had the will to live and spent a long time in hospital being treated for depression. But then . . . I don't know . . . somehow the paralysis and grief turned to rage, and I felt that I needed to understand. What had actually happened to our family? What sort of evil had seeped in? I started to make enquiries about Camilla, not because I wanted to see her again, not under any circumstances. But I wanted to understand her, the same way a parent of a murder victim wants to understand the murderer."

"What did you discover?"

"Nothing to begin with. She had covered her tracks—it was like chasing a shadow, a phantom. I don't know how many tens of thousands of kronor I spent on private detectives and other unreliable people who promised to help me. I was getting nowhere, and it was driving me crazy. I became fixated. I hardly slept, and none of my friends could bear to be with me anymore. It was a terrible time. People thought I was being obsessive and stubborn, maybe they still do, I don't know what Holger Palmgren told you. But then . . ."

"Go on?"

"Your story on Zalachenko was published. Naturally the name meant nothing to me, but I started to put two and two together. I read about his Swedish identity, Karl Axel Bodin, and about his connection with Svavelsjö Motorcycle Club, and then I remembered all the dreadful evenings towards the end, after Camilla had turned her back on us. At the time I was often woken up by the noise of motorbikes, and I could see those leather vests with that awful emblem from my bedroom window. It didn't surprise me that she mixed with those sorts of people. I no longer had any illusions about her. But I had no idea that this was the world she came from—and that she was expecting to take over her father's business interests."

"And did she?"

"Oh yes. In her own dirty world she fought for the rights of women—at least for her own rights—and I know that it meant a lot to many of the girls in the club, most of all to Kajsa Falk."

"Who is she?"

"A lovely looking sassy girl; her boyfriend was one of the leaders. She spent a lot of time at our home during that last year, and I remember liking her. She had big blue eyes with a slight squint, and a compassionate, vulnerable side behind her tough exterior. After reading your story I looked her up again. She didn't say a word about Camilla, though she was by no means unpleasant. I noticed that her style had changed: the biker girl had become a businesswoman. But she didn't talk about it. I thought I'd hit another dead end."

"But it wasn't?"

"No. About a year ago Kajsa looked me up of her own accord, and by then she had changed again. There was nothing reserved or cool about her. This time she was hounded and nervous. Not long after that she was found dead, shot at Stora Mossens sports centre in Bromma. When we met she told me there had been a dispute over the inheritance after Zalachenko's death. Camilla's twin sister, Lisbeth, came away more or less empty-handed—apparently she didn't even want the little that she got—while the majority of the assets fell to Zalachenko's two surviving sons in Berlin, and some to Camilla. She inherited part of the trafficking business you wrote about in your report, and that made my heart bleed. I doubt Camilla cared about those women, or felt any compassion for them. But still, she didn't want to have anything to do with those activities. She said to Kajsa that only losers bother with that sort of filth. She had a completely different, modern vision of what the organization should be doing, and after hard negotiation she got one of her half-brothers to buy her out. Then she disappeared to Moscow with her capital and some of the employees who wanted to follow her, Kajsa Falk among them."

"Do you know what sort of business she was setting up?"

"Kajsa never got enough of an insight to understand it, but we had our suspicions. I think it was to do with those trade secrets at Ericsson. By now I'm almost certain Camilla got Kjell to steal and sell something valuable, presumably by blackmailing him. I've also found out that in her first years with us she asked some computer geeks at school to hack into my computer. According to Kajsa, she was more or less obsessed with hacking. Not that she learned anything about it herself, not at all, but she was forever talking about the money one could make by accessing bank accounts and hacking servers and stealing information. She must have developed a business along those lines."

"That sounds possible."

"It was probably at a very high level. Camilla would never settle for anything less. According to Kajsa, she soon found her way into influential circles in Moscow, and among other things became the mistress of some rich, powerful member of the Duma—with him she began to forge connections with a strange crew of top engineers and criminals. Because she wound them round her little finger, she knew exactly where the weak point in the domestic economy was."

"And that was?"

"The fact that Russia is little more than a petrol station with a flag on top. They export oil and natural gas, but manufacture nothing worth mentioning. Russia needs advanced technology."

"She wanted to give them that?"

"At least that's what she pretended. But obviously she had her own agenda. I know that Kajsa was impressed by the way she built alliances and got herself political protection. She probably would have been loyal to Camilla forever if she hadn't become scared."

"What was she scared of?"

"Kajsa got to know a former elite soldier, a major I believe, and just lost her bearings. According to confidential information that Camilla had access to via her lover, the man had carried out a few shady operations for the Russian government. Among other things he had killed a well-known journalist, I presume you've heard of her, Irina Azarova. She'd taken a line against the government in various reports and books."

"Oh yes, truly a heroine. A horrible story."

"Absolutely. Something went wrong in the planning. Azarova was supposed to meet a critic of the regime in an apartment on a backstreet in a suburb southeast of Moscow, and according to the plan the major was supposed to shoot her as she came out. But no-one knew that the journalist's sister had developed pneumonia, and Irina had to look after two nieces aged eight and ten. As she and the girls walked out of the front entrance the major shot all three of them in the face. After that he fell into disgrace—not that anybody was particularly bothered about the children, but public opinion was getting out of hand and there was a risk that the whole operation would be uncovered and turned against the government. I think the major was afraid he'd be made a scapegoat. He was also dealing with a load of personal problems at the same time. His wife took off, he was left alone with a teenage daughter, and I believe there was even a possibility of his being evicted from his apartment. From Camilla's perspective that was a perfect setup: a ruthless person whom she could use, and who found himself in a vulnerable situation."

"So she got him on board."

"Yes, they met. Kajsa was there too, and the strange thing was that she immediately took a liking to this man. He wasn't at all what she'd been expecting, nothing like the people she knew at Svavelsjö M.C., who were killers. He was very fit and had a brutal look about him, but he was also cultivated and polite, she said, somehow vulnerable and sensitive. Kajsa could tell that he felt terrible about shooting those children. He was a murderer, a man whose specialty had been torture during the war in Chechnya, but he still had his moral boundaries, and that's why she was so upset when Camilla got her claws into him—almost literally. She dragged her nails across his chest and hissed like a cat, 'I want you to kill for me.' Her words were charged with sexual tension and with the skill of the devil she awakened the man's sadism. The more gruesome his descriptions of his murders, the more excited she became. I'm not sure I understood it, but it scared Kajsa to death. Not the murderer himself—Camilla. Her beauty and allure managed to bring out the predator in him."

"You never reported this to the police?"

"I asked Kajsa over and over. I told her she needed protection. She said she already had it and she forbade me to talk to the police. I was stupid enough to listen to her. After her death I told the investigators what I'd heard, but I doubt they believed me. It was nothing but hearsay about a man without a name in another country. Camilla was nowhere to be found in any records, and I never discovered anything about her new identity. At any rate Kajsa's murder is still unsolved."

"I understand how painful this all must be for you," Blomkvist said.

"You do?"

"I think so," he said, and was about to rest a sympathetic hand on her arm.

He was brought up short by his mobile buzzing in his pocket. He hoped it was Zander. But it was Stefan Molde. It took Blomkvist a few seconds to identify him as the person at the NDRE who had been in touch with Linus Brandell.

"What's this about?" he said.

"A meeting with a senior civil servant, an American who's on his way to Sweden. He wants to see you as early as possible tomorrow morning at the Grand Hôtel."

Blomkvist made an apologetic gesture in Fru Dahlgren's direction.

"I have a tight schedule," he said, "and if I'm to meet anybody at the very least I want a name and an explanation."

"The man is Edwin Needham, and it's about someone using the handle Wasp, who is suspected of serious crimes."

Blomkvist felt a wave of panic.

"OK," he said. "What time?"

"Five o'clock tomorrow morning would work."

"You've got to be joking!"

"Regrettably there's nothing to joke about in all this. I suggest you be punctual. Mr. Needham will see you in his room. You'll have to leave your mobile at reception, and you'll be searched."

Blomkvist got to his feet and took his leave of Margareta Dahlgren.

PART 3

ASYMMETRIC PROBLEMS

NOVEMBER 23–DECEMBER 3

Sometimes it is easier to put together than to put asunder.

Nowadays computers can easily multiply prime numbers with millions of digits. Yet it is extremely complicated to reverse the process. Numbers with only a few hundred digits present huge problems.

Encryption algorithms like RSA take advantage of the difficulties involved in prime number factorization. Prime numbers have become secrecy's best friends.

CHAPTER 25

NOVEMBER 23–24

It had not taken long for Salander to identify the Roger whom August had been drawing. She had seen a younger version of the man on a website showing former actors from Revolutionsteatern in Vasastan. He was called Roger Winter. He had had a couple of major film roles at the beginning of his career, but lately had ended up in a backwater, and was now less well known than his wheelchair-bound brother Tobias, an outspoken professor of biology who was said to have distanced himself altogether from Roger these days.

Salander wrote down Roger Winter's address and then hacked into the supercomputer NSF MRI. She also opened the programme with which she was trying to construct a dynamic system for finding the elliptic curves which were most likely to do the job, and with as few iterations as possible. But whatever she tried, she was unable to get any closer to a solution. The NSA file remained impenetrable. In the end she went and looked in on August. She swore. The boy was awake, sitting up in bed writing something on a piece of paper, and as she came closer she could see that he was doing more prime number factorizations.

"It's no good. It's not getting us anywhere," she muttered,

and when August began to rock back and forth hysterically once again she told him to pull himself together and go back to sleep.

It was late and she decided that she should rest for a while too. She took the bed next to his, but it was impossible to sleep. August tossed and turned and whimpered and in the end Salander decided to say something to try to settle him. The best she could think of was, "Do you know about elliptic curves?"

Of course she got no answer. That did not deter her from giving as simple and clear an explanation as she could.

"Do you get it?" she said.

Still August did not reply.

"OK, then," she went on. "Take the number 3,034,267, for example. I know you can easily find its prime number factors. But it can also be done using elliptic curves. Let's take curve $y = x^3 - x + 4$ and point $P = (1.2)$ on that curve, for example."

She wrote the equation on a piece of paper on the bedside table. But August did not seem to be following at all. She thought about those autistic twins she had read up on. They had some mysterious way of identifying large prime numbers, yet could not solve the simplest equations. Perhaps August was like that too. Perhaps he was more of a calculating machine than a genuine mathematical talent, and in any case it didn't matter right now. Her bullet wound was aching again and she needed some sleep. She needed to drive out all her old childhood demons which had come to life again because of the boy.

. . .

It was past midnight by the time Blomkvist got home, and even though he was exhausted and had to get up at the crack of dawn he sat down at his computer and Googled Edwin Needham.

There were quite a few Edwin Needhams in the world, including a successful rugby player who had made an extraordinary comeback having had leukaemia. There was one Edwin Needham who seemed to be an expert on water purification, and another who was good at getting himself into society photographs and looking daft. But none of them seemed right for someone who could have been involved in cracking Wasp's identity and accusing her of criminal activity. There was an Edwin Needham who was a computer engineer with a PhD from MIT, and that was at least the right line of business, but not even he seemed to fit. He was now a senior executive at Safeline, a leading business in computer virus protection, and that company would certainly have an interest in hackers. But the statements made by this Ed, as he was known, were all about market share and new products. Nothing he said rated higher than the usual clichéd sales talk, not even when he got the chance to talk about his leisure pursuits: bowling and fly fishing. He loved nature, he said, he loved the competitive aspect . . . The most threatening thing he seemed capable of doing was boring people to death.

There was a picture of him, grinning and bare-chested, holding up a large salmon, the sort of snap which is a dime a dozen in fishing circles. It was as dull as everything else, and yet, gradually Blomkvist began to wonder whether the dullness might be the whole point. He read through the material again and this time it struck him as something concocted, a façade. Slowly but surely he came to the opposite conclusion:

this was the man. You could smell the intelligence service a mile off, couldn't you? It felt like NSA or CIA.

Once again he looked at the photograph with the salmon, and this time he thought he saw something very different. He saw a tough guy putting on an act. There was something unwavering about the way he stood and grinned mockingly into the camera, at least that is what Blomkvist imagined, and again he thought of Salander. He wondered if he ought to tell her about this meeting. But there was no reason to worry her now, especially since he did not actually know anything, so instead he decided to go to bed. He needed to sleep for a few hours and have a clear head when he met Needham in the morning.

Pensively he brushed his teeth and undressed and climbed into bed. He realized he was more tired than he could have imagined and fell asleep in no time. He dreamed that he was being dragged under and almost drowned in the river Needham had been standing in. Afterwards he had a vague image of himself crawling along the riverbed surrounded by flopping, thrashing salmon. But he cannot have slept for long. He woke with a start and the growing conviction that he had overlooked something. His mobile was lying on the bedside table and his thoughts turned to Zander. The young man must have been on his mind all along.

Linda had double-locked the door. There was nothing odd about that—a woman in her situation had to take security precautions. It still made Zander feel uncomfortable, but he put that down to the apartment, or so he tried to convince himself. It was not at all what he had been expecting. Could this really be the home of one of her girlfriends?

The bed was broad but not especially long, and both the headboard and the footboard were made of shiny steel latticework. The bedspread was black, which made him think of a bier and he disliked the pictures on the walls—mostly framed photographs of men with weapons. There was a sterile, chilly feel to the whole place.

On the other hand he was probably just nervous and exaggerating everything, or looking for an excuse to get away. A man always wants to kill the thing he loves—hadn't Oscar Wilde said something like that? He looked at Linda. Never before had he seen such an extraordinarily beautiful woman, and now she was coming towards him in her tight blue dress which accentuated her figure. As if she had been reading his mind she said, "Would you rather go home, Andrei?"

"I do have quite a lot on my plate."

"I understand," she said, kissing him. "Then you must of course go and get on with your work."

"Maybe that would be best," he muttered as she pressed herself against him, kissing him with such force that he had no defence.

He responded to her kiss and put his hands on her hips, and she gave him a shove. She pushed him so hard that he staggered and fell backwards onto the bed, and for a moment he was scared. But then he looked at her. She was smiling as tenderly now as before and he thought: This was nothing more than a bit of rough play. She really wanted him, didn't she? She wanted to make love with him there and then, and he let her straddle his body, unbutton his shirt, and draw her fingernails over his stomach while her eyes shone with an intense glow and her large breasts heaved beneath her dress. Her mouth was open. A trickle of saliva ran down her chin and she whispered something he could not at first hear. "Now, Andrei," she whispered again. "Now!"

"Now?" he repeated uncertainly, and felt her tearing off his trousers. She was more brazen than he had expected, more accomplished and wildly lascivious than anybody he had met.

"Close your eyes and lie absolutely still," she said.

He obeyed and could hear her fiddling with something, he was not sure what. Then he heard a click and felt metal around his wrists, and realized he had been handcuffed. He was about to protest, he did not really go in for that sort of thing, but it all happened so fast. With lightning speed, as if she had experience, she locked his hands to the headboard. Then she bound his feet with rope and pulled tight.

"Gently," he said.

"Don't worry," but then she gave him a look he did not like and said something in a solemn voice. He must have misheard. "*What?*" he said.

"I'm going to cut you with a knife, Andrei," she said, and fixed a large piece of tape across his mouth.

Blomkvist was trying to tell himself not to worry. Why would anything have happened to Zander? No-one—apart from Berger and himself—knew that he was involved in protecting the whereabouts of Salander and the boy. They had been extremely careful with that piece of information, more care-

ful than with any other part of the story. And yet . . . why had
there been no word from him?

Zander was not someone who ignored his phone. On the
contrary, he normally picked up on the first ring whenever
Blomkvist called. But now there was no way of getting hold of
him, and that was strange, wasn't it? Or maybe . . . again Blomkvist tried to convince himself that Zander was busy working
and had lost track of time, or in the worst case had dropped
his mobile. That was probably all it was. But still . . . after all
these years Camilla had appeared out of nowhere. Something
must be going on, and what was it Bublanski had said?

"*We live in a world in which paranoia is a requirement.*"

Blomkvist reached for the telephone on the bedside table
and called Zander again. He got no answer this time either,
so decided to wake their new staff member, Emil Grandén,
who lived near Zander in Röda bergen in Vasastan. Grandén
sounded less than enthusiastic but promised to go over to
Zander's right away to see if he was there. Twenty minutes
later he rang back. He had been banging on Zander's door
for a while, he said, and he definitely wasn't at home.

Blomkvist got dressed and left his apartment, hurrying
through a deserted and storm-lashed Södermalm district
up to the magazine offices on Götgatan. With any luck, he
thought, Zander would be lying asleep on the sofa. It would
not be the first time he had nodded off at work and not heard
the telephone. That would be the simple explanation. But
Blomkvist felt more and more uneasy. When he opened the
door and turned off the alarm he shivered, as if expecting to
find a scene of devastation, but after a search of the premises
he found no trace of anything untoward. All the informa-

tion on his encrypted e-mail programme had been carefully deleted, just as they had agreed. It all looked as it should, but there was no Zander lying asleep on the office sofa, which was as shabby and empty as ever. For a short while Blomkvist sat there, lost in thought. Then he rang Grandén again.

"Emil," he said, "I'm sorry to harass you like this in the middle of the night. But this whole story has made me paranoid."

"I can understand that."

"I couldn't help hearing that you sounded a bit stressed when I was talking about Andrei. Is there anything you haven't told me?"

"Nothing you don't already know," Grandén said.

"What do you mean?"

"I mean that I've spoken to the Data Inspection Authority too."

"What do you mean, you too?"

"You mean you haven't—"

"No!" Blomkvist cut him short and heard Grandén's breathing at the other end of the line become laboured. There had been a terrible mistake.

"Out with it, Emil, and fast," he said.

"So . . ."

"Yes?"

"I had a call from a Lina Robertsson at the Data Inspection Authority. She said that you'd spoken and she agreed to raise the level of security on your computer, given the circumstances. Apparently the recommendations she'd given you were wrong and she was worried the protection would be insufficient. She said she wanted to get hold of the person who'd arranged the encryption for you ASAP."

"And what did you say?"

"That I knew nothing about it, except that I'd seen Andrei doing something at your computer."

"So you said she should get in touch with Andrei."

"I happened to be out at the time and told her that Andrei was probably still in the office. She could ring him there, I said. That was all."

"Jesus, Emil."

"She sounded really—"

"I don't care how she sounded. I just hope you told Andrei about the call."

"Maybe not right away. I'm pretty snowed under at the moment, like all of us."

"But you told him later."

"Well, he left the office before I got a chance to say anything."

"So you called him instead."

"Absolutely, several times. But . . ."

"Yes?"

"He didn't answer."

"OK," Blomkvist said, his voice ice-cold.

He hung up and dialled Bublanski's number. He had to try twice before the chief inspector came to the telephone. Blomkvist had no choice but to tell him the whole story— except for Salander and August's location.

Then he called Berger.

Salander had fallen asleep, but she was still ready for action. She was in her clothes, with her leather jacket and her boots on. She kept waking up, either because of the howling storm or because August was moaning in his sleep. But each time she dozed off, she had short, strangely realistic dreams.

Now she was dreaming about her father beating her mother, and she could feel that fierce old rage from her childhood. She felt it so keenly that it woke her up again. It was 3:45 a.m. and those scraps of paper on which she and August had written their numbers were still lying on the bedside table. Outside, snow was falling. But the storm seemed to have calmed and nothing unusual could be heard, just the wind rustling through the trees.

She felt uneasy, and at first she thought it was the dream lying like a fine mesh over the room. Then she shuddered. The bed next to her was empty—August was gone. She shot out of bed without making a sound, grabbed her Beretta from the bag on the floor, and crept into the large room next to the terrace.

The next moment she breathed a sigh of relief. August was sitting at the table busy with something. Without wanting to disturb him she leaned over his shoulder and saw that he was not writing new prime number factorizations, or drawing fresh scenes of abuse. He was sketching chess squares reflected in the mirrors of a wardrobe, and above them could be made out a threatening figure with his hand outstretched. The killer was taking shape. Salander smiled, and then she withdrew.

Back in the bedroom she sat on the bed, removed her pullover and the bandage, and inspected the bullet wound. It didn't look good, and she still felt weak. She swallowed another couple of antibiotic pills and tried to rest. She may even have gone back to sleep for a few moments. She was aware of a vague sensation that she had seen both Zala and Camilla in her dream, and the next second she became aware of a presence, though she had no idea what. A bird flapped its wings outside. She could hear August's laboured breathing in the kitchen. She was just about to get up when a scream pierced the air.

By the time Blomkvist left the office in the early morning hours to take a taxi to the Grand Hôtel, he still had no news of Zander. He tried again to persuade himself that he had been over-reacting, that any moment now his colleague would call from some friend's place. But the worry would not go away. He was vaguely aware that it had started snowing again, and that a woman's shoe had been left lying on the sidewalk. He took out his Samsung and called Salander on the RedPhone app.

Salander did not pick up, and that did not make him any calmer. He tried once more and sent a text from his Threema app: <Camilla's after you. Leave now!> Then he caught sight of a taxi coming down from Hökens gata. The driver gave a start when he saw him—at that moment Blomkvist looked dangerously determined. It did not help that he failed to respond to the driver's attempts to chat. He just sat back there in the darkness, his eyes bright with worry.

Stockholm was more or less deserted. The storm had abated but there were still white-crested waves on the water. Blomkvist looked across to the Grand Hôtel on the other side and wondered if he should forget about the meeting with Mr. Needham and drive straight out to Salander instead, or at least arrange for a police car to swing by. No, he couldn't do that without warning her. Another leak would be disastrous. He opened the Threema app again and tapped in:

```
<Shall I get help?>
```

No answer. Of course there was no answer. He paid the fare and climbed out of the taxi lost in thought. By the time he was pushing through the revolving doors of the hotel it was 4:20 in the morning—he was forty minutes early. He had never been forty minutes early for anything. But he was burning up inside and, before going to the reception desk to hand in his mobiles, he called Berger. He told her to try to get hold of Salander and to keep in touch with the police.

"If you hear anything, call the Grand Hôtel and ask for Mr. Needham's room."

"And who's he?"

"Someone who wants to meet me."

"At this time of day?"

Needham was in room 654. The door opened and there stood a man reeking of sweat and rage. There was about as much resemblance to the figure in the fishing photograph as there would be between a hungover dictator and his stylized statue. Needham had a drink in his hand and looked grim, unkempt, and a little bit like a bulldog.

"Mr. Needham," Blomkvist said.

"Ed," Needham said. "I'm sorry to haul you over here at this ungodly hour, but it's urgent."

"So it would seem," Blomkvist said drily.

"Do you have any idea what I want to talk to you about?"

Blomkvist shook his head and sat down on a sofa. There was a bottle of gin and some small bottles of Schweppes tonic on the desk next to it.

"No, why would you?" Needham said. "On the other hand it's impossible to know with guys like you. I've checked you out. You should know that I hate to flatter people—it leaves a bad taste in my mouth—but you're pretty outstanding in your profession, aren't you?"

Blomkvist gave a forced smile.

"Can we just get to the point?" he said.

"Just relax, I'll be crystal clear. I assume you know where I work."

"Not exactly," he answered truthfully.

"In Puzzle Palace, SIGINT City. I work for the world's spittoon."

"The NSA."

"Damn right. Do you have any idea how fucking insane you have to be to mess with us, Mikael Blomkvist, do you?"

"I have a pretty good idea," he said.

"And do you know where I think your girlfriend really belongs?"

"No."

"She belongs behind bars. For life!"

Blomkvist gave what he hoped was a calm, composed little smile. But in fact his mind was spinning. Did Salander hack the NSA? The mere thought terrified him. Not only was she in hiding, with killers on the hunt for her. Was she also going to have the entire U.S. intelligence services descend on her? It sounded . . . well, how did it sound? It sounded totally off the wall.

One of Salander's abiding characteristics was that she never did anything without first carefully analyzing the potential consequences. She did not follow impulses or whims and therefore he could not imagine she would take such an idiotic risk if there was the slightest chance of being found out. Sometimes she put herself in harm's way, that was true, but there was always a balance between costs and benefits. He refused to believe that she had gotten herself into the NSA, only to allow herself to be outwitted by the splenetic bulldog standing in front of him.

"I think you're jumping to conclusions," he said.

"Dream on, dude. But you might be able to save your girlfriend's skin if you promise to help me with one or two things."

"I'm listening," he said.

"Peachy. Let me begin by asking for a guarantee that you won't quote me as your source."

Blomkvist looked at him in surprise. He had not expected that.

"Are you some kind of whistle-blower?"

"God help me, no. I'm a loyal old bloodhound."

"But you're not acting officially on behalf of the NSA."

"You could say that right now I have my own agenda. Sort of doing my own thing. Well, how about it?"

"I won't quote you."

"Great. I also want to make sure we agree that what I'm going to tell you now will stay between us. You might be wondering why the hell I'm telling a fantastic story to an investigative journalist, only to have him keep his trap shut."

"Good question."

"I have my reasons. And I trust you, don't ask me why.

I'm betting that you want to protect your girlfriend, and you think the real story is elsewhere. Maybe I'll even help you with that, if you're prepared to cooperate."

"That remains to be seen," Blomkvist said stiffly.

"Well, a few days ago we had a data breach on our intranet, our NSANet. You know about that, don't you?"

"More or less."

"NSANet was created after 9/11, to improve coordination between our own intelligence services and those in other English-speaking countries—known as the Five Eyes. It's a closed system, with its own routers, portals, and bridges, and it's completely separate from the rest of the Internet. We administer our signals intelligence from there via satellite and fibre optic cables and that's also where we have our big databases and store classified analyses and reports: from Moray-rated documents, the least sensitive, all the way up to Umbra Ultra Top Secret, which even the President of the United States isn't allowed to see. The system is run out of Texas, which by the way is idiotic. But it's still my baby. Let me tell you, Mikael Blomkvist, I worked my ass off. Hammered away at it day and night so that no fucker could misuse it, never mind hack it. Every single little anomaly sets my alarm bells ringing, plus there's a whole staff of independent experts monitoring the system. These days you can't do a goddamn thing online without leaving footprints. At least that's the theory. Everything is logged and analyzed. You shouldn't be able to touch a single key without triggering a notification. But . . ."

"Someone did."

"Yes, and maybe I could have made my peace with it. There are always weak spots; we can always do better. Weak spots keep us on our toes. But it wasn't just the fact that she managed to get in. It was how she did it. She forced our server and created an advanced bridge, and got into the intranet via one of our systems administrators. That alone was a damn masterpiece. But that wasn't all: then the bitch turned herself into a ghost user."

"A what?"

"A ghost. She flew around in there without anyone noticing."

"Your alarm bells didn't go off?"

"That damn genius introduced a Trojan unlike anything else we knew, because otherwise our system would have identified it right away. The malware then kept upgrading her status. She got more and more access and soaked up highly classified passwords and codes and started to link and match records and databases, and suddenly—bingo!"

"Bingo what?"

"She found what she was looking for, and then she stopped wanting to be invisible. She wanted to show us what she'd found, and only then did my alarm bells go off: exactly when she wanted them to."

"And what did she find?"

"She found our hypocrisy, Mikael, our double-dealing, and that's why I'm sitting here with you and not on my fat ass in Maryland, sending the Marines after her. She was like a thief breaking into a house just to point out that it was already full of stolen goods, and the minute we found that out she became truly dangerous—so dangerous that some of our senior people wanted to let her off."

"But not you."

"Not me. I wanted to tie her to a lamppost and flay her

alive. But I had no choice except to give up my pursuit and that, Mikael, seriously pissed me off. I may look calm now, but you should have seen me . . . Jesus!"

"You were hopping mad."

"Damn right. And that's why I had you come here at this godforsaken hour. I need to get hold of Wasp before she flees the country."

"Why would she run?"

"Because she went from one crazy thing to the next, didn't she?"

"I don't know."

"I think you do."

"What makes you so sure she's your hacker in the first place?"

"That, Mikael, is what I'm going to lay on you now."

But he got no further.

The room telephone rang and Needham picked up right away. It was reception looking for Mikael Blomkvist, and Needham handed him the receiver. He soon gathered that the journalist had been given some alarming news, so it was no surprise when the Swede muttered a confused apology and ran out of the room. But Needham would not let him get away that easily. He grabbed his coat and chased after him.

Blomkvist was racing down the corridor like a sprinter. Needham did not know what was going on, but if it had something to do with the Wasp/Balder story, he wanted to be there. He had some trouble keeping up—the journalist was in too much of a hurry to wait for the lift and instead hurtled down the stairs. By the time Needham reached the ground floor, panting, Blomkvist had already retrieved his mobiles and was engrossed in another conversation while he ran on towards the revolving doors and out into the street.

"What's happening?" Needham said as the journalist ended his call and tried to hail a taxi further down the street.

"Problems!" Blomkvist said.

"I can drive you."

"Like hell you can. You've been drinking."

"At least we can take my car."

Blomkvist slowed his pace and turned to Needham.

"What is it you want?"

"I want us to help each other."

"You'll have to catch your hacker on your own."

"I no longer have the authority to catch anybody."

"OK, so where's the car?"

As they ran to Needham's rental car parked over by the Nationalmuseum, Blomkvist hurriedly explained that they were heading out to the Stockholm archipelago, towards Ingarö. He would get directions on the way and was not planning to observe any speed limits.

CHAPTER 26

NOVEMBER 24—MORNING

August screamed, and in the same instant Salander heard rapid footsteps along the side of the house. She grabbed her pistol and jumped to her feet. She felt terrible but ignored it.

As she rushed over to the doorway she saw a large man appear on the terrace. She thought she had a split-second advantage, but the figure did not stop to open the glass doors. He charged straight through them with his weapon drawn and shot at the boy.

Salander returned fire, or perhaps she had already done so, she did not know. She was not even conscious of the moment in which she started running towards the man. She only knew that she had crashed into him with a numbing force and now lay on top of him right by the round table where the boy had been sitting moments before. Without hesitation she headbutted the man.

The contact was so violent that her skull rang, and she swayed as she got to her feet. The room was spinning and there was blood on her shirt. Had she been hit again? She had no time to think. Where was August? No-one at the table, only pencils and drawings, crayons, prime number calculations. Where the hell was he? She heard a whimpering by the refrigerator and yes, there he was, sitting and shaking, his knees drawn up to his chest. He must have had time to throw himself to the floor.

Salander was about to rush over to him when she heard new, worrying sounds from outside, voices and branches snapping. Others were approaching, there was no time to lose. In a blinding flash she visualized the surrounding terrain and raced over to August. "Come on!" she said. August did not budge. Salander picked him up, her face twisted in pain. Every movement hurt. But they had to get away and August must have understood that too because he wriggled out of her grasp and ran alongside her. She sprang over to the table, grabbed her computer, and made for the terrace, past the man on the floor who raised himself groggily and tried to catch hold of August's leg.

Salander considered killing him. Instead she kicked him hard in the throat and stomach and threw away his weapon. Then she ran across the terrace with August and down towards the steep rocky slope. But suddenly she thought of the drawing. She had not seen how much progress August had made. Should she turn around? No, the others would be here any moment. They had to get away. But still . . . the drawing was also a weapon, and the cause of all this madness. She left August with her computer on the rock ledge she had identified the night before. She then launched herself back up the slope and into the house and looked on the table, and at first she could not see it. Drawings of that bastard Westman were everywhere, and rows of prime numbers.

But there—there it was, and above the chess squares and the mirrors there was now a pale figure with a sharply defined scar on his forehead, which Salander by now recognized only too well. It was the same man who was lying on the floor in front of her, moaning. She whipped out her mobile, took a photo and sent it to Bublanski and Modig. She had even scribbled a line at the top of the paper. But a second later she realized that was a mistake.

They were surrounded.

Salander had sent the same word to Blomkvist's Samsung as she had to Berger: CRISIS. It hardly left room for misunderstanding, not coming from Salander. However he looked at it, it could only mean that she and August had been discovered, and at worst they were under attack even now. He floored the accelerator as he passed Stadsgårdskajen and emerged onto the Värmdö road.

He was driving a new silver Audi A8, with Needham sitting next to him. Needham looked grim, and every now and then tapped something into his mobile. Blomkvist was not sure why he had allowed him to come along. Maybe he wanted to discover what the man had on Salander, or no, there was something else as well. Maybe Needham could even be useful. In any case he could hardly make the situation worse. The police had by now been alerted, but he doubted they would be able to assemble a unit quickly enough—especially as they were sceptical about the lack of information. Berger had been the focal point, trying to keep them all in contact with each other, and she was the only one who knew the way. He needed all the help he could get.

He was approaching Danviksbron. Needham said something, he did not hear what. His thoughts were elsewhere. He thought of Zander—what had they done to him? Why the hell had he not come along for a beer? Blomkvist tried his number again. He tried calling Salander too. But nobody answered.

"Do you want me to tell you what we have on your hacker?" Needham said.

"Yes . . . why not."

But they did not get anywhere this time either. Blomkvist's mobile rang. Bublanski.

"I hope you realize that you and I are going to have a lot to talk about later, and you can count on there being legal consequences."

"I understand."

"But for now I'm calling to give you some information. We know that Lisbeth Salander was alive at 4:22. Was that before or after she texted you?"

"Before, just before."

"OK."

"How can you be so specific about the time?"

"She sent us something extremely interesting. A drawing. I have to say, Mikael, it exceeded our hopes."

"So she was able to get the boy to draw."

"Oh yes. I have no idea what technical issues, if any, might arise in terms of admissibility of evidence or what objections a clever defence lawyer might raise. But as far as I'm concerned there's no doubt this is the murderer. The drawing is incredibly vivid, with that extraordinary mathematical precision again. In fact there's also an equation written at the bottom of the page, I have no idea if it's relevant to the case. But I sent the drawing to Interpol. If the man is anywhere in their database, he's toast."

"Are you going to send it to the press as well?"

"We're debating that."

"When will you be at the scene?"

"As soon as possible . . . hold on a second."

Blomkvist could hear another telephone ringing in the background, and for a minute or so Bublanski was gone on another call. When he returned he said briefly:

"We've had reports of gunfire out there. It doesn't sound good."

Blomkvist took a deep breath.

"Any news on Andrei?" he said.

"We've traced his mobile signal to a base station in Gamla Stan, but no further. We've had no signal at all for a while now, as if the mobile had been smashed or just stopped working."

Blomkvist drove even faster. Fortunately the roads were empty at that hour. At first he said very little to Needham, just a brief account of what was going on, but in the end he could not hold back. He needed something else to think about.

"Will you tell me what you've found out?"

"About Wasp? For a long time, zip. We were convinced we'd reached the end of the line," Needham said. "We'd left no stone unturned, and still got nowhere. In a way it made sense."

"How so?"

"A hacker capable of a breach like that should also be able to cover all tracks. I realized we wouldn't get anywhere by conventional means. So I skipped the forensic bullshit and went straight for the big question: Who had the chops to pull this off? That question was our best hope. There's hardly anyone out there with that level of ability. In that sense, you could say that the hacker's skill worked against them. Plus, we had analyzed the rootkit itself, and . . ."

Needham looked down at his mobile.

"Yes?"

"It had artistic qualities. Personal style, you might say. Now we just had to find its author, and so we started to send posts to the hacker community. There was one name, one handle, which came up time after time. Can you guess which one?"

"Maybe."

"It was Wasp. Sure, there were other names, but Wasp stood out. I ended up hearing so much mythical bullshit about this person that I was dying to crack their identity. We read every word Wasp had written online, studied every operation that had Wasp's signature on it. Soon we were certain that Wasp was a woman, and we guessed that she was Swedish. Several of the early posts were written in Swedish, which isn't much to go on, but since there was a Swedish connection in the organization she was tracking, and Frans Balder was Swedish, it was at least a place to start. I got in touch with the NDRE, and they searched their records, and then in fact . . ."

"What?"

"They had a breakthrough. Many years earlier they investigated a hacker operation that used that very handle, Wasp. It was so long ago that Wasp wasn't even particularly good at encryption yet."

"What happened?"

"Wasp had been looking for data on individuals who'd defected from other countries' intelligence services, and that was enough to trigger the NDRE's warning system. Their investigation led them to a psychiatric clinic for children in Uppsala, to a computer belonging to the head physician there, a man named Teleborian. Apparently he'd done some work for the Swedish Security Police, so he was above suspicion. Instead the NDRE concentrated on some mental health nurses who were targeted because they were . . . well, to be blunt about it, immigrants. It was such a stupid strategy. Anyway, nothing came of it."

"I can imagine."

"So I asked a guy at the NDRE to send over all the old material, and we sifted through it with a different mindset. You know, you don't have to be big and fat and shave in the mornings to be a good hacker. I've met twelve- and thirteen-year-olds who are crazy good. It was obvious to me that we should look at every child in the clinic at the time. I had three of my guys investigate each one of them, inside and out, and do you know what we found? One of the children was the daughter of former spy and arch-villain Zalachenko, who was known to our colleagues at the CIA. Then everything got really interesting. As you probably know there are some overlaps between the network the hacker was investigating and Zalachenko's old crime syndicate."

"That doesn't necessarily mean it was Wasp who hacked you."

"Of course not. But we took a closer look at this girl, and what can I say? She has an interesting background, doesn't she? A lot of information about her in the public record has been mysteriously deleted, but we still found more than enough and . . . I don't know, I could be wrong, but I get the feeling we're on the right track. Mikael, you don't know shit about me. But I know what it's like for a kid to see extreme violence at close quarters. And I know what it's like when society doesn't lift a finger to punish the guilty. It hurts like hell, and I'm not at all surprised that most children who experience it go under. They turn into destructive bastards themselves."

"Yes, unfortunately."

"But just a few grow to be as strong as bears, Mikael, and they stand up and fight back. Wasp was one of those, wasn't she?"

Blomkvist nodded pensively and pressed down on the accelerator a little more.

"They locked her up and kept trying to break her. But she kept coming back, and do you know what I think?"

"No."

"She got stronger each time. She became positively lethal. I bet she hasn't forgotten a single thing that happened. It's all etched into her, isn't it? And maybe that's at the bottom of this whole goddamn mess."

"You still haven't told me what you want," Blomkvist said bluntly.

"I want what Wasp wants. I want to set some things right."

"And get your hands on the hacker."

"I want to meet her and give her a piece of my mind and plug every last damn hole in our security. But above all I want to retaliate against certain people who wouldn't let me finish my job because Wasp exposed them. I have reason to believe you're going to help me with that."

"Why?"

"Because you're a good reporter. Good reporters don't want dirty secrets to go on being dirty secrets."

"And Wasp?"

"Wasp is going to get a chance to do her worst. You're going to help me with that too."

"Or else?"

"Or else I'll find a way of putting her inside, and making her life hell again, I swear."

"But for now all you want to do is talk to her?"

"No fucker is going to be allowed to hack into my system again, so I need to understand exactly how she did it. I want you to give her that message. I'm prepared to let your girl-friend go free if she'll sit down with me and explain."

"I'll tell her. Let's just hope . . ."

"That she's still alive," Needham said. They turned left at high speed in the direction of Ingaröstrand.

It was rare for Holtser to get things so wrong.

He had this romantic delusion that you could tell from a distance if a man was likely to succeed in close combat. That was why he had not been surprised when Kira's attempted seduction of Blomkvist had failed. Orlov and Bogdanov had been completely confident. But Holtser had had his doubts having seen the journalist for only one giddy second in Saltsjöbaden. Blomkvist looked like a problem. He looked like a man who could not be fooled or broken so easily.

With the younger journalist it was different. He looked like the archetypal weakling, yet nothing could have been further from the truth. Zander had resisted for longer than anyone Holtser had ever tortured. Despite excruciating pain he had refused to break. His eyes shone with a grim determi-nation which seemed buttressed by a higher principle, and at one point Holtser thought they would have to give up, that Zander would rather endure any suffering than talk. It was not until Kira solemnly promised that both Berger and Blomkvist from *Millennium* would be made to suffer the same that Zander finally caved.

By then it was 3:30 in the morning. Holtser knew that he would always remember the moment. Snow was falling over the skylights. The young man's face was dried out and hollow-eyed. Blood had splashed up from his chest and flecked his mouth and cheeks. His lips, which for a long time had been covered with tape, were split and oozing. He was a wreck, but still you could tell that he was a beautiful young man.

Holtser thought of Olga—how would she have felt about him? Wasn't this journalist just the kind of educated man she liked, someone who fights injustice, takes the side of beggars and outcasts? He thought about that, and about other things in his own life. After that he made the sign of the cross, the Russian cross, where one way leads to heaven and the other to hell, and then he glanced over at Kira.

She was lovelier than ever. Her eyes burned with light. She was sitting on a stool by the bed wearing an elegant blue dress—which had largely escaped the bloodstains—and said something in Swedish to Zander, something which sounded soft and tender. Then she took him by the hand. He gripped hers in return. He had nowhere else to turn for comfort. The wind howled outside in the alley. Kira nodded and smiled at Holtser. Snowflakes fell on the window ledge.

Afterwards they were sitting together in a Land Rover on the way out to Ingarö. Holtser felt empty, and was not happy with the way things were going. But there was no getting away from the fact that his own mistake had led them there, so he sat quietly, listening to Kira. She was strangely excited and spoke with searing hatred of the woman they were about to confront. Holtser did not think it was a good sign, and if he could have brought himself to do so he would have urged her to turn back and get the hell out of the country.

But he said nothing as they drove on in the darkness. Kira's sparkling, cold eyes frightened him, but he pushed away the thought.

He had to at least give her credit: she had been amazingly quick to put two and two together. Not only had she worked out who had hurtled in to save the boy on Sveavägen. She had also guessed who would know where the boy and the woman had disappeared to, and the person she came up with was none other than Mikael Blomkvist. They were baffled by her reasoning. Why would a reputable Swedish journalist harbour a person who appeared from nowhere and abducted a child from a crime scene? But the more they examined the theory, the more it held together. Not only did the woman— whose name was Lisbeth Salander—have close ties to the reporter, but something also happened at the *Millennium* offices.

After the murder in Saltsjöbaden, Bogdanov had hacked into Blomkvist's computer to try to find out why Balder had summoned him to his home in the middle of the night. Getting access to his e-mail had been easy enough. But that now stopped. When was the last time it had been impossible for Bogdanov to read someone's e-mails? Never, so far as Holtser was aware. Blomkvist had suddenly become much more careful—right after the woman and the boy disappeared from Sveavägen.

That in itself was no guarantee that the journalist knew where they now were. But as time went on there were more indications that the theory might be right, and in any case Kira did not seem to need ironclad evidence. She wanted to go for Blomkvist. Or, if not him, then someone else at the magazine. More than anything she was obsessive in her determination to track down the woman and the child.

Maybe Holtser could not understand the subtleties of Kira's motives. But it was for his benefit that they were going to do away with the boy. Kira chose to take significant risks for Holtser, and he was grateful, he really was, even though now in the car he felt uneasy.

He tried to draw strength from thinking about Olga. Whatever happened, she must not wake up and see a drawing of her father on all the front pages. He tried to reassure himself that the hardest part was behind them. Assuming Zander had given them the right address, the job should be straightforward.

They were three heavily armed men, four if you counted Bogdanov, who spent most of the time staring at his computer as usual. The team consisted of Holtser, Bogdanov, Orlov, and Dennis Wilton, a gangster who had been a member of Svavelsjö M.C. but now worked for Kira. Four men against one woman who was probably asleep, and was also protecting a child. It shouldn't be a problem, not at all. But Kira was almost manic:

"Don't underestimate Salander!"

She said it so many times that even Bogdanov, who always agreed with everything she said, began to get irritated. Of course Holtser had seen how fit and fast and fearless the woman had been on Sveavägen. But the way Kira described her, she must be some kind of superwoman. It was ridiculous. Holtser had never met a woman who could remotely match him—or even Orlov—in combat. Still, he promised to be careful. First he would go up and check out the terrain and prepare a strategy. They would not be drawn into a trap. He stressed this many times over, and when finally they arrived at an inlet next to a rocky slope and a jetty he took command. He told the others to get ready in the shelter of the car while he went ahead to locate the house.

Holtser liked early mornings. He liked the silence and the feeling of transition in the air. Now he was walking along, leaning forward and listening. It was reassuringly dark—no lights were on. He left the jetty behind him and came to a wooden fence with a rickety gate, next to an overgrown prickly bush. He opened the gate and started to climb steep wooden stairs holding the handrail on the right.

Soon he was able to make out the house above. It lay hidden behind pine trees and aspens and was only a dark outline, with a terrace on the south side. On the terrace were some glass doors which they would have no trouble breaking through. At first he saw no major difficulties. He was moving almost soundlessly and for a moment he considered finishing off the job himself. Maybe it was even his moral responsibility. It should be no more difficult than other jobs he had done, on the contrary. There were no policemen this time, no guards, nor any sign of an alarm system. True, he did not have his assault rifle with him, but then there was no need for

it. The rifle was excessive, the result of Kira's heated imagination. He had his pistol, his Remington, and that was more
than enough.

Suddenly—without his usual careful planning—he started
moving along the side of the house, up to the terrace and the
glass doors. Then he stiffened, without at first knowing why—it
could have been a sound, a movement, a danger he had only
half sensed. He looked up at the rectangular window above
him, but from his position he could not see into it. He kept still,
now less and less sure of himself. Could it be the wrong house?

He resolved to get closer and peer in, and then . . . he was
transfixed in the darkness. He was being observed. Those eyes
which once before had looked at him were now staring glass-
ily in his direction. That is when he should have reacted. He
should have sprinted around to the terrace, gone straight in,
and shot the boy. But again he hesitated. He could not bring
himself to draw his weapon. Faced with that look, he was lost.

The boy let out a shrill scream which seemed to set the
window vibrating, and only then did Holtser tear himself
out of his paralysis and race up to the terrace. Without a
moment's reflection he hurtled straight through the glass
doors and fired with what he thought was great precision,
but he never found out whether he hit his target.

An explosive shadowlike figure came at him with such
speed that he hardly had time to brace himself. He knew that
he fired another shot and that someone shot back. In the
next instant he slammed onto the floor with his full weight, a
young woman tumbling over him with a rage in her eyes that
was beyond anything he had ever seen. He reacted instinctively and tried to shoot again. But the woman was like a wild
animal. She threw her head back and . . . Crack!

When he came to he had a taste of blood in his mouth and his pullover was sticky and wet. He must have been hit. Just then the boy and the woman passed him, and he tried to grab hold of the boy's leg. At least he thought he did. But suddenly he was gasping for breath.

He no longer understood what was going on. Except that he was beaten, and by whom? By a woman. That insight became a part of his pain as he lay on the floor amid broken glass and his own blood, breathing heavily, his eyes shut. He hoped it would be over soon. When he opened his eyes again he was surprised to see the woman still there. Had she not just left? No, she was standing by the table, he could see her thin boyish legs. He tried his utmost to get up. He looked for his weapon, and at the same time caught a glimpse of Orlov through the window. He moved once more to attack the woman.

But before he could do anything the woman grabbed some papers and stormed out. From the terrace she threw herself headlong into the trees. Shots resounded in the dark and he muttered to himself, "Kill the bastards." But it was all he could do to get to his feet, and he cast a dull glance at the table in front of him.

There was a mass of crayons and paper which he looked at without really focusing. Then it was as if a claw took hold of his heart. He saw an evil demon with a pale face raising his hand to kill. It took a second or so for him to realize that the demon was himself, and he shuddered. Yet he could not take his eyes off the image.

Only then did he notice something scribbled at the top:

Mailed to police 4:22.

CHAPTER 27

NOVEMBER 24—MORNING

When Aram Barzani of the Rapid Response Unit made his way into Gabriella Grane's house at 4:52 he saw a large man dressed in black spread-eagled on the floor next to the round table.

He approached cautiously. The house seemed to have been abandoned, but he was not taking any risks. There were recent reports of a fierce gunfight up at the house and he could hear the excited voices of his colleagues outside on the steep rock slope.

"Here!" they shouted. "Here!"

Barzani did not understand what was going on, and for a moment he hesitated. Should he go to them? He decided to first see what condition the man on the floor was in. Broken glass and blood lay all around, and the table was strewn with torn-up pieces of paper and crushed crayons. The man on the ground was crossing himself feebly. He was mumbling something. Probably a prayer. It sounded Russian, Barzani caught the word "Olga." He told the man that a medical team was on its way.

"They were sisters," the man said in English.

But it sounded so confused that Barzani attached no

importance to it. Instead he searched through the man's clothes, made sure that he was unarmed, and thought he had probably been shot in the stomach. His pullover was soaked in blood, and he looked alarmingly pale. Barzani asked what had happened. He got no reply, not at first. Then the man gasped out another strange sentence.

"My soul was captured in a drawing," he said, and seemed to be about to lose consciousness.

Barzani stayed for a few minutes to watch him, but when he heard from the ambulance crew he left the man and went down to the rocky slope. He wanted to discover what his colleagues had been shouting about. The snow was still falling and it was icy underfoot. Down by the water voices could be heard and the sound of more cars arriving. It was still dark and hard to see and there were many uneven rocks and straggly pines. The landscape was dramatic and steep. It could not have been easy to fight in this terrain and Barzani was gripped with foreboding. He noticed that it had become strangely quiet.

But his team members were not far away behind an over-grown aspen. He felt afraid—a rare occurrence for him—when he saw them staring down at the ground. What had they seen? Was the autistic boy dead?

He walked over slowly, thinking about his own boys, six and nine now. They were crazy about football—did nothing else, talked about nothing else. Björn and Anders. He and Dilvan had given them Swedish names because they had thought it would make their lives easier. What kind of people come out here to kill a child? He was gripped by a sudden fury. But in the next moment he breathed a sigh of relief.

There was no boy there, but two men lying on the ground,

apparently both shot in the stomach. One of them—a brutal-looking type with pock-marked skin and a stubby boxer's nose—tried to get up but was pushed down again. His face betrayed his humiliation and his right hand was shaking with pain or rage. The other man, who was wearing a leather jacket and had his hair in a ponytail, seemed in worse shape. He lay still and stared in shock at the dark sky.

"No evidence of the child?" Barzani said.

"Nothing," his colleague Klas Lang answered.

"And the woman?"

"No sign of her."

Barzani was not sure if this was good news and he asked a few more questions. But no-one knew what had happened. The only certainty was that two automatic weapons, Barrett REC7s, had been found thirty or forty yards away, towards the jetty. They were assumed to belong to the men, but when asked how they had ended up there, the man with the pock-marked face spat out an incomprehensible answer.

Barzani and his colleagues spent the next fifteen minutes combing the terrain. All they could find were further signs of combat. More and more people began to arrive on the scene: ambulance crew, Detective Sergeant Modig, two or three crime scene technicians, a succession of regular policemen, and the journalist Mikael Blomkvist, who was accompanied by a massive American with a crew cut who immediately commanded everyone's respect. At 5:25 they were informed that a witness was waiting to be interviewed down by the seashore and parking area. The man wanted to be addressed as K.G. He was actually called Karl-Gustav Matzon. He had recently bought a new-build on the other side of the water.

According to Lang, he needed to be taken with a grain of salt: "The old boy has a very vivid imagination."

Modig and Holmberg were standing in the parking area, trying to make sense of what had happened. The picture so far was fragmented and they were hoping that the witness K.G. Matzon would bring a measure of clarity to the night.

But when they saw him coming towards them along the shoreline, that seemed less and less likely. K.G. Matzon was resplendent in a Tyrolean hat, green checked trousers, and a red Canada Goose jacket and he was sporting an absurd twirly moustache. He looked as if he were trying to be funny.

"K.G. Matzon?" Modig asked.

"The very same," he said, and without any prompting—maybe he realized that his credibility needed a boost—he explained that he ran True Crimes, a publishing house which produced books on notable crimes.

"Excellent. But right now we'd like a factual account, not some sales pitch for a forthcoming book," Modig said, to be on the safe side.

Matzon said of course he understood. He was after all a "respectable person." He had woken up at a ridiculous hour, he said, and lain there listening to "the silence and the calm." But just before 4:30 he heard something which he immediately recognized as a pistol shot, so he quickly got dressed and went onto his terrace—which had a view of the beach, the rock promontory, and the parking area where they were now standing.

"What did you see?"

"Nothing. It was eerily quiet. Then the air exploded. It sounded as if a war had broken out."

"You heard more shots?"

"There were cracks of gunfire from the promontory on the other side of the inlet and I stared across, stunned, and then . . . did I mention I was a birdwatcher?"

"No, you didn't."

"Well, it's made my eyesight very good, you see. I've got eagle eyes. I'm used to pinpointing tiny details far off, and I'm sure that's why I noticed a small dot on the rock ledge up there, do you see it? The edge of it sort of cuts into the slope like a pocket."

Modig looked up at the slope and nodded.

"At first I couldn't tell what it was," Matzon continued. "But then I realized it was a child, a boy I think. He was sitting up there in a crouch and trembling, at least that's how it seemed to me, and then suddenly . . . my God, I'll never forget it."

"What?"

"Someone came racing down from above, a woman, and she leaped into the air and landed so violently on the rock ledge that she all but fell off it. After that they sat there together, she and the boy, and just waited, waited for the inevitable. And then . . ."

"Yes?"

"Two men appeared holding assault rifles and shot and shot. As I'm sure you can imagine, I threw myself to the ground. I was scared I'd get hit. But I couldn't help looking up at them all the same. You see, from where I was the boy and the girl were clearly visible, but they were invisible to the men standing at the top, at least for the moment. It was obvious to me that it was only a matter of time before they were discovered and there was no escape. As soon as they left the rock ledge the men would see them and kill them. It was a hopeless situation."

"But we've found neither the boy nor the woman up there," Modig said.

"That's just it! The men got closer and closer—they only needed to lean forward to see the woman and the child. In the end they could probably have heard them breathing. But then . . ."

"Yes?"

"You're not going to believe this. That man from the Rapid Response Unit definitely didn't."

"Well, go ahead and tell me, and we can worry later about whether it's believable."

"When the men stopped to listen, maybe they sensed they were very close, the woman leaped to her feet and shot them. Bang, bang! Then she rushed forward and threw their weapons away. It was like an action film, and after that she ran, or rather rolled, almost fell down the slope with the boy to a BMW standing here in the parking area. Just before they got into the car I saw that the woman was holding something, it looked like a computer bag."

"Did they drive off in the BMW?"

"At a fearful speed. I have no idea where they went."

"OK."

"But that's not all."

"What do you mean?"

"There was another car there, a Range Rover, I think, black, a new model."

"And what happened to that one?"

"I was busy ringing the emergency services, but just as I was about to hang up I saw two more people coming down from the wooden stairs over there, a tall skinny man and a woman. I didn't get a good look at them from that distance. But I can tell you two things about that woman."

"Yes?"

"She was a twelve-pointer, and she was angry."

"Twelve-pointer meaning beautiful?"

"Or at least glamorous, classy. You could see it a mile off. But, boy, was she furious. Just before they got into the Range Rover she slapped the man, and the weird thing is: he hardly reacted. He just nodded as if he thought he deserved it. Then he got behind the wheel and they were gone."

Modig noted everything down, realizing that she had to get out a nationwide search bulletin for both the Range Rover and the BMW without delay.

Gabriella Grane was drinking a cappuccino in her kitchen on Villagatan and thinking that she was holding it together, all things considered. But she was probably in shock.

Helena Kraft wanted to see her at 8:00 a.m. in her office at Säpo. Grane guessed that she wouldn't just get the sack. There would be judicial consequences too, which would pretty much ruin her prospects of finding another job. At thirty-three, her career was over.

And that was by no means the worst of it. She had known that she was flouting the law and had taken a conscious risk. But she had done it because she believed it was the best way to protect Frans Balder's son. Now, after the shoot-out at her summer place, no-one seemed to know where the boy was.

He might be injured, or even dead. Grane was racked by the most devastating feelings of guilt: first the father and then the son.

She got up and looked at the clock. It was 7:15 and she needed to get going to give herself time to clean out her desk before the meeting with Kraft. She made up her mind to behave with dignity, to not make any excuses or beg to be allowed to stay. Her Blackphone rang, but she couldn't be bothered to answer. Instead she put on her boots and her Prada coat and an extravagant red scarf. If she was going under, she might as well go with a bit of panache. She stood in front of the hall mirror and touched up her makeup, wryly giving herself the victory sign, as Nixon had when he resigned. Then her Blackphone rang again. This time she picked up reluctantly. It was Casales at the NSA.

"I just heard," she said.

Of course she had.

"How are you feeling?"

"How do you think?"

"Like the worst person in the whole world?"

"Pretty much."

"Who'll never get another job?"

"Spot on, Alona."

"In that case let me tell you, you have nothing to be ashamed of. You did the right thing."

"Are you trying to be funny?"

"This isn't the time for jokes, sweetheart. You have a mole on your team."

Gabriella took a deep breath. "Who is it?"

"Nielsen."

Gabriella froze. "Do you have proof?"

"Oh yes, I'll send it all over in a few minutes."

"Why would Nielsen betray us?"

"I guess he didn't see it as a betrayal."

"What on earth did he see it as, if not betrayal?"

"Collaborating with Big Brother maybe, doing his duty by the leading nation in the free world, what do I know?"

"So he gave you information."

"He helped us to help ourselves, actually. He gave us information about your server and your encryption. It's not as outrageous as it sounds. Let's face it, we listen in on everything from the neighbours' gossip to the prime ministers' phone calls."

"But this time the information was leaked a stage further."

"In this case it seeped out like we were a funnel. I know, Gabriella, that you didn't exactly stick to the rule book. But I'm absolutely convinced that you were in the right, and I'll make sure your superiors get to hear it. You could see that there was something rotten in your organization, so you couldn't act within it, yet you were determined not to shirk your responsibility."

"But it went wrong."

"Sometimes things go wrong, no matter how careful you are."

"Thanks, Alona, it's nice of you to say so. But if anything has happened to August Balder, I will never forgive myself."

"Gabriella, the boy is OK. He's cruising around in a car somewhere with Miss Salander, in case someone's still chasing them."

Grane could not take it in. "What do you mean?"

"That he's unhurt, babe, and thanks to him his father's murderer has been caught and identified."

"You're saying August is alive?"

"That's right."

"How do you know?"

"Let's just say I have a very well-placed source."

"Alona . . ."

"Yes?"

"If what you say is true, you've given me back my life."

After hanging up, Grane rang Kraft and insisted that Mårten Nielsen be present at their meeting. Reluctantly, Kraft agreed.

It was 7:30 in the morning when Needham and Blomkvist made their way down the steps from Grane's summer house to the Audi in the parking area by the beach. Snow lay over the landscape and neither of them said a word. At 5:30 Blomkvist had gotten a text message from Salander, as brisk and to the point as ever.

<August unhurt. We'll keep our heads down awhile longer.>

Again Salander had not mentioned her own state of health. But it was an incredible relief to hear about the boy. Afterwards Blomkvist had been questioned at length by Modig and Holmberg and he told them every detail of what he and the magazine had been doing over the past few days. They were not particularly well disposed towards him, yet he got the feeling that somehow they understood. Now, an hour later, he was walking past the jetty. Up the slope a deer scampered into the forest. Blomkvist settled into the driver's seat and waited for Needham, who came loping along in his wake. The American's back was giving him trouble.

On the way towards Brunn they found themselves in traffic. For several minutes no cars were moving and Blomkvist thought of Zander, who was constantly on his mind. They had still not had any sign of life.

"Can you get something noisy on the radio?" Needham said.

Blomkvist tuned into 107.1 and got James Brown belting out what a sex machine he was.

"Give me your phones," Needham said.

He stacked them next to the speakers at the back of the car. He clearly meant to talk about something sensitive, and Blomkvist had nothing against that—he had to write his story and needed all the facts he could get. But he also knew better than most that there's no such thing as a leak without an agenda. Although Blomkvist felt a certain affinity with Needham and even appreciated his grumpy charm, he did not trust him for one second.

"Let's hear it," he said.

"You could put it this way," Needham began. "We know that in business and industry there's always someone taking advantage of inside information."

"Agreed."

"For a while we were pretty much spared that in the world of intelligence, for the simple reason that we guarded different kinds of secrets. The dynamite was elsewhere. But since the end of the Cold War, that's changed. Surveillance in general has become more widespread. These days we control huge amounts of valuable material."

"And there are people taking advantage of this, you say."

"Well, that's basically the whole point. Corporate espionage helps keep companies informed about the strengths and weaknesses of the competition. It's a grey area. Something that was seen as criminal or unethical decades ago is now standard operating procedure. We're not much better than the NSA, in fact maybe we're even . . ."

"The worst?"

"Just take it easy, let me finish," Needham said. "I'd say we have a certain moral code. But we're a large organization with tens of thousands of employees and inevitably there are rotten apples—one or two very highly placed rotten apples I was thinking of handing you."

"Out of the kindness of your heart, of course," said Blomkvist with a touch of sarcasm.

"OK, maybe not entirely. But listen. When senior management at our place crosses the line and gets into criminal activities, what do you think happens?"

"Nothing very nice."

"As you know, there's a corrupt unit at Solifon, headed up by a man called Zigmund Eckerwald, whose job it is to find out what the competing tech companies are up to. They not only steal the technology but also sell what they steal. That's bad for Solifon and maybe even for the whole Nasdaq."

"And for you too."

"That's right. It turns out that our two most senior executives in industrial espionage—their names are Jacob Barclay and Brian Abbot—get help from Eckerwald and his gang. In exchange the NSA helps Eckerwald with large-scale communications monitoring. Solifon identifies where the big innovations are happening, and our idiots pluck out the drawings and the technical details."

"I assume the money this brings in doesn't always end up in the state coffers."

"It's worse than that, buddy. If you do this sort of thing as a state employee, you make yourself very vulnerable, especially because Eckerwald and his gang are also helping major criminals. To be fair, at first they probably didn't know their clients were major criminals."

"But that's what they were?"

"Damn right. And they took advantage too. I could only dream of recruiting hackers at their level of expertise. The essence of this illegal business is to exploit information, so you can imagine: once they realized what our guys at the NSA were up to, these criminals knew they were sitting on a goldmine."

"So they were in a position to blackmail."

"Talk about having the upper hand. Our guys haven't just been stealing from large corporations. They've also plundered small family businesses and solo entrepreneurs who are struggling to survive. It wouldn't look too good if everything came out. So as a result the NSA is forced to help not just Eckerwald and Solifon, but also the criminals."

"You mean the Spiders?"

"You got it. Maybe for a while everyone stays happy. It's big business and the money's rolling in. But then a little genius pops up in the middle of the action, a certain Professor Balder, and he's just as good at ferreting around as he is at doing everything else. So he finds out about this scheme, or at least part of it. Then of course everyone's scared shitless and decides that something has to be done. I'm not entirely clear on how these decisions got made. I'm guessing our guys hoped legal threats would be enough. But when you're in bed with a bunch of criminals . . . The Spiders prefer violence. They probably drew our guys into the plan at a late stage, just to bind them in even more tightly."

"Jesus."

"I would never have gotten to know any of this if we hadn't been hacked," said Needham.

"Another reason to leave the hacker in peace."

"Which is exactly what I'm going to do, so long as she tells me how she did it."

"I don't know how much your promises are worth. But there's another thing I've been wondering about," Blomkvist went on.

"Shoot."

"You mentioned two guys, Barclay and Abbot. Are you sure it stops with them? Who's their boss?"

"I can't give you his name, unfortunately. It's classified."

"I suppose I'll have to live with that."

"You will," Needham said inflexibly. At that moment Blomkvist noticed that traffic was starting to flow again.

CHAPTER 28

NOVEMBER 24—AFTERNOON

Professor Edelman was standing in the parking lot at the Karolinska Institute wondering what in heaven's name he had let himself in for. He was embarking on an arrangement which would mean his having to cancel a whole series of meetings, lectures, and conferences.

Even so he felt strangely elated. He had been entranced not just by the boy but also by the young woman, who looked as if she had come straight from a street brawl but who drove a brand-new BMW and spoke with chilling authority. He had barely been aware of what he was doing when he said, "Yes, sure, why not," to her questions, although it was obviously rash.

The only grain of independence he had shown was to have declined all offers of compensation. He was going to pay his own travel and hotel expenses, he said. He must have felt guilty. But he was moved to take the boy under his wing, and his scientific curiosity was piqued. A savant who both drew with photographic exactitude and could perform prime number factorization—how absolutely riveting. To his own surprise he even decided to skip the Nobel Prize dinner. The young woman had made him take leave of his senses.

. . .

Hanna Balder was sitting in the kitchen on Torsgatan, smoking. It felt as if she had done little else aside from sit there and puff away with a pit in her stomach. She had been given an unusual amount of support, but she had also been getting an unusual amount of physical abuse.

Lasse Westman could not handle her anxiety. It detracted from his own martyrdom. He was always flying into a rage and yelling, "Can't you even keep track of your own brat?" Often he lashed out with his fists or threw her across the apartment like a rag doll. Now he would probably go crazy. She had spilled coffee all over the *Dagens Nyheter* culture section, and Lasse was already worked up because of a theatre review he found too sympathetic to actors he did not like.

"What the hell have you done?"

"I'm sorry," she said quickly. "I'll wipe it up."

She could tell from the set of his mouth even before he knew it himself that he would hit her, and she was so well prepared for his slap that she did not say one word or even move her head. She could feel the tears welling up and her heart pounding. But actually that had nothing to do with the blow.

That morning she had received a call which was so perplexing that she hardly understood it: August had been found, had disappeared again, and was "probably" unharmed— "probably." It was impossible for Hanna to know if she should be more worried, or less. Hours had gone by without further news.

Suddenly she got to her feet, no longer caring whether she would get another beating or not. She went into the living room and heard Lasse panting behind her. August's drawing paper was still lying on the floor and an ambulance was wailing outside. She heard footsteps in the stairwell. Was someone on their way here? The doorbell rang.

"Don't open. It'll be some bloody journalist," Lasse snapped.

Hanna did not want to open either. Still, she could not very well ignore it, could she? Perhaps the police wanted to interview her again, or maybe, maybe they had more information now, good news or bad news.

As she went to the door she thought of Frans. She remembered how he had stood there saying that he had come for August. She remembered his eyes and the fact that he had shaved off his beard, and her own longing for her old life, before Lasse Westman—a time when the telephone rang and the job offers came flooding in, and fear had not yet set its claws into her. She opened the door with the safety chain on and at first she saw nothing; just the lift door, and the reddish-brown walls. Then a shock ran through her, and for a moment she could not believe it. But it really was August! His hair was a tangled mess and his clothes were filthy. He was wearing a pair of sneakers much too big for him, and yet: he looked at her with the same serious, impenetrable expression as ever. She would not have expected him to turn up on his own. But when she undid the safety chain she gave a start. Next to August stood a cool young woman in a leather jacket, with scratch marks on her face and earth in her hair, glaring down at the floor. She had a large suitcase in her hand.

"I've come to give you back your son," she said without looking up.

"Oh my God," Hanna said. "My God!"

That was all she managed to say. For a few seconds she was completely at a loss as she stood there in the doorway. Then her shoulders began to shake. She sank to her knees and, forgetting that August hated to be hugged, she threw her arms around him, murmuring, "My boy, my boy," until the tears came. The odd thing was: August not only let her do it, he also seemed on the verge of saying something, as if he had learned to talk on top of everything. But before he had the chance, Lasse was standing behind her.

"What the hell . . . well, look who's here!" he growled, as if he wanted to carry on with their fight.

But then he got a grip on himself. It was an impressive piece of acting, in a way. In the space of a second he began to radiate the presence which used to make women swoon.

"We get the kid delivered to our front doorstep," he said to the woman on the landing. "How convenient. Is he OK?"

"He's OK," the woman said in a strange monotone, and she walked into the apartment with her suitcase and her muddy boots.

"Just come right on in," Lasse said in an acid tone.

"I'm here to help you pack, Lasse."

This was such a strange reply that Hanna was convinced she had misheard. Lasse did not seem to understand either. He just stood there looking stupid, his mouth wide open.

"What did you say?"

"You're moving out."

"Is this some kind of joke?"

"Not at all. You're leaving this house, right now, and you're not coming anywhere near August ever again. You've seen him for the last time."

"You must be insane!"

"Actually I'm being unusually generous. I was planning on throwing you down the stairs, but instead I brought a suitcase, thought I'd let you pack some shirts and pants."

"What kind of a freak are you?" Lasse shouted, both bewildered and beside himself with rage. He bore down on the woman with the full weight of his hostility, and Hanna wondered if he was going to take a swipe at her as well.

But something stopped him. Maybe it was the woman's eyes, or possibly the fact that she did not react like anyone else would have done. Instead of backing off or looking frightened she only smiled at him, and handed him a few crumpled pieces of paper from an inside pocket.

"If ever you and your friend Roger should find yourselves missing August, you can always look at this and remember," she said.

Lasse turned over the papers, confused. Then he screwed up his face in horror and Hanna took a quick look herself. They were drawings and the top one was of . . . Lasse. Lasse swinging his fists and looking profoundly evil. Later she would hardly be able to explain it. It was not just that she now understood what had been going on when August had been alone at home with Lasse and Roger. She also saw her own life more clearly and soberly than she had in years.

Lasse had looked at her with exactly that twisted, livid face hundreds of times, most recently a minute ago. She knew this was something no-one should have to endure, neither she nor August, and she shrank back. At least she thought she did, because the woman looked at her with a new focus. Hanna eyed her uneasily. They seemed on some level to understand each other.

"Am I right, Hanna, he's got to go?" the woman asked.

The question was potentially lethal, and Hanna looked down at August's oversize shoes.

"What are those shoes he's wearing?"

"Mine."

"Why?"

"We left in a hurry this morning."

"And what have you been doing?"

"Hiding."

"I don't understand—" she began, but got no further.

Lasse grabbed hold of her violently.

"Why don't you tell this psychopath that the only one who's leaving is her!" he roared.

Hanna cowered, but then . . . It may have been something to do with the expression on Lasse's face, or the sense of something implacable in the young woman's bearing. Hanna heard herself say, "You're leaving, Lasse! And don't ever come back!"

It was as if someone else were speaking in her place. After that things moved quickly. Lasse raised his hand to strike her, but no blow came, not from him. The young woman reacted with lightning speed, and hit him in the face two, three times like a trained boxer, felling him with a kick to the leg.

"What the hell!" was all he was able to say.

He crashed to the floor, and the young woman stood over him. Hanna realized how long and how desperately she had wished Lasse Westman out of her life.

Bublanski longed to see Rabbi Goldman.

He also longed for some of Modig's orange chocolate, for his new Dux bed, and for springtime. But right now it was his job to get some order into this investigation. It was true that, on one level, he was satisfied. August Balder was said to be unharmed and on his way home to his mother.

Thanks to the boy himself and to Lisbeth Salander, his father's killer had been arrested, even though it was far from certain that he would survive his injuries. He was in intensive care at Danderyd Hospital. He was called Boris Latvinov but had for some time been using the name Jan Holtser. He was a former elite soldier from the Soviet army, a major, and his name had cropped up in the past in several murder investigations, but he had never been convicted. He had his own business in the security industry, and was both a Finnish and Russian citizen, and a resident of Helsinki; no doubt someone had doctored his government records.

The other two people who had been found at the summer house on Ingarö had been identified by their fingerprints: Dennis Wilton, an old gangster from Svavelsjö MC who had done time for both aggravated robbery and assault; and Vladimir Orlov, a Russian with a criminal record in Germany for procuring, whose two wives had died in unexplained circumstances. None of the men had yet said a word about what happened, or about anything at all. Nor did Bublanski hold out much hope that this would change. Men like that tend to hold their tongues in police interviews. But then those were the rules of the game.

What Bublanski was unhappy about, though, was the feeling that these three men were no more than foot soldiers and that there was a leadership above them linked to the upper echelons of society in both Russia and in the United States. He had no problem with a journalist knowing more about his investigation than he did. In that respect he was not proud. He just wanted to move ahead, and was grateful for all information, whatever its source. But Blomkvist's discerning approach to the case had pointed up their own shortcomings and reminded Bublanski of the leak and the dangers to which the boy had been exposed because of them. On this score his anger would never subside, and perhaps that explains why he was so irritated at Helena Kraft's eager efforts to get hold of him—and the head of Säpo was not the only one. The IT people at the National Criminal Police were also after him, as were Chief Prosecutor Richard Ekström and a Stanford professor by the name of Steven Warburton from the Machine Intelligence Research Institute, who wanted to talk about "a significant risk," as Amanda Flod put it.

That bothered Bublanski, along with a thousand other things. And there was someone knocking at his door. It was Modig, who looked tired and was wearing no makeup, revealing something different about her face.

"All three prisoners are having surgery," she said. "It'll be a while before we can question them again."

"Try to question them, you mean."

"I did manage to have a brief word with Latvinov. He was conscious for a while before his operation."

"Did he say anything?"

"Just that he wanted to talk to a priest."

"How come all lunatics and murderers are religious these days?"

"While all sensible old chief inspectors doubt the existence of their God, you mean?"

"Now, now."

"Latvinov also seemed dejected, and that's a good sign, I think," Modig said. "When I showed him the drawing he waved it away with a resigned expression."

"So he didn't try to claim it was a fabrication?"

"He just closed his eyes and started to talk about his priest."

"Have you discovered what this American professor wants, the one who keeps calling?"

"What . . . no . . . he'll only talk to you. I think it's about Balder's research."

"And Zander, the young journalist?"

"That's what I came to talk about. It doesn't look good."

"What do we know?"

"That he worked late and was spotted disappearing down past Katarinahissen accompanied by a beautiful woman with strawberry- or dark-blond hair and expensive clothes."

"I'd not heard that."

"They were seen by a man called Ken Eklund, a baker at Skansen. He lives in the *Millennium* building. He said they looked as if they were in love, or at least Zander did."

"You think it could have been some sort of honey trap?"

"It's possible."

"And this woman, might she be the same one who was seen at Ingarö?"

"We're looking into that. But I don't like the idea that they seemed to be heading towards Gamla Stan. Not only because we picked up Zander's mobile phone signals there. That revolting specimen Orlov, who just spits at me whenever I try to question him, has an apartment on Mårten Trotzigs gränd."

"Have we been there?"

"Not yet. We've only just located it. The apartment was registered in the name of one of his companies."

"Let's hope there's nothing unpleasant waiting for us there."

Westman was lying on the floor in the entrance hall on Torsgatan, wondering how he could be so terrified. She was just a chick, a pierced punk chick who hardly came up to his chest. He should be able to throw her out like some little rat. Yet he was as if paralyzed and it had nothing to do with the way the girl fought, he thought, still less with the fact that her foot was planted on his stomach. It was something about her look or her whole being that he could not put his finger on. For a few minutes he lay there like an idiot and listened.

"I'm reminded of the fact," she said, "that there's something really wrong in my family. We seem to be capable of the most unimaginable cruelties. It may be a genetic defect. Personally, I've got this thing against men who harm children and women, and that makes me dangerous. When I saw August's drawings of you and your friend Roger, I wanted to hurt you, badly. But I think August has been through enough, so there's a slight chance that you and your friend might get off more lightly."

"I'm—" Westman began.

"Quiet," she said. "This isn't a negotiation, it's not even a conversation. I'm just setting out the terms, that's all. Legally, there are no problems. Frans was wise enough to register the apartment in August's name. This is how it's going to be: You have precisely four minutes to pack your things and get out. If you or Roger ever come back here or contact August in any way, I'll make you suffer so much that you'll be incapable of doing anything nice again, for the rest of your lives. In the meantime, I'll be preparing to report you to the police with full details of the abuse you've subjected August to. As you know we have more than the drawings to go on. We have testimonies from psychologists and experts. I'll also be contacting the evening papers to tell them that I have material which substantiates the image of you that emerged in connection with your assault on Renata Kapusinski. Remind me, Lasse, what was it that you did? Bite through her cheek and kick her in the head?"

"So you're going to go to the press."

"I'm going to go to the press. I'm going to cause you and your friend every conceivable disgrace. But maybe—I'm saying maybe—you can hope to escape the worst of the humiliation so long as you're never again seen near Hanna and August, and if you never again harm a woman. As a matter of fact I couldn't give a shit about you. Once you leave, and if you live like a shy and timid little monk, you may be all right. I have my doubts—as we all know, the rate of re-offending for violence against women is high, and basically you're a bastard, but with a bit of luck, who knows . . . Got it?"

"I've got it," he said, hating himself for saying so.

He saw no way out, he could only agree and do as he was told, so he got up and went into the bedroom and quickly packed some clothes. Then he took his coat and his mobile and left.

He had nowhere to go. He had never felt more pathetic in his life. Outside an unpleasant sleety rain lashed into him.

. . .

Salander heard the front door slam and footsteps receding down the stone stairs. She looked at August. He was standing still with his arms straight down by his sides, staring at her intently. That troubled her. A moment ago she had been in control, but now she was uncertain, and what on earth was the matter with Hanna Balder?

Hanna seemed about to burst into tears, and August . . . on top of everything else he started shaking his head and muttering. Salander just wanted to get out of there, but she stayed. Her work was not yet complete. Out of her pocket she took two plane tickets, a hotel voucher, and a thick bundle of notes, both kronor and euros.

"I'd just like, from the bottom of my heart—" Hanna began.

"Quiet," Salander cut in. "Here are some plane tickets to Munich. Departure is at 7:15 this evening so you've got to hurry. I've organized transport to take you directly to Schloss Elmau. It's a nice hotel not far from Garmisch-Partenkirchen. You'll be staying in a large room on the top floor, in the name of Müller, and you'll be there for three months to start with. I've been in touch with Professor Edelman and explained to him the importance of absolute confidentiality. He'll be making regular visits and seeing to it that August gets good care. Edelman will also arrange for suitable schooling."

"Are you serious?"

"I'm deadly serious. The police now have August's drawing and the murderer has been arrested. But the people behind the attacks are still at large; it's impossible to know what they might be planning. You have to leave this apartment at once. I'm busy with a few other things, so I've arranged for a driver to take you to Arlanda. He's a bit weird-looking, maybe. But he's OK. You can call him Plague. Have you got all that?"

"Yes, but . . ."

"Forget the buts. Just listen: You mustn't use your credit card or your own mobile, Hanna. I've fixed an encrypted mobile for you, a Blackphone, in case there's an emergency. My number is already programmed in. I'll pick up all the costs of the hotel. You'll get a hundred thousand kronor in cash, for unforeseen expenses. Any questions?"

"It sounds crazy."

"Not to me."

"But how can you afford this?"

"I can afford it."

"How can we . . ."

Hanna looked completely bewildered, as if she were not sure what to believe. Then she began to cry.

"How can we ever thank you?" she struggled to say.

"*Thank* me?"

Salander said the words as if they were incomprehensible. When Hanna came towards her with outstretched arms she backed away, and with her eyes fixed on the hallway floor she said:

"Pull yourself together! Get a grip and get off whatever stuff you're on, pills or anything else. That's how you can thank me."

"I will . . ."

"And if anyone gets it into their head that August needs to be put in some home or institution, I want you to fight back as hard and as ruthlessly as you can. Aim for their weakest point. Be a warrior."

"A warrior?"

"Exactly. Don't let anyone—"

Salander stopped herself. They were not perhaps the greatest words of farewell, but they would have to do. She turned and walked towards the front door. She did not get far. August started to mutter again, and this time they could make out what the boy was saying.

"Not go, not go . . ."

Salander had no good answer to that either. She just said: "You'll be OK," and then added, as if talking to herself, "Thanks for the scream this morning." There was silence for a moment, and Salander wondered if she should say more. But instead she slipped out.

Hanna called after her: "I can't tell you what this means to me!"

But Salander heard nothing. She was already running down the steps to her car. When she reached Västerbron, Blomkvist called on the RedPhone app to say that the NSA had tracked her down.

"Tell them hi and that I'm on their tracks too," she said.

Then she drove to Roger Winter's house and scared him half to death. After that she drove back to her place and set to work with the encrypted NSA file, without coming any closer to a solution.

Needham and Blomkvist had worked a long day in the hotel room at the Grand. Needham's story was fantastic and Blomkvist would be able to write the scoop *Millennium* so badly needed, but his feeling of unease did not abate. It was not just because Zander was still missing. There was something about Needham that did not add up. Why had he turned up in the first place, and why was he putting so much energy into helping a small Swedish magazine, far from all the centres of power in the United States? Blomkvist had undertaken not to disclose the hacker breach, and had half promised to persuade Salander to talk to Needham. But that hardly seemed enough.

Needham behaved as if he were taking enormous risks. The curtains were drawn and their mobiles were lying at a safe distance. There was a feeling of paranoia in the room. Confidential documents were laid out on the bed. Blomkvist was permitted to read them, but not to quote from or copy them. And every now and then Needham interrupted his account to discuss various aspects of the right to protect journalistic sources. He was obsessive about ensuring that the leak could not be traced back to him, and sometimes he listened nervously for footsteps in the corridor or looked out through a gap in the curtains to check that no-one was out there watching the hotel, and yet ... Blomkvist could not help feeling that most of it was play-acting.

He became more and more convinced that Needham knew exactly what he was doing, and was not even especially worried about someone listening in. It occurred to Blomkvist that Needham was playing a part with the backing of his superiors. Maybe he himself had also been given a role in this play which he did not yet understand.

Therefore he paid close attention not just to what Needham said, but also to what he did not. He considered what Needham might be trying to achieve by going public. There was undoubtedly a certain amount of anger in the mix. Some "bastards" in a department called Protection of Strategic Technologies had prevented Needham from nailing the hacker who had gotten into his system, because they didn't want to be exposed with their pants round their ankles, and that infuriated him, he said. Blomkvist had no reason not to believe him, still less to doubt that Needham genuinely did want to exterminate these people, to "crush them, grind them to pulp under my boots." But there were other aspects of the story he was not quite so comfortable with. It felt as if Needham were wrestling with some kind of self-censorship.

From time to time Blomkvist went down to the lobby just to think, or to call Berger or Salander. Berger always answered on the first ring and, even though they were both enthusiastic about the story, Zander's disappearance haunted their conversations.

Salander did not pick up all day, until eventually he got hold of her at 5:20. She sounded distracted, and informed him that the boy was now safe with his mother.

"And how are *you*?" he said.

"OK."

"Not hurt?"

"Nothing new at least."

Blomkvist took a deep breath.

"Have you hacked into the NSA's intranet, Lisbeth?"

"Have you been talking to Ed the Ned?"

"No comment."

He would say nothing, even to Salander. Protection of sources was even more important to him than loyalty to her.

"Ed isn't so dumb after all," she said.

"So you have."

"Possibly."

Blomkvist felt the urge to ask her what the hell she thought she was doing. Instead, as calmly as he could, he said:

"They're prepared to let you off if you'll agree to meet them and tell them how you did it."

"Tell them that I've got more than they think."

"OK. But would you consider meeting . . ."

"Ed?"

How the hell did she know, Blomkvist thought. Needham had wanted to be the one to reveal himself to her.

"Ed," he repeated.

"A cocky bugger."

"Pretty cocky. But would you consider meeting him if we provide guarantees that you won't be arrested?"

"There are no such guarantees."

"I could get in touch with my sister Annika and ask her to represent you."

"I've got better things to do," she said, as if she did not want to talk about it anymore.

He could not stop himself from saying, "This story we're working on . . . I'm not sure I understand all of it."

"What's the problem?" Salander said.

"First of all, I don't understand why Camilla has surfaced after all these years."

"I suppose she'd just been biding her time."

"How do you mean?"

"She probably always knew she would be back to get revenge for what I did to her and Zala. But she wanted to wait until she had built up her strength on every level. Nothing is more important to Camilla than to be strong, and she must have seen an opportunity, a chance to kill two birds with one stone. At least that's my guess. Why don't you ask her next time you have a drink together?"

"Have you spoken to Holger?"

"I've been busy."

"Thank God you got away," Blomkvist went on.

"I made it."

"But aren't you worried that she could be back at any moment?"

"It has occurred to me."

"OK, good. You do know that Camilla and I did nothing more than walk a short way down Hornsgatan?"

Salander did not answer.

"I know you, Mikael" was all she said. "And now that you've met Ed, I guess I'll have to protect myself from him too."

Blomkvist smiled to himself.

"Yes," he said. "You're probably right. Let's not trust him any more than we absolutely have to. I don't want to become his useful idiot."

"Doesn't sound like a role for you, Mikael."

"No, and that's why I'd love to know what you discovered when you accessed the NSA intranet."

"A whole load of compromising shit."

"About Eckerwald and the Spiders' relationship with the NSA?"

"That and a bit more besides."

"Which you were planning to tell me about."

"I might do, if you behave yourself," she said with a teasing tone, and that only made him feel happy.

Then he chuckled, because at that moment he realized what Ed Needham was trying to do. It hit him so forcefully that he had a hard time keeping up his act when he returned to the hotel room, but he went on working with the American until ten that night.

CHAPTER 29

NOVEMBER 25—MORNING

Vladimir Orlov's apartment on Mårten Trotzigs gränd was neat and tidy. The bed was freshly made with clean sheets and the laundry basket in the bathroom was empty. Yet there were signs that something was not quite right. Neighbours reported that some moving men had been there the morning before and a close inspection revealed bloodstains on the floor and on the wall above the headboard. The blood was compared to traces of saliva in Zander's apartment and the match confirmed.

But the men now in custody—the two still capable of communicating—claimed to have no knowledge of bloodstains or of Zander, so Bublanski and his team concentrated on getting more information on the woman who had been seen with him. By now the media had published columns and columns about not only the drama on Ingarö but also about Andrei Zander's disappearance. Both evening newspapers and *Svenska Morgon-Posten* and *Metro* had carried prominent photographs of the journalist, and there was already speculation that he might have been murdered. Usually that would jog people's memories and prompt them to remember anything suspicious, but now it was almost the exact opposite.

Such witness accounts as came in and were thought to be credible were peculiarly vague, and everyone who came forward—except for Mikael Blomkvist and the baker from Skansen—took it upon themselves to remark that they could not imagine the woman guilty of any crime. She had apparently made an overwhelmingly good impression on everyone who had encountered her. A bartender called Sören Karlsten, who had served the woman and Zander in Papagallo on Götgatan, went on and on boasting that he was a good judge of character and claimed to be absolutely certain that this woman "would never hurt a soul."

"She was class personified."

She was just about everything personified, if one were to believe the witnesses, and from what Bublanski could see it would be virtually impossible to produce a police sketch of her. The witness accounts all depicted her in different terms, as if they were projecting their ideal image of a woman onto her, and so far they had no photographs from any surveillance camera. It was almost laughable. Blomkvist said that the woman was without a shadow of a doubt Camilla Salander, twin sister of Lisbeth. But going back in the records for many years, there was no trace of her. It was as if she had ceased to exist. If Camilla Salander was still alive, then it would be under a new identity.

Bublanski especially did not like that there had been two unexplained deaths in the foster family she left behind. The police investigations at the time were deficient, full of loose threads and question marks which had never been followed up.

Bublanski read the reports, ashamed that out of some bizarre respect for the family's tragedy his colleagues had failed to get to the bottom of the glaring problem that both the father and the daughter had emptied their bank accounts just before their deaths, or that in the very week he had been found hanged the father had started writing a letter which began:

"Camilla, why is it so important to you to destroy my life?"

This person who seemed to have enchanted all the witnesses was shrouded in ominous darkness.

It was now 8:00 in the morning and there were a hundred other things Bublanski should have been attending to, so he reacted with both irritation and guilt when he heard that he had a visitor. She was a woman who had been interviewed by Modig but who now insisted on meeting him. Afterwards he wondered if he had been exceptionally brusque, maybe because all he was expecting was further problems.

The woman in the doorway had a regal bearing but was not tall. She had dark, intense eyes which gave her a melancholy look. She was dressed in a grey coat and a red dress that looked a bit like a sari.

"My name is Farah Sharif," she said. "I'm a professor of computer sciences and was a close friend of Frans Balder's."

"Yes, of course," said Bublanski, suddenly embarrassed. "Take a seat, please. My apologies for the mess."

"I've seen worse."

"Is that so. Well. To what do I owe this honour?"

"I was far too naïve when I spoke to your colleague."

"Why do you say that?"

"Because I have more information now. I've had a long conversation with Professor Warburton."

"He's been looking for me too, but it's been so chaotic, I haven't had time to call him back."

"Steven is a professor of cybernetics at Stanford and a leading researcher in the field of technological singularity. These days he works at the Machine Intelligence Research Institute, whose aim is to ensure that artificial intelligence is a positive help to mankind rather than the opposite."

"Well, that sounds good," said Bublanski, who felt uncomfortable whenever this topic came up.

"Steven lives somewhat in a world of his own. He found out what happened to Frans only yesterday, and that's why he didn't call sooner. But he told me that he had spoken to Frans as recently as Monday."

"What did they discuss?"

"His research. You know, Frans had been so secretive ever since he went off to the States. I was close to him, but not even I knew anything about what he was doing. I was arrogant enough to think I understood some of it at least, but now it turns out I was wrong."

"In what way?"

"Frans had not only taken his old AI programme a step further, he had also developed fresh algorithms and new topographical material for quantum computers."

"I'm not sure I follow."

"Quantum computers are computers based on quantum mechanics. They are many thousand times faster in certain areas than conventional computers. The great advantage with quantum computers is that the fundamental constituent quantum bits—qubits—can superposition themselves."

"They can *what*?"

"Not only can they take the binary positions one or zero

as do traditional computers, they can also be both zero and one at the same time. For the time being quantum computers are much too specialized and cumbersome. But—how can I best explain this to you?—Frans appeared to have found ways to make them easier, more flexible and self-learning. He was onto something great, at least potentially. But as well as feeling proud of his breakthrough, he was also worried—and that was the reason he called Steven Warburton."

"Why was he worried?"

"In the long term, because he suspected his creation could become a threat to the world, I imagine. But more immediately because he knew things about the NSA."

"What sort of things?"

"I don't know anything about that aspect of his discoveries. He somehow stumbled upon the messier side of their industrial espionage. But I do know this: It's no secret that the organization is working hard specifically to develop quantum computers. For the NSA that would be paradise, pure and simple. An effective quantum machine would actually enable them to crack all encryptions, all digital security systems. Then no-one would be safe from that organization's watchful eye."

"A hideous thought," said Bublanski with surprising feeling.

"But there is an even more frightening scenario: if such a thing were to fall into the hands of major criminals," Farah Sharif said.

"I see what you're getting at."

"So I'm keen to know what you've managed to get hold of from the men now under arrest."

"Unfortunately nothing like that," he said. "But these

men are not exactly outstanding intellects. I doubt they would even pass secondary school maths."

"The real computer genius got away?"

"I'm afraid so. He and a female suspect have disappeared without a trace. They probably have a number of identities."

"Worrying."

Bublanski nodded and gazed into Farah Sharif's dark eyes, which looked beseechingly at him. A hopeful thought stopped him from sinking back into despair.

"I'm not sure what it means," he said.

"What?"

"We've had IT guys go through Balder's computers. Given how security-conscious he was, it wasn't easy. You can imagine. But we had a spot of luck, you might say, and what we soon realized was that one computer must have been stolen."

"I suspected as much," she said. "Damn it!"

"Wait, I haven't finished. We also understood that a number of machines had been connected to each other, and that occasionally these had been connected to a supercomputer in Tokyo."

"That sounds feasible."

"We can confirm that a large file, or at least something big, had recently been deleted, although we haven't been able to restore it."

"Are you suggesting Frans might have destroyed his own research?"

"I don't want to jump to any conclusions. But it occurred to me while you were telling me all this."

"Don't you think the perpetrator might have deleted it?"

"You mean that he first copied it, and then removed it from Balder's computers?"

"Yes."

"I find that hard to believe. The killer was only in the house for a very short while, he would never have had time— let alone the ability—to do anything like that."

"OK, that sounds reassuring, despite everything," Sharif said doubtfully. "It's just that . . ."

"Yes?"

"I don't think it fits with Frans's character. Would he really destroy the greatest thing he'd ever done? That would be like . . . I don't know . . . chopping off his own arm, or even worse, killing a friend, destroying a life."

"Sometimes one has to make a big sacrifice," Bublanski said thoughtfully. "Destroy what one loves."

"Or else there's a copy somewhere."

"Or else there's a copy somewhere," he repeated. Suddenly he did something strange: he reached out his hand.

Farah Sharif did not understand. She looked at the hand as if she were expecting him to give her something. But Bublanski decided not to let himself be discouraged.

"Do you know what my rabbi says? That the mark of a man is his contradictions. We can long to be away and at home, both at the same time. I never knew Professor Balder, and he might have thought that I was just an old fool. But I do know one thing: we can both love and fear our work, just as Balder seems to have both loved and run away from his son. To be alive, Professor Sharif, means not being completely consistent. It means venturing out in many directions all at the same time, and I wonder if your friend didn't find himself in the throes of some sort of upheaval. Maybe he really did destroy his life's work. Maybe he revealed himself with all his inherent contradictions towards the end, and became a true human being in the best sense of the word."

"Do you think so?"

"We may never know. But he had changed, hadn't he? The custody hearing declared him unfit to look after his own son, yet that's precisely what he did. He even got the boy to blossom and begin to draw."

"That's true, Chief Inspector."

"Call me Jan. People sometimes even call me Officer Bubble."

"Is that because you're so bubbly?"

"No, I don't think so somehow. But I do know one thing for sure."

"And what's that?"

"That you're . . ."

He got no further, but he did not need to. Farah Sharif gave him a smile which in all its simplicity restored Bublanski's belief in life and in God.

At 8:00 a.m. Salander got out of her bed on Fiskargatan. Once again she had not managed to get much sleep, not only because she had been working on the encrypted NSA file without getting anywhere at all. She had also been listening for the sound of footsteps on the stairs and every now and then she checked her alarm and the surveillance camera on the landing.

She was no wiser than anyone else as to whether her sister had left the country. After her humiliation on Ingarö, it was by no means impossible that Camilla was preparing a new attack, with even greater force. The NSA could also, at any moment, march into the apartment. Salander was under no illusions on either point. But this morning she dismissed all that. She went to the bathroom with resolute steps and took off her top to check her bullet wound. She thought it was finally beginning to look better, and in a mad moment she decided to take herself off to the boxing club on Hornsgatan for a session.

To drive out pain with pain.

Afterwards she was sitting exhausted in the changing room, with hardly the energy to think. Her mobile buzzed. She ignored it. She went into the shower and let the warm water sprinkle over her. Gradually her thoughts cleared, and August's drawing reappeared in her mind. But this time it wasn't the illustration of the murderer which caught her attention—it was something at the bottom of the paper.

Salander had only a very brief glimpse of the finished work at the summer house on Ingarö; at the time she had been concentrating on sending it to Bublanski and Modig. If she had given it any thought at all, then like everyone else she would have been fascinated by the detailed rendering. But now her photographic memory focused on the equation August had written at the bottom of the page, and she stepped out of the shower deep in thought. The only thing was, she could hardly hear herself think. Obinze was raising hell outside the changing room.

"Shut up," she shouted back. "I'm thinking!"

But that did not help much. Obinze was absolutely furious, and anyone other than Salander would understand why.

Obinze had been shocked at how weak and half-hearted her effort at the punchbag was, and had worried when she began to hang her head and grimace in pain. In the end he had surprised her by rushing over and rolling up the sleeve of her T-shirt, only to discover the bullet wound. He had gone crazy, and evidently hadn't calmed down yet.

"You're an idiot, do you know that? A lunatic!" he shouted.

She was too tired to answer. Her strength deserted her completely, and what she had remembered from the drawing now faded from her mind. She sank down on the bench in the changing room next to Jamila Achebe. She used to both box and sleep with Jamila, usually in that order. When they fought their toughest bouts it often seemed like one long, wild foreplay. On a few occasions their behaviour in the shower had not been entirely decent. Neither of them set much store by etiquette.

"I actually agree with that noisy bastard out there. You're not right in the head," said Jamila.

"Maybe," Salander answered.

"That wound looks nasty."

"It's healing."

"But you needed to box?"

"Apparently."

"Shall we go back to my place?"

Salander did not answer. Her phone was buzzing again in her black bag. Three text messages with the same content from a withheld number. As she read them she balled up her fists and looked lethal. Jamila decided it might be better to have sex with Salander another day instead.

. . .

Blomkvist had woken at 6:00 with some great ideas for the article, and on his way to the office the draft came together in his mind with no effort at all. He worked in deep concentration at the magazine and barely noticed what was going on around him, although sometimes he surfaced with thoughts of Zander.

He refused to give up hope, but he feared that Zander had given his life for the story, and he did what he could to honour his colleague with every sentence he wrote. On one level he intended the report to be a murder story about Frans and August Balder—an account of an eight-year-old autistic boy who sees his father shot, and who despite his disability finds a way of striking back. But on another level Blomkvist wanted it to be an instructive narrative about a new world of surveillance and espionage, where the boundaries between the legal and the criminal have been erased. The words came pouring out, but still it was not without its difficulties.

Through an old police contact he had gotten hold of the paperwork on the unsolved murder of Kajsa Falk, the girl-friend of one of the leading figures in Svavelsjö MC. The killer had never been identified and none of the people questioned during the investigation had been willing to contribute anything of value, but Blomkvist nevertheless gathered that a violent rift had torn apart the motorcycle club and that there was an insidious fear among the gang members of a "Lady Zala," as one of the witnesses put it.

Despite considerable efforts, the police had not managed to discover who or what the name referred to. But there was not the slightest doubt in Blomkvist's mind that "Lady Zala" was Camilla and that she was behind a whole series of other crimes, both in Sweden and abroad. It was not easy to find any evidence, though, and that exasperated him. For the time being he referred to her in the article by her codename Thanos.

Yet the biggest challenge was not Camilla or her shadowy connections to the Russian Duma. What bothered Blomkvist most was that he knew Needham would never have come all the way to Sweden and leaked top secret information if he were not bent on hiding something even bigger. Needham was no fool, and he knew that Blomkvist was not stupid either. He had therefore avoided making any part of his account too pretty.

On the contrary, he painted a fairly dreadful picture of the NSA. And yet . . . a closer inspection of the information told Blomkvist that, all in all, Needham was describing an intelligence agency which both functioned well and behaved reasonably decently, if you ignored the revolting bunch of criminals in the department known as Protection of Strategic Technologies—as it happens the self-same department which had prevented Needham from nailing his hacker.

The American must have wanted to do serious harm to a few specific colleagues, but rather than sink the whole of his organization, he preferred to give it a softer landing in an already inevitable crash. So Blomkvist was not especially surprised or angry when Berger appeared behind him and handed him a TT telegram with a worried expression.

"Does this scupper our story?" she said.

The telegram read:

TWO SENIOR EXECUTIVES AT THE NSA, JACOB BARCLAY AND BRIAN ABBOT, HAVE BEEN ARRESTED ON SUSPICION OF SERIOUS FINANCIAL MISCON-

DUCT AND ARE ON INDEFINITE LEAVE AWAITING
TRIAL.

"THIS IS A BLOT ON THE REPUTATION OF OUR
ORGANIZATION AND WE HAVE SPARED NO EFFORT
IN TACKLING THE ISSUES AND HOLDING THOSE
GUILTY TO ACCOUNT. ANYONE WORKING FOR THE
NSA MUST HAVE THE HIGHEST ETHICAL STAN-
DARDS AND WE UNDERTAKE TO BE AS TRANSPAR-
ENT DURING THE JUDICIAL PROCESS AS WE CAN,
WHILE REMAINING SENSITIVE TO OUR NATIONAL
SECURITY INTERESTS," NSA CHIEF ADMIRAL
CHARLES O'CONNOR HAS TOLD AP.

The telegram did not contain very much apart from the long
quote; it said nothing about Balder's murder and nothing
that could be linked to the events in Stockholm. But Blomkvist understood what Berger meant. Now that the news was
out, the *Washington Post* and the *New York Times* and a whole
pack of serious American journalists would descend on the
story, and it would be impossible to anticipate what they
might dig up.

"Not good," he said calmly. "But not a surprise."

"Really?"

"It's part of the same strategy that led the NSA to seek me
out: damage control. They want to take back the initiative."

"How do you mean?"

"There's a reason why they leaked this to me. I could tell
right away that there was something odd about it. Why did
Needham insist on coming to talk to me here in Stockholm,
and at five in the morning?"

"You think his actions were sanctioned higher up?"

"I suspected it, but at first I didn't get what he was doing. It just felt off. Then I talked to Salander."

"And that clarified things?"

"I realized that Needham knew exactly what she'd dug up during her hacker attack, and he had every reason to fear that I would learn all about it. He wanted to limit the damage. I suspect he gave me just enough to keep me happy and let me have my scoop and to prevent me from digging any deeper."

"He's in for a disappointment, then."

"Let's at least hope so. But I can't see how to break through. The NSA is a closed door."

"Even for an old bloodhound like Mikael Blomkvist?"

"Even for him."

CHAPTER 30

NOVEMBER 25

The text message had said <Until next time, sister!>
Salander could not work out if it had been sent three times
in error or if it was an absurd attempt to be overexplicit. It
made no difference now anyway.

The message was evidently from Camilla, but it added
nothing to what Salander already knew. The events on Ingarö
had only deepened the old hatred—she was certain Camilla
would come after her again, after having gotten so close.

It was not the wording of the texts that upset Salander
so much as the thoughts it brought to mind, the memory
of what she had seen on the steep rock slope in the early-
morning light when she and August had crouched on the
narrow ledge, gunfire rattling above them. August had not
been wearing a jacket or shoes and was shivering violently
in the falling snow as the seconds went by. Salander realized
how desperately compromised their situation was. She had a
child to take care of and a pathetic pistol for a weapon, while
the bastards up there had assault rifles. She had to take them
by surprise, otherwise she and August would be slaughtered
like lambs. She listened to the men's footsteps and the direc-

tion they were shooting in, even their breathing and the rustle of their clothes.

But the strange thing was, when she finally saw her chance, she hesitated. Crucial moments went by as she broke a small twig into pieces on the rock ledge in front of them. Only then did she spring to her feet right in front of the men and, taking advantage of that brief millisecond of surprise, she fired two, three times. From experience she knew that moments like these burn an indelible impression on your mind, as if not only your body and muscles are sharpened, but also your perception.

Every detail shone with a strange precision and she saw each ripple in the landscape in front of her, as if through a camera zoom. She noted the surprise and fear in the men's eyes, the wrinkles and irregularities in their faces and clothes, and the weapons which they were waving and firing off at random, narrowly missing their targets.

But her strongest impression did not come from any of that. It came from a silhouette further up the slope which she caught out of the corner of her eye. Not menacing in itself, it still made more of an impact on her than the men she had shot: it was her sister. Salander would have recognized her half a mile away, even though they had not seen each other in years. The air itself was poisoned by her presence and afterwards Salander wondered if she should have shot her too.

Camilla stood there a moment too long. It was careless of her to be out on the rock slope in the first place, but presumably she could not resist the temptation of seeing her sister executed. Salander recalled how she half squeezed the trigger and felt a holy rage beating in her chest. Yet she hesitated for a split second, and that was enough. Camilla threw herself behind a rock and a scrawny figure appeared on the terrace and started shooting. Salander jumped back onto the ledge and tumbled down the slope with August.

Now, walking away from the boxing club, thinking back to it all, Salander's body tightened in readiness for a new battle. It struck her that perhaps she should not go home, but leave the country for a while. Something else drove her back to her desk, though: what she had seen in her mind's eye in the shower, before reading Camilla's texts, which was now occupying her thoughts more and more. August's equation:

$$N = 3034267$$

$$E : y^2 = x^3 - x - 20; P = (3.2)$$

From a mathematical point of view, there was nothing unique or outstanding about it. But what was so remarkable was that August had started with the random number she had given him at Ingarö and taken that further to develop a considerably better elliptic curve than the one she herself had made. When the boy had not wanted to go to sleep, she had left it on the bedside table. She had not gotten any answer then, nor even the slightest reaction, and she had gone to bed convinced that August understood nothing about mathematical abstractions, that he was only a kind of human calculator of prime number factorizations.

But, my God . . . she had been wrong. August had stayed up in the night not just drawing; he had also perfected her own mathematics.

She did not even take off her boots or leather jacket, she just stomped into her apartment and opened the encrypted NSA file along with her programme for elliptic curves.

Then she rang Hanna Balder.

· · ·

Hanna had scarcely slept because she had not brought any of her pills with her. Yet the hotel and its surroundings still cheered her. The breathtaking mountain scenery reminded her of how cramped her own existence had become. Slowly she began to unwind, and even the deep-seated fear in her body was beginning to let go. But that could have been wishful thinking. She also felt slightly at sea in such extravagant surroundings.

There had been a time when she would sail into rooms like these with perfect self-assurance: *Look at me, here I come.* Now she was timid and trembling and had difficulty eating anything even though the breakfast was lavish. August sat beside her, compulsively writing out his series of numbers, and he was not eating either, but he drank unbelievable volumes of freshly pressed orange juice.

Her new mobile rang, startling her. It had to be the woman who had sent them here. Nobody else had the number so far as she knew. No doubt she just wanted to know if they had arrived safely so Hanna answered cheerfully and launched into an effusive description of how wonderful everything at the hotel was. She was brusquely interrupted:

"Where are you?"

"We're having breakfast."

"In that case stop now and go up to your room. August and I have work to do."

"Work?"

"I'm going to send over some equations I want him to take a look at. Is that clear?"

"I don't understand."

"Just show them to August, and then call me and tell me what he's written."

"OK," said Hanna, nonplussed.

She grabbed a couple of croissants and a cinnamon bun and walked with August to the lifts.

It was only at the outset that August helped her. But it was enough. Later she could see her mistakes more clearly and make new improvements to her programme. Deep in concentration she worked on for hour after hour, until the sky darkened outside and the snow began to fall again. Then suddenly—in one of those moments she would remember forever—something strange happened to the file. It fell apart. A shock ran through her. She punched the air.

She had found the secret keys and cracked the document, and for a little while she was so overcome by this that she hardly managed to read. Then she began to examine the contents, and her amazement grew with every passing moment. Could this even be possible? It was more explosive than anything she had imagined and the reason it had all been written down could only have been that someone believed the RSA algorithm was impenetrable. But here it was, all that filth in black and white. The text was full of internal jargon and strange abbreviations and cryptic references, but that was not a problem for Salander since she was familiar with the subject. She got through about four-fifths of the text before the doorbell rang.

She chose to ignore it, probably only the postman. But then she remembered Camilla's text message and checked the camera on the landing via her computer. She stiffened.

It was not Camilla but her other nemesis, the one she had almost forgotten with everything else that was going on. Ed the fucking Ned. He looked nothing like his pictures online, but he was unmistakable all the same: grumpy and determined. Salander's brain started ticking. How had he managed to track her down? What should she do? The best she could come up with was to send the NSA file off to Blomkvist on their PGP link.

Then she shut down her computer and hauled herself to her feet to open the door.

What had happened to Bublanski? Sonja Modig was at a loss to understand it. The pained expression he had been wearing in recent weeks had vanished and now he smiled and hummed to himself. It's true that there was plenty to be pleased about. The murderer had been caught, August Balder had survived, despite two attempts on his life, and Frans Balder's conflict and connection with the research company Solifon were becoming clearer.

But many questions remained, and the Bublanski she knew was not one to rejoice without good reason. He was more inclined to self-doubt, even in moments of triumph. She could not understand what had gotten into him. He walked around the corridors beaming. Even now, as he sat in his office reading the dull report on the questioning of Zigmund Eckerwald by the San Francisco police, there was a smile on his lips.

"Sonja, my dear, there you are!"

She decided not to comment on the unwonted enthusiasm of his greeting and went straight to the point.

"Jan Holtser is dead."

"Oh no."

"And with him went our last hope of learning more about the Spiders."

"So you think he was about to open up?"

"There was a chance, at least."

"Why do you say that?"

"He broke down completely when his daughter showed up."

"I didn't know. What happened?"

"He has a daughter called Olga," Modig said. "She came from Helsinki when she heard that her father had been injured. But when I talked to her and she realized that Holtser had tried to kill a child, she went berserk."

"In what way?"

"She stormed into him and said something incredibly aggressive in Russian."

"Could you understand what she was saying?"

"Something like he could die alone and she hated him."

"Strong words, then."

"Yes, and afterwards she told me that she would do everything in her power to help us with the investigation."

"How did Holtser react?"

"That's what I was saying. For a moment I thought we had him. He was totally destroyed, had tears in his eyes. I'm not big on that Catholic teaching which says that our moral worth is determined just before we die, but it was almost touching to see. This man, who had done so much evil, was crushed."

"My rabbi . . ." Bublanski began.

"Please, Jan, don't start with your rabbi now. Let me continue. Holtser started saying what a terrible person he had been, so I told him that he should as a Christian take the opportunity to confess, and tell us who he was working for. At that moment I'm convinced he came close. He hesitated and his eyes flitted from side to side. But instead of confessing he began to talk about Stalin."

"Stalin?"

"About how Stalin didn't only punish the guilty but also their children and grandchildren and the entire family. I think he was trying to say that his boss was the same."

"So he was worried about his daughter."

"However much she may have hated him, he was. I tried to tell him that we could get the girl into a witness protection programme, but Holtser had started to drift away. He fell unconscious and died an hour later."

"Anything else?"

"Only that someone we're beginning to think may be a superintelligence has vanished and that we still have no trace of Andrei Zander."

"I know, I know."

"We've made progress on one front at least," Modig said. "You remember the man identified by Amanda on August's drawing of the traffic light?"

"The former actor?"

"That's right, he's called Roger Winter. Amanda interviewed him for background information, to find out whether there was any relationship between him and the boy or Balder, and I don't think she expected to get much out of it. But Winter seemed badly shaken and before Amanda had even started to put pressure on him he confessed to a whole catalogue of sins."

"Really?"

"And we're not talking innocent stories. You know, West-man and Winter have been friends since they were young men at Revolutionsteatern and they used to get together to drink in the afternoons at the apartment in Torsgatan when Hanna was out. August would sit in the next room doing his puzzles, and neither of the men paid him much attention. But on one of these occasions the boy had been given a thick maths book by his mother—it was clearly way above his level, but he still leafed through it frantically, making excited noises. Lasse became irritated and grabbed the book from the boy and threw it in the bin. It seems August went completely crazy. He had some sort of fit, and Lasse kicked him several times."

"That's appalling."

"That was just the beginning. After that August became very odd, said Roger, and took to glaring at them with this weird look. One day Roger found that his jeans jacket had been cut into tiny pieces, and another day someone had emptied out all the beer in the fridge and smashed the bottles of spirits. It turned into some kind of trench warfare. I sus-pect that Roger and Lasse in their alcoholic delirium began to imagine all sorts of strange things about the boy, and even became scared of him. The psychological aspect of this isn't easy to understand. Roger said it made him feel like shit, and he never talked about it with Lasse afterwards. He didn't want to beat the boy, but he couldn't stop himself. It was as if he got his own childhood back, he said."

"What on earth did he mean by that?"

"It's not altogether clear. Apparently Roger Winter has a

disabled younger brother. Throughout their childhood Roger was a constant disappointment, while his brother was showered with praise and distinctions and appreciated in every possible way. I guess that bred some bitterness. Maybe Roger was subconsciously getting his own back on his brother. Or else . . ."

"What?"

"He put it in an odd way. He said it felt as if he were trying to beat the shame out of himself."

"That's sick."

"Yes. Strangest of all is the way he suddenly confessed everything. It was almost as if he wanted to be arrested. Amanda said he was limping and had two black eyes."

"Peculiar."

"Isn't it? But there's one other thing which surprises me even more," Modig said.

"And what's that?"

"That my boss, that brooding old grouch, has become a little ray of sunshine."

Bublanski looked embarrassed.

"So it shows."

"It shows."

"Well, yes," he stammered. "It's just that a woman has agreed to come out to dinner with me."

"You haven't gone and fallen in love, have you?"

"It's just dinner," Bublanski said, blushing.

Needham knew the rules of the game even if he did not enjoy it. It was like being back in Dorchester. Whatever you did, you could not back down. If Salander wanted to play hard-ball, he would show her hardball. He glared at her. But it did not get him very far.

She glared back and did not say a word. It felt like a duel, and in the end Needham looked away. The whole thing was ridiculous. The girl had been unmasked and crushed, after all. He had cracked her secret identity and tracked her down, and she should be grateful that he wasn't marching in with the Marines to arrest her.

"You think you're pretty tough, don't you?" he said.

"I don't like surprise visits."

"I don't like people who break into my system, so we're square. Maybe you'd like to know how I found you?"

"I couldn't care less."

"It was via your company in Gibraltar. Not too smart to call it Wasp Enterprises."

"Apparently not."

"For a smart girl, you make a lot of mistakes."

"For a clever boy, you work for a pretty rotten organization."

"You got me there. But we're a necessary evil in this wicked world."

"Especially with guys like Jonny Ingram around."

He was not expecting that. He really was not expecting that. But he would not let it show.

"You have a good sense of humour," he said.

"It's hilarious. To have people murdered and to work together with villains in the Russian Duma making mega-bucks and saving your own skin; that's comical, isn't it?" she said.

For a moment he could barely breathe. He could no longer keep up the pretence. Where the hell had she gotten that from? He felt dizzy. But then he realized—and it slowed his pulse a little—that she was bluffing. If he believed her even for one second it was only because in his worst moments he too had imagined that Ingram might be guilty of something like that. But Needham knew better than anyone that there was not a shred of evidence of such a thing.

"Don't try to bullshit me," he growled. "I have the same material you do and a lot more besides."

"I wouldn't be so sure of that, Ed, unless you too have the private keys to Ingram's RSA algorithm?"

Needham looked at her and told himself that this could not be true. Surely she could not have cracked the encryption? Not even he, with all the resources and experts at his disposal, had thought it was worth trying.

But now she was suggesting . . . Impossible. Maybe she had a mole in Ingram's inner circle? No, that was just as far-fetched.

"This is how it is, Ed," she said in a new authoritative tone. "You told Blomkvist that you would leave me in peace if I told you how I carried out my data breach. It's possible you're telling the truth there. It's equally possible that you're lying, or that you won't have any say in the matter anyway. You could get the sack. I don't see any case for trusting you or the people you work for."

Needham took a deep breath.

"I respect your attitude," he said. "But I'm a man of my word. Not because I'm a decent person. I'm a vengeful maniac, just like you, young lady. But I wouldn't have survived as long as I have if I let people down when it mattered. You can either believe that or not. I swear to you, though, I will make your life hell if you don't open up."

"You're a tough guy," she said. "But you're also a proud bugger, aren't you? You need to make absolutely sure that no-one ever gets wind of my breach, whatever the cost. As to that, I'm ridiculously well prepared. Every detail could be made public before you even have time to blink. I don't in fact want to do it, but I *will* humiliate you if I have to."

"You're full of shit."

"I wouldn't have survived either if I was full of shit," she said. "I hate this society where we're watched over all the time. I've had enough of Big Brother and authorities in my life. But I'm prepared to do something for you, Ed. If you can keep your trap shut, I can give you information that will put you in a stronger position, and help you clear out the corruption in Fort Meade. I'm not telling you anything about my breach—only because it's a matter of principle for me. But I can help you get your own back on the bastards."

Ed stared at the strange woman in front of him. Then he did something which would surprise him for a long time.

He burst out laughing. He laughed until he cried.

CHAPTER 31

DECEMBER 2–3

Levin woke up in a good mood at Häringe castle after a long conference about the digitalization of the media, which had ended with a big party where the champagne and hard liquor had flowed. A failure of a trade union representative from the Norwegian newspaper *Kveldsbladet* had remarked spitefully that Serner's parties "grow more lavish the more people you sack," and made a bit of a scene, which resulted in Levin getting red wine on his tailor-made jacket. But he was happy to let him have that. Especially since it had enabled him to get Natalie Foss up to his hotel room in the small hours. Natalie was twenty-seven and sexy as hell, and despite the fact that he was drunk, Levin had managed to have sex with her both last night and this morning.

Now it was already 9:00 and his mobile was pinging and he had more of a hangover than he could afford, bearing in mind all the things he had to do. On the other hand he was a champion in this discipline. "Work hard, play hard" was his motto. And Natalie—how many fifty-year-olds could pull a bird like that? But now he had to get up. He was dizzy as he lurched to the bathroom for a pee. Then he checked his share portfolio. It was a good way to start hungover mornings. He picked up his mobile and went into Internet banking.

Something must have gone wrong, some technical mishap he could not understand. His portfolio had crashed, and as he sat there shaking and skimming through his assets he noticed something peculiar. His large holding in Solifon had as good as evaporated. He was beside himself as he went into the stock exchange sites and saw the same headline everywhere:

THE NSA AND SOLIFON CONTRACTED FOR THE MURDER OF PROFESSOR FRANS BALDER. *MILLENNIUM* MAGAZINE REVELATIONS SHOCK THE WORLD

What he did next is unclear. He probably yelled and swore and banged his fists on the table. He vaguely remembered Natalie waking up, asking what was going on. But the only thing he knew for sure was that he kneeled for a long time over the toilet bowl, vomiting as if there were no end to it.

Grane's desk at Säpo had been tidied. She would not be coming back. Now she sat there for a little while, leaning back in her chair and reading *Millennium*. The first page was not what she had expected from a magazine serving up the scoop of the century. It was black, elegant, sombre. There were no pictures. At the top it said:

IN MEMORY OF ANDREI ZANDER

And further down:

THE MURDER OF FRANS BALDER AND THE STORY OF HOW
THE RUSSIAN MAFIA GOT TOGETHER WITH THE NSA AND
AMERICA'S LEADING TECHNOLOGY COMPANY

Page two consisted of a close-up of Zander. Even though Grane had never met him, she was moved. Zander looked beautiful and a little vulnerable. His smile was searching, tentative. There was something at once intense and unsure about him. In an accompanying text Erika Berger wrote about how Zander's parents had been killed by a bomb in Sarajevo. She went on to say that he had loved *Millennium* magazine, the poet Leonard Cohen, and Antonio Tabucchi's novel *Sostiene Pereira*. He dreamed of a great love and a great scoop. His favourite films were *Dark Eyes* by Nikita Mikhalkov and *Love Actually* by Richard Curtis. Berger regarded his report on Stockholm's homeless as a classic piece of journalism. And even though Zander hated people who offended others he himself refused to speak ill of anyone. The piece went on:

As I write this, my hands are shaking. Yesterday our friend and colleague Andrei Zander was found dead on a freighter in Hammarbyhamnen. He had been tortured, and had suffered terribly. I will live with that pain for the rest of my life.

But I am also proud to have had the privilege of working with him. I have never met such a dedicated journalist and genuinely good person. Andrei was twenty-six years old. He loved life and he loved journalism. He wanted to expose injustices and help the vulnerable and displaced. He was murdered because he tried to protect a small boy called August Balder and, as we reveal in this issue, one of the biggest scandals in modern times, we honour Andrei in every sentence. In his report, Mikael Blomkvist writes:

"Andrei believed in love. He believed in a better world and a more just society. He was the best of us."

The report ran to more than thirty pages of the magazine and was perhaps the best piece of journalistic prose Grane had ever read. She sometimes had tears in her eyes but still smiled when she came to the words:

Säpo's star analyst Gabriella Grane demonstrated outstanding civic courage.

The basic story was simple. A group of individuals under Commander Jonny Ingram—who ranked just below the NSA head, Admiral Charles O'Connor, and had close contacts with the White House and Congress—had begun to exploit the vast numbers of trade secrets in the hands of the organization for their own gain. He had been assisted by a group of business intelligence analysts at Solifon's research department "Y."

If the matter had stopped there, it would have been a scandal which was in some way comprehensible. But the course of events followed its own evil logic when a criminal group—the Spiders—entered the drama. Mikael Blomkvist had evidence to show how Jonny Ingram had gotten together with the notorious Russian Duma member Ivan Gribanov and "Thanos," the mysterious leader of the Spiders, to plunder tech companies of ideas and new technology worth astronomical sums of money, and to sell it all. But they really plumbed the depths of moral depravity when Professor Frans Balder picked up their tracks and it was decided to eliminate him. That was the most astonishing part of the story. One of the most senior executives at the NSA had known that a leading Swedish researcher was going to be murdered and did not lift a finger to prevent it.

It was not the account of the political quagmire that most engaged Grane, but rather the human drama. There Blomkvist's gifts as a writer were on full display. She shuddered at the creeping realization that we live in a twisted world where everything, both big and small, is subject to surveillance, and where anything worth money will always be exploited.

Just as she finished reading she noticed someone standing in the doorway. It was Helena Kraft, beautifully dressed as always.

Grane could not help remembering how she had suspected Kraft of being the leak in the investigation. What she had taken to be guilty shame had been Kraft's regret at the unprofessional way in which the investigation was being conducted—at least that is what she had been told during their long conversation after Mårten Nielsen confessed and was arrested.

"I can't begin to say how sorry I am to see you go," Kraft said.

"Everything has its time."

"Do you have any idea what you're going to do?"

"I'm moving to New York. I want to work in human rights, and as you know I've had an offer on the table from the U.N. for some time."

"It's a loss for us, Gabriella. But you deserve it."

"So my betrayal's been forgiven?"

"Not by all of us, I can assure you. But I see it as a sign of your good character."

"Thanks, Helena. Will I see you later at the Pressklub-ben's memorial for Andrei Zander?"

"First I have to do a presentation for the government on this whole mess. But later this evening I'll raise a glass to young Zander, and to you, Gabriella."

Alona Casales was sitting at a distance, contemplating the panic with an inward smile. She observed Admiral O'Connor crossing the floor, looking like a bullied schoolboy rather than the head of the world's most powerful intelligence organization. But then all the powerful figures at the NSA were feeling pathetic today, all except Needham.

Needham was not in a good mood either. He waved his arms around and was sweaty and bilious. But he exuded all his usual authority. It was obvious that even O'Connor was afraid of him. Needham had come back from Stockholm with real dynamite, had caused a huge argument and insisted on a complete shake-up throughout the organization. The head of the NSA was not going to thank him for that; he probably felt like sending Needham to Siberia immediately and forever.

But there was nothing he could do. He looked small as he approached Needham, who did not even bother to turn in his direction. Needham ignored the head of the NSA in the same way he ignored all the other poor bastards he had no time for, and plainly nothing improved for O'Connor once the conversation got going.

For the most part Needham seemed dismissive and, even though Casales could not overhear, she could imagine what was being said, or rather, what was not being said. Over the course of her own long conversations with Needham he refused to say one word about the way he got hold of the information. He was not going to compromise on a single point, and she respected that.

Needham seemed determined to milk the situation for all it was worth, and Casales solemnly swore that she would stand up for integrity in the agency and give Needham as much backing as she could if he ran into any problems. She also swore to herself that she would call Gabriella Grane in a final bid to ask her out, if rumours were true that she was on her way over here.

Needham was not in fact deliberately ignoring the NSA head. But neither was he going to interrupt what he was doing— yelling at two of his controllers—just because the admiral was standing at his desk. Only after about a minute did he address him and then in fact he said something friendly, not to ingratiate himself or compensate for his nonchalance, but because he really meant it.

"You did a good job at the press conference."

"Did I?" said the admiral. "It was hell."

"Well, you can thank me, then, for giving you time to prepare."

"Thank *you*? Are you kidding? Every news site around the world is posting pictures of Ingram and me together. I'm guilty by association."

"In that case for Christ's sake keep your own people in line from now on."

"How dare you talk to me like that."

"I'll talk however the hell I want. We're in the middle of a crisis and I'm responsible for security. I don't get paid for being polite."

"Watch what you say . . ." O'Connor began.

But he was thrown when Needham suddenly stood up, big as a bear, either to stretch his back or assert his authority.

"I sent you to Sweden to clean all this up," the admiral went on. "Instead when you came back everything was a complete disaster."

"The disaster had already happened," Needham snapped. "You know it as well as I do."

"So how do you explain all the shit that ended up in that Swedish magazine?"

"I explained it to you a thousand times."

"Right, your hacker. Guesswork and bullshit."

Needham had promised to keep Wasp out of this mess, and it was a promise he meant to keep.

"Top-quality bullshit, don't you think?" he said. "That damn hacker, whoever he may be, must have cracked Ingram's files and leaked them to *Millennium*. That's bad, I agree. But do you know what's worse? What's worse is that we had the chance to cut the hacker's balls off and put an end to the leaking. Instead we were ordered to shut down our investigation. Let's not pretend you went out of your way to stand up for me then."

"I sent you to Stockholm."

"But you called off my guys and our entire investigation came to a grinding halt. Now the rail is cold. And how much good would it do us if it came out that some lousy little hacker had taken us for a ride?"

"Not much, probably. But we can still make trouble for *Millennium* and that reporter Blomström, believe you me."

"It's Blomkvist, actually. Mikael Blomkvist. Be my guest. You'd win a lot of popularity contests if you marched in on Swedish territory and arrested the world's most celebrated journalist right about now," Needham said. The admiral muttered something inaudible and stormed off.

Needham knew as well as anyone that O'Connor was fighting for political survival and could not afford to make any reckless moves. He himself was fed up with working his fingers to the bone, and he loped over to Casales to chat with her instead. He was in the mood for something irresponsible.

"Let's go get hammered and forget this whole fucking mess."

Hanna Balder was standing on the little hill outside Hotel Schloss Elmau in her snow boots. She gave August a push and watched him whizz down the slope on the old-fashioned wooden toboggan the hotel had lent them. He came to a stop near a brown barn. Even though there was a glimmer of sunshine, a light snow was falling. There was hardly any wind. In the distance the mountain peaks touched the sky and wide-open spaces stretched out before her.

Hanna had never stayed in such a wonderful place, and August was recovering well, not least thanks to Charles Edelman's efforts. But none of it was easy. She felt terrible. Even here on the slope she had stopped twice and felt her chest. Withdrawal from her pills—benzodiazepines—was worse than she could have imagined. At night she would lie in bed curled up like a shrimp and examine her life in the most unsparing light, sometimes banging her fist against the wall and crying. She cursed Lasse Westman, and she cursed herself.

And yet . . . there were times when she felt strangely purified and occasionally she came close to being happy. There were moments when August would work quietly on his equations and his number series and would even answer her questions—albeit in monosyllables and somewhat odd terms.

The boy was still an enigma to her. Sometimes he spoke in numbers, in high numbers to the power of even higher numbers, and seemed to think that she would understand. But something had changed. She would never forget how she had seen August sitting at the desk in their hotel room that first day, writing out long winding equations which poured from him with amazing fluency, and which she photographed and sent on to the woman in Stockholm. Late that evening a text message had come in on Hanna's Blackphone:

```
<Tell August we've cracked the code!>
```

She had never seen her son so happy and proud. Even though she had no idea what it was all about and never mentioned it, even to Charles Edelman, it meant the world to her. She began to feel proud too, immeasurably proud.

She developed a passionate interest in savant syndrome, and when Charles was staying at the hotel they often sat up after August had gone to bed and talked into the small hours about her son's abilities, and about everything else too.

She was not sure it had been such a good idea to jump

into bed with Charles. Yet she was not sure it had been a bad idea either. Charles reminded her of Frans. They formed a little family of sorts: she; August; Charles; the rather strict but kind teacher, Charlotte Greber; and the Danish mathematician Jens Nyrup who visited them. Their whole stay was a voyage of discovery into her son's remarkable universe. As she now sauntered down the snowy hill and August got up from the toboggan, she felt, for the first time in ages: She would become a better mother, and she would sort out her life.

Blomkvist could not understand why his body felt so heavy. It was as if he were trying to move through water. And yet there was a commotion going on out there, a victory celebration. Nearly every newspaper, website, radio station, and TV channel wanted to interview him. He did not accept any of the requests. When *Millennium* had published big news stories in the past, he and Berger had not been sure whether other media companies would latch on to them. They had needed to think strategically, make sure they were syndicated in the right places and sometimes even share their scoop. Now none of that was necessary.

The news broke with a bang all by itself. When NSA head Charles O'Connor and U.S. Secretary of Commerce Stella Parker appeared at a joint press conference to apologize publicly for what had happened, the last lingering doubts about the story's credibility were dispelled. Now a heated debate was raging on editorial pages around the world about the consequences and implications of the disclosures.

But in spite of all the fuss and the telephones which never

stopped ringing, Berger had decided to arrange a last-minute party at the office. She felt they deserved to escape from the hullaballoo for a little while and raise a glass or two. A first print run of fifty thousand copies had sold out the previous morning and the number of hits on their website, which also had an English version, had reached several million. Offers of book contracts poured in, their subscription base was growing by the minute, and advertisers were lining up.

They had also bought out Serner Media. Berger had managed to push the deal through a few days earlier, though it had been anything but easy. Serner's representatives had sensed her desperation and taken full advantage, and for a while she and Blomkvist had thought that it would prove impossible. Only at the eleventh hour, when a substantial contribution came in from an unknown company in Gibraltar, bringing a smile to Blomkvist's face, had they been able to buy out the Norwegians. The price had been outrageously high, given the situation, but it was still a minor coup when a day later the magazine's scoop was published and the market value of the *Millennium* brand rocketed. They were free and independent again, though they had hardly had time to enjoy it.

Journalists and photographers had even hounded them during Zander's memorial at Pressklubben. Without exception they had wanted to offer congratulations, but Blomkvist felt smothered, and his responses had not been as gracious as he would have liked them to be. The sleepless nights and headaches continued to plague him.

Now in the late afternoon of the following day, the furniture in the office had been hurriedly rearranged. Cham-

pagne, wine, beer, and catered Japanese food had been set
out on the desks. And people started to stream in, first the
staff and freelancers, then a number of friends of the magazine, not least Holger Palmgren. Mikael helped him out of
the lift and the two embraced.

"Our girl made it," said Palmgren, with tears in his eyes.

"She generally does," Blomkvist replied with a smile. He
installed Palmgren in the place of honour on the sofa and
gave orders that his glass was to be kept filled.

It was good to see him there. It was good to see all sorts
of old and new friends. Gabriella Grane was there too, and
Chief Inspector Bublanski, who should probably not have
been invited, in view of their professional relationship and
Millennium's status as independent watchdog over the police
force, but Blomkvist had wanted to include him. Officer
Bubble spent the whole evening talking to Professor Farah
Sharif.

Blomkvist drank a toast with them and the others. He was
wearing jeans and his best jacket, and unusual for him he had
quite a lot to drink. But he could not shake off that empty,
leaden feeling and that was because of Zander, of course.
Andrei was constantly in his thoughts. The moment in the
office when his colleague had so nearly taken up his offer of
a beer was etched in his mind, a moment both humdrum
and life-determining. Memories of the young man flashed
up all the time, and Blomkvist had difficulty concentrating
on conversations.

He had had enough praise and flattery—the only tribute
that did affect him was Pernilla's text: <you do write for
real, Pappa>—and occasionally he glanced over towards

the door. Naturally Lisbeth Salander had been invited, and
would have been the guest of honour had she turned up.
Blomkvist had wanted to thank her for the handsome contribution during the Serner dispute. But there was no sign of
her. What did he expect?

Her sensational decrypted document had allowed him to
unravel the whole story, and had even persuaded Needham
and the head of Solifon, Nicolas Grant, to give him more
details. But he had heard from Salander only once since
then: when he had interviewed her—to the extent that was
possible—over the RedPhone app about what had happened
out at the summer house on Ingarö.

That was a week ago now and Blomkvist had no idea
what she thought of his article. Maybe she was angry that
he had dramatized it. He had no choice but to fill in the
blanks around the meagre answers she gave. Or perhaps she
was furious because he had not mentioned Camilla by name
but had simply referred to her as a Swedish-Russian woman
known as Thanos. Or else she was disappointed that he had
not taken a harder line across the board. It was impossible
to know.

The situation was not improved by the fact that Chief
Prosecutor Ekström really did appear to be considering a
case against Salander: unlawful deprivation of liberty and
seizure of property were the charges he had cooked up.

Eventually Blomkvist got fed up with it all and left the
party without saying goodbye. The weather was awful and
for lack of anything better to do he scrolled through his text
messages. There were congratulations and requests for interviews and a couple of indecent proposals. But nothing from
Salander. He switched off his mobile and trudged home with

surprisingly heavy steps for a man who had just pulled off the scoop of the century.

Salander was sitting on her red sofa on Fiskargatan, gazing emptily out at Gamla Stan and Riddarfjärden. It was a little over a year since she had started the hunt for her sister and her father's criminal legacy, and there was no denying her success on many counts.

She had tracked down Camilla and dealt the Spiders a serious blow. The connections with Solifon and the NSA had been severed. Ivan Gribanov, the Duma member, was coming under tremendous pressure in Moscow, Camilla's hit man was dead and her closest henchman, Jurij Bogdanov, and several other computer engineers were wanted by the police, forced to go underground. But Camilla was alive somewhere out there. Nothing was over. Salander had only winged her quarry and that was not enough. Grimly she looked down at the coffee table, where a packet of cigarettes and her unread copy of *Millennium* lay. She picked up the magazine and put it down again. Then she picked it up once more and read Blomkvist's report. When she reached the last sentence she stared for a while at the new photograph next to his byline. Then she jumped to her feet and went to the bathroom to put on some makeup. She pulled on a tight black T-shirt and a leather jacket and went out into the December evening.

She was freezing. It was crazy to be wearing so little, but she did not care. She cut down towards Mariatorget with quick steps, turned left into Swedenborgsgatan, and walked into a restaurant called Süd, where she sat down at the bar and alternated between whisky and beer. Since much of the clientele came from the world of culture and journalism, it was hardly surprising that many of them recognized her. Guitarist Johan Norberg, for example, who wrote a regular column for *We* and was known for picking up on small yet significant details, observed that Salander was not drinking as if she enjoyed it, but rather as if she had to get it out of the way.

There was something determined about her body language, and a cognitive behavioral therapist who happened to be sitting at a table nearby wondered if Salander was even aware of anyone else in the restaurant. She hardly looked around the room and seemed to be preparing herself for some kind of operation or action.

At 9:15 she paid in cash and stepped into the night without a word or gesture.

Despite the cold, Blomkvist walked home slowly, deep in gloom. A smile only crossed his lips when he ran into some of the regulars outside the Bishops Arms.

"So you weren't washed up after all!" Arne, or whatever his name was, bellowed.

"Maybe not quite yet," Blomkvist replied. For a moment he considered having a last beer inside and chatting with Amir.

But he felt too miserable. He wanted to be alone, so he continued to the entrance door of his building. On the way up the stairs he was overcome by a vague sense of unease, maybe as a result of all he had been through. He tried to dismiss it, but it would not go away, especially when he realized that a light had blown on the top floor. It was pitch-black up there.

He slowed his steps and sensed a movement. There was a flicker, a weak sliver of light as if from a mobile, and a figure like a ghost, a slight person with dark flashing eyes, could be made out.

"Who's that?" he said, frightened.

Then he saw it was Salander.

He brightened at first and opened his arms, but she looked furious. Her eyes were rimmed with black and her body seemed coiled, as if prepared for an attack.

"Are you angry with me?" he said.

"Quite."

"Why is that?"

Salander took a step forward, her face shining and pale, and he remembered her gunshot wound.

"Because I come to visit, and there's no-one at home," she said. He walked towards her.

"That's a bit of a scandal, isn't it?" he said.

"I'd say so."

"What if I ask you in now?"

"Then I suppose I'll have to accept."

"In that case, welcome," he said, and for the first time in ages a broad smile spread across his face.

A star fell outside in the night sky.

ACKNOWLEDGMENTS

My sincere thanks to my agent, Magdalena Hedlund; Stieg Larsson's father and brother, Erland and Joakim Larsson; my publishers, Eva Gedin and Susanna Romanus; my editor Ingemar Karlsson; and Linda Altrov Berg and Catherine Mörk at Norstedts Agency.

I also owe thanks to David Jacoby, senior security researcher at Kaspersky Lab, and Andreas Strömbergsson, professor of mathematics at Uppsala University, as well as to Fredrik Laurin, digger-in-chief at Ekot, Mikael Lagström, V.P. services at Outpost 24, the authors Daniel Goldberg and Linus Larsson, and Menachem Harari.

And of course to my Ann.

ALSO AVAILABLE IN THE

MILLENNIUM SERIES

THE GIRL WITH THE DRAGON TATTOO
by Steig Larsson

Harriet Vanger, a scion of one of Sweden's wealthiest families, disappeared over forty years ago. All these years later, her aged uncle continues to seek the truth. He hires Mikael Blomkvist, a crusading journalist recently trapped by a libel conviction, to investigate. He is aided by the pierced and tattooed punk prodigy Lisbeth Salander. Together they tap into a vein of unfathomable iniquity and astonishing corruption.

Crime Fiction

THE GIRL WHO PLAYED WITH FIRE
by Steig Larsson

Mikael Blomkvist, crusading publisher of the magazine *Millennium*, has decided to run a story that will expose an extensive sex trafficking operation. On the eve of its publication, two people are brutally murdered, and the fingerprints found on the murder weapon belong to his friend, the troubled genius hacker Lisbeth Salander. Blomkvist, convinced of Salander's innocence, plunges into an investigation. Meanwhile, Salander herself is drawn into a murderous game of cat and mouse, which forces her to face her dark past.

Crime Fiction

THE GIRL WHO KICKED THE HORNET'S NEST
by Stieg Larsson

Lisbeth Salander lies in critical condition in a Swedish hospital, a bullet in her head. But she's fighting for her life in more ways than one: if and when she recovers, she'll stand trial for three murders. With the help of Mikael Blomkvist, she'll need to identify those in authority who have allowed the vulnerable, like herself, to suffer abuse and violence. And, on her own, she'll seek revenge—against the man who tried to kill her and against the corrupt government institutions that nearly destroyed her life.

Crime Fiction

THE GIRL WHO TAKES AN EYE FOR AN EYE
by David Lagercrantz

Lisbeth Salander seizes on a chance to unearth her mysterious past once and for all. She will let nothing stop her—not the Islamists she enrages by rescuing a young woman from their brutality; not the prison gang leader who passes a death sentence on her; not the deadly reach of her long-lost twin sister, Camilla; and not the people who will do anything to keep buried knowledge of a sinister pseudoscientific experiment known only as the Registry.

Crime Fiction

VINTAGE CRIME / BLACK LIZARD
Available wherever books are sold.
www.vintagebooks.com